FREE FIRE ZONE
DENNIS MAULSBY

Published by Prolific Press Inc.
Harborton, VA

Printed in the USA

Free Fire Zone
Dennis Maulsby
©2016 Dennis Maulsby
All Rights Reserved. *No part of this publication may be reproduced,stored in a retrieval system, or transmitted, in any form, by electronic, mechanical, photocopying, recording, or otherwise, without prior written permission from the publisher.*
Published by Prolific Press Inc. Harborton VA.
ISBN: 978-1-63275-082-2
Edited by Glenn Lyvers
Printed in the USA

Contents...

About the Author:

Dennis Maulsby is a retired bank president living in Ames, Iowa with his wife, Ruth, a retired legal secretary; and his dog, Charlie, a retired CIA operative. His poetry and short stories have appeared in *Lyrical Iowa,* the *Des Moines Register, The North American Review, Haiku Journal, Spillway, The Hawai'i Pacific Review, The Briarcliff Review,* and other journals. His short story, *The Night of the Pooka* recently won first prize in the 2015 Montezuma All-Iowa Fiction Contest.

His first book of poetry, *Remembering Willie, and all the others* won silver medal book awards from the Military Writers Society of America (2005) and the Branson Stars & Stripes organization (2009). The book is included in the Library of Congress' Veterans' History Project. Maulsby's second book of poetry *Frissons,* published in 2011, consists of traditional American-style haiku and senryu. *"Near Death/Near Life,"* a third book of poetry, was released by Prolific Press in May of 2015.

Acknowledgements ...

Grateful acknowledgement is made to the publishers of books, periodicals and anthologies in which these poems and stories or earlier versions of them have appeared:

Poems: The Ames Progressive: "Waiting For Nam"; Near Death/Near Life: "Valkyrie"; Spillway Magazine and Near Death/Near Life: "Quantum Many Worlds"; Peregrine (Honorable mention award) and Near Death/Near Life: "Sweat-dreams"; The Briancliff Review (Pushcart Prize nominee) and Near Death/Near Life: "Isle Royale Hunted"; Near Death/Near Life: "Monsoon Malarial Dreams 1967"; Near Death/Near Life: "Memorial Day in the Garden"; Perfume River Poetry Review and Near Death/Near Life: "We"; Near Death/Near Life: "Reflections"; Near Death/Near Life: "Kill-Zone Requiem"; Near Death/Near Life: "Wonderland"; Remembering Willie and Near Death/Near Life: All the Thousands 1964-1975".

Story: First place award 2014 War to End All Wars contest for flash fiction extract entitled: Frozen Chosin".

Foreword

There are a handful of poets from the Vietnam War who have managed to capture the realism and emotional turmoil of that conflict. Dennis Maulsby is on the top of that very short list. In this book, he combines his poetic talents in a series of short stories that weave a tapestry of imagination and creative fantasy.

These short stories force us to look at the war, our own lives, how we treat veterans, and our belief systems. These tales take you on a journey of mind and spirit. You might feel safer if you mentally "lock and load" to protect yourself. The stories are powerful and moving.

Readers will follow the fictional life of Lieutenant Teigler as he travels to Vietnam and into a kind of *"Twilight Zone."* Is Teigler insane, cursed, blessed, or some kind of blemished, immortal spiritual warrior? There is nothing simple about this character, as you will discover. Is he the hero or a villain, an enlightened sage, or is he working for the devil? We, the readers, witness nightmares, dreams, and delusions from the *"Free Fire Zone"* of the author's heart and mind. The title of this book seems so absolutely correct and right.

Dennis was stationed in Trang Bang. In the spring of 2002, I journeyed back to that hamlet, visited the Cao Dai Temple, and spoke with the brother of the young girl who was made famous by the magazine cover—running naked from that temple, burned by napalm, arms sorrowfully outstretched. There is a lot of sadness in the history of that small village. For one thing, there appears to have been little way for Americans to ever have truly secured that place. A VC stronghold then, and the site of many intense battles, the author surely felt the stresses and fears of that time and place. It is hard to believe that I could stand on that same road and even worship in the temple there without fearing for my own life. Time does heal some wounds but it always leaves a scar! Sufferers from PTSD and the horrors of war, especially among the survivors of combat in Vietnam, will find this book, although a fantasy, emotionally based in the real world. For those who still struggle with nightmares and flashbacks, these short stories may be a kind of therapy.

It is odd that it sometimes takes the world of fantasy and poetry to paint the picture of the emotional experience of war. Dennis brilliantly precedes each new short story with a poem. This made the whole reading experience a multidimensional emotional trip for me, and it added a surreal layer to these unique stories.

As with real life, we may never fully understand the author's Lieutenant Teigler, nor the war, but we all can recognize common pain and suffering—physical, emotional, and spiritual.

W. H. "Bill" McDonald Jr.

Vietnam Veteran - 128th Assault Helicopter Company; Founder and first president of the Military Writers Society of America.

Preface

In his ecstasy of power, he is mad for battle …
Pure frenzy fills him. - Achilles in the Iliad.

Welcome to the *Free Fire Zone*, also known as a free kill zone. In Vietnam, it was enemy territory, all the friendlies and neutrals moved out. Anyone found inside the zone was considered hostile—a legitimate target that could be killed on sight, no questions asked. Each of the stories in this book originates from this zone, any subject, any genre fair game. These stories are works of fiction, the characters and plots, creatures of my imagination. If they resemble real people or events, it is, as they say, strictly coincidental. However, a few slivers of autobiographical material have slipped in. Most of the background and descriptions of Vietnam's people and places come from my year there.

I was a military intelligence officer assigned to what were called radio research units, a cover for electronic intelligence gathering. My first six months in country were spent living in Trang Bang, a village located on Highway One west of Saigon. You know this village better than you think. In 1972, a famous picture was taken of a young girl running naked down the road out of that village, her clothes burned off by napalm, the province's Cao Dai Temple in the background.

Struggling against memories of war is the fate of all soldiers returned from killing places. The fighting in Iraq and Afghanistan will create another generation of afflicted men and women. For those of you who have never made this journey, I hope you will welcome them back. Listen to their stories. For you veterans, try the creative act, whatever that might be for you. It is the most powerful therapy I have discovered.

For Bill McDonald,
whose example and encouragement made things happen.

Special thanks to all our armed forces, both at home and abroad, active, retired, and to all those who came before...

With gratitude to my wife, Ruth, who read and analyzed this entire book — much of it more than once — and whose devotion has always pollinated my dreams.

Thanks to Mary Helen Stefaniak and Karen Bender for knowledge gained in Iowa Summer Writing Festival workshops.

Thanks to Pat Beiber, Leonard Joy, Linda Voit, Mary Teresa Fallon, R.J. Crum, Rick Hildreth and Robin Sprafka, and Eric Mayne who helped critique this book. And to the members of the Des Moines Barnes & Noble Writers Group, the Society of Great River Poets, and all the others who listened and suggested changes, corrections, and deletions.

Waiting for Nam 1967

Our last night nearly died
of smoke inhalation
(duffle ignited by the motel in-wall heater).
Early morning, left from Oakland,
in flight to Southeast Asia, white men
expecting the privileges of our race.

Thirty minutes to refuel in Hawaii.

Walked around the terminal
(just to say we'd been there):
wrinkled travelers crumpled near
cheap shops, gum and candy on the floor,
whiffs of disinfectant and urine …

Seven thousand eight hundred
forty-one air miles, no movies,
plugged toilets, under-powered air,
coffin seating—six by three by three,
waiting for Nam.

Below us the Philippines,

laughing tan people
in rainbow buses.
Past southern China,
farmers, pant legs up,
in black-mud-wet fields tended
ducks and hogs. Newly mutated
flu virus passed from drake to boar,
then infected the world.

Like a shout in a culvert pipe,

a ripple of fear
racked the plane—on each wingtip
a camoed F-4 Phantom fighter jet.
The pilot squawked,
"We're within intercept range of China,
need the protection."
Visions of Mig-17 cannon
breaking the plane open, freeing us
for a last, long dive to Mother Ocean.

Waiting for Nam.
Swooped in over Cam Ranh Bay—white beaches,
surfers, mirrored tin-roofed hooches,
red dust roads, high black columns of burning shit …
At the officers' club, in our third
sweat-soaked uniform, we pressed
cold San Miguels to our foreheads,
listened to short-timers' bad advice.

0900, two hours after dawn, a crowd hunkered

in the grass beside the airstrip
seeking transport to Saigon. A C-130 cargo plane
squatted with its ramp down, a crazy quilt of people rushed
into its gray-green interior to create Noah's Ark:
Vietnamese soldiers with wives, rifles, and children,
grandmothers with leg-tied chickens,
a boy and a monkey,
Americans with flak jackets and pistols,
whores in black pants and aproned dresses.
Everyone hip to hip on the deck, waiting for Nam.

Someone handed out
cigarettes, mothers breast-fed babies,
grandmothers exposed black teeth.

The monkey pissed on an officer's leg,

smiles hid behind hands.
Crewmembers, earphones on, stumbled
through on errands—a typical day in the Republic.
Tan Son Nhat Airport concrete, a bake oven,
children's hands sought our pockets, lost a Zippo.
Other hands grabbed boots, "Shine, GI?
Number one job, twenty P."
Taxi drivers hawked black market PX deals:
"Make you money, GI. Help me, my baby
killed by Viet Cong."
Pimps made their pitch.
"You no like *flickee flic*. You *dinky dau*.
Okay, Cheap Charlie, for you only five dollar."
Smoky streets, a crush of three-wheel Lambrettas,
scooters, cyclos, ox carts, and olive-drab trucks.
Spices and hydrocarbons burnt nostrils.

Women walked by in tight long-sleeve blouses,
waist-length black hair, already looking good.

Battalion Headquarters—all sandbags,

machine guns—inside, shadow men,
waiting for Nam.

Free Fire Zone

The black came—blacker than black—not just the absence of light, a blackness of sound, a blackness of mind and soul…. It crept in, as it always did, after the rocket attacks in those morning hours that one wanted to believe were inviolate. It grew so thick the pulse of its organs could be felt against the skin. The blackness filled every surface and irregularity. The slow tide would crest the earth berm, leak through the sandbagged bunkers to touch booted feet, and then rise to groins and chests. It filled the barrels of rifles, pressed cloth against flesh, pushed out the air as it entered pores, noses, and ears, until its acid velvet was all there was.

I prayed that while it had our bodies and minds, it would not take our souls. If by some chance God let us return, I knew it would still be inside us, marking us as lepers to wives and lovers, parents, friends, and, worst of all, to each other.

Pain in my knuckles brought me back a little. I pulled my fist back from the sandbagged wall. We'd go out soon. I listened to the breathing of the others. The acrid odor of confined male fear burned my nostrils. I assured myself we were safe. The sides of the bunker were built into a ten-foot-high earth berm. The exposed front face consisted of four thicknesses of alternating sandbags pounded with mallets into rock-hard walls. Overhead, rough-cut wood beams topped with perforated steel runway panels supported layers of sandbags. Similar bunkers looked out every fifty meters; their weapons ports aligned for interlocking fire. From a fan of claymore mines cemented in front, wires ran back to stacked detonators. Farther out, rows of barbwire entanglements the height of a tall man sealed us in.

Even so, the threat of ground attack was not the danger tonight. Charlie's artillery rockets had delay fuses. They dug in deep, cratering the runways at the airstrip. They would also bust through bunker roofs before exploding. I didn't want to be one of those, my blood leaking into the grasping dirt, suffocating while I listened to the muffled shouts of the men above trying to dig me out.

The attacks came three or four times a week—always in the early hours—the enemy didn't want you rested. After months of sleep deprivation and adrenaline highs, soldiers became emotionally bruised and unfocused, susceptible to delusions and neurotic behavior. I should know.

~~~OOO~~~

Two of us crept out from the doglegged entrance and along the blast shield. Our minds remembering the base camp layout: wood barracks with corrugated metal roofs, NCO Club, the two-story barn of a communications center with semitrailers attached like little pigs suckling a sow, and at the far end of the compound, the motor pool garage and its detached office, which had been the latest victim of a Katyusha rocket. One pierced the outer sheet metal and punched a perfect 122-millimeter hole in the corner of an army-issue steel desk. The Chinese-made weapon then exploded out its ass-end and shot-gunned the twenty-foot sidewall of the garage next-door. It looked like a giant cheese grater.

We listened for a few minutes at the rear of the bunker. Our job, to check for any survivors who might have been hit by that first salvo of rockets. We quietly slipped away from the berm, moving slowly as we scanned for infiltrators. It took a few minutes at that pace to pass through an area kept clear of brush and weeds. If the enemy broke through the perimeter, they would be in the open, exposed to fire from our fallback positions. Sergeant Ratcliff scuffed along to my rear. I would have felt better if he walked in front or at my side—his behavior had grown increasingly erratic in the last two months.

As we entered the company area near one of the barracks, he whispered, "Wait a minute." He moved under the eaves of the building. After a few seconds, I heard the patter of liquid hitting wood then dirt. My nose twitched as I caught the hot odor of urine.

I jumped, his voice in the dark almost directly in my ear.

"That felt good, El Tee."

"Goddamn, Rat, don't you ..."

"Hey—just imagining me in my dress blues pissing on your grave."

Forcing down the wad of acid in my throat, I moved us on. *No use challenging him without witnesses.* Like mirror images, we crept down the center aisle of the first barracks running a hand over the bottom of each iron cot to see if anyone had been hit in their bunks.

I heard a half-suppressed chuckle.

"You know about the warrant officer in the helicopter unit that got fragged last week? It did severe damage to his family jewels—don't think he'll ever worry about being a diaper changer."

The story had spread all over camp. Fragging, rolling a hand grenade under the bunk of a disliked officer, or NCO, was on the rise. I had already been threatened once during a run-in with Private Willis. A number of enlisted men had complained about being bullied and threatened by the ex-football lineman. Ratcliff, as his squad leader, should have made the first move on Willis. The sergeant seemed both afraid of the huge blond-haired man and distracted by personal problems. I caught the over six-footer out in the open one day with no one around.

"I—am—tired—of—your—shit, Willis! I am going to watch you. You will find your ass in the Long Binh Junction stockade unless I see a change."

His hairline and ears skinned back, then compressed together, eyes squinty, nostrils flared. He looked around to make sure no one else was near.

"And, you might get a night visit. I know where you bunk."

"You and me ... why should we wait? Let's go down behind the motor pool and have this out right now! Just you and me."

"I ain't dumb. For hitting an officer you'll have me court-martialed."

I had him now. If he was worried about a trial, he couldn't be serious. Pressing my advantage, I said, "We'll take off our shirts. You won't see my bars. Just you and me."

"No, no, Sir." He took a pace back.

Two nights later, we met again. I lay in bed sweat-soaking my army-issue green boxers and reading a mystery novel, trying to get so wrapped in it I would forget for just a moment where I was. A nervous knock vibrated my door, then a louder one.

"Come," I said.

Willis stepped in. He came to a reasonable facsimile of attention and said, "I need to speak with you, Sir."

"Right now?"

"Yes, Sir, please."

"Wait for me at the door facing the road. I'll be with you in a minute."

~~~OOO~~~

Click ... click. My wits snapped back in the blackness; we cleared the last of the barracks. *Click ... click.* My soldier's mind recognized the sound of the safety on the sergeant's rifle being switched on and off. *Click ... click.* Rat's reflex started to creep me out. Or, did he plan something extreme? His actions became more peculiar every day. I tried to alert my superiors, but the old sergeants' network protecting him threw up a wall a second lieutenant couldn't penetrate. Besides, he only focused his rage on me. To everyone else he appeared normal. *Click ... click.* My only chance—get him to go off in front of others.

The *click ... clicks* came closer together. The pressure of the shelling and our isolation in the dark accelerated his mania. *Click ... click.* My palm came up to rest on the grip of my forty-five. *Click ... click.* I'd never get it out and cocked in time. *Click ... click.* The muscles in my back and chest twitched, already anticipating the impact of spinning copper-jacketed slugs ripping finger-sized holes on their way in, and then exiting through fist-sized cavities on the other side.

I tripped. The *click ... click* stopped. I fell on something soft wrapped in a nylon poncho liner—a body. I tried to sound normal, but my voice shook.

"Rat, we've got one." My hands patted the body searching for wounds. Ashamed, I felt grateful for the casualty's presence. The flesh felt warm through the quilted liner. My hands found no blood. The body belched, out came an overwhelming whiff of alcohol tinged with vomit.

"Shit, the bastard is drunk and passed out," I said, in a voice that went from a whisper to normal volume.

At that moment, the all clear sounded. Men stumbled out of nearby shelters talking and waving flashlights. Taking advantage of the distraction, I stepped back over the body, got behind Rat, and pulled my pistol. I made the safety *click* and one more *click* as the hammer came back to full cock. He heard. His rifle clattered as it hit the hard-packed red dirt. He shouted something inarticulate, causing the flashlights to swing our way. In the light, I saw Rat bend down and grasp wads of the drunk's blanket and clothing in his fists. Surprisingly strong, he raised the soldier off the ground and hurled him about five feet to land in a crumple.

"You. You fucking son-of-a-bitch ... you son-of-a-bitch ... bitch."

I knew, as sure as I was born of woman, another few seconds without having tripped and Rat would have killed me. I picked up his rifle, felt the friction heat where his hands had rubbed the grip and trigger guard. Reholstering my pistol, I left him shaking in the dark.

~~-OOO-~~

Four hours later, I mulled over my situation at breakfast. I reflected on what I knew about him. In exchange for no questions asked about where his surplus hot water heater went, the mess sergeant secured Ratcliff's personnel file. Rat, an old-timer, had found a home in the Army beginning with Korea. According to the file, he experienced the very sharp end of some nasty business during the latter part of that "police action," when it degenerated into something like WWI, the hills and ridges along the 38th parallel honeycombed with trenches and bunkers.

Pushed out of their positions by Chinese human wave attacks, our guys counterattacked to retake them. The GIs called it "knee to groin" combat—soldiers shot, knifed, and strangled each other close enough to smell each other's breath and feel hot blood run between their fingers. These actions chewed up whole battalions, leaving those remaining only able to form a single company out of shell-shocked survivors.

Thinking back, I recalled our first meeting. Ratcliff met me at Tan Sun Nhut Airport, another green dehydrated replacement. In country six months, his faded jungle fatigues, worn nylon-leather boots, and scarred M-16 gave him the look of the veteran warrior. I presented the reverse image: unarmed, in sweat-soaked cotton stateside uniform and scuffed black jump boots.

After a salute and a handshake, he offered me an automatic pistol with web belt and issue holster. I refused and pulled my personal weapon out of my duffle bag: Grandfather's WWII Colt .45-caliber model 1911 A1. The hand-me-down weapon had gone to war with three generations of Teiglers. Its weight strapped to my hip generated the only reassuring feeling of the day.

The first part of our journey began in a canvas-topped three-quarter ton truck. As hard sprung as all military vehicles, it gave our collective kidneys a pounding. We passed by hundreds of brick and stucco two-story buildings in the Saigon suburbs; all so alike one could travel in circles for hours and not know the difference. The street traffic was exactly the opposite. Vehicles of every type and description packed together from ox carts and diverse-colored Lambretta scooters to olive drab army trucks and black Citroen sedans left over from the French. The cars' low-slung, not quite aerodynamic bodies and miniature cowcatcher grills reminded me of old European detective movies once popular on late-night TV. The city air became foggy with the blue-white choking smoke of burned motor oil veined with the smell of unwashed bodies, manure, and garlic.

Both traffic and air lightened up once we hit farmland. The truck rolled down a highway built up to shed water during the monsoons. From this vantage point, muddy rice paddies stretched back to the vanishing point on both sides, some being worked by men and women in rolled-up black pants and woven rice straw hats. About every five miles, a nest of farmhouses would drift past.

The truck slowed, pulled over to the shoulder, and stopped next to a small wooden table near one of the farmhouses. Local kids offered fresh-cut pineapple on bamboo skewers. It brought back memories of being six years old and selling Kool-Aid in front of our old gray two-story to folks walking from the bus stop. The sergeant bought a slice for each of us. I spotted the mother watching out a window. As we pulled away, I waved. She withdrew a fish-pale hand allowing the curtain to close.

"Like salt?" Ratcliff offered a C-ration salt packet. "It's good that way."

"This sure tastes sweet." The sugar content caused my teeth to ache.

"Ripened in the field," he mumbled between bites. "And Asian pineapple is smaller and sweeter than those big ones they grow in Hawaii."

"You stationed in The Islands?"

"Ya, me and my bed-hopping ex with the 25th Infantry," he said, wiping juice from his chin.

"Sarge, what's it like here?" I asked, my question taking advantage of his willingness to talk.

"The usual. It's full of stinks, can't tell the friendlies from the bad guys, but the beer is good. Everyone has some kind of scam or side business going. Can't keep drugs and booze away from the troops. Half the year it rains like hell, impossible to keep dry, your clothes and boots get eaten off your body by fungus and mold. You don't want to know about the other half of the year."

"What about the South Vietnamese?"

"The women start looking good after your first ninety days. However, the skinny is that the pros have penicillin resistant strains of VD. Get a case and they don't let you go home to spread it around."

"Sounds delightful." My scrotum pulled my testicles up tight against my body. "When do we get to the company?"

"Another thirty minutes by truck and ten minutes by helicopter, if we catch one today. No scheduled flights in country, Sir."

We managed to hop the last chopper of the day. A very, very informal affair; we scrambled in and sat on aluminum-framed sway-bottomed canvas seats. The doorless bird took off and gained altitude fast—altitude provided a little safety. It was cool at that height and refreshing for a new guy. From this vantage point, the country even looked pretty, with patchwork rectangles formed by rice paddies, rubber tree plantations, and rivers blending into occasional wooded areas. After a time, we left farmland behind and flew over dense green acres of jungle divided into random segments by a crooked brown river and its tributaries.

Suddenly the helicopter banked right and descended fast. I felt my body lift off the seat and the pineapple of an hour ago rise in my throat. The pilots' hands and arms moved in practiced patterns, their eyes locked on something we couldn't see from the back. I glanced at Sergeant Ratcliff, sitting nearest the door. The "G" forces of the dive pushed his eyebrows up to his hairline. The wind of our descent caused my eyes to water and for a few blinks, I couldn't see anything. The chopper came to a stop, hovering near the west bank of the murky river. The pilot pointed and shouted something drowned out by the blade noise. His warrant officer co-pilot remained hunched over the controls keeping the craft stable.

I rubbed my eyes and tried to focus on his lips. He shouted, "Shoot, shoot them! Goddamn it! Shoot!"

My head followed his point. Kneeling in a sampan on the river ten feet away were two Vietnamese—old grandfathers—dressed in dirty white loincloths and straw coolie hats—each with a paddle laid across his lap gripped in a callused hand. They stared straight ahead, chins up, lips compressed. I could see white eyebrows and wispy beards. Their chests were hairless and their thinness was accentuated by skin stretched tightly over their ribs. The only thing in the boat was a large bag of rice, no weapons.

I gulped—we hovered too near the river, too near the grandfathers. The chopper blades cut the air no more than six feet over their heads. The prop wash caused the surface of the water to shiver out from a center point below us in concentric circles. The water appeared mysterious, muddy, and deep.

"This is a free fire zone. You kill anything that moves, no questions asked. They are Viet Cong! Jesus, shoot them!" the lieutenant pilot screamed, his lips twisted and pulled back.

My eyes snapped back to his face. Unable to reconcile this order with the peasants' passive behavior, I was like a computer that had received two equally strong but opposite commands. I sat helpless.

The sergeant's body slumped forward in slow motion as if his innards were flowing out like corn from a cut feedbag.

He moved his weapon up. I shouted, "No!"

Too late, each pop, pop, pop of the gun firing was punctuated by the wink of sun off empty brass spinning out the rifle's ejection port. I looked down and saw only the wet, glistening boat bottom.

This sin we shared—could this have been the breaking point for Rat? I felt guilty as hell about the incident and I had only been a bystander—how was he dealing with it? I made a vow to visit the helicopter unit and talk to those pilots as soon as I could rig it. Downing my plastic cup of reconstituted coffee, I left the mess hall, walked across the compound to chat with the captain. First, I needed to wangle some in-country rest and recreation.

A red ochre colored dust covered everything outside. Clouds of it drifted over the camp every time a truck or jeep drove by. Breathing it twenty-four hours a day caused congestion. Sneezing expelled bloody-looking phlegm—a plague upon the entire camp. No one found relief from the dust or the heat. The communications intercept building contained the only air-conditioned space. Its overburdened machines barely kept the operators from passing out and the transistors from frying.

Enemy activity had been very light. Calling in favors from the captain, I received permission for a daylight-only visit to Saigon, with Willis as my driver. Throughout the trip, the private was so watchful. Any observer would have thought I was a Mafia Don and he my *protezione* bodyguard. Our destination: Vinh's high-class massage parlor. We entered the interior eager to wallow in its special pleasures. Overhead fans evaporated our sweat.

Our company commander's recommendation had led us to the place, a brick and stone building of European design, not the average American's image of Southeast Asia. After ten minutes of soap, water, and scrubbing, we relaxed in individual hot tubs, a cold brown bottle of *Ba Moi Ba* beer in hand. A heavy perfume, almost lilac, rose from the steaming water—we weren't going to be able to hide our indiscretions later.

I heard splashing. Willis completed a deal with his attendant. His weightlifter's muscles pumped up as he rose from the water. The size of his erection caused doubt to flicker across her face as they left the room. I started to discuss price with my companion when a truck backfired outside. In the pause, I remembered about the antibiotic resistant strains of VD. In spite of her best efforts to convince me, I refused to proceed. I don't know who felt the most disappointed. Of course, she only lost money.

I waited in the lobby and made small talk with the off-duty whores. They wanted to know about life in the U.S. What did we eat, did everyone really have cars, and what were American women like? Were they as big and hairy as GIs? I got a few laughs describing them as even hairier, with stuck out teeth, and constantly demanding sex. Not even inexperienced Vietnamese women believed that last part. Females all over the world must go to the same secret school where they learn how to see through the lies and fables of men. A half hour later, Willis ran out of money.

"Lieutenant, sorry you had to wait," he said, rolling up his sleeve.

"Well, Willis, while you played hide the kielbasa, I gathered valuable intelligence from these enemy agents." My hands inscribed an imaginary circle around my female companions. Their reaction ran the gamut of fright and puzzlement, then laughter. In fact, it was likely that at least one did pass information to the Viet Cong.

The two of us swaggered to the jeep, waved goodbye, and left for base camp. We were almost back when Willis noticed the padlock on the gas cap had vibrated open. A few months ago, headquarters ordered all vehicles to have straps welded on the gas caps and the filler pipe so they could be locked.

American trucks and jeeps possessed extra-wide-mouthed filler pipes, so you could top off their tanks in the field from gas cans without needing a funnel. The enemy had discovered a standard American hand grenade would fit in the pipe nicely. They snapped a rubber band around the grenade and the safety spoon, pulled the pin, stuck the banded grenade into the pipe, and replaced the cap. Gas slowly dissolved the rubber band, igniting a firebomb that produced a napalm effect that incinerated everything nearby, starting with the soldier's ass in the seat above the tank.

I told him to slow to a stop. We would gently dismount to keep gas splash to a minimum. If we had a grenade in the pipe, it could only be a few minutes away from an explosion. The jeep sat lonely on the road about a klick from the main gate. I sent Willis to hustle a bomb expert, hoping not to look too foolish if it was a false alarm.

Rice paddies crowded the land on both sides of the road—nice and open. If Charlie attacked before help returned, he would be seen well in advance. I unsnapped the brown leather strap that kept my forty-five in its shoulder holster, and squinted through the late afternoon sun. Today, the only apparent observer was a farmer tending a water buffalo in the distance.

Willis returned, dragging a skinny specialist fifth class. The specialist's sour red face and stiff body language betrayed his reluctance. He wouldn't have gone along with this for a second Louie, whose life span in combat measured less than two minutes—hardly worth the effort. Willis, with his superior pectorals, however, refused to take no for an answer. I met them twenty meters from the innocent-looking jeep.

"What makes you think the vehicle is booby-trapped?" The specialist looked at me as if pointing out the real booby. Picking up the lilac scent from our recent bath, he frowned.

"We know the lock was secure when we last filled the tank. It came loose on our way back from Saigon."

"It sounds like you are overly suspicious, with government-issue lowest-bid locks, what do you expect?"

"I don't care who made the locks, the private and I are not touching that vehicle until it has been cleared." Willis and I exchanged determined glances.

"Shit. Well, I'll drive it back myself," he said and started walking toward the jeep. I moved to the side of the road and motioned Willis to follow. We lay down. The bomb expert made eleven paces. As if by signal, when he put his heel down on step number twelve the jeep erupted in a shower of flame and metal fragments. We leapt up from the ditch where we had taken cover to roll the specialist over and over to put out his burning clothes.

My faith restored in army locks, I wondered how someone got it open without cutting it off. Why hadn't the staff at Vinh's noticed a native fooling with our vehicle? It was bad for your business and personal health to have customers blow up after leaving your establishment. Once we filed an after-action report, poor Vinh would find himself strapped naked in a chair in the basement of Saigon police headquarters, testicles tickled with electricity, and forcefully asked questions he couldn't answer.

Another GI with a key wouldn't have aroused suspicion. Who had been the culprit … Ratcliff? If so, in his hurry he hadn't made sure the lock completely latched—we had been warned. For a brief moment, the thought of going AWOL pranced seductively in my mind. Narrow escapes these last few days had used up all the luck hoarded up to see me through my one-year tour. This must end.

Checking Ratcliff's barracks, I found his bunk untouched and covered with several days' worth of dust. At the orderly room, the first sergeant stayed mute about Rat's whereabouts. I noticed the louder we argued the deeper the wrinkles became on his forehead. They pulled down his receding hairline, where wearing a helmet for twenty years had rubbed a permanent bald spot.

The captain opened the door of his office, cut off the shouting, and waved me in. Hands on my shoulders, he pushed me into a chair. He settled his olive-drab butt in a swivel chair, forearms resting on the desktop, hands clasped. I waited.

In the absence of voices, one heard the background night noise of the jungle: thousands of insects of varying sizes beat against the screens, fragile barriers against such determination. We stared at each other. When he saw my skin return to its natural tint, he asked, "Lieutenant, what is your problem with Sergeant Ratcliff?"

"I believe he is trying to kill me," I said in a voice that sounded overly dramatic.

His eyes widened and cheeks puffed out. He started to rise, but changed his mind. The captain squinted, looked at the ceiling, and then dropped his line of vision to the desktop. Putting on a thoughtful face, he knocked his gold West Point ring twice on the desktop. I relaxed; the ring knocks meant a decision.

Faced with my refusal to leave it alone, he said, "We don't know where the man is. The sergeant's been missing for two days."

After hearing the full story, he gave me permission to warn the pilots of the helicopter that had flown Ratcliff and me through the free fire zone. It took a while, completing a successful landline call in Vietnam rated high on the list of near impossibilities. The country's telephone exchange consisted of pre-World War II French switchboards. Real live women operators, most with little command of English, plugged in wires by hand to make connections. Asian culture also played a role. Rather than lose face by admitting they didn't understand our request, they tied us to a random number. Further eroding the system, every Nam, Loi, and Minh in Saigon illegally connected black market phones dropping the signal strength until we could hardly hear whoever was on the other end.

"Eighth Field Artillery, Sergeant Broder here," came an operatic voice heralding another wrong number.

"Sergeant, I'm sorry to bother you. This is my fifth wrong connection."

"I've had my share of those," he replied with a bass chuckle. "Since we are connected is there anything I can do for you before we go our separate ways?"

"You know, an idea just struck me. Your unit owns the real heavy artillery, 175s and eight-inchers, right?"

"On the button, Sir," he said.

"Can I call in an artillery strike on the Saigon telephone headquarters?"

"I have never met you, but I can tell from your request you are an evil man—but my kind of evil. While I am sorely tempted, I must refuse." The humor in his voice was evident.

I cranked the phone and tried again. This time the bookies had to pay. After identifying my outfit and myself, I got the duty officer for the 171st Aviation Transport Unit on the horn. "Lieutenant, I am calling to alert you of an AWOL sergeant that could be stalking two of your people. He and I participated in an incident involving one of your choppers three months ago."

"Got any names or helicopter ID numbers?" he asked.

"I've racked my brains," I said, "and I think the pilot was a Lieutenant Smith and with him a Warrant Officer De ... something."

"WO DeVille ... son-of-a-bitch! He got fragged a week ago...he's dead."

My knuckles whitened on the handset. "I heard you had someone wounded."

"That was the situation when he went to the MASH unit. Something suspicious happened there resulting in his death. It's being investigated."

"It's possible our missing sergeant could be involved."

"Before they hauled him off to the hospital, DeVille muttered something about the murder of two elderly Vietnamese civilians," he said.

"My God, the sergeant and I were with them on that occasion. The sergeant did the shooting."

"Our warrant officer didn't remember who they transported or we would have warned you. Looks like someone is covering his tracks by getting rid of witnesses." His voice shaky, "One or both of our suspects may be dead already."

After "captain ring knocker" turned out extra military police for the gate and perimeter guard, he opened a bottle of rust-colored Japanese scotch, its geisha girl label covered in red-on-yellow kanji characters. "From the way your tan just disappeared, I think you could benefit from a bit of this."

As the minutes passed, we drank a lot more than a bit. I still felt reluctant to believe Ratcliff was trying to kill me. As the shooter, he must have been consumed with guilt. No wonder he acted crazy, but Lieutenant Smith gave the order. The sergeant or the lieutenant—one of them the murderer—and if the one got the other it would be my turn next.

After the guards reported the area secure, the captain led me to the officers' barracks. I remember dropping on my bunk fully clothed. He removed my boots before turning out the light.

Only a few hours had passed when the shouting and banging started. I swam slowly up out of a drunkard's sleep to awaken confused and slow-witted. I fumbled the light to the on position. Something heavy in the hallway rammed against the wall, shaking the room and spider-webbing the plasterboard.

The weight shifted and boomed against the wall on the other side of the hall. My door slammed open. I could see two men gripping each other. They moved in a jerky macabre dance—one arm around each other's backs, the fingers of their free hands interlocked around something vaguely resembling a small pineapple.

Bleary-eyed and dazed, I tried to focus on the faces of the two as they twisted back and forth. I recognized Private Willis, then in an ice-water moment, Lieutenant Smith. Willis, taller and more muscled than his opponent, barely held his own. Smith must have been loaded to the gills with adrenaline.

When I recognized the object they were holding, my own glands started pumping. The two squeezed a hand grenade missing its pin! Willis must have been coming to see me, and surprised Smith, who was about to roll the grenade under my bunk. I slapped my cheeks in an attempt to clear my head. I must intervene.

Before that could happen, hands fumbled, losing their grip. The safety spoon flew off, bounced off the concrete floor with a metallic ping. We had five seconds!

I saw something that would brand my memory forever. Willis twisted Smith's grenade hand inward and pulled their bodies together, tighter than any lovers' embrace. An ancient "fight or flight" instinct rushed forward. Time seemed to slow down—it was so compressed that tears for Willis were forming even as I tried to dive to safety. I felt the explosion more than heard it. The bodies muffled the noise. The pressure wave slapped my skin like the rough discipline of an abusive father. I felt knives in my legs and buttocks and a slicing, cutting pain on the top of my head.

My first breath drew in acrid blue smoke. I couldn't see out of one eye. Coughing, I reached up and felt blood running where a flap of my scalp had peeled back. With ringing ears, I pushed myself around. The door and walls were peppered with holes. What remained of Smith lay half through the doorway. Draped across his legs in the hall was Willis.

I belly-crawled toward them. Someone turned on a flashlight. I got a good look with my unbloodied eye. "Oh, God, oh, God, fuck ... fuck —"

They were both gutted. The grenade had gone off at stomach level. Not all the blood and body parts coating me were mine. I vomited what was left of the scotch on the floor. Someone put a towel on my head for a compression bandage.

"Stay with us, Lieutenant. They've called the medics," Sergeant Ratcliff said, his gnarled hands pressed the cloth. "I tracked the son-of-a-bitch for days. I checked the maps at HQ—not any free fire zone where he ordered the shooting."

~~~OOO~~~

It was daylight by the time they stitched my scalp together and picked the shrapnel out of my backside. The medics ticketed me for a recovery hospital in Japan. They assured me I had the proverbial million-dollar wounds. I would probably not return to Nam. The words held no meaning.

I would give a million, my life, and everything else I owned to get Willis back. Two weeks later, in a blue hospital robe with the Japanese version of "Blue Suede Shoes" playing from overhead speakers, I translated Ratcliff's cramped handwriting. Willis, DeVille, and Smith's families received official letters saying they died in combat fighting for their country. They would be given military funerals in their hometowns, the families presented with flags and medals.

"Obedient to Their Laws"

"Go tell the Spartans, stranger passing by, that here, obedient to their laws we lie."— Simonides.

Unstrung dolls … lie alone or clustered
in the mud along the trail.

Leaves, harvested by the ambush,
cover, soften crumpled body shapes.
Blue smoke curls in places the sun penetrates.

A whistle blows.
Low-pitched voices echo among the trees.
Shadows shake the underbrush.

I cough—taste vomit and blood.
A downy-cheeked soldier, elephant grass
stuck in his helmet net,
looks down tight-lipped.

The dead time between thoughts grows,
sweat stings my eyes. I blink
to keep focused.
My feet begin to twitch,
little animals seeking refuge.

He releases the spring-loaded bayonet
on his Chinese red stock rifle.
It snaps erect—a strange, thin phallus.
Laughter comes from my throat,
surprising us both.

His brows lift, he fixes the retaining ring
on the bayonet, locking it in place.

I am about to be violated.

The Ambush

aptain Parker had been awake since midnight. His drift into sleep interrupted when one of the base camp howitzers fired, evoking a shout of *"incoming"* from a green replacement just arrived from the States. This was the second time tonight. New guys couldn't tell the difference between outgoing artillery rounds and those inbound. Old-timers' bodies knew the difference. They didn't shout or hit the floor when American guns fired. They even slept through friendly fire. He heard the murmur of voices explaining to the new guy that if one heard a boom and a swishing noise the shell was outbound and if a swish and a boom incoming.

The fire from the big guns paused for varying intervals, which meant they didn't have a specific target—they were merely laying out a pattern of harassment and interdictory rounds designed to disrupt enemy movement. Charlie moved a lot of men and equipment under the cover of darkness. In theory, shells exploding on his supply lines at random locations and intervals should slow him down.

He thought about turning on the light and reading. That would keep him up too late and he'd pay the price in the morning. After adjusting the pillow, Parker worked on relaxing tight muscles in his neck. He took several deep even breaths. They didn't help. The room and entire officers' quarters reeked of sweat. The odor permeated the walls and mattresses. One could separate out the types of sweat: the ammonia odor of fear combined with plain old heat-sweat, but a noticeable absence of the sultry blended male-female kind. The peppery, metallic stink of sweat laced with adrenaline was the worst.

The faces of his men marched across his mind. They formed a grunt or infantry company, the Army's tip of the spear-point. Units like his did the fighting. Parker worried constantly about men and equipment. There was never enough. No miser could ever lust for gold as much as he yearned for a fully staffed company of veterans. Hell, even fifty percent veterans would do. Besides the losses from battle, sickness, and accidents, the rotation policy allowed for too much turnover. Experienced survivors went stateside after a year of duty. No recipe for success, the constant influx of green troops, especially draftees, created casualties at disproportionate rates.

Good leaders could reduce losses. He thought about his sergeants, mostly competent men, but again about half of them inexperienced. The officers were another sad story. The executive officer had proved to be a good administrator but possessed little fighting experience. In his second tour, his Senior Lieutenant Jesus Santos, the first platoon commander, knew the terrain and the enemy. The other three, with one exception, college boys fresh out of ROTC, not even a West Pointer or mustang among them. Their time with the company would be a crapshoot. The life span of a new second Louie in combat hit a new low in Vietnam—two-and-a-half minutes.

The exception came with some unusual baggage. Lieutenant Teigler, a recent returnee from a hospital stay in Japan, was a loner and an enigma. His first trip to Nam in an undercover intelligence unit only lasted six months.

Something strange happened to get him transferred to the infantry. The intelligence branch did not ordinarily allow men with top-secret clearances out of their grasp. His records were conspicuously empty of details. Questions about his background remained unanswered since no one in the company or even at battalion level possessed the security clearance or the need-to-know. The only clue to any suspicious activity came in the form of a leftover copy of a cover letter from a report prepared by the Criminal Investigation Division (CID) office in Saigon. The report itself was missing. By chance, Parker knew the signer of the letter. Sergeant Cozeen had been an instructor at a riot suppression course he had taken at Fort Gordon. He'd check with him tomorrow.

~~~OOO~~~

The monsoon rain beat at the men. Great gray pillars of rain stomped over everything. The triple canopy jungle surrounding the patrol never got dry. Water trickled off millions of exposed plant surfaces to make background noise unique to the season and place. One could hear the percussion of drops landing on leaves like a thousand brushed snare drums. Water fell on the top foliage, then dripped downward from leaf to leaf accumulating until one heard the thrup, thrup, thrup noise of rivulets slapping the spongy jungle floor. Flesh could take the constant soaking, but standard issue leather boots rotted out after three months.

So far, it had been one of those usual patrols; no sign of the enemy. One man took a pungee stick in his calf from a pit trap. Two others hauled him back, reducing the group to nine. The remaining men dealt with the damp misery by focusing on family, girlfriends, or the chance the next mail call would bring something good. Everyone drifted off in his own little world, lulled by the drumming, drumming, drumming of the rain. The dreams were better than reality, but not being alert in the here-and-now could get you killed.

It happened fast—the detonation of a mine blasting air and steel balls down the trail, sweeping away Sergeant Brant and two eighteen-year-old privates—then the crazy roar of automatic weapons. The confetti of bullet-shredded plants showered skin, clothes, and the falling, jerking bodies of the dying.

Seconds became minutes as the brain flushed ancient survival drugs into arteries. Lieutenant Teigler saw the melting faces of the soldiers to his sides—plastic skin and putty muscles twisted into fear and pain. Bits of flesh and liquid sprayed out as slugs erupted from their backs.

They were killing his men! He felt anger rise and burst. This time it was no ancient "fight or flight" instinct that emerged, but a wholly separate creature. Pure rage unlocked a deeply buried reptile, an ancient animal that dwells invisibly in the core of all men, a creature that knows no fear, no mercy, and no restraint, only the madness of the moment.

Sergeant Washington, to his left, bumped against him. Blood exploded from the man's head, splattering Teigler's face. Bullets jerked the soldier upright, bringing the machete sheathed over his right shoulder within reach. Teigler's claws closed on the hilt. It slid out of the sheath as the sergeant's hundred eighty pounds of dead meat dropped to the trail floor. A copper-jacketed slug sparked off the blade sending a painful shock up the lieutenant's arm.

A low guttural hiss began to form in his throat as his eyes shrunk to mere slits above lips forming a rictus—the machete grew into his sinews and bone. He rushed into the brush, slipping through resisting growth, running toward the enemy's green tracer bullets.

Pausing out of the kill zone, possessed by a newly released personality, the panting body crouched and cocked its head left then right, listening for the direction of the firing. It was behind them. Leaping forward, the reptile saw smoke and steam rising over a prone enemy firing an overheated rifle. The steel-claw blade flashed down between the Viet Cong's neck and shoulder, then three more times chopping open the skull.

The creature stripped off the belt containing canteen, compass, and bandage. The bloody nylon shirt came ripping off. Shooting continued to the man-reptile's right. Bare-chested, it scurried toward the sound and the rising mists of weapons smoke. The eleven or twelve Viet Cong in the ambush force remained laid out in a firing line at ten-foot intervals. Thick brush isolated them from each other. The angry flame in its mind grew overtones of green and blue, pleasure and disappointment. This was too easy.

~~~OOO~~~

The helicopter lowered itself slowly into the giant doughnut-hole-shaped clearing hacked and blasted out of the jungle; the rotors missed the surrounding growth by only a few meters on each side. Captain Parker spotted Lieutenant Santos and his radioman leaning forward against the rain-filled prop wash, one hand holding their boonie hats. Hopping off the bird's left skid, he moved in a half-crouch until he cleared the whirling chopper blades.

"What in the hell is going on?" he said. "Why am I out here?"

"Captain," Santos said after a pause, "decisions need to be made that exceed my authority. Let me show you."

In the ten minutes it took to reach the ambush site, Parker adjusted to the jungle. The green amorphous mass became individual plants, the sour must-rot odor grew bearable, and he could more clearly pick up human voices against the rain's white noise.

Santos halted on the trail. "I've secured the area. Our wounded evacuated, the dead and the survivors are still here. The action started at this location. From the physical signs and the survivors' stories, the patrol proceeded in proper formation. The point man missed any sign of the VC. They appear to have been planted in this spot for as long as five days. It would have been a miracle if he had spotted them."

"From the way the foliage is shredded," Parker said, "it looks like they got hit first with one of those Chinese-made shotgun mines."

Santos nodded, "That was the signal for the others to open fire with rifles and automatic weapons. The enemy spread their men over a hundred-foot front in the area to our right. From the prone position they swept their weapons back and forth spraying bullets in a zone between two and four feet above the ground."

"I've seen it before, the victims get hit in the legs first and then several more times as they fall through the cloud of metal. Where's Teigler? Your radio report said he and two others made it."

Santos's tan face paled. He motioned the captain to follow him and moved into the brush. "Here's where the lieutenant departed from the patrol. You can see the broken twigs and crushed vegetation left in his wake. At this point, he overran the ambush, stopped to get his bearings, and then attacked, rolling up the VC's left flank."

Parker stared at the first enemy body, the head a red-gray pudding of blood and crushed bone. The smell of voided bowels and already rotting blood roiled up about him. His nose and lips twitched. Santos pulled at his sleeve. They moved, not talking, past nine more bodies all with the same death wounds. They found number eleven fifty feet on looking as if he had run, but not fast enough. The final body must have been the Viet Cong leader.

"The killing of this one took some time," Santos said. "We found his right arm still clutching a jammed AK-47 about twenty feet back, then the second limb near here. He took a while to bleed out. It appears that was the plan."

The VC leader's body lay at an angle across the trail, torso twisted by its final convulsions. To Parker, it looked like a discarded alien slug-creature, minus arms, face a wooden witch mask, and black-stone eyes staring. The captain felt the morning's breakfast in his stomach turn sour and start to rise. With an effort, he forced it back. "Where's Teigler? How many know about this?"

"Sergeant Kolwalski has him under guard. No one besides the sergeant, my radioman, and you know. Not even the patrol survivors have any idea."

"Have your platoon dig in. You'll remain here for another day. I'll have rations, water, and anything else you need flown out. Keep the area isolated. Mark the positions of our dead and chopper the bodies back to camp. Don't touch anything else. Get the exec on the radio. We need the CID investigators out here, especially Sergeant Cozeen. Take me to Teigler."

The soldiers stared at the man sitting on the ground, arms around his knees. Hunched over and shaking, his body, especially the naked upper torso, was covered and clotted with what looked like sticky, bloody raw hamburger. The rain failed to penetrate the coating—his tears had done a better job. Two lighter runnels showed on each side of his nose.

The captain thought about the sequence of events resulting in his causalities and the enemy dead. "You son-of-a-bitch, abandoning your men to hare off in the bush! You violated every fucking rule of combat. I'll have your ass."

Teigler didn't respond. He sat, eyes closed, head resting on his knees, arms flaccid alongside his calves. Muscles in his cheek and back twitched at random. The foursome stood waiting for an answer—an explanation.

The captain twisted his fingers into fists. "Are you some kind of fucking psychopath? We are soldiers. We take out or capture the enemy. We don't murder like serial killers. You need to be locked up with a shrink. You will never serve in my company again."

Silence crept in as heavy as the rain running from the men's clothes, radio, and rifles. Teigler opened his eyes, stared past their knees into the jungle. Coiled on a low tree branch, a mottled green snake raised its head, their golden eyes locked—the reptile's tongue flickered in recognition.

Valkyrie

her hair shivers in the light
airs from the trees

those courtesan hips summon,
a samba quilted from women's music.

she sways close, pale fox eyes clever,
wills my heart to stutter.

phoenix four,
this is alpha one.
fast movers inbound,
eta, two mikes,
over.

I lay full length, broken,
metallic blood scent
fogs red-crusted grass.
nearby,
my wounded radioman,
his beaten-dog whimpers
worm-crawl into my ears.

phoenix four,
this is alpha one.
napalm drop on your position,
over.

ah!
the rush,
this fiery rush,
her passion
melts my skin, so hot …

my eyes flash into liquid crystal.

A Chat with Uncle Ho

stumble over jungle roots, the only one still movin'—'Merican or Viet Cong—from an ambush gone way balls-up. Gunfire stutterin' and claymore pellets buzzin', why, we must of shot enough to kill each other a dozen times. The El-Tee left us, run off into the bush. All those round-eyed and slant-eyed boys screamin' and cryin', it was more than I could bear.

My daddy always said I was soft hearted. He told me it was part of the gift, me bein', accordin' to him, the seventh son of a seventh son.

"Boy, you'll have the sight. You will see behind those curtains closed to us. Your mam's family traces back to Old Wales and many of her folk came to these hills knowin' the meanin' of dreams and the craftin' of potions and charms."

The monsoon rain started slammin' down again bruisin' my shoulders, the kind of rain that soaks you through and through, but gives no relief from the heat—no relief from the mud and stinks. Don't make no difference, I guess, my uniform nothin' but slicked down rags and boot soles flappin' with every step. I raised my hands. They were wrinkled and pale. The skin between my thumb and forefinger so pale and thin you could look through and see jungle leaves and stalks.

After wanderin' lost for a while, I started followin' a trail of smoke. Funny how things can burn in a country so wet. Not much like home though, too hot, too wet, lots of bugs—some real ugly fist- sized ones too.

Finally, broke outta the jungle onto a road, in the ditches dead women and children tumbled together with red-black patches crusted on their skin—awful quiet, their torn soaked bodies overlappin' like Gran's crazy quilts.

Up a ways, there was a clearin' with tumbled rubbish where hooches had stood, their thatch still smokin' and glowin'. The smell was god-awful, jungle decay mixin' with burnin' garbage, manure, and grease.

An old man was hunkered down in soft ashes and smoke, as still and quiet as could be. He wore one of those funny-shaped rice straw hats and a rain cape made the same. He was lucky, the drops was fallin' like a mother's hard tears. Splattin' and makin' the embers hiss, they probably kept him from bein' fried. Feathers of ragged smoke from the fires drifted cross his wrinkled skin, coatin' him with oil that smelt like burnt pig. His wispy beard and moustache were blackened and clotted.

I stood quiet for a while, waitin' for him to talk, rememberin' to show respect for older folks. Then I asked, "What's this place called?" He didn't stir. "Is there a town or base nearby?" I couldn't tell if'n he heard.

I took three steps back toward the road when he says, "The name doesn't matter."

Encouraged, I ask, "Who are you, Granfather?"

He muttered somthin' about 'Mericans and says, "You can call me Uncle Ho. Do you know who you are, spirit child?"

"Uncle Ho, what happened here?"

"We have witnessed your coming and going … Chinese, Mongols, French, communists, Americans …"

As he was talkin', I could see pictures of old-timey men and women fightin' an' strugglin'.

"Your bodies melt away and your souls wander. And you? Why are you still with us?"

"Uncle Ho, won't it stop sometime?"

I caught a flash in the corner of my eye. I turned and saw a good-sized lizard skitter across the road into the jungle. When I looked back, Uncle Ho had gone. I returned to the road, it had to go somewhere, didn't it? Around the first bend, I thought I saw the back of another soldier, his hair blond like mine. His clothes and boots like mine. The road narrowed. I started walkin' faster and so did he. Jungle closed in on the road. I started shoutin' and runnin'.

We clawed at bushes an' branches, our bare arms moved through them without bein' cut and scratched, our shouts echoed. His shirt rode up. I could see three bullet-flowered wounds in his back. It brought back the memory of pain in my chest and stomach. My palms felt for the pain, came away crusted, sticky, and red. The soldier and road were gone, only hot, thick jungle all around—dark even in broad daylight.

"O, Jesus, not me?"

---OOO---

A Huey jinked overhead one way then another as the pilots of the heavily loaded medevac navigated their army green helicopter between marching pillars of monsoon rain.

"John," the pilot said, "I just caught the flash of a white face." The lieutenant started to move his control stick to induce a turn.

"Probably not, El-Tee," replied the co-pilot warrant officer. "We just picked up the last of the bodies from Lieutenant Teigler's ambushed patrol—all accounted for."

"No other of our troops in the area?"

"None for kilometers, no natives either—for some reason they stay away from this patch. Nothing human down there."

Quantum Many Worlds

My sleeping men lie scattered
among desert scrub in quilted camo blankets.
Their lovers, in 5.56 and 7.62 millimeters,
held close.

It is a time of waiting—that last hour
of morning when nocturnal animals and spirits
are almost at rest. Yet, we day creatures
remain hushed, hidden, until slapped
by the hot Afghan sun. In the stillness,

I dream of multiple copies of me, acting
their parts in alternate times and places—
our worlds stacked side by side
like an infinite deck of cards. From their faces

flashes of gunfire, the rush
of adrenaline, the smell of copper,
rising in mist from cooling flesh.
The acid of dawn burns exposed skin.

Alien worlds and madness
spiral shut. Shadows cut back
and forth among Rīgestān dunes, whisper
in Pashtu. Black gunmetal rasps
against gravel and sand. My eyes
snap open, glass-empty.

The Monitor

Nasty dark visions woke me. It was almost that early hour when the Viet Cong launched their attacks, while the cover of night still masked their approach and the coming dawn let them see their targets. With luck and proper timing, they would be inside the wire slicing our bacon, before we could react.

I rubbed my bristly cheek and chin. My fingers came away coated with greasy body oil and dirt. Skin exposed during the night itched from wall-to-wall insect bites—couldn't tell if they came from crawling or flying ones. I pushed up from the sandbagged floor, adjusted my boonie hat, and snugged down the strap on the shoulder holster securing my GI .45 automatic.

The gun fired a heavy, jacketed bullet about the diameter of the average male trigger-finger. An immediate man-killer, accurate at the same range one could throw a bowie knife. It fired reliably in a monsoon downpour or after being immersed in jungle mud for a week.

My passion for the weapon began at an early age with intensive schooling by Marine and Army veterans: my father and grandfather. I was reintroduced to the pistol at a Fort Benning, Georgia target range. Its kick-like-a-mule reputation frightened my fellow trainees. I whispered as I picked it up, "We're not going to hurt each other now, are we?" The butt shaped and merged to my hand like Excalibur fit Arthur's. The two of us qualified as an expert hybrid-killing machine.

Its reputation and three-pound weight were comforting, especially since Okie, Caber, and I remained the only Americans in the unit. Operating independently, we three had broken all the speed records in getting to the top of our various superiors' shit lists. At their first opportunity, they shipped us out to operate as advisors to a *Ruff-Puff* South Vietnamese outfit.

Ruff-Puff was GI mocking slang for their real designation: Regional/Popular Forces. RF/PF units consisted of young married men living with their families in fortified villages. Under the command of the province chief, they guarded population centers and road junctions, did short-range patrolling, and operated as auxiliaries during local maneuvers of regular army units.

The lack of training and WWII hand-me-down weapons made my heart skip a beat every time I imagined them in combat. Their corporals and sergeants, jumped-up local boys, received rank through family connections rather than through merit or experience. The few native officers assigned were exiles, whose problems with drink, petty corruption, or lack of political favor left them to rot at the bottom of the South Vietnamese military pyramid. Supposedly compensating for all the shortcomings, the rear echelon motherfuckers in Saigon believed these amateurs' motivation would be superior—these boys and old men—all that stood between a Viet Cong attack and their families.

However, this time, all the wives and kiddies had stayed behind. Yesterday, twenty of us luckless bastards jumped off trucks to defend a fortified tower and bunker complex, which guarded a major road junction. The French built the tower, a two-story concrete phallic monstrosity, during their last years as a failing colonial power. It ran twenty feet in diameter, its white skin pierced with firing ports on the first and second levels.

The Vietnamese had added cube-shaped sandbagged bunkers, connected by trenches, in an oval around the tower. Fifty feet out, they staked out what little barbwire survived their leaky supply channels. Over time, the woven hemp fabric of the sandbags became bleached gray by unrelenting sun and stained red where monsoon rains leached out some of their dirt filling. Windblown plant seeds germinated in the cracks between the bags adding shaggy patches of green.

From the roads, the whole mess looked like one of those Civil War iron ships called monitors—bunkers and trenches mimicked the hull and the tower the gun turret. However, while the ship's armor offered good resistance to weapons of the period, today's technology made our protection significantly less capable.

We had driven by the installation at other times and talked about how impossible it would be to defend. The egg-shaped layout meant that the bunkers on the ends possessed blind spots not covered by interlocking fire from the other positions. The east end of the fortification lay too near the tree line. The enemy would have to cross only a short piece of open ground to the protection of drainage ditches alongside the road. From there, it was a few meters to three strands of thinly stretched wire.

The VC's rocket-propelled grenades or RPGs would have no problem piercing the bunker walls. They carried automatic weapons and would be supported by mortar fire. The communists also possessed an intelligence gathering system that knew every inch of our little home, including the names and ancestry of our troops and weapons. Hell, those people knew more about who fathered us than we did.

In spite of all those advantages, the enemy possessed a major flaw. While Charlie studied Mao's little guerilla book, he hadn't read about how "no plan survives first contact with the enemy." He frequently called off attacks if the opening move became spoiled.

I crept out of the far-west bunker into the darkness. The air wasn't any fresher outside, with its smell of rotting plants and human excrement, but at least it wasn't laced with Vietnamese cigarette smoke. Okie swore that instead of tobacco, the locals smoked a mixture of old ground-up wrestlers' shorts and stinkweed. I bent over to move through the trench—the Vietnamese didn't dig deep enough to cover six footers. Patches of red mud sucked at my boots, filled in the half-inch tread, which caused me to slip even on the dry parts.

Pushing aside a tattered green poncho, I entered the tower's hollow belly. A single flashlight bulb wired into a spare radio battery cast angular, tessellated shadows off walls and equipment. The light source hit the two men inside at an angle, illuminating only their cheeks and foreheads. It left black shadows hovering in their eye sockets. They looked like animated skulls. I hoped it wasn't an omen.

At the radio, Okie listened to communication checks and chatter on our frequency, to his right stood Uncle Ho. No one knew his real name. The elderly native with his traditional scraggly white beard and moustache looked the spitting image of the great leader of the North. The old man and his grandson, Nam, had latched onto us when we discovered them begging in the local outdoor market. They were the sole survivors of an enemy attack on their village up north, near the border between the Vietnams. The locals shunned the pair. Village gossips spread rumors that Ho was some kind of shaman with the power to see and talk with the dead.

Okie, as one might guess, came from Oklahoma, his dark eyes and crow-black hair gifts from a Cherokee grandmother. His prior gang experience predisposed him to small, tightly knit groups with strong leaders. In Viet Nam, he got neither. Personnel were constantly being rotated out—most soldiers only there for a year. Worse, officers spent six months out, six months in. They led a combat unit for the first half of their tour and then took a staff position for the remainder. The turnover of experienced leaders and infantrymen left the constantly green replacements confused about whom to follow when it became their turn to "ride the dragon." After his platoon caught hell in a couple of balls-up firefights, Okie's bad attitude placed him at the top of his grunt company's transfer list.

"Is Caber up and about?" I asked.

"He crept in shortly after midnight and sacked out upstairs, but I heard him taking a piss off the side of the tower a few minutes ago," Okie said.

Red-haired, reaching six-foot-five and 230 pounds, Robert Bruce MacDonald owed fealty to the most international of the Scottish clans. His nickname, Caber, came from wins in the Scottish Highland Games in one of the heavy events: the caber toss. The competitors took a short run forward vertically balancing a 19-foot-long, 130-pound piece of timber, which they flipped end over end. I watched it done once at a clan gathering in Texas. Never did figure out how it was scored.

Caber's fall from regulation-grace resulted from the Army's discovery that he conducted more family than military business. If they thought this transfer would slow down his black market activities, they misjudged both his ability and the ingenuity of his relatives. The MacDonald Clan and their numerous dependents owned various commercial ventures, most legitimate, wherever in the world capitalism was allowed to flower. Before being caught, Caber had almost cornered the Southeast Asian market in booking rock bands for military units, and a sideline renting porno films.

For me, this assignment was a last chance. In the middle of a massive buildup, the Army needed every half-assed trooper. During my first assignment, I had been one of several witnesses to the murders of two elderly Vietnamese men. The killer started eliminating us to avoid prosecution. The final death toll was five, including the killer and my best friend, who sacrificed himself to save me. I was sent to an infantry unit as part of a cover-up, where I led a patrol almost wiped out by an enemy ambush. The attacking Viet Cong unit was killed off one-by-one. The relief force reported I stalked and killed almost a dozen enemies with a machete.

My recollection only included feeling helpless as my men were shot down, then reptilian rage and fear so red and powerful it burned out any coherent memories of the next thirty minutes. My psychiatric evaluation resulted in a diagnosis of multiple personality disorder. All I knew, someone, or something used my body when I wasn't there. Unfortunately, the colonel in charge of reassignments didn't believe in such fairytales. He transferred me to the only place that didn't care.

Okie, Caber, and I all came together for the first time in a two-room, brown-roofed house used as a combination aid station and advisors' living quarters. It was located behind the ten-foot-high, earth-bermed, heavily guarded walls of the province chief's compound. Two Vietnamese army medics ran a medical clinic in the outer room. Boot prints and trash littered the floor. I couldn't tell if there was grout between the tiles or just solid green mold and bacteria colonies. The medics sat stiffly in their chairs, forearms resting on an official-looking table. Behind them, a lonely half-bottle of iodine and some aspirin tins sat on the shelves of a glass cabinet.

The boom of a pistol fired in close quarters echoed off the walls. I crouched. My hand went to the butt of my Colt. The medics hadn't jumped. They looked down at the floor with guilty smiles, a Vietnamese cultural rule: never look a superior in the eye, it showed disrespect.

I strode into the second room. Its furnishings consisted of a rickety field desk, two chairs, and three wood and canvas bunks with mosquito netting hung from cross bars at the ends—everything, including wood, clothing, and bags in the popular decorator shade of olive drab. Light entering from unglazed screened windows reflected off cream-colored plaster on the walls. Paired wires looped through a hole punched in one of the screens to power a naked light bulb hung from a hook centered in the ceiling,

The men in the room remained in their original positions, one prone on a bunk, a nudist magazine rolled in one hand. The other lay back in a chair, feet up on the desk, held a smoking .357 caliber revolver. Splayed on the floor, white bellies up, lay two dead finger-length green lizards. I didn't notice any holes in the lizards or the walls.

"You shooting blanks?" I asked.

"Only with the pistol," he said.

I met his stare, on the edge of disrespect—a test. After a long minute, he pulled his feet off the desk. He said, "Nothin' to do 'round here. I pulled the slugs out of the cartridges and poured in melted wax. You can pop lizards without damagin' anythin'."

"It's nothing to me," I responded, "but the locals allow those bug-eaters to live in their houses." During my first visit to a Vietnamese home, they served hot tea. I almost baptized my gonads with it when I witnessed the creatures run along the floor, up the wall, and across the ceiling, their tiny claws catching invisible footholds in the plaster.

After depositing my duffle bag at the foot of the unoccupied bunk, I dropped my butt on its lumpy mattress, and opened an army-issue map case. I dumped out three manila-colored personnel files. The two soldiers' lack of courtesy reaffirmed my conclusion that any attempt to get them under military discipline would only cause rebellion. They were both the products of tight-knit societies with unique rituals and beliefs. I would build on their experience.

"Fellow screw-ups," their eyebrows went up, "my name is Lieutenant Rod Teigler. I have had the pleasure of reading your 201 files," I said. "In this kind of unit, where Americans are few, and a snap decision by one of us could result in the death of the others, I don't believe in keeping any secrets. During the next half hour, I am going to report to the province chief and check out the scenery. Here's my file. I want you both to read it. When I return I will answer any questions—and, I mean *any* questions—you care to pose about my personal or professional history. When you finish with me, I hope you will allow each other access to your files, which took a very generous bribe to procure, and a similar question and answer period.

~~~OOO~~~

A fully developed head cruncher racked me. It was my fault. On the way back from the province chief's office, I remembered some ancient folklore from my high school Latin class. We had read *Caesar's Commentaries* on his military campaign in Gaul. He observed Gallic tribesmen debated solutions to their problems twice: once sober and once drunk. I stopped by the marketplace, purchased two cases of *Ba Moui Ba*, Vietnamese beer. That night we tried the Old Gallic route in trading personal information. As one might suspect, the conversation stayed a little stiff until we broached the second option.

After the beer was gone, my new comrades pulled out hard stuff from hidden places. Things got *real* lively. Fortunately, excessive consumption struck us harmless before we decided to burn down the village and chase the locals' daughters through the bush.

I managed to pry open one gummy eye. Through the blinding mid-morning light, I saw one of the tiny lizards crawling across the ceiling. If Okie shot this one, I would kill him. I took a sniff. Magnified by the humid air, the smell consisted of a nose-boggling combination of bad breath and male foot odor, laced with a touch of vomit. Without moving, my head raced in and out on a mad tide, crashing against rocks.

Maybe my plan worked. From what I recalled, we had gained enough blackmail material about each other to ensure our mutual destruction ... hmm, cooperation. However, it would take a day or two to recover—such the price of male bonding.

The memory faded. In spite of my fanatical desire to be somewhere else, I was back at the crossroads, in the dark, waiting the enemy. I noticed a size-thirteen pair of boots descending from the tower's second level. "Let's go over the plan once more. Caber?"

"I took delivery of the goods after sunset last night. The caltrops are about two inches in height," he said, handing out samples.

The devices looked like large versions of the *jacks* the neighborhood girls used to play with. Four sharpened steel prongs arranged at angles allowed them to present one spike upright no matter how they landed when tossed on the ground.

"Uncle Ho, these are an old European invention which will make anyone who steps or lands on them very unhappy."

"No," Ho said, "not European, Chinese have first."

"Okay," I said, no time to pursue that line further. "Are they in place and will whoever made them keep the secret?"

"No problem, El-Tee," Caber responded. "Father MacDonald's folks are loyal to him and seventy miles to the north."

"Father MacDonald? You have a relative who's a priest? No, don't answer."

"All of these bad boys are placed in the far side ditches on the roads to the east and south," Caber said, "the most likely avenues of attack. While slipping through the dark, spreading our little spiny-metal friends, I detected VC scouts in the tree lines. In spite of a very strong impulse, I left their fucking necks unbroken."

"Okie?"

"Well, El-Tee," he drawled, "the men moved the Brownin' .30 caliber machine gun from its daylight position and built a nice little nest in one of the connectin' trenches. In its place, we left a black-painted wooden mockup. I'm sure the enemy will blow that bunker first, thinkin' the gun is still there, but … *xin loi* … sorry about that.

"And, my task is completed," I said. "The gas cans stolen … borrowed from a generous engineer company are now full up with Mother Teigler's special recipe of gasoline, ivory flakes, diesel oil, and other ingredients I will not disclose until the patent comes through. The two hand grenades taped to the back of each can detonate with wires extending from the pull-rings to this tower. These infernal devices are a scaled-down version of a French napalm-type mine called a *fougass*."

"No," Ho said, "not French, Chinese make first."

"El-Tee," the other two said, "you a truly evil man. We salute you."

"Since the main attack will come against our weakest point closest to the tree line, I buried four of the fougass outside the trenches facing east, where their blast patterns will overlap. The village men positioned two more inside the abandoned end bunker.

"Uncle Ho will detonate them. The napalm should travel thirty or forty feet, the metal fragments farther. The ivory flakes will cause the burning fuel to stick to clothing, weapons, and skin.

"Whoever gets a dose, even a small one, will only think about going home to beg his mama to kiss his booboos. Anyone not touched should have their minds seriously fucked over watching torched, screaming comrades run by."

"As instructed," Okie said, "I'll be backin' up Uncle Ho to ensure no VC breaks into the defended part of our trenches."

"I will command the machine gun," Caber said, paused and smiled, "with the secondary mission of taking over in case you get wasted, El-Tee."

"Well, don't be so happy about it. Looks like we've got the basics covered," I replied. "Keep your men shooting, be attentive as they are new to combat and may get buck fever. Remember, take plenty of initiative, if Charlie gets any advantage—*any at all*—they'll nail our balls to the rafters of their …."

Interrupted by a loud metallic click, I glanced in Ho's direction. He finished snapping a sixteen-inch bayonet on the barrel of his Remington M-97 12-gauge pump shotgun. Modified for close-in fighting in the trench warfare of WWI, pumping the action while holding the trigger depressed allowed the gun to empty its eight-round magazine like an automatic weapon. The weapon was his baby. He kept it clean enough to eat off of.

"No questions? Go to your positions." I made a major effort to bleed confidence from my eyes into theirs. If we didn't believe we would win, no number of tricks would help. The four of us slapped hands together and chanted, "Kill VC!"

~~~OOO~~~

My eyes detected light on the horizon. We would be hit soon. Walking down the line, I stopped at each position to make sure all appeared awake with weapons ready. I took a long look at Uncle Ho's grandson Nam. Head movements jerky, his hands twisted the sling on his carbine. I made a mental note to check on him again. The inspection completed, I settled in the south-facing bunker. This would be the focal point of Charlie's diversionary attack. He would keep our attention focused here, while his main force knocked out the unsupported east bunker and rolled us up with an advance down our own trenches.

The village boys squatted in spider holes, complete with covers, dug deep into the bunker floors next to the outside walls. When rocket-propelled grenades pierced the sandbags, they would be out of the stream of superheated gas and metal these weapons generated. The bunkers also offered mortar round protection.

Numbers scrolled in my head. I counted down the last sixty seconds before sunrise. A few repressed hisses and groans came from the roadsides. Caltrops had stuck the Viet Cong who crawled out of the tree lines into the ditches—first blood went to us.

The count got down to fifteen when we heard the *whump* and felt the earth-jerk of enemy mortar shells exploding. They'd stop once their men charged. I flopped into my hole in time to avoid the first RPG detonation. My ears rang from the *blam* of the explosion. I felt a pulse of skin-blistering heat. Bits of heat-fused dirt stung my back like little shotgun pellets.

Whistles blew, followed by shouting. Charlie's infantry was coming.

The Browning cut loose, so far, so good. I watched it create a knife-blade spread of slugs at 400 rounds per minute, cutting down two men in loose black clothing. A third man's shock and pain was obvious as thirty-caliber bullets blew through his lungs and stomach. Gravity pulled him into the barbwire web.

Without knowing how it got there, I held my forty-five. My body felt feverish. Something else shared my head with me. I tried to push out a reptilian coldness. A stranger's roar burst from my mouth.

Our village boys clustered at the gun ports shooting and yelling. I saw rolling flashes in my peripheral vision—fougass being detonated. High-pitched screams came from that direction. Ho's shotgun barked twice. A twist of exploded air carried the smell of burnt human-pork mixed with nitrates and gasoline.

The attack in front petered out. A grenade exploded to my left rear. It was too close and didn't sound like one of ours. My body slithered down the trench. I couldn't feel my feet hit the ground. My eyes tunnel-visioned.

I entered the next bunker. The creature inside me made a split-second decision. The pistol in my hand bucked. A bullet went through the firing port and knocked back an enemy about to drop in a second grenade. The first had killed two of the three villagers and left the air fouled with a blue acrid haze. The one left alive was Nam, frozen on the floor beside his dropped weapon. He smelled of urine.

My left hand grabbed his web belt and threw him at the gun port. I forced him to look at two guerillas firing AK-47s as they ran toward us. Fragments of dirt and rock from their bullet strikes flew through the opening, felt like needles sticking our cheeks. I pushed his weapon forward, shouted his name, and fired it. Nam came out of his daze. I put his hands on the carbine. Without further coaching, he fired off a full magazine, replaced it, fired three more rounds—no VC left.

The thirteen-year-old turned away, pressed his cheek against the gunstock, his shoulders quivered. Dirt and black grit from expended explosives mixed with sweat filled the lines and pores on his skin. My eyes felt like bad acupuncture victims. The cunning scaly one in my mind left. The cold vestige of its personality made me nauseous.

The attack ended, my world quiet. I slumped, loose-spined against the sandbags, exhausted—an empty sack of skin. It took two shaky tries to get the pistol on safe and back in its holster.

"El-Tee, are you all right?"

Caber filled the doorway. I waved one hand, lowered my chin, and swallowed back a spoonful of stomach acid before saying, "If you're here it must be over, what were our causalities?"

"Okie and Ho are fine, we've got three wounded, and I see two bodies here."

"The enemy?"

"Fucking A! We kicked their ass good. The Browning got five, Ho fried three, and you guys got three. They carried off the wounded and dead who weren't under our guns."

"Get a situation report off to HQ on the radio."

I looked down at the dead. A feeling of relief rose in my mind. Someone else would notify their wives and mothers, my Vietnamese not up to the task. A flush of guilt followed—I would be there when they were told.

Uncle Ho came wearing a stiff Asian face looking for Nam. I noticed his jaw muscles relax when the boy moved. The skin around the old man's black eyes crinkled as they focused on me.

He stroked his mustache and beard, as close as he would ever come to a thank-you.

Sweat-dreams

Near my hunting boots, a broke-back rabbit jerks.

blood smell knife-pricks my nostrils   soldiers' bodies
twitch in the grass

A fire-black, glass-shattered Chevy squats in a ditch.
Shadows chase the wrecker's strobe light.

a rocket-propelled grenade's magma-hot sun
overturned smoked jeep   faces burned off

The syrup-thick stink of a packing plant's butchered hogs
flushes through the car vents.

my Vibram-soled jungle boots deadlift mud   repetition
after repetition   slog between day-old bullet-flowered corpses

In the corral's dry, gray dust a dead cow, ballooned up
with August heat, waits the knacker's truck.

dead soldiers' swollen innards burst   flies deposit
human grease on my hands and face

The Assassin

The sun burned plants, earth, and men, the air stove hot. I could smell my own stink, that leftover adrenaline stink, when I moved. The hands on my army-issue watch read 0830.

In the background, cleanup squads moved bodies and stacked captured weapons. Some tied cloths around their faces, mostly to keep out the flies, the heat would soon push the blood-and-shit odor past what a normal nose could endure. Leaking body fluids left slick red mud around the dead, requiring each foot to be carefully placed.

An enemy's crisped body still smoked where fougass napalm had caught him. I hunkered down for a close-up look. When skin and body fat had been consumed, the flames stopped. But fire hadn't killed this one. A spray of number four buckshot had blown away the muscle and flesh on the man's back, chopped his spine, and shredded a kidney. White bone shards stood out in contrast to the red and gray of tissue and organs.

Ho's shot came as an act of unintended mercy. Burns this extensive were a soldier's worst nightmare—even morphine hardly dented the pain. Given the primitive medicine available to the Viet Cong, this one would have pleaded for death within the first hour.

Behind me I heard retching and Caber's voice. "Jesus Christ, Lieutenant, did you know what that fucking stuff would do?"

Nodding, I stood and staggered through the gate, stopped outside the perimeter wire. I kept my back to the tower, not wanting to see more, but the burnt-shit smell remained glued in my nostrils. My eyes watered from the stench—mostly from the stench. I kicked at a tuft of grass clinging to the red soil at the top of the roadside ditch.

My ears filled with the mixed noises of a crowd in motion. Normal domestic traffic moved through the crossroads: people on foot and bicycles, oxcarts, three-wheeled Lambrettas, and motor scooters—all moving like they had places to go and people to see. I caught the flashes of a few brown faces as they glanced at the carnage behind me and quickly looked away. In Vietnam, people learned not to attract attention after events like this. Enemy agents mingled among the innocent in such crowds. Government police would question anyone looking too interested. After force-filling a suspect's belly with water, a few gut punches later, detainees begged to confess.

Scanning the traffic, a bad feeling welled up. Something was different—stood out. My eyes locked on a city girl on a bicycle, dressed in an *ao dai*—a long-sleeved, one-piece blouse and ankle-length skirt slit waist-high on the sides. Loose-fitting white silk slacks showed underneath. A *non la* cone-shaped straw hat wobbled on her head. Her feet protected from the bike's rough metal pedals by pink plastic sandals imported from Singapore.

I wondered what attracted my attention as she cycled closer. Her long black hair and svelte body were attractive, but not more so than several others on the road. And I remained too fucked up from immediate combat stress to be horny—that compulsion would come roaring in later. She closed to about ten feet when it hit me. Her eyes never left me. Outside of whores, women in this culture would rather be beaten than stare at a man. She stopped, straddled her bike, the tension in her body obvious.

I licked dry lips. My hands came up palms out as though to warn her off. She looked over my shoulder, seemed to focus on something. I half-turned to see what it could be. In my side vision, I saw her reach under the front panel of her skirt.

Twisting back, I grabbed at the pistol in my shoulder holster. The strap wouldn't release. I tore at it. She was in trouble too, her weapon caught in the cloth of her skirt. We looked like a couple of prize fools, she fumbling in her crotch and me tugging at my chest. Who says the Dark Angel doesn't have a sense of humor?

I stopped, the pistol butt cold in my hand. Christ! Was there no fucking relief from this unending killing? My mind cherished the peace of death. I relaxed and waited.

From the rear, shouts in English called up a deep buried, adrenaline-released survival persona. It wasn't me. The snake returned. As a hopeless spectator, I felt muscles coil. The holster strap broke and the forty-five came loose.

The gun leveled. Her eyebrows lifted. It surprised both of us when it boomed. The heavy slug punched through the girl's chest and kicked her out of her sandals and off the bike.

The backward motion freed up her weapon, a snub-nosed revolver. It fired as she fell, whether on purpose or caused by a dying twitch, I couldn't tell.

Pain! Every nerve in my head and neck tried to leap out through my skin.

I clawed back to consciousness thirty minutes later as a medevac chopper dropped me at Cu Chi's 12th Evacuation Hospital. After a quick look-over, the doctor assured me I would live. The assassin's bullet gone high, plowed a furrow in my scalp, and nicked my skull. In the following days, all the doctors' drugs wouldn't stop the memories: the killings too intimate, too immediate. Not the arcade shooting of our training—the target appeared. You shot. It dropped cleanly and antiseptically out of sight.

Awake or asleep, the same sequence: burning, screaming soldiers, Vaseline-slick intestines hanging out of a man wrapped in barbwire. The muddy fields ripe with the churning odor of cooked and minced human meat. The girl blown off her feet, blood spraying out. The tuning fork hum of the bike frame as it struck the pavement, her bare child-size toes twitching—

I could never go back again.

The Appointment

I saw Death again today
standing in the middle of the block,
just on my way to work.

His clothes, dark shadow rags.
He smiled and waved,
withered fingers splayed.

Blank faced I stared
at that perfect stalker.
Perhaps, it was my time.

He wore a porkpie hat,
pulled down tight,
curls escaping around the edges.

Appearance not fashionable,
he didn't care
ultimate damn iconoclast.

He leaned forward, rubbed his chin
and rasped: "Remember,
I'll come when you make the appointment.

When your soul knows,
way beyond doubt, you are ready.
Friend, you've been so close at times."

Stickball in Brooklyn

he Reverend Captain A. C. Charles, Jr. walked out of his office at the 12th Evacuation Hospital careful to stay on the wooden boardwalks built with lumber from discarded artillery shell shipping boxes. The ground on either side mushed by the monsoon rain, had the look and consistency of rotten bloody oatmeal. Smells worse, he thought. During the afternoon's rounds, he would try to convince more ambulatory GIs to attend Sunday's service.

One patient in particular retained his interest. Lieutenant Teigler and he had fascinating past discussions on religious topics, such as St. Paul's letters, situation ethics, and other subjects. Teigler also related some firsthand knowledge of Vietnam's unique Cao Dai religion picked up during his current assignment. I think today I will ask about his perception of evil. He has experienced it in combat, of course.

~~~OOO~~~

"Evil, you say, Chaplain? Well I know the source, while I have been on the sharp end of the Devil's hi-jinx often enough, I only met him face to face one time. Let me set the scene for you. We start over three years ago and on the other side of the planet."

The street view was monotone, but with every line and curve of the curbs and streetlights sharply drawn. The townhouses lining both sides, pen and ink drawings, desperate for a wash of color but only getting the yellow pall of an urban sun. Cars lined both sides of the street, their sheet metal as fragile as tissue, leaving only a lane and a half down the middle. Here and there, they displayed crinkled fenders and missing hubcaps—old raggedy men showing off war wounds and football scars.

A pickup game of stickball was in progress with *Old Nick* challenging the kids on the block, although I didn't know who *he* was at the time. The game was simple but had dozens of variations. This one had three players: a batter, a pitcher, and a fielder. The batter hit a pitched tennis ball with the sawed-off three feet of a broomstick. One was called out after the traditional three strikes, or if the two others caught the ball before it touched the ground.

Lucifer could put a lot of power into the ball and spit out a real pithy line of patter he had picked up over the ages. Some of his Latin jibes were incredibly funny, most of which he had gotten off the walls of whorehouses and public urinals in Alexandria, Egypt, the intellectual center of the old Roman Empire. I guess those old scholars knew how to put a word or two together.

He had only mastered half the game, possessing no talent at fielding. The ball eluded him by spinning under cars or flying off fire hydrants at unexpected angles. Once it even went down a sewer grate. He loudly blamed it on the intervention of a vengeful God. Otherwise, Nick held his temper well, but when he worked up a sweat chasing the ricochets, you could detect the odor of brimstone.

~~~OOO~~~

My army buddy, Dante Cagliostro had put me up at his Brooklyn home during our holiday leave. Dante and I were both blends of the immigrant populations of The Republic, although the gene pools that produced us were different. Being from the Midwest, my bloodlines consisted primarily of German and New England Quaker pioneers. The early mixing of the two in the crucible of the extreme weather and primitive conditions of the prairie created some of the world's most stubborn people. Dante's Polish mother and Italian father's ancestors migrated to America during poor economic and political times in the old countries.

We would never be mistaken for brothers, Dante being blond, average height, blue-eyed and pudgy of face and body, while I provided the contrast as a thin six-footer with black hair and dark eyes. His personality was outgoing and expressive. A great storyteller, he constantly moved his hands and body—a trait emphasized by the Italian heritage—to accent points in conversation. My genes and upbringing ran to the opposite, more cynical.

For all the physical and cultural differences, we meshed well intellectually, having both smashed the Army's version of the I.Q. test. The military absorbed and manipulated us in all the little ways armies had learned from the days of the Caesars to the present. The computers threw us together with ten others due to our language ability and electronics background. Our group worked in D.C. on a top-secret code-word project concerning the simultaneous translation of Russian voice-radio messages. While the idea was worthy, the equipment of the period failed to live up to the task. We knew it was only a matter of time before the project closed and we went our separate ways.

Since it was over eight hundred miles to my parents' house in Iowa, I frequently received invites to visit the East Coast homes of the other team members over holidays. The Cagliostro's two-story townhouse blended into the heart of a borough that retained vestiges of the melting pot: Polish hair salon, Jewish bakery, Italian restaurant, and Irish used car lot.

An elevated portion of the subway bisected the neighborhood, running level with my second-floor guestroom. Shortly before the graffiti-covered trains became visible, a rumble-tide smacked against the outside walls, vibrations traveled through the floors, up the furniture legs increasing in intensity until the windowpanes hummed. During the sleepless minutes they created, I watched the faces of the passengers rush by only twenty feet away. They might as well have been mannequins, since their moment in view was so brief they looked frozen in position. I splayed my fingers and waved them in front of my eyes. It made the passing trains look like the flickering frames of an old silent movie. In my imagination, I gave the passengers personalities and fashioned a variety of plots where hero and heroine defeated the villain once more.

Our first morning, Dante and I set out to handle his mother's errands. He introduced me to various folks on the block. They quickly swept us into the relaxed warm embrace of the local culture—none of the scorn and rejection we felt in other places because of the war. The air was flush with the exotic bakery smell of fresh bagels, a treat still rare in the Midwest. When we sniffed carefully, we also caught the lighter sugar-cinnamon odor of pastry. The elevated trains clacked by from time to time, their back draft inflated our pant legs and blew dirt and bits of paper hip high.

As we walked from place to place, we garnered more than the usual once-over by the local maidens. The draft had swept the area clean of eligible men. We poor specimens, not used to being under the microscope, wilted somewhat in the face of such scrutiny. However, they must have reached a consensus on our potential, since we didn't see any of them again after those first few hours. In my mind's eye, I could see a redheaded chairperson calling for a vote of the assembled bachlorettes in the back room of the bakery. "All right, all those in favor of waiting for the better-quality men to return, raise your right hand. Motion carried. No further business appearing, we are adjourned."

This rejection didn't seem to apply to Dante's youngest cousin, Ethel, whose breasts had recently achieved apple size. She wondered whether massage would accelerate their growth and hovered around with suggestions of experiments she thought the two of us should try—an entry-level Lolita. However, besides being underage, Ethel hadn't yet lost her baby fat. It was impossible to get serious with someone who possessed the secondary sexual characteristics of a marshmallow. I decided she would have to wait for a future prince charming.

We weren't left completely without female companionship. The local mother's network got busy and arranged dates for us with a couple of "nice girls." First stop: dinner at the Italian restaurant.

The brick exterior of the building needed a tuck here and there and paint peeled off wood-framed dirty windows. It made me reluctant to enter, my Midwest mindset placing the structure in the wrong-side-of-the-tracks-gyp-joint category. The inside, however, possessed greater charm: the tables and walls dressed up in reds and gold's, the lighting warm and the white-jacketed staff welcoming.

I learned later that the outsides of the borough's buildings were maintained in a beggarly fashion in order to fool the tax assessor. Your property assessment remained stable, unless you took out a building permit. Make any obvious changes to the outside you were forced to buy a permit and your taxes went up. Improvements on the inside stayed between you and your brother-in-law contractor, who, if he wanted a normal sex life, kept his mouth shut. This still seemed strange since the assessors would probably visit the inside of local businesses in the normal course of their lives. I finally reflected that even in Iowa, with its Germanic attention to rules, we knew enough to bend when cultural demands conflicted with regulation. Perhaps too far at times.

The staff seated and fussed over the *belle donnes* and left us to gradually blend into the Etruscan hum of this Old World establishment. After two years of army food, just reading the menu became the mental equivalent of one fine orgasm. The ordering was unique and simple. The waiters encouraged us to try a portion of anything on the menu in whatever order we wished, although they recommended beginning with the antipasto and ending with dessert. Large boats of marinara sauce were provided and refilled as necessary during the meal. Our first dish: *insalata* with vinegar and olive oil dressing.

After a few bites, I noticed what I had earlier assumed was some strange Mediterranean vegetable actually had tentacles.

"Dante," I said, "is this what I think it is?"

"It's calamari," he replied in brotherly fashion. "Eat it, it's good." And, so it was.

I turned to my date with a break-the-ice joke about how the squid tasted good, but difficult to get down, what with the tentacles grabbing lips in a last-ditch attempt not to be eaten. She rewarded me with a smile and the usual hard-wired female rejoinder about male crudity. I was glad to have finally established communication with this tall, slender blonde. When we first met on the steps of her apartment building, her body language and wet palm when we shook hands indicated a high degree of nervousness. The mothers chose another cousin for Dante, but one far enough removed to escape the incest taboo. A brunette with a quick mind, she physically broadcast an energy that could recharge any man's batteries at fifty paces. Her hips moved with enough power to break rock.

By the end of the meal, the place, the food, and the conversation gave us all a warm bonded feeling. Even the blonde contributed periodically to the flow of talk and joking. Upon leaving, we took Dante's suggestion to ride the subway to Central Park, although it rang alarm bells in my mind with images of pickpockets and muggers. The station was dirty, its walls and benches scarred with wear and vandalism. The lighting was bright and the activity level up. It felt safer than I expected. The platform and cars were stuffed to capacity with young people, all of us going to the same destination. It hit me, for kids without easy access to autos this was the New York equivalent of cruising Main Street.

Outside of a few couples, the crowd appeared evenly divided into small gender-separate clusters, that spent the travel time hotly eyeing each other, adjusting clothing, and trying various antics to show cool. I wondered if our ancient mothers and fathers back on the African veldt had similarly advertised their charms and availability. Courting activity became even more intense at the park. A full moon projected Escher shadows from rocks and breeze-ruffled trees. The place was packed. Kids must have been spilling out of subway stations in the vicinity for hours. The air became visibly misted with teen hormones—breathing too deep made your head spin.

"Central Park is entirely manmade," Dante began in a tourist guide voice. We pushed our way through the press between the lake and the boathouse, the crowd like a huge seething monster made of nothing but elbows and knees.

"Every tree, every rock and bit of grass was put in its specific spot by plan," he grunted, as an odd elbow accidentally found his ribs. "Building began in the 1800s. The park is a tribute to Victorian era vanity; they could manipulate God's universe to match their taste."

"You don't like it?" I queried.

"I love it, but it isn't real. It's a special effect, don't you think? You've lived closer to the natural world than I."

"Yes ... yes, it's missing roughness, species competition, the smell isn't right. Lordy, it's an 800-acre landscaped garden maintained by Japanese gardeners."

Our editorial comments came to a halt as we reached the edge of a crowd which had achieved critical mass. Dozens of running pairs broke out of the tangle—a giant puffball shooting its spores across meadows and woods. The triggers of night and the pack-induced attraction of male and female made the result irresistible.

I felt my hand pulled by the blonde ... without fear or thought, we ran, our fingers locked, our legs moved without sensation, as though we floated at speed. I felt a bass growl of joy rise in my throat and heard it answered by her soprano snarl close by—animals in season. An alternating magnetic lust-pulse spun us around, brought our heartbeats into harmony. Our lips came together. Hers engorged, softer than any I had ever tasted. Female nipples, hard little pearls, pierced my skin, blew fire inside me.

Over the blood rush booming in my ears, I could hear sobs. Shoulder length hair covered my neck and chin. I felt warm tears collect, pool on my flesh. In this release of anguish, I could sense anger and betrayal. Palms and fists beat once, twice against my chest. My arms came up to fold us into each other, a great sweet surge of protective maleness swirled up out of me to wrap around us. I armored us against whoever caused her pain. A last guttural muffled wail, she quieted. For long minutes, we remained standing silent in the space we had created.

Stepping out from behind a shadow-mottled boulder, Dante said, "Are you guys okay? It's time to go home."

The next day over breakfast, I related the enormity of the feelings the blonde evoked in me to Dante. He told me our date had been a sort of coming-out-event for her. She and her mother had recently escaped from sexual abuse.

"Goddamn it, Dante, I'm no psychia…"

"She's already got one, she needed the company of a normal man."

"Son of a bitch, I could have messed her up worse!"

Dante's eyes softened, his voice slowed. "My friend, you did just fine."

He put a hand on my shoulder. "The boys are playing stick ball down the block, let me introduce you to the game." (Which brings us back, Padre, to the beginning of the story.)

~~~OOO~~~

We watched the action in the narrow street for twenty minutes before the players took a break. Dante sat on the curb, shoulders down, staring at one of them. His hands twitched from time to time. He became strangely evasive about answering my questions, clearly not wanting to talk. The batter dropped his stick to rattle on the pavement and walked toward us. Smiling, hands in pockets, he shuffled over, reddish sockless feet in tattered sneakers. The sweat broke out on Dante's brow, even though we sat in the shade.

"Well, hello pilgrim," the voice coarse and scratchy, as if from a lifetime of too much drink. Thick-stemmed black hair peppered his exposed skin, which looked as though it had recently been sandpapered. In the air, a sulfur and nitrate scent reminiscent of the rifle and grenade ranges of basic training.

"Nothing to say to an old friend of the family?" He smiled, exposing yellowed teeth. "Introduce me to your companion."

Dante looked at me with raised eyebrows and a sick look. "I hope you believe what I am going to say, because the strength of your faith is about to be severely tested."

"He's got to make up his own mind," the squat man said. "Free will, you remember?"

Dante's head dropped, his lips compressed, "Rod, meet the creature, renowned in story and song as *Lucifer, Old Nick, Beelzebub* ... also addressed in these parts as simply, *the Devil.*"

Perhaps, it was my imagination, but the sidewalk became hot, the air grew sticky, and I suffered the worst case of compressed vision I had ever experienced. The whole world necked down to the three of us, confined in a space six feet square.

"At your service," himself said to me.

My toes and fingers went cold and my throat shut down, I sat there trying not to gape, unable to speak, or draw a breath. Dante's comments gave me some time to adjust.

"I should have known he'd be hanging around. He's been pestering my family for centuries. The Cagliostros were *alchimisti* back in the 1700s in Palermo. One of them almost made a deal with him for the recipe for changing lead into gold. And, I'm named after a famous ancestor on the other side of the family, Dante Alighieri."

My tongue and tonsils uncrossed, I blurted, "Not the guy who wrote 'Dante's Inferno.'"

"The very same—one of the few to visit hell and return unscathed. Since both sides of the family escaped, Old Nick feels we remain his personal challenge. He's a constant pest."

"Your family is more resistant than most, a rare genetic anomaly," Nick said, hunkering down to face us. "Kind of like inheriting resistance to cholesterol. You and your relatives can be exposed to me and not get your souls clogged." He scrunched forward, his body violated my personal space. "By the way, in case the question crossed your mind, I don't give autographs."

A lick of terror ran up my spine. An adrenaline flush pushed my heart and eyes to flutter at redline. I calmed a bit as the coin flipped by the ancient wattle-necked reptile in me came up fight instead of flight.

"Not interested," I slurred, my tongue still slow to respond. *What a conceited asshole,* the old scaly snake in my mind helpfully volunteered. A breeze began, evaporating sweat, cooling my body. My senses expanded out to normal range. I felt better.

"Right, of course, I have something to offer that is much better." He raised a hand palm up, signaling the start of negotiations.

"For an entity as old as you," I said studying his palm, "your lifeline doesn't look very long. But I guess it's all relative when your span of years is near infinite."

"Good, good technique, trying to break my pitch?"

"Not me ... just curious."

"I want you to know I study my potential clients' backgrounds and needs in great depth before I make an offer."

"Needs, not wants? The Creator provides for our needs."

I had to give him credit, he shrugged off my attempts to be playful and proceeded like the vastly experienced salesperson he was. Cutting to the chase, his offer was to make me a successful writer: poet, essayist, playwright, novelist, I could do all these. Any form of writing in which I wished to indulge would be published and receive acclaim.

A sufficiency of money would be forthcoming, but *he* allowed, that in his reading of my needs, fame as an author appeared primary and wealth secondary. A side benefit—the intellectual women to whom I was always attracted, and with whom I had always been unsuccessful, would vie for my attention. (Well, you know. It's like John Wayne said when asked by Barbara Walters why he always married women of Latin or Spanish decent, "Every man picks his own poison.") As I sat silent, enjoying silk-sheet pictures in my mind, he upped the ante with movie contracts for the novels.

I came out of my reverie looking for pen and blood, ready to sign, when he finally said, "All right, all right, I never even offered this to Tom Clancy, but when they make the movie versions they will faithfully follow the plots of your books."

"Damn, sounds good, where do I sign?"

"No blood, no pen and parchment, I'm an old-fashioned man. All we need is a handshake," he said softly.

His arm came up and mine automatically started to respond, then I noticed Dante squirming beside me. In a moment of hesitation, my last night's experience with the blonde came flooding back to fill me with pure tender passion, pushing out any feelings of avarice. I knew I could not accept gifts from someone who embodied the evil she'd experienced whether he was directly responsible or not. I stood, dropped my arm, and walked away, Dante by my side grinning.

"It's a woman, isn't it? They're always saving your scrawny asses," *the Devil* shouted. "You don't deserve it, but I'll give you a free one, so you'll know what you have just fucked away."

Surprised, we turned and stared at him still squatting in the gutter among discarded Kleenex, dead bugs, and candy wrappers.

He rose, stepped back, and said, "You will never be killed by an enemy bullet."

I turned to Dante. "What a bunch of bullshit!"

"I'm sure that was not meant as a favor," he responded looking over my shoulder at the empty space Nick had occupied.

~~~OOO~~~

"So, Padre, afterwards it all happened as predicted. Our research group disbanded shortly after our return to the National Security Agency. While the rest of the gang went to Berlin to contribute to the Cold War, I went to Infantry Officer Candidate School at Ft. Benning to graduate as a hundred and eighty-day wonder. Ten months after my seven-thousand-mile journey to this fine Republic of Vietnam, you find me in your MASH unit with a bullet wound to the head. The docs all say, a mere scratch, which will heal soon, leaving only a scar as a reminder, unnoticeable to everyone, except the beautiful women who run their fingers through my hair. After all, Nick didn't say enemy bullets wouldn't wound me—only that they wouldn't kill me.

"Now, hang on a minute, don't be eager to leave. I have something else I'd like to tell you. Something you'll want to pass on through your channels. Lying in bed all this time has permitted me to think out the circumstances surrounding the Devil's offers. You remember the literature you gave me, especially the book by St. Augustine? See if this logic sounds reasonable to you.

"First, St. Augustine starts with God as the only one who can create. Oh, we mess with and reassemble in different ways what He created, but we don't really start with *nothing*. Neither man, nor the Devil can truly create anything.

"Second, God is not affected by time. The good saint says before the act of creation there was no time. It took what scientists call the Big Bang, God's act of creation, before time started. Amazing how the more we know, the more science and religion seem to come together. So, He created time and therefore is not affected by it. God's angels are probably not affected by it either, since they do his bidding along the entire timeline.

"Third, we know from the history of human interaction with the Devil, this former angel will do everything in his power to subvert us from grace. His deals, no matter how innocent appearing, become masterpieces of betrayal.

"Okay, okay, I'm about to get to the point. What would be the ultimate betrayal? A deal so one-sided only a supernatural being could even imagine it?

"Since Nick cannot create anything, how can he change what God makes available for us? What if as a former angel, not affected by time, he knows what our futures are?

"The ultimate betrayal—if we fulfill our destinies—would be for him to offer to guarantee us what we will achieve anyway without his help! We give away our immortal souls and get absolutely nothing in return. Of course, not all of us achieve our goals. He can't offer success to everyone. Even so, I bet he makes a few hundred thousand worthless deals a year. Ah, I see from your expression you get the picture.

"No, I can't discuss it further. I'm still tired. I'll be back in the field with my unit by the end of the week. I need some additional quiet time to think. I won't be killed by an enemy bullet, but I could be crippled ... yet, if he really foresaw a successful writing career, I must survive ..."

Gentled Man

Unspeakable horror
Interwoven with blinding flashes
Primitive yet exotic beauty
With hands purposely quiet
And gentled at his sides
But should there be threats
Those hands could activate
And decimate an oncoming foe

*~ Corrine Kahl, published poet, member of the Society
of Great River Poets, Burlington, Iowa. Poem written
about the author.*

Shoot Out at Miners' Luck

State Patrol Sergeant Jon W. Cozeen raised his forearms from the top rail of the fence and flicked white paint specks off his sleeve. He pushed his holstered Glock back to clear his jacket. The day's events had kept his attention for most of the last hour. He rested one foot on the lowest crossbar of the arena fence, watching through silvered aviator-style sunglasses. After a month of cooling temperatures, the day had turned out unusually sunny and warm. This part of the state remained overdue for its first big snowfall. The sun warmed him from the calves up, but the ground was less comforting, the cold finally worked its way through the soles of his shiny-brown trooper boots.

Not used to standing so long anymore, he thought, as he rocked a little, breaking earth contact, sitting on my ass too much in a heated patrol car. He listened a moment as the radio in his cruiser spit out a brief exchange between the dispatcher and a unit on the way to an accident over on County 41.

An interesting weekend, he mused. Cowboy black powder shooters and reenactors swarmed in from considerable distances to participate in the first annual Big Fall Shoot 'Em Up. The merchants of the small mountain town of Elwood leaped on the bandwagon, hoping this new event would bring bucks into the area to replace the waning profitability of its forty-year-old rodeo. The festivities began with a day of cowboy action shooting events. A group called SASS, the Single Action Shooting Society, restaged Old West type shooting scenarios for fun and competition. Participants in period costumes walked or rode through the courses firing black powder pistols, shotguns, and rifles at targets representing bad guys—timing and accuracy determined the winners.

Under pressure from local campaign donors, the governor ordered the members of his reluctant patrol office to provide range safety and security. Senior Sergeant Cozeen purposely volunteered for this last day, featuring pioneer working animal demonstrations and contests. Besides being a student of the American West and its technology, he wanted to keep an eye on one of today's contestants. He focused his full attention back into the arena as the judges announced the winner of the large mule-jumping contest. His man accepted the $500 first prize astride a brushed-slick brown mule, which he put through a few celebratory dressage routines. The mule stepped backward, then moved sideways left to right, spun in a circle toward the stands, and reared on its hind legs, all without its rider appearing to move a muscle or give a command. The bleacher crowd gave him some tepid applause, which petered out quickly. Most of the locals knew this guy.

The breeze shifted. The odor of animal sweat and manure caught the patrol officer's nostrils. On its heels came the blended smell of concession stand popcorn and nachos. Both his eyebrows and the hair on the back of his neck went up, as the mounted man rode his way. As the pair approached, he could hear the creak of leather and click of the tack's metalwork. Cozeen cast a historian and stockman's eye over an outfit not seen in this neck of the woods for over a hundred years.

Hmmm. Tack: snaffle bit and trained to neck rein—the mule has a tender mouth. McClellan cavalry saddle on a regulation blue saddle blanket with yellow stripes ... blunt horse head spurs fixed on calf-high black leather boots—doesn't want to cut his animal.

Costume: light blue trousers with yellow leg stripe, dark blue fatigue blouse with embroidered captain's bars ... cartridge belt supporting a butt-forward holster—he will use a cross-draw.

Hat: a black wide-brimmed campaign model with gold and black cord and crossed saber emblem.

Weapons: looks to be a pair of Schofield black powder Smith & Wesson .45s—one at the waist (antique original $8,000 to $10,000) and one on the saddle (modern reproduction $700 to $800)—and a trapdoor Springfield twenty-gauge shotgun conversion carried in a saddle boot.

All in all, the perfect picture of an 1970's cavalry officer.

Cozeen put both feet on the ground and stumbled back as the rider forced the mule's head into his space. The cavalryman looked down from his mount, poker faced, black eyes staring. The animal's ears flicked forward and then back, picking up on its rider's hidden emotions. In its right ear a gold ring flashed.

"Amazing, Lieutenant Teigler," Cozeen said, "I don't think I would have believed a mule could clear a six-foot bar from a standing start without seeing it myself."

"Hybrid vigor, Sergeant, hybrid vigor. I didn't know your curiosity extended to jumping." His voice picked up a hard edge. "Or, are you here for the usual reason?"

"Well, I'm not here to congratulate you on promoting yourself to captain, nor to talk about old times in Nam. How's your alter ego holding up?"

"So you're still a sergeant, after almost eighteen years."

Rod Teigler removed his tan buckskin gauntlets and slapped them across his upper leg. The mule snorted, curled its lips to expose spade-shaped teeth, and scuffed the arena sawdust with one hoof.

Cozeen looked around to make sure they were out of earshot. "I was in charge of the army criminal investigation. I read the psychiatrist's analysis. I sense the shadow of your other personality in your published poetry and fiction."

Teigler's face and body showed no emotion but the mule shifted its weight from one back leg to the other, doing a kind of rumba step, acting out the rising anger of its rider.

"But nothing's happened," he said. "I don't deserve this. Year after year, you and your boys watching my every move …"

"And, we'll continue until there is no longer a threat, however long it takes. You're a ticking bomb. I just hope the fuse doesn't get shorter as you get older."

Man and mule watched the trooper stride stiff-legged back to the patrol car, muscles tense, as if he felt their eyes burn his back. "He sees the blackness in me, but not the blackness in himself," Teigler thought, remembering the event that brought about their first meeting.

Back at the office, Cozeen, feet on the desk, sucked on a mug of thick, bitter, end-of-the-day coffee. He winced at the metallic aftertaste, and put on an even more sour face at the entrance of their youngest rookie patrol officer.

"Sergeant, I watched that Teigler guy yesterday like you asked. He did real good on the ride-through shooting course. He hit every target in record time. Real smooth, that mule of his, real smooth. Don't think I've ever seen one that big."

"You mean Sal."

"Who?"

"His mule is named Sal, a gaited mule, part Tennessee Walker. Once she gets into her running walk, he's got a very stable gun platform."

"The boys tell me you and that character go way back."

"O'Connell, take a chair. I guess I need to brief you on Teigler," he sighed. "I've told everyone else, and you need to hear the story from me."

Staring at a wall calendar picture of the rainforest, Cozeen began his recollections. He had been stationed in Saigon, the then capital of the Republic of South Vietnam, with the Military Police Criminal Investigation Division. During his second tour of duty in 1967, he investigated a number of strange events, whose only common thread was one officer.

"After interrogating the man, everything seemed to square with the history in his 201 file. Lieutenant Rod Teigler spoke in the flat twangy Midwest tones of his youth. His I.Q. tests qualified him for MENSA and any job the Army offered. He possessed a special aptitude for languages and electronics. With a farm boy's affinity for weapons, he shot expert the first time with any kind of boomer the service placed in his hands. Facing the draft after college, he enlisted in the Army's version of Military Intelligence. They spent a lot of time and tax money honing his skills.

"About halfway through his first enlistment, he applied for a commission and transferred to Infantry Officer Training School at Fort Benning, Georgia. Six months later, he became one of one hundred forty-four to receive gold bars graduating fourth in his class out of three hundred thirty-four starters.

"MI took him back. Forty-five days later he squeezed his six-foot plus frame into a seat on a big bird bound for Viet Nam. He spent only a few months in country before the fun started. First came a supposedly innocent involvement in the murders of two elderly natives and three Americans. He spent time in Japan recovering from wounds received during that fracas. He volunteered to go back, but this time, MI wouldn't touch him with a ten-foot pole. Reassigned to a grunt outfit, his patrol walked into an ambush the third time out. Some real strange shit happened. We debriefed one of the survivors right behind him on the trail. By his account, a Chinese-made shotgun mine kicked off the attack, wiping out the leading half of the American unit. The second half of the patrol, farther back on the trail, took automatic weapons fire from brush to their right.

"Our survivor watched Teigler drop his unfired M-16, take up a machete from a dead trooper and run straight down the gun barrels of the VC. As Teigler's back disappeared into the jungle, the man to the rear of our witness got hit and spun with his trigger depressed, accidentally killing the last American sergeant. With no leadership, the two remaining privates dropped and prayed. Thirty minutes later, a relief force choppered into a landing zone half a klick away.

"As they swept over the site, they found ten dead VC in their original ambush positions, all dispatched with multiple heavy blade slashes to the head and shoulders. They followed a blood trail through the jungle. Near body number eleven, whose arms had been forcible removed, they found Teigler, bare-chested, collapsed, tears washing runnels in the blood and gore crusted on his body hair and clothes.

"Well, they didn't know what to do with him. On the one hand, his record listed more confirmed kills than 99 percent of our troops. On the other, he deserted his men when he should have been organizing them to take out the ambush. In addition, his methods resembled a serial killer more than a soldier. The brass finally decided to sweep the matter under the carpet, although Teigler would be sent for psychiatric evaluation.

"I wasn't privy to all the records of their conversations, only the doctor's summary. My criminology courses had not prepared me for his conclusion."

Cozeen paused and raised the coffee cup to his lips, grimacing as the now cold liquid washed over his tongue. He sputtered, and drops fell on his uniform. He pulled a tissue out of his right-hand desk drawer and dabbed at the spots.

"Sarge, don't stop now," O'Connell said, leaning forward, both hands on the edge of the desk.

"The short version is that Teigler most likely suffers from multiple personalities. The doc's notes identified at least one and possibly another."

"You mean, like the full moon comes out and he changes into a monster?"

"Not exactly, but now that you mention it, not too far off, except the trigger is not the moon but extreme stress. Pressure the guy enough and you get a killer personality in charge of his body. Appears this happens to combat veterans more often than people imagine."

"Did they find out who the other personality was?"

"Using hypnosis, the psychiatrist uncovered the being who did the blade work on the VC. Seems like Teigler's mind houses an ancient reptilian creature the doctor called the perfect warrior. Once released, its sole function is to kill the enemy anyway it can: knives, clubs, teeth—a true berserker."

"You mean he's crazy berserk?"

"The doctor explained that in Viking days berserker warriors went insane in battle. They charged the enemy foaming at the mouth, swords cutting and hacking. Sometimes they attacked naked to show contempt for the other side. There are stories of them fighting on after receiving wounds that would kill a normal man."

"Do you believe such crap?"

"No … no, I don't. But violent animal instincts exist in each of us that come out under the right circumstances," Cozeen said, remembering his own actions during the Tet Offensive.

"That's the guy I watched yesterday? Holy shit! He sure seemed regular."

"And that wasn't the end of the story." Cozeen leaned back again and stared for a moment at a cobweb in the corner. "The Army sent him back out into the field as an advisor to some South Vietnamese Regional Forces along with a couple of other American screw-ups they wanted to lose."

"Well, he survived. He's back here now."

"Yes, indeed, but it got worse. One night the province chief put him in charge of an under-strength, under-weaponed platoon of green South Vietnamese village boys. Their assigned mission, to defend a poorly fortified position near a road junction. They got hit with a company-size attack at dawn. His group of misfits wiped out a load of VC before the enemy called off the attack."

"Sounds pretty heroic to me, Sarge."

"Nothing is normal with this guy."

Cozeen related the CID's investigation of a subsequent event. "Shortly after the attack, when the crossroads filled with the civilians they were there to protect, he pistol-shoots this young girl right off her bicycle. One of the most precise hits I ever saw. The forty-five-auto round entered below her left breast slightly to the middle—her heart blown into mush."

"You were the investigating officer."

"I talked with him at the 12th Evacuation Hospital. He claimed she went for a revolver hidden under her skirt. The two of them staged a little quick draw contest resulting in a head wound for him and reincarnation for her. The problem: we could find no weapon other than his. Teigler's wound could have been self-inflicted. Of course, at least fifty South Vietnamese civilians on the roads witnessed the shootout, but weren't willing to talk."

Cozeen remembered the confusion at headquarters. Another heroic situation befuddled by an unexplainable event. Teigler had added to his personal body count under suspect circumstances.

"Only by using considerable persuasive talent did Teigler get out with an honorable discharge, instead of spending his remaining years in an asylum at government expense."

"Well, boss," O'Connell said, "how in the hell did the problem come to roost here?"

Cozeen sat the cup down on the desk and rubbed sweaty hands on his thighs. O'Connell could hear the rasp of calloused skin on the cavalry twill of the uniform.

"He was pretty shaken up after all that, probably infected with a hefty dose of post-traumatic stress disorder. No one got treatment back then. The Army just dumped Viet vets back into society. A lot of them are still living as homeless loners or in isolated small packs. Teigler took his meager combat pay and bought twenty acres of isolated land. He built a cabin and put out a *not welcome* mat."

"That his place 'cross the pass out in back of the Wilson's ranch?"

"The very one. It's wide open. He can see you coming a mile away. The first five years or so, he pretty much lived as a hermit, only came to town once a month for supplies. He started freelance writing, made some money. Must have been good therapy too, since lately he's gone public, showing up as a nineteenth century cavalryman at re-enactments and shooting contests."

O'Connell detected a touch of envy in Cozeen's speech; it made him wonder just how recovered the sergeant was from his own war experience.

"I assume he got the fancy mule about then."

"Careful, son," Cozeen replied, "when you assume you make an *ass* out of *u* and *me*. He originally rode a horse. The ass came later."

"I've never seen one like it, especially with a gold earring."

"Teigler got the mule cheap in spite of its many talents. It had a bad habit of kicking anything moving behind it, then tossing its rider. Evidently, something spooked it bad as a colt. It became skittish to the rear. Mules do learn quickly, both good and bad behav…"

"So how did it get the ring in its ear?"

Cozeen ran the fingers of his right hand through his hair twice and put his feet on the floor. "Hold on, I am about to tell you. The frustrated owner took a low bid from Teigler when no one else would buy her. The lieutenant saddled and bridled the mule right there on the spot. When Sal bucked, he took her right ear in his mouth and bit a hole through it with his dogteeth. It's an old Apache trick. Really gets an animal's attention."

"That stopped the kicking?"

"Not only cured it, but somehow the act started to bond them together. That's one of the few ways you can read him. He rarely shows outward emotion, but she feels what he feels and she ain't as good at hiding it. Later, since the hole in her ear didn't close, Teigler inserted a gold ring. Sometimes he even clips on a miniature gold jingle bell—*and she will have music wherever she goes.*"

"Well, the Shoot 'Em Up is over. What do we do about him?"

"I followed his truck and horse trailer out to Miners' Luck Pass. He's headed back to his spread, probably close to the highest point even as we speak."

"We've lost track of him?"

"Well, sonny, he can only come out of there one of two ways: turnaround and come back, or go out the east exit. I called Sheriff Miller. He's parked in a pullover on the other side. Teigler will get followed home when he leaves the pass. Besides, the weather satellite says one nasty storm is in progress up there. No reason for us to go through that."

~~~OOO~~~

The FM jazz station on Teigler's truck radio finally lapsed completely into static after a mile or so of fading in and out. Some peculiarity of this area ate up most of the electromagnetic spectrum. Try as you might, no radio, TV, or cell phone would work for the next several miles. The mountain seemed to act like a giant capacitor, soaking up energy. The storm must be charging it with billions of volts. He wouldn't want to be around if it decided to discharge all at once.

Besides this quirk, he remembered the strange stories originating on this mountain, starting with an old Indian legend of a curse. From time to time, folks traveling through reported seeing odd-looking people and animals, which vanished when approached. After the new highway routed traffic lower down the slope, the sightings dried up. So far, his big dually truck proved itself master of the snow. It accumulated fast. At first, big clumps of flakes, then the wind picked up and blew them into small hard pellets intermixed with occasional sleet. Windblown particles hit the truck's windshield and sheet metal in waves, sounding like the rattle of shotgun pellets.

Visibility kept dropping. Teigler worked to keep the vehicle and trailer on the move and as close to the right as possible. The original construction crew bulldozed the road out of the mountainside, leaving a shear drop-off on the outside edge. He began to worry about Sal. The wind chill must be dropping the temperature in the trailer.

Snow accumulated faster than the wipers could handle. Ice built up under the rubber and lifted them off the glass, leaving wide bands of smeary water and ice crystals. He needed to stop and shake them clear. Rod pushed the brake pedal medium hard; the truck started to slow, then glided sideways.

Pumping the brakes, he cussed aloud and prayed silently. The front left fender hit something; the screeching sound of metal on metal caused his teeth to grate. Damn if they weren't riding the guardrail on the cliff side. If made of softer material, his grip would have permanently imprinted his fingerprints on the steering wheel.

Teigler could feel the rail bend as the full weight and forward motion of the truck-trailer pushed against it. Just before it came to a rest, he heard a *whinny - hee - haw* from Sal as the floor in the trailer went from level to a thirty-degree lean. The engine choked to a halt.

He sat a few minutes in silence before unclenching his teeth. The sweat continued to flow. Rod loosened his coat to cool off, not wanting to lose the insulating value of his clothes in below-zero weather. He must have driven straight across a curve, and hit the rail on the far side.

I must be shocked silly, he thought, sounds like a story problem in the math section of the SAT test. "Now, what the hell do I do?" he said aloud, his breath visible in the cooling cab air.

Options appeared few. He could start the truck and try to drive off the rail. Not a good choice, since any further disturbance might cause it to collapse, sending vehicle and trailer tumbling thousands of feet downward. He could start the truck, run the heater, and wait out the storm. This assumed the weight of the snow piling up on the rig wouldn't push them over, or the exhaust pipe wouldn't clog with snow and gas him. This choice also didn't help Sal, outside of her blanket, no other source of heat in the trailer. The accident left them positioned slightly beyond the highest point in the pass, which meant within only a few miles stood a state-maintained heated rest stop. He could go for help, but what about Sal's chances while he hoofed it?

"Hoofing it? Of course," he said. "Sal will do the hoofing. Hell, she's a big sixteen-hands-plus mule. She can wade through deeper snow than I can."

Teigler emerged from the truck minutes later in modern long underwear covered by his 1875 wool cavalry uniform, a reproduction of a Plains soldier's curly buffalo coat draped from shoulders to calves. Made from a thick old bull hide, it weighed over twenty pounds. A fur ear-flapped cap and shearling mittens completed the outfit. It took another fifteen minutes to ease Sal, along with her saddle and bridle, out of the trailer and cinch her up. He rolled up his blanket and Sal's and tied them behind the saddle. Rod strapped on the guns. Such treasures couldn't be left behind. In one coat pocket he placed a hoof pick, a pointed metal hook with a hand-sized grip.

He'd need it to remove snow and ice that would pack up in the mule's hoofs.

He robbed the Vaseline out of Sal's show kit and smeared three fingers worth over the exposed portions of his face and the mule's muzzle. Teigler mounted and adjusted the buffalo coat, which was slit up the back to allow for the saddle. Now with his legs up in the stirrups, the coat flaps hung down to cover everything down to the ankles. Those old-timers sure knew how to protect themselves from the elements, he thought.

With a "Hup, Sal," they started through snow, which had already accumulated as high as the mule's shins.

Visibility closed down to about thirty feet. The wind gusted, throwing up blinding clouds of white as they traversed unprotected areas. During the next half hour, Teigler spent plenty of time regretting his decision. Conditions continued to deteriorate. He couldn't see more than a few feet ahead. The snow in places now reached well up the animal's forelegs. He wondered whether they still remained on the road, or were headed in the right direction. Or, even how far they had traveled.

He hoped the mule's better senses would keep them out of trouble. Rod's hands kept the reins slack, giving Sal her head. They would need shelter soon; toes and fingers had lost sensation. Numbness crept up from his extremities. He hunched over the mule's neck, holding on with his forearms and thighs. Sal stopped, up to her chest in a thick-packed drift built up between two wind-eroded rock spires. She picked up on his fear. He couldn't dismount, he'd never be able to get back in the saddle, might not even be able to stand. Sal must move.

Okay, first thing—get my emotions under control. Teigler thought about his despair, the times when he had been ready to let go. War-driven guilt remained a constant companion. He had killed so many, lost so many. Almost pulled over into an on-coming semi one night—suicide by trucker. His arms felt disconnected, moving the steering wheel into the oncoming lane without conscious control. The thought of waiting as the cold crystallized his blood was sweet—no pain—just floating off.

Then he remembered Sal; could he let her go? He took stock. The dreams and the dark thoughts didn't come so often now, the writing was good therapy. Anger over his weakness rose in his throat. Damn my demons!

Teigler analyzed their situation. Packed snow pinned the mule's chest and legs. Sal must be encouraged to leap out of the drift. She needed to redo her winning jump of earlier in the day. "Up, Sal, up," he whispered. He worked his cold-slowed jaws up and down and wiggled his tongue. He tried the command again. She remained too frightened and confused to respond.

Rod remembered her song. He had taught himself to play the guitar three years ago, another attempt at therapy. Too much of a novice to play anything sophisticated, he concentrated on folk music. The horse barn included an attached fenced paddock, which joined on both sides of the cabin. Sal came right up to the back porch when he rocked and strummed.

"I had a mule, her name was Sal," his voice cracked, then firmed. "Fifteen miles on the Erie Canal. She's a good ol' worker and a good ol' pal." He tried to belt it out. "… you bet your life I'd never part with Sal,— up, Sal, up."

The mule's body quivered. She pawed and kicked the snow making space— then the leap. They landed on top of the drift. The snow under Sal's belly kept her hoofs from touching the ground—man and animal hung up. She kicked and got her back feet on something solid. Rearing, she attacked the drift, and leaped once more. The two bodies, generating just enough magnetic field, closed a circuit between the two rock spirals. The air and snow around the two turned blue and crackled. The mountain's massive accumulation of electricity discharged.

Teigler smelled ozone and felt ice picks dance on his nerve endings. Every synapse in his body closed. Legs froze around the barrel of the mule. They broke out. Teigler felt amazed he was still in the saddle, his last thought before passing out.

He woke to a creaking, groaning noise. Teigler looked up with one eye, the other refused to work, the eyelashes iced shut. Sal pushed against a wooden door, tall enough to admit them mounted. It groaned under their combined weight and opened wide enough for her to push through into the dark interior. Once at the back of the building, she stopped and waited for her rider to dismount. His mind gave the command to his body, but nothing happened. Sal, sensitive as always, shifted sideways quickly. Teigler came crashing off. The hay on the floor cushioned the fall, but he hit hard enough to get his joints unlocked and blood flowing.

He took a deep breath. "Thanks, I needed that."

Teigler lay there a moment waiting for his senses to adjust to the dark. He heard rustling and breathing noises ... smelled the tart-apple scent of horses. As his eyes adjusted, he saw stalls and a second floor haymow—a stable. Warmed above zero by animal heat it was out of the chill of the wind. He felt grateful. He spotted a kerosene lamp hanging on a nail. Tried to stand. Got dizzy. Decided to crawl. On the second attempt, he got the lamp and the tin of big wooden matches next to it. He smoothed the buffalo coattails under his butt, sat down, and draped the rest around his knees making a miniature tent. On his third clumsy try the lamp lit.

He placed it under the coat. Caught under the robe, the heat provided immediate relief. Removing the mittens with his teeth, he pulled his arms out of the sleeves, and held his hands inside over the lamp. It felt like needles were being jammed in them as they warmed. Boots and socks off, he did his feet next, with similar teeth-gritting results. In the lamplight, he checked for any signs of frostbite. The hands appeared all right, but a couple of toes looked discolored.

Boots back on, Teigler kicked blown snow away from the inside of the partially opened stable door and shouldered it closed. After removing Sal's saddle and bridle, he cleaned hard packed snow from her hoofs with the hoof pick and replaced the tool in his pocket. He began to wipe her down with handfuls of straw. When he turned to her hindquarters, he noticed her tail was missing the last three inches. It smelled like a combination of burned hair and the ozone odor that tickles nostrils after a lightning strike. Puzzling out what had happened would have to wait. Since she was otherwise undamaged, Teigler threw on her blanket and led her to an empty stall. He broke the film of ice on a water bucket and let her drink. Two scoops of corn and three of oats from stored sacks completed his job as stable boy. Teigler checked his watch; about half past four, this time of year it got dark fast. He'd better move before he became isolated in the lonely blackness.

"Well, girl, I'm going to find out where we are. People have to be close," he said. "I'll write when I get work."

Sal looked up from munching and rewarded him with a snort. Snow continued to fall, but not as heavily. The wind changed from a constant blow to periodic gusts. Partial shapes of buildings could be discerned. To the left of the stable about a hundred feet off, three small one-story buildings sharing common walls lined up. They possessed the typical second-story false front of old-fashioned pioneer design. Facing them, across what Teigler took to be a street, sat a larger, more imposing full two-story structure. The wind swirled along its roof. Chunks of heavy snow tumbled off, carrying with them the smell of wood smoke. He would go there.

~~~OOO~~~

Across the way, in the saloon, Angel Jones calculated, for the tenth time in the last four days, the odds of her survival. The same answer came—little to no chance. She looked again at the faces of the three men and the other woman at the table. On her left, Little Bill eased his chair back, a middle-aged man with a mouthful of stumpy, broken teeth. His rotten breath clouded the air every time he laughed, not the kind of laugh that made you want to join in. Moses Smith, the Missourian, elbows on the table, sat with his back to the bar, studying his poker hand. The oldest and the shortest, for fifty years he had blackened the name his Bible-thumping mother hoped would be his example to live by. Angel could read his lips as he named each card to himself. She shook her head, thinking, it's a wonder he ain't figured out how his friends always know what he's a'holdin'.

Chub, his only name, lounged to her right facing Little Bill and the front doors. Like the name implied, his vast lump of flesh had taken constant effort to accumulate over three decades. Although he possessed a cherub-like face, of the five outlaws, he enjoyed inflicting hurt the most. Bald on top, Chub compensated with a full beard and mustache, the lip hair rough trimmed by his Bowie knife, so as not to interfere with food going in. The rest of the men had week-old stubble on their faces. Angel rubbed a cheek with a bad case of whisker burn.

Betsy Allen, the lost soul of the group, huddled in the corner. As the village's schoolteacher, she had gathered her few students for the first time just this year. They used the back room in this saloon since there weren't enough young'uns to justify a regular schoolhouse. A shy stick-to-herself young woman, she repulsed all the local boys courting attempts. Betsy stayed over the winter when most people left for the lower valley to avoid the snow. Even the mine closed for the season, only leaving two guards. The general store owner, Mr. Delgado remained every year. He offered Betsy room and board and a small salary to help out. However, his real reason was to provide a "decent woman" to keep his wife company over the heavy snow months, Angel, the dance hall girl, being the only other female planning on staying.

Mrs. Delgado, being a God-fearing, upright woman, did not care to be forced into any relationship with a "soiled dove." Well, neither of the Delgados would ever worry about the quality of their neighbors again. Angel felt a touch of concern about Betsy. Her clothes, torn or barely pinned together, hung loose off thin shoulders. Sticky strands of uncombed, mousy brown hair drooped over her forehead and ears. The girl's nose had been broken and both eyes blackened during one of the rougher sessions she experienced during the last four days. I tried to tell her not to fight, Angel thought, although any of these three or the other two down at the mine office might have beat her just for fun.

Cursing her fate, Angel regretted her decision to stay. At the time, it had seemed like a good idea. She possessed a goodly poke of coin and gold dust. The saloon owner would pay her top dollar to keep the place until spring. She thought a couple of months' rest from being pawed and bruised by miners and ranch hands would suit her just fine. One more summer and she would have squirreled away enough money to go anywhere and do about anything she wanted. The chances of that looked mighty slim now.

The gang rode in four days ago, chased by a posse and the blizzard. They quickly secured the few of them, killing the mine guards and Mr. Delgado in the process. Angel, Mrs. Delgado, and Betsy remained alive to provide entertainment. On the third day, the Delgado woman died hard from internal bleeding, her naked body thrown out the back door. While hauling water and firewood this morning, Angel saw a frozen arm sticking up out of the snow. She knew better than to ask where the men's bodies had been cached. Jeb Donovan, the gang's leader, had got his start fifteen years ago in "Bloody Kansas," when private militias and criminal gangs raided both sides of the Kansas/Missouri border. During the ensuing War Between the States, both Union and Confederate forces posted bounties on him and his followers as the lowest of the low.

Donovan took no chances. His only talent lay in finding the most unprotected areas to steal, burn, and rape, whether civilian or military. Most recently, they had robbed the bank at Elwood, killing a clerk, and two depositors for good measure. Donovan and his second-in-command, Davy Moore, were holed up down at the mine office. They hadn't availed themselves of the women. Angel felt sure the two possessed an attraction for each other that excluded the ladies.

"Teacher, put some more wood in the stove," Chub said over the clink of coins and rustle of cards. "Angel, fetch me another bottle of the good stuff from behind the bar."

The two women rose to complete their chores. As she approached the group on the way back, Angel fought back the urge to choke on the men's sour body odor. Their new clothes, boots to hats, from the rifled general store couldn't hold back the smell of decaying layers of dirt, grease, and long unchanged underwear. She returned to her chair and tried again to think of some way out. No one could survive long outside in this storm. When the blizzard stopped, the gang would leave and she and Betsy wouldn't get far.

The sound and vibration in the floor of stomping feet on the porch of the saloon interrupted her thoughts. Someone pawed and shook the double front doors. They all glanced up. Whoever it was started kicking snow away from the door to allow entry. The men went back to their cards. It must be Jeb or Davy. With a snap of broken ice, one of the double doors opened. A blast of snow and wind temporarily formed a cloud around a bundled-up figure. The man pushed the door shut by leaning back on it.

Angel's eyes widened. Oh, my God, a stranger! How in the hell could anyone get here through this storm? The man turned right and leaned a shotgun up against the wall.

Chub, facing the door, said, "What the …"

Taking their cue from him, the others turned. The man unbuttoned his buffalo coat. As it fell open, the group let out a collective grunt. His uniform made him a soldier, a captain of cavalry. A pistol protruded from his belt.

The gang members stayed frozen in place, their mouths open. Kicking the snow off his boots, the captain walked over to the potbellied stove, turned his back on the group, and spread the sides of the coat wide to catch the heat. He sniffed a few times, made a face, as his nostrils filled with the room's odor. Woof, Teigler thought, smells like an old, overheated men's locker room complete with backed-up toilets.

The man spoke for the first time. "Folks, I hope you don't mind if I take advantage of your fire. What town is this?"

Angel appraised him at over six-foot-tall and near 200 pounds. His voice an easy-to-the-ear baritone, she couldn't place his accent. He sounded like an educated man, but he strung his words together in a strange fashion. The outlaws also noticed his height. Little Bill motioned to Chub, then pointed at the stranger.

Chub pushed the chair back, stood, and pulled a foot-long, rusty Bowie knife from its sheath. He had developed quite a liking for knife work over the years. If faced with a choice, he'd use a blade over firearms every time.

The big man glided over to the captain with a practiced silence. With a lunge, his left arm went around the man's neck pulling him back into the right-hand knife. Chub hadn't allowed for the thick buffalo hide. The first stab missed. His hand and weapon became a confused frenzy wrapped in the heavy coat.

He pulled back, stabbed again searching for the kidney. The coat resisted his thrust. The knife penetrated the coat but not the layers of clothes underneath.

Grunting from the pressure on his throat, the stranger's hands came up. He gripped Chub's arm, loosened the chokehold.

The third time was the charm. An inch and a half of bowie knife blade slid between the man's ribs. Almost immediately, a roar came out of the victim. Everyone jumped. Chub hesitated, arm drawn back for a final thrust.

The captain's right boot came up, then smashed down to crush the outlaw's instep. Chub screamed. The gripping left arm was pried off. The cavalryman spun around. His right arm shot forward palm up to catch Chub under his nose. The outlaw's head snapped back. Angel heard a tearing sound and a crunch. The fat man dropped.

His face transformed into a non-human rictus of rage, the stranger covered the distance from the stove to the table in time to greet the other two attempting to rise. Moses received his attention first. The bone edge of the stranger's left forearm, backed by two hundred pounds of bone and meat in motion, caught him in the Adam's apple. The outlaw's body was lifted off its feet and tossed to the side.

Angel's mind held no doubt that Moses' throat had been crushed. He would choke to death. Still in his chair, Little Bill managed, in spite of the captain's speed, to pull his Colt. He fired as Moses crumpled to the floor and the man rushed him. The bullet didn't slow his trip to hell.

A hand grabbed his hair. A blue-clad knee pinned his gun hand against the table. Out of his right coat pocket the stranger pulled a metal hook. He drove it into the side of Little Bill's head just above the ear. His arm lifted again and again, the blows not stopping until he was exhausted. The bloody hoof pick clattered to the floor.

Afraid to move, Angel and Betsy sat frozen in place during the melee. The faces, hands, and clothes of the two women and the stranger were coated with blood splatter. Using his grip on Bill's hair, the captain pulled the body's dead weight out of the chair and collapsed into it himself.

Angel noticed Chub still quivering and moaning. She grabbed a billet of wood from the stack near the stove and with a feeling of satisfaction, her farm girl arms finished the job the captain had started. Then she hunkered down, grinned, and watched Moses choke red-faced until his air ran out. In terms of vengeance, she was an Old Testament creature. Betsy rushed to a corner, fists pushed against her lips. Her eyes tightly closed, sobs and moans escaped from her mouth. Angel searched the gang members, collected their weapons, and placed them on the table. She stared at the stranger, still hesitant to approach. In her years in mining and railroad towns, she had witnessed this kind of fighting madness, but never the speed and the simple moves that put the gang members down. Most men took a lot of killing.

The tendons in the stranger's neck relaxed, the smoky amber color in his eyes faded into dark brown, cheeks and lips quivered. The captain gasped, clutched his wounded side. He looked at the dead ones. Tears poured down his face. The captain's mouth twisted. He turned his head to one side and vomited. Angel decided to leave him alone a few more minutes. She rousted Betsy from her corner and shook her. Together they hauled the bodies out the back door. On her return, she poured hot water from a kettle kept on the stove into a porcelain basin and set it down in front of the stranger.

"My name's Angel. What's your name, Captain?" she said, keeping her voice soft. The man started to shake. He tried to lift his hands.

"It's all right. They're gone. You saved us."

Dipping part of her petticoat in the water, she cleaned his face and hands of blood and grease.

"Good … feels good," he gasped, gagging back a second urge to vomit.

She got him out of the buffalo coat. It became obvious where Little Bill's bullet had gone. The coat had flared out making the stranger look wider. The shot went through the left side of the hide without touching his body. The knife wound was another matter. After removing his army jacket and peeling back his long johns, she found where the Bowie had notched two ribs and punched through into the flesh beneath. She cleaned it with water and bound it with a whiskey-soaked bandage. Angel hoped the knife hadn't gone in too far. Any kind of penetrating wound in that area of the body usually resulted in fever and death within a few days. The captain's shaking grew worse. He was going into shock. She grabbed some blankets from the back room and wrapped him. Following orders, Betsy put more wood in the stove. They heated up the morning's leftover coffee. Angel poured for all.

~~~OOO~~~

Rod felt sick, mouth tasting of bitter bile. The waves of nausea slowed, the thick black coffee a help. It reminded him of the stuff his German grandmother used to make. In the early hours, before the men got out of bed, you could hear her turning the crank on the antique wood and cast iron grinder. Grounds and water were placed in a blue enameled pot, which sat on the stove all day. It got boiled to the point that when poured you about needed scissors to snip it from the spout. He knew what had just happened. It was the ambush in Nam all over again, some visceral thing, not himself, in control of his body. His awareness supplanted, crushed down deep inside, helpless, only seeing things far off, like looking through the wrong end of binoculars.

He hated it!

One of these times, he would not come back, his body an eternal prison, confining his screaming soul. Maybe Cozeen had it right. He was a blight on the land. Rod examined the two women drinking coffee across the table. They looked as if they had been recently and continuously misused in hard ways, especially the younger one, who sported purple-green facial bruises and probably a broken nose. Hair in tangles, she rubbed at crusty stuff in the corners of her eyes. Slouched over the coffee cup, staring into the black liquid, her hands clenched and unclenched.

Angel, the older one, appeared much more experienced and able to talk sense. A few strands had pulled loose from her tied-back medium-blonde hair. The woman's wide mouth seemed about to break into a smile. Her blue eyes, however, held a toughness around the edges. He had seen it before in the faces of bar girls around military bases, a professional, calculating face, one used to making customers think they were welcome, while being fleeced. There was no lace around this woman's soul.

"My name is Rod Teigler," he said. "Where in the name of God am I? Who were those men?"

Her answers came in a rush. "Captain, let me report to you like a soldier. We been prisoners of the Donovan gang ever since the blizzard started. You probably got word from your superiors about them bein' in the area. They robbed the bank in Elwood. Of the six of us winterin' over, Betsy and me are the only two left alive."

"I came from Elwood today," he said, "no Donovan gang there and no bank robbery."

"Then what do you call this?" she said as her hands lifted a full canvas sack from the floor and smacked it down on the table. On its face stenciled in bold black script: Bank of Elwood.

Rod focused on the sack. "And what town is this?"

"It ain't a real town. We call it Miners' Luck. They struck silver here a few years ago, but not enough to draw any sizable crowd."

Teigler looked around the room, noting the kerosene lamps, potbellied stove, and the old-fashioned guns on the table, nothing modern anywhere. The saloon atmosphere began to feel spooky.

"Which one was Donovan?"

"None," Angel said. "He's one of two left. They're holed up down the street."

Still shaking, his hands pulled out the .45s and checked their loads—five good rounds per cylinder, each pistol with an empty chamber under the hammer. The actions moved easily. Thank God, the cold hadn't affected their operation.

"Are they likely to come over here?"

"Not in the dark. With wind and snow this bad, they could pass us within yards and not see the buildin'. But they'll be comin' in the mornin'. From the signs, it's likely to clear for a while at dawn."

"Do you have a phone or CB radio?"

Angel just stared at him, as though he had spoken Apache. Teigler fumbled in his pockets for his cell phone, hoping the cold hadn't killed the battery. He opened the keypad cover, pulled out the antenna, and held down the PWR button. Both women gasped, as the phone lit up and played its hello music. You would have thought he had performed magic. Unfortunately, the signal strength indicator stayed flat—no calling out.

"Captain, that some kind of watch?" Betsy said. "I've seen 'em play music, but never one with a light inside."

"So, what do we do? We can't get help," he said, ignoring her.

"Well, Sir," Angel said, "I don't know what the Army way might be, but you are goin' to have to kill 'em."

She went on to explain their problem. They couldn't leave. The cold and the blizzard made it impossible. Once the storm quit, Donovan would be desperate to ride out before the posse on his trail caught up. The outlaw wouldn't want to leave with the bank money setting on the table. Even if given the loot, he would want no witnesses to tell what he had done or where he had gone. Donovan didn't know about his dead companions, or the captain's arrival. They just needed a good plan to take advantage of that.

Only half-listening to her speech, Teigler looked again at the Old English print on the canvas moneybag, a typeface out of style decades ago. A nasty, far-out creepy thought entered his mind. He scooped up some of the coins left on the table by the poker players. While not an expert, he knew the money of his captain persona's era. In his hands lay Carson City gold double eagles, seated Liberty half-dollars, Indian head pennies, and even a Civil War two-cent piece. All in mint condition.

"What year is it?" he said, breaking into Angel's monologue.

She stopped, responding with a puzzled frown.

He reached across the table, a rough hand on each shoulder and said, "What year?"

She pushed his hands aside, locked her eyes to his, and said, "Eighteen seventy-seven."

Teigler slumped back in his chair. She must be right. The speech, the dress, the weapons, the artifacts … all consistent with the period. When the mountain released its massive accumulated energy, did it open a portal to the past? Had it matched his clothing and frame of mind to the year?

His mind wrestled with the shock. Angel pushed the idea of a plan again. Retreating inside himself, Teigler refused to talk. She knew men like him, men baptized in blood and loss at such places as Shiloh, the Wilderness, and Chickamauga, minds burned and scarred. Some committed suicide or sought out death by leaping into high-risk situations. The captain might let Donovan kill him tomorrow. As her last chance, a God-given chance, she couldn't let that happen.

The two women prepared a good supper, frying steaks cut from the side of beef hanging frozen on the back stoop. Fried potatoes and canned peaches completed the menu. Angel tried to get a whisky or two in Teigler, but he only took a sip. Strangely, he neither smoked nor chewed tobacco, unlike most men she knew. Well, only one sin remained to try. Fortunately, she knew that one rather well. Angel sang songs in her most husky voice, starting with "Barbara Allen" and progressing to "Sweet Betsy from Pike," "Arkansas Traveler," and "Brennan on the Moor." As the last song ended, she began to massage his neck and shoulders. In spite of how lean he looked, Angel could feel considerable muscle.

Teigler allowed her to guide him into the back room. She made short work getting him stripped and into her bed. The captain had obviously not lain with a woman in a long time. His responses seemed clumsy, but with hard-muscled snake-like twists, the act itself went quickly, almost violently, as if some inner alien creature drove him. He fell asleep five minutes later. Angel crept out to the main room with pillows and blankets for Betsy. The teacher would stay there for the night. There was still work to do on Teigler. Both women needed him ready at daylight.

In the early hours, Angel went to work on him again; this time was good for her too. It took longer and Teigler was gentle, a vast change from her encounters of the last four days. In the dreamy afterglow, she thought about his hands. It seemed wrong, the way his hands could rise up and kill so easily, and yet remain capable of pleasuring intensely, almost effortlessly. She managed to get him to pillow talk afterwards. What Angel heard shocked and frightened her. She shivered beside him. In normal circumstances, any frontier woman would have thought him crazy.

According to the captain, he came from a time a century from now. Confirming her suspicion, he had experienced war, but one thousands of miles away, a wet jungle place of heat, bugs, and death. In his world, a person could travel great distances in horseless carriages, trains, and even fly at hundreds of miles per hour. Most people lived in cities rather than small towns and farms. Voices and pictures could be sent into every home. He confessed to not being a captain in the cavalry.

Teigler explained that in the future her time would be revered. Modern people would outfit themselves in the old clothes, study the old ways, and join groups to act out how they had lived. It all sounded so convincing. Angel asked about the women of this future and especially those in her line of work. He said women all had the vote and many were elected to public office, although a woman hadn't made president yet. She learned sisters-in-arms existed in those times yet to come. Teigler said the best ones worked in places called Las Vegas or Reno. Still without a plan, both fell asleep in the hour before dawn. When the pair woke, they discovered they weren't going to surprise Donovan and his surviving partner after all.

"Betsy's gone," Angel shouted from beside the bar. Rod rushed into the room long-johned and barefooted, pistol in hand. They searched the saloon and looked out back. The sun began to appear over the mountains, brightening the interior of the saloon. No snow in the air, the blizzard was catching its breath. In the new light, a fresh trail in the snow stretched all the way to the mine office down the street.

"Why the hell would she go to Donovan?" Angel said. "She suffered more than any of us at the hands of the gang."

Reacting to his companion's blank expression, he said, "Some people held hostage get crazy enough to actually like their captors, even to the point of resisting rescue."

She shook her head in disbelief. "So what now?"

"I guess we wait and see what they do. In the meantime, I want you to get familiar with the shotgun I brought. We also need food and coffee. I don't think we'll have to wait long."

~~~OOO~~~

"That can't be right," Davy said, running his fingers through his sandy-colored hair. "There is no one alive could kill those three like she described. Not those three."

"Well, we wouldn't have heard cannon fire yesterday, what with the wind and snow," Donovan replied. He rubbed one scarred shoulder, and raised craggy eyebrows. "What happened to those boys don't matter now. We have to decide whether we leave between the storms with our share of the loot, or go after Angel and her soldier."

"We rode too many a year with those men to leave without gettin' even," Davy said, "and, I want the rest of the cash."

"I don't know. I'm gettin' me a bad feelin'."

"You're gettin' old. I'm goin' up there."

"No, you're not," Donovan said. "We both go, and we do it my way. Oh, and before we kill them we get shut of the teacher."

~~~OOO~~~

Teigler scanned the brilliantly lit street from the saloon's front windows. The village laid out east to west. The rising sun's reflection off the snow made his eyes sting. Donovan had sent the school marm back with a message. They needed to meet in the street and resolve the issue, just the two of them—winner take all. It was a trap, of course. According to Angel, Donovan would hedge his bets. However, at two to one, he and Angel couldn't wait for the outlaws to figure out some other more devious plan. Teigler accepted. Betsy went back with his response. Angel begged him to reconsider. He told her not to worry. He had practiced this kind of showdown many more times than Donovan. The outlaws' options appeared limited, given the town's simple layout.

He figured it would be some variation on back shooting. Donovan would keep his attention while Davy took him out from behind. The million-dollar question: from where would that shot come? They couldn't use the roofs; there must be four to five feet of snow on them. The east end of the saloon or one of the windows across the street offered the best locations. Teigler would bet on the windows. Even though she had used one on her family's farm, Angel dry fired the shotgun a number of times. Comfortable with its weight and how to aim, she would cover his back.

It was almost time to go out. He would have the sun in his eyes, as well as the blinding reflection from the snow. He took soot from the coal oil lamp chimneys and coated his eyelids and the flesh around them to reduce the glare.

"You puttin' on war paint?" Angel said, running the fingers of one hand up his cheek into the frosted black hair on his temples.

He hugged her and put some under her eyes. "You're a member of the tribe now." Without thinking about it, her body relaxed in his arms. She resisted the urge to press closer and put her head on his chest. Scolding herself, she pushed away, not wanting to feel that way about any man.

"I'm going to open the window by the door so you can shoot through it. Keep your attention on the windows across the street—not on me and Donovan."

Teigler thought about the gunfight. Chances of victory improved if you could get a psychological leg up on your opponent—get him angry or frightened, prone to mistakes. Maybe like the old Samurai, he could gain dominance by staring down his opponent. He would face the outlaw in his uniform, no coat, and no hat. He'd carry a Smith & Wesson in each hand— none of this fast-draw nonsense. He stepped out the door.

Donovan closed his engraved gold pocket watch, stepped over the teacher's sprawled, broken body and opened the door. Davy would be in position now. The sun would be at his back, another advantage. He began to feel better. He had outlasted most of the Civil War gangs. No reason he couldn't go on for a long time yet. The deep snow slowed movement. Donovan moved sideways around several drifts higher than his head to work his way up the street. The wind blew in fits and starts. It would whisk up powdery snow from the roofs to temporarily obscure his vision. One gust hit Donovan as he approached the saloon almost taking his hat. He stopped, close enough. With his back to the sun, his shadow projected a good eight feet in front of him.

"Soldjer boy, you get out here, my breakfast is a waitin'."

He spotted something blue move out of a swirl-devil of snow. The air cleared and Donovan got his first good look. The captain was a tall one, probably five or six inches over him. He wore no hat. Black circles around his eyes made his face look like a skull.

Jeb felt a sudden loss of confidence. His opponent didn't speak, just stood there with two .45 Smith & Wesson pistols loose at his sides. The soldier's eyes stared flat and hot. Standing in snow above his knees, the man's body appeared to float above the ground.

Donovan tried not to meet his eyes. The outlaw wanted to make up an insult to hurl, but his mind could only focus on the gray and blue clad boys he had bushwhacked—the men and women he had slaughtered. He heard their cries in the wind. Was the captain an avenging angel? Spits of snow melted on his cheeks, tears of the dead.

Donovan refocused. It seemed as though they had been standing there for hours. He jumped as a shotgun blast shattered a window up the street to his right. A high-pitched scream pierced the air as glass and buckshot sprayed the back shooter.

A dropped rifle clattered on wooden planks. The soldier spun left, raised his guns. Flame and grimy cotton smoke spit out both barrels. Inside the store, Davy let out a gurgle, followed by a thump as his body hit the floor.

Donovan raised his Colt and fired just as an eddy of snow obscured his target. The revolver jumped in his hand, followed by the crack of the bullet. He thought he heard a grunt. He ran forward a dozen steps, and then another. Donovan stopped, his eyes tried to bore through the suspended snow. The wind dropped. The air cleared.

Blood crashed through his temples. He could hear and feel his heart thump his ribcage. The soldier was gone, no sign of him. Donovan gulped cold air. A streak of numbing fear ran through the outlaw's mind.

Then came relief, he figured he must have killed him, the body dropped into the deep snow. He walked closer to the saloon, his shadow advancing in front of him. Jeb began to feel jubilant. He survived. As the only one left, he would have all the money. He would go to Mexico and live the good life. The old Donovan must go. A new man would take his place. Maybe a rancher, or … maybe even a banker, the boys would have gotten a kick out of that. He stopped near where the captain had stood. Another step, the outlaw's shadow rested on the disturbed area where he must have fallen.

Out of the snow, piercing his shadow, rose two slender gun barrels. For a split second, Donovan didn't recognize what they were. Flame and smoke blew out.

He realized his shadow had betrayed him. Donovan's stomach took a punch. Part of his left kidney spewed out behind him. He rocked back then forward. His knees buckled. The pistols fired again. He took a bullet in the right arm and one in the chest. The twisting 230-grain soft lead slugs blossomed when they hit resistance.

Ballooning through his flesh, the shock waves liquefied organs and shredded muscle. Two of the four bullets remained in his body after smashing bone. Donovan and his dreams died before he hit the welcoming snow. The wind picked up, dry white particles swirled into new patterns. Soft hands brushed the snow off Teigler's face.

~~~OOO~~~

Teigler woke three days later in Elwood Community Hospital. He tried to jerk upright and paid for it with a slap of pain. His head seemed filled with the echoes of doors slamming and slamming and slamming … Someone handed him a glass of water with a straw. He took a drink and focused his eyes on the ceiling until the pain fell below monster level.

"So, Lieutenant, where you been?" a familiar voice said.

"Well, Sergeant Cozeen, I'm not back from Scarborough Fair."

In the course of the ensuing conversation, Teigler learned that he and a blonde woman had showed up at the pass rest stop riding double on his exhausted mule. His companion held his unconscious body in the saddle. They arrived during a break in the storm. Another day passed before it finally blew out and they got him to the hospital.

"The doctors and I are very curious," Cozeen said. "You had two wounds crudely bandaged with what looked like parts of an old lace petticoat. The docs swear one is a stab wound, which pierced your peritoneum. For that you should be grateful for antibiotics. In an earlier age, it would have killed you. They also took a bullet out of your upper chest. I identified it as .32-20 caliber, a cartridge last used in a rare version of the black powder 1873 Colt revolver."

"Well, you're the historian," Teigler said, adjusting his hospital blanket. "I accept your expert opinion."

"Your buffalo coat had several new odd-size buttonholes in it at random locations. The blood on it wasn't all yours. Your guns had been fired. Did you have a private quarrel with one of the other Shoot 'Em Up participants? We checked on all the reenactors, none missing or injured."

"I'm neither a historian nor an attorney," Teigler responded, "but I do know no *corpus delecti* equals no case."

Biting his lip, Cozeen looked out at the snow-flocked trees and bushes. "It's a mystery worthy of the great Sherlock," he muttered.

"You know what the man said," Teigler responded. "When you have eliminated the impossible, whatever remains, however improbable, must be the truth." A look of concern flashed across his face. "Tell me about the woman and my mule. Are they okay?"

"Sal came through fine, she's in my barn—very tired but no major damage. One strange thing, the last six inches of tail hair is all frizzled, burnt by what looks like an electrical discharge. The woman sat by your bed until you were out of trouble, then disappeared. The hospital called me the day after she left. One of the nurses said the blonde left a message. She was going to the first place you mentioned to find her sisters. She figured you would follow her if you wished."

Teigler leaned back in relief, a smile on his face.

"One other point," Cozeen said. "When I went through your possessions, your wallet was shy of the $500 mule jump prize money. My suspicion—the gal made off with it."

Teigler laughed, "She earned every dollar of that money. I'm glad she found a replacement grubstake. Incidentally, I have a few questions for you. One, was there a settlement called Miners' Luck in the area? And two, did the Donovan Gang ever pass through here?"

Cozeen got a thoughtful look on his face. "To number one, yes, that's how the pass got its name. But, there's nothing left of it now—not even a splinter. When the only vein of workable silver played out in 1898, they abandoned the buildings and burned them to the ground. To number two, yes. That group of sadists disappeared without a trace right after Elwood's only bank robbery back in the late 1870s."

Teigler looked out the window and thought to himself, Angel had left the bank loot behind. Sal hardly made it, burdened with the two of us. The gold was too heavy. Whoever made it back first to the mine in the spring couldn't resist temptation. They disposed of the outlaw bodies so they could keep the treasure. Everyone else believed the gang escaped with the loot. All of it except my souvenirs …

Cozeen broke the silence. "Are these historical facts relevant?" "Oh yes! By the way, get my coat, will you? I have an early Christmas present for you, Lawman," Rod said.

Cozeen held out the heavy coat. Teigler reached into one of the sleeves and pulled out a new-looking canvas bag. He tossed it to the patrol officer with a tight-lipped, screw-you grin. Cozeen's eyes bulged as he read the print on the outside. He felt something hard through the canvas. He reached inside, and pulled out two shiny brand new Carson City gold double eagles.

Isle Royale Hunted

Hidden in undergrowth, curious as death, yellow eyes watch.
Last night surrounded by the wash, wash, wash of lake water,
they loped through the pinewoods, their shadows feather-drifting
across mossy ground—owl wings riding on whispers. Across from
the narrow beach, its rocks hot, green-algaed apples,

a boat is laced to the dock. The brown sugar, tung-oiled hull
lifts and tugs against mooring lines. A bare-chested,
blue-jeaned graybeard works on the cambered teak deck.
Muscles knotted, he furls sails dyed crimson
with Chinese ox-blood. The sun wrings bright spots
out of the water to dance over sail and man.
Scarred medic's hands become mottled red, slick again
with wound-flowered flesh and fluids. His topaz eyes
remember crawling among the wounded, bodies scattered
in bullet-cut elephant grass, jungle all around.
A ghost soldier's back arches, flooded lungs and mouth gush.

A short-legged, wirehaired terrier peers over the bow,
wide black eyes curious marbles. He huffs,
nose wrinkles on and off, thinks big dog thoughts.
His jaws open in a yawn of pink tongue, crenellated teeth.
The dog imagines himself hustling down the island's
dark, paw-soft paths, scents of wild things songs in his nostrils.

Man and dog sense wolves in their dreams. In jungle and pines,
quick gray-black grinning muzzles seek them.

Old Reptile

I arrived early at the tennis courts. My old buddy Bob had argued me into a quick match between events. He and I returned to our small birth town in Iowa for the high school class of 1960's fortieth reunion. As a result of many months in Nam nearly three decades ago, I had lost the ability to cope with group social events. The more numerous and more in motion the humanity, the more impossible it became to assess risk and secure the perimeter. Only Bob's threat of blackmail brought me back—he knew too many secrets.

So here I waited, in whites, idly spinning a borrowed racket, exposed to a summer sun demanding the gray bleached asphalt release its surface moisture. In the late-morning quiet, bird song and a goldfinch flash caught my attention.

The park was old. As third graders, Bob and I had attended its dedication fifty years ago, its small acreage dozed out of the trees and marshy ground near the river. Leaning back on the rental Chevy's red fender, I let my eyes wander over the familiar park boundaries. The mature trees at the far end were gone, victims of age and fungus-carrying bark beetles. I tried to reconstruct where they had stood, triggering an uneasy memory of a day when we sheltered under their protection, so many years ago. I remembered …

~~~OOO~~~

…an amber afternoon at the park with empty tennis courts, deserted baseball diamond, and limp paddle-ball ropes. Blurry blast furnace-like heat ripples rose from the parking lot in response to the slap of the Iowa summer sun. Mirage-like, the ripples seemed to flow down the blacktop path, until they disappeared into elm and cottonwood shade.

Under the trees, gray wooden picnic tables and a tilted shed with a creaking Dutch door furnished a refuge for a dozen preteens, whose exhausted mothers had exiled them for the afternoon. Two high school girls, outfitted in city park department white blouses and tan shorts, tried to impose order. At first, they allowed us to tumble about and around them, to paw at their hips and legs, until their German heritage demanded discipline and they diverted us into other games.

A couple of kids moved sweaty chess pieces, while others braided the last lanyards or bracelets of the season. Recently, Bob and I had acquired a growing interest in gender differences. That day we spent our time in activities, which allowed our attention to focus on the movements of these older ... more developed girls. There was a mystery, but our future part in it escaped us. The telephone in the shed rang.

"Okay, everyone go home—now," the head counselor said. She waved the black handset. "There's a tornado comin' ... go on, git!"

We rumbled out of the playground, a train of kids at a fast walk, each one shunted off as the procession reached his house. No one talked, our minds full of images springing from stories of storms past, chickens sucked into milk bottles with their legs dangling out, straw pounded like nails into wooden power poles, a hog razored in half by a wind-powered sheet of corrugated steel, and Aunt Inez crippled for life—caught in the business end of the funnel!

Finally alone, fear flushed me from the cover of the trees and bushes of an older neighborhood into the raw space of our new housing development. I could see our place as I raced up the last section of dusty, unpaved road.

The sound of my breathing and heartbeat grew unnaturally loud. I stopped. Itchy sweat trickled down my sides. There was no movement of air, no bird song, no rustle of leaves.

I scanned the area, no people, dogs, bikes, or cars. Looking back, I saw, hanging suspended above each of my footprints, a kicked-up puff of dust. Lungs worked harder, taking in heavy liquid air. My own sweaty ammonia scent filled the space around me. The sky seemed immense, a great bowl filled with raw curds of ragged clouds. Colors faded, everything brown-toned and one dimensional like an old tintype. The tornado was very close.

My sneakered feet felt locked to the ground, body and thoughts frozen, helpless before the approaching winds. My consciousness slid down into the lowest portion of my brain, that place where our ancient scaly reptile ancestor lurks with all its hardwired survival instincts. From a deep well came a snarl of defiance and a leap into my consciousness.

My arms and legs twitched, lips parted, hands clenched—the hypnotic spell shattered. The hybrid creature I became sprinted, adrenaline-pumped, toward shelter. A gray-black wind-mountain full of dirt, branches, and human garbage loped down the road behind me. It shrieked and scratched at my clothes and hair.

The door to our house opened. My anxious mother hustled me into the basement. There, in the southwest corner, under the glow of the family's antique oil lamp, safe in my mother's arms, the freight train roar of the storm passed. The reptile personality faded, and I became fully human once more. I never rode out a tornado that close again. However, you clawed your way out—old reptile—more than a few times, beginning in those faraway wet and dense jungles, like those of your birth, where men hunted each other.

You kept me alive, when I wanted to die—the things you … we did and witnessed. Flesh cut open with bullets and exploded into chunks. Staring faceless bodies hung on barbwire and tree branches. A skull picked clean by insects, still wearing a pilot's helmet and sunglasses, grinned on the seat of a crashed chopper. Four friends, skin burned black, stripped to underwear, tossed in a heap beside their smoked jeep. A thirteen-year-old enemy, half our size, waving the gushing stump of an arm … I taste their blood. I cramp over, let it rush out of my mouth. The overflow stains shorts and tennis shoes, puddles red on the asphalt.

A breeze, heavy with humidity, rushes from the river, fills the foliage. From swaying uncut grass behind the courts, a thrush warbles. A monarch butterfly meanders over the hood of the red car and kisses the gray-shot hair of a kneeling man. The head shakes. The crimson and black winged insect flutters away, instinct telling it to find a more peaceful place.

A Time to Heal

A dark crocodile shadow races alongside
our helicopter gunship, skims the muddy jungle river.

It is patient.

Decades of pursuit compress,
fold the space behind me,

musty reptile breath hot on my ankles.

The years, dry leaves, ground by our running feet,
powder my hair gray, wrinkle skin.

Olive-drab shards of war memories burn.

My heart's broken spring slows,
its razor-pain ripples into silent dark.

"Have you caught up at last?"

In the blackness comes the scrabble of claws,
flint-studded caiman skin rasps fear into anger.

"Fight me, damn you!"

The thud of scaly feet grows distant.
Echoes die in the thick constricting velvet.

In my loneness, a light unshutters.

An Asian-eyed child offers a white-petaled blossom.
My scarred hand opens, a broken sword drops.

"It is perfect."

Desert Spirits

He indulged himself. Afternoon heat rose and swirled out of the gravel parking lot next to the Dairy Shack. It caused the ice cream to melt and trickle down the cone, his tongue not fast enough to lick up the cool vanilla before it lapped over his fingers. New perspiration prickled his back and chest. Rorschach sweat patterns appeared on the bleached-out blue work shirt and faded jeans. He removed a cream-colored Stetson straw, rested it on the leather bench seat of the new two-tone yellow and white Dodge 4x4 pickup.

The residual wetness, dammed up by the headband, started to evaporate and cool his forehead. The effect wouldn't last long in the dry desert air. Rod Teigler wiggled his toes inside new black water buffalo boots. Their hybrid half-riding, half-walking heels worked equally well slotted into stirrups or pushing against the sand and rock of the local game trails. He heard shoes scuffing the gravel.

"Man, that's one nice truck."

Rod's head turned, brows lifted. The words came from a thin pale man wearing a white square paper hat over slicked back dark hair and a matching apron over t-shirt and khakis. A whiff of Old Spice reached the truck before he did. The Dairy Shack owner had stepped out from behind his serving window.

"I've got a '79 model at home. Been fixin' it up, overhauled slant-six engine, new upholstery, and such. No rust, it's been a desert truck all its life—paint faded a bit though. Name's Herb, look like you've come a ways."

Teigler's tongue caught a vanilla drip just before it would have sailed off to land on his shirt belly. He decided to be cordial. "Came down through Colorado and New Mexico, thought I'd try to find peace and quiet in the Chihuahuan Desert."

The man tested the metal of the door with one hand before bending to lean his forearms on the window chrome. "You picked the right time. May and June are the hottest months of the year, hundred degrees every day, chases away the usual run of tourists. My advice, you keep plenty of water at hand, every season we lose a few city dudes. I been thinkin' about getting a slide-on camper like yours."

"Would you like to see inside?"

"No thanks. I checked 'em out at the RV dealer in El Paso. Very neat, top cranks up, bed, stove, sink—room for two. Like to get up in the mountains with the gal friend." He closed one eye in a man-to-man wink. "Very cozy."

Looking over Herb's shoulder, Rod noticed what looked like a squat bundle of rags limping toward them along the highway shoulder. The image discomforting, something coiled inside him, irritated.

Noticing his stare, the man turned his head. "Oh, that's Old Lozen, last Chihenne Apache round here, named after her famous witch woman great-great-great-grandmom."

"Does she cast spells or tell fortunes?"

"The locals believe she has *Diya*, spirit power. Claims to be able to locate bad guys, *Inda-ce-ho-ndi*, Enemies-Against-Power, she calls it. Don't believe it myself and I'm part Comanche. Lozen does a lot of beggin'. Want I should chase her off?"

"No. Can you make up a food packet? I'll pay."

"Can do. I make up lunches for some of the county highway crews. Just be a minute."

Rod watched the woman draw near. Wild scraggy hair, shot with white, held in place with a faded red cloth headband. A mishmash of castoff or donated Salvation Army specials clothed her from neck to ankles. An apron painted with cryptic triangular designs fluttered around her waist. The footgear looked authentic Apache, leather moccasins stretched from toes up to the calves, tied off with thongs. A five-foot gray walking staff cut from a cane cholla plant helped with an arthritic limp. Hung about her body were pouches and jewelry, or in her case probably amulets and desert plant medicine.

The ice cream man returned with a paper sack in hand, open for Rod's inspection. "One baloney and one cheese, a boiled egg and an apple, two dollars."

Rod handed over the money. Herb turned, advanced a few paces, and made an impatient left-handed come-here wave at the woman. He handed her the bag, made a comment, pointed toward Teigler, and returned to work, leaving them alone. Their eyes met. She stopped in the white powdery pea-gravel at the side of the truck and stared. Lozen smelled like tarbush and cactus pollen. He waited.

The medicine woman's black stone eyes pierced his mind. He started to panic, but his arms and legs felt cloaked in molasses. She fastened a gold-veined turquoise nugget to a notch on her staff, shook it.

"Come out." She whispered, "*Maganii*, show me."

Teigler felt transfixed, tried to break eye contact. The stirring inside increased and became angry. She shook the staff again and chanted:

> *Upon this earth*
> *On which we live*
> *Ussen has Power.*
> *This Power is mine*
> *For locating the enemy.*
> *I search for the Enemy*
> *Which Only Ussen the Great*
> *Can show to me.*

The ice cream cone fell out of his hands, landing between his legs on the seat. His heart felt like it took a blunt needle thrust. Muscles convulsed. The snake-creature inside leaped. Rod's eyes closed to slits, turned amber, mouth hissed open.

A muffled gasp, Lozen mumbled, "Shape-shifter … no, two half-spirits." She reversed the stone, shook her staff, and commanded, "Back."

Rod's body slumped. He struggled to get control of a wave of nausea. A callused, cool hand gripped his chin and raised his head. Panting, Teigler's eyes were once again captured by the witch.

"*Tl'iish*, you snake soldier. Inside you, old, old, very old scaled spirit wants the man. Cannot be defeated." She untied a small elk-leather medicine bag from her waist and threw it on his lap. Waddling away, Lozen looked over her shoulder. "Find harmony or die."

~~~OOO~~~

Ten minutes later, well out of the one-horse town, Rod found a side road, pulled over, and shut off the engine. Door open, he stumbled out of the truck, clothes soaked with sweat and melted ice cream. The countryside smelled of sage and creosote. He lowered and locked the camper's jacks, protesting muscles cranked the top up. Clothes went into a rope-necked green army-surplus laundry bag. Pumping water into the miniature sink, he cleaned up with a quick whore's bath. Checking the mirror, he noticed red-black half-moons under his eyes. He had bled under the skin.

A sharp spike of pain surfaced on the right side of his abdomen, third time today. The spot felt hot as he rubbed it. Collapsed naked on the bed, he loosened the ties of the witch's pouch. Rod had only seen pictures, but he recognized a dozen peyote buds, a bitter-tasting potent psychedelic. Lozen's prescription would take him and his reptile parasite into the spirit world. Was he meant to confront his nemesis?

It all started in Vietnam, killed too many, stayed too long, betrayed by his commanders, kept getting tossed into life or death events. The more killing, the more the barriers broke. The reptile personality in the brain clawed out, became stronger, increasingly berserk each time. Rod was willing to die, wanted to die, *it* didn't! Whatever acts the situation required to survive, the creature did, more than a normal man could stomach. Calling it up, would he be able to kill it, or …

~~~OOO~~~

Rod detected subtle changes in the countryside. It was logical. The Chihuahuan Desert covered a huge landmass spread over New Mexico, Texas, and Old Mexico. Traveling from the Northwest with its higher elevation and pine-covered mountains, he now descended into lower regions. Each thousand feet down displayed some differences in plant and animal life.

According to the highway signs, he was in Brewster County, The largest county in the largest state in the lower forty-eight. Some 6,200 square miles allowed a population spread of 1.43 people for each one of those square miles. Of course, most of the local folks lived in Alpine, the county seat, leaving the few other inhabitants scattered sparsely over the rest of the countryside like a reverse choke shotgun pattern on a map.

Five miles south of town, he spotted a small glass and bleached-wood building. "The Brewster County Historical Museum and Garden" was scrawled on a sign near the entrance. On a whim, he pulled the camper-laden truck into the empty gravel lot—he could use some campground directions. The late afternoon sun reflected off the sandy ground, a shock after the air-conditioned cab. Rod hustled up the narrow sidewalk and stepped into the museum.

The inside rewarded him with coolness. He heard a cheery, "Howdy, cowboy. What'll you have?"

His forward movement brought him belly-up to a glass display case, equipped with stacked color brochures, jars of prickly pear jelly, and an NCR cash register. Standing behind the counter, a head shorter than himself, stood a redhead. Her short-cut hair was striking, not the carroty orange stuff accompanied by a massive freckle infection, but a deep, dark magenta with ruby overtones. Looking down, he noticed she had just a sprinkle of freckles across a nicely shaped nose and upper cheekbones. The girl—woman—rested her forearms on the counter and stared up into his face. The pupils in her light brown eyes widened as he removed his sunglasses.

"My name's Kathleen O'Donnell Maloney; you can call me Pepper."

He breathed in her perfume. It didn't appear to come from a bottle, just real woman scent. "Rod," he croaked, "Rod Teigler." His internal reptile companion tensed, also affected by the pheromones. A species-memory flashed in its mind, giant fin-backed scaly male beasts bellowed and fought in the riverbank mud as females hissed promises on the other side.

He licked his lips. "I'd like to know more about this country, Pepper."

She moved out from behind the counter and waved him into the interior. "I'm jus' the person to handle that desire, honey. Follow me."

Teigler liked the tied-off man's blue gingham shirt and tight jeans. Looked like Pepper carried about ten pounds more than she needed, but he had always been partial to curves. And, the extra was ... all in the right places.

She flicked on the lights, and pointed to displays lining the walls. Putting on her schoolmarm face and voice, she said, "The desert we live in is characterized by the near absence of rain, usually only ten to twelve inches a year. The Sierra Madre Mountains keep the western rains out. This year we got a couple of extra inches due to larger than normal tropical storms punching northeast out of the Bay of California. Our garden is particularly lovely as a result."

Teigler thought *lovely* was an appropriate word. Usually he ignored the women around him, shut out all the little signals. After Nam, he possessed only a limited amount of affection, maybe not enough for even one other person. Yet, there was a void. He could still feel the hole in his heart from the recent death of his old mule and companion, Sal. Maybe he should try it. "Could I impose on you to give me a tour?"

"You bet, tall man." She wrinkled her nose. "I never miss a chance."

Pepper hip-swayed through the next exhibits. "The Chihuahuan is a rich desert. At least 3,500 plant species grow here. The main ones include creosote bush, tarbush, yucca, and many varieties of cacti. On the animal side, while red wolves and jaguars have been hunted out, the remaining species include bighorn sheep, rabbits, fox, coyote, and mice of all kinds. Stay away from the peccaries, those little piggies are downright mean."

Teigler felt a swirl of emotion spurt up from some deep uncapped well, magnified by the arousal of the reptile personality. Its reaction not concerned with anything but the exchange of chemical signals between them. Heady stuff, sanding away the scar tissue, making him feel more vulnerable while pushing him toward the risk he usually avoided with the opposite gender.

"Are we ready for the garden yet?"

"Now don't be in a rush, we haven't got through the lizards and snakes."

"I'd rather check out the birds and the bees."

"Well," she said drawing out the word, "the sun is going down. We better look at the garden while there is still light."

~~~OOO~~~

Rod and Pepper sat together on a concrete bench facing the setting sun. Long black shadows ran from the tops of the taller bushes and plants. The twilight temperature ran cool and silky against their skin, the air heavily perfumed with cactus blossoms. She had really given him the cook's tour. The woman knew the common and Latin names of plants, and which ones the Indians and settlers had used for food and medicine.

"How do you know so much about the desert?"

"Well," she admitted, eyes downcast, "I have my masters in biology from Texas A&M."

"This is not your full time job?"

"I was born and raised on a ranch near here. I love this country. It's like living in a cathedral. I've got a government summer grant lined up to study endangered desert lizards. During the school year, I teach at the university."

Rod stayed silent a moment. How much insight would her knowledge about reptiles give her into his situation? "I wondered why you sound like a college professor and laugh like a country girl."

"Most of the local educated folk can turn it on or off depending on the audience. When I meet an interesting man, I usually shuck the professor personality. Women outnumber men around these parts, and us lonely singles don't want to frighten any off with highfalutin' talk."

"Not to worry, for me, smart well-educated women are a turn-on. It's late, show me where there's a campground, I'll fix you dinner."

"Rod, honey, pull your camper-rig around to the back of the building—to the employee parking lot. You can set up there for the night. There's electrical plug-ins, water, and a picnic table. Tomorrow's Sunday, so there won't be any hurry to leave."

~~~OOO~~~

The pair feasted on Gala apple slices and red seedless grapes while Rod set up a two-burner Coleman stove on the outside table to fry scrambled eggs with green chilies and tomato salsa. Cold Shiner Boch beer accompanied the meal. He pulled a blue enameled percolator off the second burner. "Kona coffee, Madame, to cap off the evening? No, wait, I need one more item."

Teigler vanished into the camper and soon returned with a hooded sweatshirt and a mysterious bottle. "Put this on, my dear biologist, the desert feels a bit cool after dark. And something more to warm us," he said, waving a long-necked dark bottle.

Holding out her coffee cup, Pepper said, "Napoleon Brandy, you sure know how to treat a girl."

The two continued coffee and conversation for another half hour, snuggled together to fox the cold air. During the "stories of their lives" chatter, Pepper seemed happy to learn he too came from a rural background. She knew more about cattle and he more about hogs. Both paraded childhood memories. Teigler mentioned his military service and the time spent in Vietnam, but refused to respond with details to her probing questions. After several more cognacs, they started telling funny stories about various relatives. The laughter grew in volume, scaring off all the prowling night creatures within fifty yards. The voices finally gasped into silence.

Teigler felt huge hands squeezing his heart; his temperature flared. The reptile opened jaws, tongue flicked out tasting, the tip of its tail quivered. The woman's muscles tensed as she felt her own heart song merge into his, the sexual tension as thick, rich, and sweet as chocolate brownies. Pepper took his shaking hands and led him into the camper.

~~~OOO~~~

Rod jumped awake, sensing movement beside him. Eyes snapped open and looked into Pepper's big grin.

"Don't mind me, I was justa lookin'. Grandma always says when a man's asleep, that's when he shows you his real face."

"How did I do?"

"I liked most of what I saw, probably some hurt in there. You'll need to tell me about that sometime. You were real frisky last night. At least four trips to the well, if you get the meanin'."

Rod, the man, only remembered two times. He felt his defenses begin to rise. "Not a pest, I hope."

"Not a bit. I reckon it's been some time since you've been with a woman. Also, you have two different styles, one gentle and slow, the other a bad boy, all ropy muscles and kind'a wild, each nice in their own way. Where's the potty?"

A spike of fear ran through him. Damn, I've only met two women on this trip and both could see right through me. Was it some kind of gender instinct? He sat up. "Look under the seat cushion. You want me to step out?"

"I'm not shy. You lie back. I'll make breakfast."

Teigler lay with his hands behind his head on the built-in camper bed, his feet hanging over the edge from the ankles down. He rarely found a bed long enough to accommodate his stretched-out six foot three inch body. Pepper fried onions, thin sliced steak, and potatoes. Wearing only lace-trimmed panties and a sweatshirt, the hem lifted every time her hand worked the spatula. She was a clever woman. "So, with that name you have to be Irish," Teigler said, appreciating the view.

"Not a big deal around here, about seven percent of the population is from the Old Sod, but during St. Pat's Day, the whole damn town claims the right, so they can drink and fight. As a writer, you must have some of the blood in you."

"Irish, Scot, and Welsh." He started to sing: "I'll take you home again, Kathleen O' Donnell Maloney, across the ocean wild."

Pepper provided the next two lines, "To where your heart has ever been, since you were first my Bonnie bride."

The desert air and the company made breakfast a feast. Teigler poured some ketchup on his hash before taking a bite. He hadn't felt this good in years, his mind, muscles, and bones all relaxed, even the reptile curled head to tail at peace. The reoccurring pain in his abdomen seemed temporarily pacified.

Pepper stood, blue-patterned china cup in hand. "Sure like this Kona, I could get hooked. Let's clean up, I've got to get back to the home spread. You come too. Grandma's likely to be worried, since I didn't check in last night" She let loose one of those sunny smiles. "Had other things on my mind."

~~~OOO~~~

The yellow and white truck hummed along the two-lane bleached asphalt. Rod hummed along with it. Two dainty feet in gold-toe cotton socks rested on the dash. He reached over and massaged the inside of Pepper's thigh.

"Careful, farm boy, too much of that and I'll have to attack."

Rod gave her a twisted silent smile, indicating he would give as good as he got given the opportunity. He'd spent a memorable week at the Mahoney ranch waiting for Pepper's school year to end. Grandma Beth had a centuries-old made-from-scratch recipe for chicken and dumplings that he could really tuck into. Her Tex-Mex cooking would have left him pounds heavier except for all the extracurricular activity. Not just the lovemaking, he fixed fences, painted, done a bit of shoeing, and had ridden some hours every day getting the feel of the country. The stomach pains returned sporadically, but limited themselves to a few minutes each. He wondered if ulcers were developing.

The time at the ranch also allowed him to finally face off with his alter ego, an extremely unpleasant and bruising confrontation. He'd convinced the two women to allow him an overnight in the desert with Janey, their five-year-old white-spotted Appaloosa mare as his sole companion. They rode out at noon with horse kit, compass, extra water, blanket, matches, and Grandpa Maloney's old trail knife—half Bowie and half machete. Lozen's elk hide bag rested under his shirt. At the time, Rod thought he had picked the direction of travel at random.

~~~OOO~~~

Man and horse stopped for the evening just outside a four-foot thick man-high wall of peach-blossomed prickly pear. The extra height on horseback allowed the rider to see over the barrier. The plants grew in a circular interlocked thicket with a large open area in the middle.

"What do you think, Janey? Is this a good place?" The horse tossed its head and snorted. Rod clicked his tongue. "Here we go, girl." He neck-reined Janey back a few paces and dismounted.

Working in the fading light, Teigler pounded the horse's steel picket pin into the ground and attached a 28-foot rope to the ring at its top. The other end, clipped to a wide leather collar, he fastened to Janey's neck. The setup kept the horse from wandering, but enabled her to graze in a circle around the picket stake, to lie down comfortably, and even to roll over. The mare safely tethered, Rod removed the bridle and saddle and provided his charge with water and feed.

Using the trail knife's twelve-inch blade, he could slash through the prickly pear barrier. The last few rays of sun glinted in the mare's honey-brown eyes as the man chopped through the cactus wall and stumbled into a perfect 50-foot diameter circle. Windblown brown-sugar sand and parched gray-black stones carpeted the floor, the green of plants and colors of living creatures absent. Teigler could see the cacti had grown together on top of an old circular stone wall. Throwing his blanket close to the perimeter edge, he sat, and removed his boots and hat. Pulling ankles up, he crossed his legs and leaned back against the wall. It was too dark to gather wood for a fire, but with a full moon scheduled, it wouldn't be needed.

Teigler's fingers explored the crumbly stonework. His conclusion: built by the hands of ancient men. The walls leaned inward, and if complete would have risen to curve into a plastered dome. It had to be the remains of a kiva, a place of worship for ancient native people.

"Over two thousand years old," he said aloud to the moon, "Probably built over an earlier, much older site of spirit power."

Night swelled up like an inky liquid out of rock crevices and caves. Riding its tide flew silver-haired, big-eared bats working hordes of nocturnal insects. With no town-glow, stars winked in their multitudes, their light old beyond comprehension. A breeze traced cold fingers through his hair. The day's heat stored in the kiva floor's petrified wood and sand warmed black velvet air.

Picking up the elk hide bag, he untied the drawstrings and dumped peyote buds on the blanket. Lozen's words drifted back, "Find harmony or die."

"So, here we go." Mouthing half the peyote, he started chewing. It tasted bitter. Rod swallowed the saliva, but not the pulp. He flushed water from the canteen over the bolus and continued to chew.

After fifteen minutes, he said, "I think I've worked all the goody out of this batch." He spit out the fibrous material and began munching on the remaining buds. He drank again and waited.

A half hour passed. "Nothing so far. Did she give me bad stuff?"

Out of the silence, a ticking sound grew—noises alternating between fast taps and slow tick, tick, ticks … His skin erupted in goose bumps as his head moved from side to side, pulling in sounds from all directions. His awareness expanded. "Scorpions, desert scorpion legs tick as they scurry."

The echoing drum-thump of a passing coyote's pads came through. The belly muscles of sidewinder rattlesnakes pushing against the ground produced rough rhythmic susurrations. Kangaroo rats' feet and tails tapped the sand like drumsticks on a cymbal. Woodwind notes climbed up and down the scale as thousands of insect bellies rubbed against rock particles. Symphonic music blended and rose in tempo. "It is a cathedral."

He laughed. A deeper, separate bass laugh echoed back at him. He sensed another presence. As if the music called it, white fog began to rise from the kiva floor. It grew, coalesced, and thickened into an amorphous cloud as high as his chin.

Heat lightning crackled, shadows spiked and fluttered. The vapor boiled around Rod's body. Pain lanced through him from crotch to scalp, huge hands were tearing him apart. Lightning broke the sky. He wailed. It sliced him down the middle.

~~~OOO~~~

In the kiva, two shadows faced each other. One crouched on its hind feet, hair covering its broad chest and long arms. The other low to the ground, scaly body on four legs, tail quivering. The hairy one danced from side to side, exposed spade-like teeth, and threw sand. The lizard hissed open-mouthed and tossed its head and tail. The two raced toward each other, collided, rose up in a grotesque hug with heads locked over each other's shoulders. Toes and clawed feet scrabbled, flinging back fans of sand and pebbles. The ape bit at its opponent's neck, got a mouthful of wattle. The reptile's claws ripped simian back-flesh.

The creatures sprang apart screeching. Both had identical wounds on their necks and backs. The hairy one leaped forward, a stone in its fist cut the lizard's head. The green-mottled low-slung body whipped to one side, gator-tail lashed across meaty primate calves, tumbled the enemy. The two fighters limped away.

They began to understand. Any wound to one became a wound to the other. The pair sensed a strange, alien spirit nodding over their realization. Not through with them yet, the timeless god of the kiva caused the low-slung fog to flatten and spin.

Out of the barren floor, a heavy, boxy shape rose, pushing aside bushels of sand and rock as it elevated from an ancient grave. The intruder stood four feet tall and six feet long. Its massive muscled chest slimmed down to narrow hips with a bobtail in back, the small feline head brought into proportion by two seven-inch fangs with cutting serrated edges. Both the ape and the reptile knew its kind from long, long ago.

The great saber-toothed cat shook itself from head to tail. Sand and dirt flew off its hide, exposing the rosettes spotting its fur. It glared at its opponents, first one then the other. The mouth scythed open. It roared. The two crouched lower, adrenaline pumping.

Not so fast in a long chase, the 500-pound predator usually leapt from ambush to take large-sized prey. Pinned down by the lion's front legs and chest, the saber-like teeth daggered into neck-flesh severing blood vessels—fast kills.

The mentally-linked ape and lizard circled—one to each side of the cat—maintaining awareness of each other's position. Their joint attack, the only option for survival, must be done quickly. The enemy could sprint faster than they could over short distances.

The ape held a stone in each hand. He felt his reptile twin advance and threw a rock. It struck above a furry eye, fracturing the projecting bone. Distracted, the lion turned toward him roaring. The lizard caught the creature's right back leg in its mouth, twisted, dragging its two hundred scaly whip-wire pounds of force to dislocate the hip, bringing it down at the rear.

Racing forward, the ape jumped, clamped its legs around the cat's neck, the oblong chunk of granite locked in his right fist struck the cat's head. Body and muscle and tendon power flowed together to focus all their energy into the tip of the pointed rock.

The pounding stopped only when exhausted primate-flesh shook to a halt, the shattered saber-toothed skull stripped of its skin and meat. The blood smell of fresh-sheared copper tainted with sewer odor of voided bowels permeated the arena. The two emotionally connected survivors crawled off and lay side by side. The vaporous controlling entity inhabiting the kiva exuded a sense of satisfaction. The victors felt layered spikes of pain. Ape and reptile minds and bodies card-shuffled back into one entity.

~~~OOO~~~

Teigler's eyes burned through the lids, the desert sun already up in the ten o'clock position. He moved—yelped. From the waist down the flesh was paralyzed from sitting too long in one position. His arms grabbed his legs, rolled over. It took ten minutes to work out the kinks and the needles. Other localized pains exerted themselves. A cut on his forehead had bled into his hair, clotting it together. The act of taking off his shirt pulled off the scabs covering the claw marks on his back; it started them bleeding again. There was a monster hickey on his neck and an eight-inch long purple welt across his right leg. Evidently, what happened in the spirit world didn't stay in the spirit world. Including ... he bent to examine a seven-inch sharp-hooked tooth at rest on the granulated sand of the kiva. Ivory colored and polished, it looked fresh out of the cat's mouth. They'd take this trophy with them.

Taking a long swig from the canteen, he mentally touched the reptile. Still there, coiled head to tail, but the rage gone, the desire to fight and take control gone. The creature and he would travel to their preordained death together, but until then, they would suffer each other's existence. The half-spirits had found harmony.

~~~OOO~~~

Teigler came out of his flashback, breaking his eye-lock on the highway's flashing white lines. They were on their way. He and Pepper had planned a trip, which included ten days of travel following a loop composed of Highway 67 south to the border, then east following the Rio Grande on 170 to Big Bend National Park. After a week of exploring and fishing, the pair would turn north on 385 and back to Alpine on Highway 90. They'd return with plenty of time for Pepper to complete her summer lizard study. Listening to her shoptalk, Rod now knew more about reptiles than the average local. This familiarity helped reduce his anxiety about his internal traveling companion.

There'd been quite a ruckus at the ranch upon his return from the overnight in the desert. His make-believe story about Janey tossing and dragging him didn't set well. The toothed neck mark was received with skepticism, especially from Pepper. "A horse-hickey, that's horse-hockey in my book."

He'd stuck to his story and they'd finally let it rest, not hearing any conflicting testimony from the only other eyewitness. White stripes on the highway loped by. He thought about the days ahead. Side roads could be explored. Some dead-ended way back in the desert at cattle watering stations or trailed out at abandoned ranches. Rod clicked on the radio and played with the FM band, finally settling on a Mexican station playing polkas. The only other choices seemed to be the constant whine of female Country-Western vocalists complaining about men.

He turned to his passenger, "Do you like this music?"

"Raised with it. What's your taste?"

"Anything with its roots and inspiration in folk, includes bits of classical, rock, jazz, country, gospel ..."

Pepper broke in, "Irish bands? The Barleycorn and Dubliners."

"Where do you get their music? I've got the Clancy Brothers, Planxty, and The Sons of Erin."

Rod revved the big V-8 engine to five mph over the speed limit and set the cruise control. Taking a swig out of the fat coffee mug resting on the brown Naugahyde dash, he eased back, watching the countryside unravel, and then continued the conversation. The road remained empty and desolate for miles ahead. It would be a long way to the next outpost of civilization. Some clusters of color caught his eye from time to time, much of the desert still in late spring bloom. Pepper turned the air-conditioning fan up and adjusted the side and middle vents to surround their bodies with cool air.

Rod's stomach started bothering him again, a burning sensation on the lower right side, then achy pinpricks. Maybe it was the taco stand food they'd tried at lunch. The pain grew over the next few miles, until Bowie knives suddenly twisted in his gut. The truck swerved onto the shoulder then back across the highway. He tapped the brake releasing the cruise control. The pickup shuddered to a diagonal halt, blocking both lanes. The truck shook back and forth, reinforced 4x4 springs finally brought the rocking under control.

"Rod," Pepper gasped, untangling herself, "what's the matter?"

"My stomach. No question, I need medical help."

"Hell, honey, Shafter, the nearest town is fifty, sixty miles away."

Groaning, Teigler forced his foot to push the gas pedal, hands turned the wheel and the truck jerked back into the right lane. After the first five miles, he knew he wasn't going to make it, the pain too intense. Pepper caught a glimpse of a faded, paint-peeled sign set off a side road on the left: *Mendoza, three miles, Population 90, City of Oppor...*

The truck rumbled down the neglected road, spewing dust and gravel from the rear tires, bouncing in and out of chuckholes. Rod nearly passed out several times. Only help from the agitated snake personality inside him kept the truck going. The adobe buildings of a small town appeared over a low rise. "Thank God," he groaned, the vehicle slowed, the dust settled.

"Shit," Pepper exclaimed, "it's a ghost town."

Below boarded-up windows, wild plants grew out of cracks in the crumbled sidewalks. The aura of decay and abandonment reflected in chipped blistered paint, tumbleweed pyramids nestled against walls, and glass-fanged windows. Rod slumped forward, chest hitting the steering wheel, pushed against the wide chromed horn button in the middle. His last thought through the blaring honk, *I hope that isn't Gabrielle's trumpet.*

~~~OOO~~~

"Take it easy, son." An old man's face appeared above his.

Rod looked around, he lay stretched out on a table in a white-painted room with stainless-steel-faced cabinets. Pepper held his hand. A sink with hospital swan-necked faucet and wide pedal-ended hot and cold handles leaned crooked against one wall. He took a deep breath, smelled antiseptic tainted with horse and cow sweat. Stomach still felt twisted but the intensity was muffled, slightly below the limit of his pain threshold.

"You're in my surgery. I've given you a shot of morphine. It's your appendix—ninety percent sure. It has to come out and soon."

Rod nodded to show he understood. "What now?"

"More bad news, son. I'm a veterinarian. Good with cattle and horses, but not people. I'm also the last resident on the once great and upcoming town of Mendoza."

"Jesus!"

"We've got an option, Rod … your name, right? I checked your wallet and noticed you have a VA card. There's a Veterans Administration Hospital another ten minutes out in the desert. Our road dead ends there."

Rod moaned and tried to sit up. Pepper helped pull him upright.

"Grab onto my shoulders, let's get you into my truck."

The doc's rust-splotched Ford truck popped, creaked, and groaned as it leaned into a curve. Teigler rode with one hand over his stomach and one braced against the dash. Pepper cushioned him from slamming up against the passenger side door. Rod wished death would come soon and end the pain. Someone or something was chain-sawing his side. The old doc hadn't quit talking since they started, maybe an effort to distract them.

"Yes, sir, last man in these parts. Ply my trade with the few ranches in the area, mostly cattle and horses but sometimes a dog or cat or two. I can't retire, nothing saved, and I'm still in the clutches of three ex-wives."

Already nauseous, Teigler's nose was overwhelmed with the cab's smell of manure and sick animals. The carpet on the driver's side had holes worn through to expose heel-polished metal. His palm on the dash felt the grit of the ages, layers of dust and sand built up over the years. Not sure he would be able to tell when they got there, with the windshield spider-webbed in one corner and covered with sun-baked dirt.

"Good place we're going, been there since 1879, big Victorian-style three story. Porches round about each level, ten-foot ceilings inside, lots of gingerbread decoration outside. My great grandpa helped build the place, the best carpenter in the Chihuahuan. The place started out as a tuberculosis sanatorium. Of course, in those days, they called the disease *consumption*. Some famous folk took treatment there, maybe even Doc Holiday."

The truck started running rough, engine sputtering. It died. Pepper and the old geezer swore, baritone and mezzo soprano voices in harmony. He turned the key. The starter clacked several times. He pumped the gas pedal. The engine rattled, dieseled, and then fired on all cylinders. Their trip continued.

"During the Great War, Uncle Sam acquired the property. Must have been a division worth of soldiers shipped in that had been gassed in the trenches—bunch of them still in the cemetery. Got real active again in World War II, used as a physical therapy center for amputees."

Distorted through the grimy windshield, Teigler saw they were approaching a large white structure that jutted up some forty feet. The truck dry-skidded to a halt near a new-looking glass and concrete guard shack next to a double chain-link gate. A ten-foot high chain-link fence with sentry towers at the corners surrounded the facility. Angle iron strung with razor wire bent inward at the top. Looks like they want to keep people in, Teigler noted.

Several isolated wood and metal buildings stood outside the fence in back. A sign fastened to the chain link read: U.S. Department of Veterans Affairs, Chihuahuan Treatment Center. Painted on the right side was a seal emblazoned with an eagle, wings outstretched, talons holding two U.S. flags. A uniformed armed guard stepped out and held up a hand with palm out.

Doc cranked down a gravel-dusted window. "Got an emergency. This fellow needs treatment now or he'll die."

"Friend, this is a hospital for the criminally insane, a lock-down treatment center for the military's most violent mental cases, psychopaths. We don't take patients off the streets."

"This is a veteran. He has a VA card. You don't take him, he passes, and some congressman is going to be mighty upset."

The guard's brow wrinkled. His mouth opened and shut. "Wait, I'll call in."

A few minutes later, the gate swung open. The guard waved them in. "Drive around to the back entrance."

~~~OOO~~~

The ring-necked lizard lay still in the sand under yucca plant shade. Puffing up his throat sack in irritation, he listened to a clumsy black-tailed jackrabbit thumping twenty feet away. The sound died out. Ring-neck leaped up on his hind legs and raced, back feet only, across the hot sand to flop on his belly in a cluster of cholla. The lizard froze, goggle-eyes scanned for insects and enemies. Startled, he heard voices.

The reptile-Teigler cleared away the fragments of its desert dream and listened. The man it inhabited was asleep and non-resisting, tubes in his arms. People were talking at the bedside.

"Well, Patricia, how is our unexpected guest doing?"

"Normal for what he's been through. I believe the appendectomy was successful. You got him in time, Dr. Ralls."

"The question now is what do we do with him and his friends? This intrusion into our operation is most unwelcome. The horns of a dilemma?"

"We had to take him in. That old man would have raised hell with the authorities."

"Not sure we can let these folks go. The next time the man visits a real VA hospital, he'll likely discover our secret. For now, let's collect more information. I've prepared some close-enough-to-pass entrance forms and questionnaires. Shut off the sedation and when he wakes, fill them out. I'll question the others."

Teigler's nose wrinkled, catching the odor of bleach and antiseptic cleaning solution. The smell tickled. He coughed. A set of cool fingers pressed against his forehead. His eyes squinted, too bright. The room was all done in hospital white. Bleached bone white—appropriate, he thought. A pleasant, but sharp-nosed female face appeared in focus attached to a hand now resting on his.

"Just relax," she said, "nurse's orders."

"So, what the hell happened?"

"Your appendix went over to the enemy. We've removed it and you're doing fine."

"What about Pepper and the old man ... my rig?"

"If Pepper's your girlfriend, she's out in the lounge. The old man is with her. The doctor is bringing them up to speed on your condition. When the veterinarian goes back to Mendoza, a couple of our staff will ride back with him to retrieve your truck."

She cranked up the bed into a sitting position and handed him a glass of water with a bent plastic straw. Settling in a chrome-legged fiberglass chair, the nurse picked up a clipboard and took a silver ballpoint from the pocket of her gray scrubs.

"Now, let's get some information, shall we? We have your name and address from your driver's license."

"The address is not current. Just sold that property and haven't put down roots anywhere else yet."

"Anyone we should notify?"

"No, relatives are either dead or distant."

"No wives, current, or ex? Children?"

"None to the first … and none I know of to the second."

"Were you traveling for business or pleasure?"

"Entirely for pleasure. No business. Just footloose and fancy free."

"Anyone we should call that might be expecting you to visit or return at a given time?"

"Depends on how long. We're on the first day of a ten-day trip. My girl's grandmother should be called if the delay is too long."

"Well, that should do for the moment. You'll be with us for at least two days. Your appendix was badly infected and removed at the last minute. You're shot full of antibiotics and painkillers." She stood and adjusted the drip rate on one of his bottles. "We have you in an isolated ward. You will not be allowed to leave this area." The nurse moved toward the door. "This facility provides treatment to the military's most extreme mental cases. Most of them are psychotic and very dangerous."

Rod's eyelids felt very heavy. A thought buzzed through his mind. She hadn't asked for his VA account number. Usually it's the first question out of their mouths at sign-in.

The snake stirred, felt puzzled. What was putting the man to sleep? Its senses had detected strong undercurrents of threat from the white-clothed humans. It uncoiled and stretched out into the slumbering body, feeling a glove-like tightness. Eyes popped open. It listened and sniffed. Hiding under the overlay of cleaning fluid came the thick crawling odor of human blood and raw tissue. Anger rose, they must get out. The body sluggish, it got an arm to rise, then lost control—the arm flopped back down. The needles, they must come out.

Footsteps clicked down the hall outside, growing louder. Shadows of feet appeared under the door. A key clicked against pin tumblers in the lock, the brass knob twisted. The reptile closed the eyes and slumped back. A guard pushed the door wide, allowing the doctor and a second man to enter.

"I'm going to start your orientation here, Mr. Louis Bataglia, since I will soon need your help with this situation."

"I'm not doin' shit, like I want to be here."

"Your Uncle Vito issued explicit orders. Without my approval, you will not leave. Not bad enough you had to get rough with one of his nieces, your own cousin, but killing one of Chicago's finest really iced the cake."

"The bitch squealed. She had the cop waiting on the front steps."

"Instead of giving you up or something more drastic, Vito listened to his sister, your mother, and sent you here. You should be grateful. I'm supposed to turn you into something useful to this operation. Listen and learn."

Red-faced, the man clenched his jaw muscles. "Okay, but I ain't no kid, Doc, don't disrespect me."

The doctor began his story. Both Louis and the hidden reptile listened. "Are you familiar with organ transplants?" A head nodded. "For centuries, parts of one person surgically placed into another caused a violent reaction. The receiving body rejected the new part. The patient died. In 1980, ciclosporin came on the market and dramatically reduced organ rejection."

"So what does that have to do with the price a' pizza on State Street?"

"As the success rate increased, the demand for organs skyrocketed. All kinds of organs: hearts, livers, lungs, kidneys, arteries, ..."

"Okay, okay, enough, but I still don' get it."

"The dons in New York, Chicago, and L.A. finance this place. Whenever possible, they don't kill enemies anymore—they ship them to me. We harvest the organs and sell them through several layers of shell companies to private clinics and hospitals. What's left is buried in the soldier's cemetery with a fake name."

"Makes my fuckin' stomach turn. So, how much do we make?"

"Heart, seventy to eighty thousand; lung, forty to fifty thousand each; liver, sixty to seventy thousand, and so on. So far, we've processed a dozen units. The gross to date: $3.8 million."

"Well, that's good money ... but not big money."

"We've only been operational for a few months, multiply by four for an annual take of over fifteen million. Overhead and personnel costs are low. We pay nothing for raw material. We have room for forty more contributors here, which could increase the annual gross to $60 million."

"Son of a bitch, used to be a hit was all cost, now killing our enemies pay big returns. I think I like this."

"Now that you have the picture, Lou, let me introduce you to a thorn in our side needs to be extracted."

The snake-man lay silent and attentive. The men talked. They were satisfied the world would not miss the three intruders. The man before them already helpless, his two companions in the lounge drinking rohypnol-laced coffee would soon be out. Lou and the nurse would take the old man and his truck back to the vet's office in Mendoza. A heart attack drug would be injected through his navel. In a few days, some customer would find him slumped over his desk.

The remaining two healthy young bodies would be mined to fill new orders. Tomorrow, the nurse, hair dyed red, and Lou both dressed in the couple's clothes, would drive the camper truck to Mexico. Periodic stops to shop or eat on the way would establish a false credit card trace. Once across the border, they would burn the truck and camper, destroy the clothes and personal items, and return under different identities. Anyone looking for Rod and Kathy might get as far as the dead-end in Mexico. The men departed, both in a good mood.

The room was quiet again, the only noise the low-key whistle of air coming from the overhead duct. The reptile managed to get one arm raised to the mouth. It bit down on the tubing and jerked out the needle. After a short rest, the other was removed. The body felt lead-weight heavy. Every five or ten minutes, it tried to raise an arm or leg. A half hour passed before it could sit up. The guard outside mouthed a two-syllable yawn. It must be late night or early morning.

Feet slipped over the bedside, hips pushed off, and the body fell to one knee. The legs were rubbery, pain in the side. Hands ripped off the clumsy one-piece hospital garment. Two stitches in the incision had pulled loose. A little blood trickled down the right thigh. The creature stood and walked, at first using the bed as a support, then by itself as the drug flushed out of veins and arteries. No windows in this interior room. The walls stayed rock-solid when the reptile pressed against them, old-fashioned plaster and lath, no way to break through without tools and a lot of noise. It picked up the saber-tooth from the pile of Rod's possessions on a side table and pried up a piece of floor tile, found concrete underneath, a Victorian precaution to slow the spread of fire from floor to floor. Pacing silently, anger welled up. They were caged.

The reptile leaped up on the bed, examined the ceiling. It was false. Lower than the ten feet the old man described, it consisted of two by three foot rectangular tiles resting on aluminum T-bars anchored to the original ceiling with wire. Pushing a tile sideways, the arms did a sinuous pull-up for a quick look, found enough space between the old and new ceilings to crawl. Each sidewall was pierced by an old-fashioned wooden-framed vent opening into the next room, which allowed for air circulation in the days before air conditioning.

Lowering itself back, the reptile made a neck sling for the tooth out of gown ties. One bounce on the bed sent the creature's upper body to rest on the T-bar frame—hips and legs slithered up. The tile slid back. The wooden louver's screws pulled easily out from old rotten wood. No fake ceiling in the adjacent room. The reptile went through feet first, lowering the body slowly with shaking arms. There were bloody scratches on its sides from crawling over the ceiling support wires. After fifteen minutes, its eyes adjusted to the dark, faint light from stars and moon crowded the area with shadows. It was in a storage room. Old tables leaned against the walls. Near the door stood a number of modern oxygen tanks.

This outside room had tall double-hung windows. Shrunk-up oak sashes, exposed to the desert air for over a century, fit loosely in their frames. The creature tugged at the cast-iron pocket-lift window handles. They pulled off in its hands. Sealed tight with decades of paint, the bottom sash resisted any effort to open. The lizard climbed up on the sill and pried at the upper sash with the saber-tooth, felt it drop a few inches. Pushing down allowed the weight of the 200-pound body to help lever open an escape hole. The creature passed through and paused on the outside limestone sill, listening and smelling. Lowering itself with outstretched arms, it dropped to the first floor porch deck. Another stitch pulled out.

Taking two paces, it vaulted over the railing to land on the ground below. The tooth tapped silently against its chest as it slowly crept to the nearest guard tower. The desert night was cool. Hat pulled down, the guard held his jacket lapels closed with one hand. The other held a shotgun vertical by the fore stock.

Naked feet made no sound on iron rungs as the reptile ascended, but a floor plank creaked. The guard whirled, bringing up the gun. The ivory tooth flashed as it took out his throat, but didn't prevent a last reflex movement of the guard's trigger finger. The shotgun fired, blowing a peeled back hole in the galvanized metal roof.

Coils of razor wire filled the space between the tower and fence. The reptile slung the dead man across the wire, skittered across the still warm body, and lowered itself to the ground, hanging from the dangling arms of the corpse.

Floodlights snapped on, illuminating the perimeter—a bell rang. The escapee closed one eye to preserve its night vision and limped from shadow to shadow, keeping out of the sight of the three other corner towers. The fugitive stumbled past the outbuildings, one of which smelled of motor oil and gasoline.

Light through the windows of the pole barn used as a garage lit up a car, a jeep, and a backhoe. A smaller metal building's walls vibrated against his palms, diesel exhaust fumes from the generator inside puffed out of a stack in the roof. The floodlights also illuminated the canvas-covered engine and propeller of a light aircraft tied down in an open area west of the buildings.

The escapee scuttled across a narrow gravel airstrip. Entering desert growth, it slowed to avoid spiny plants. Dawn found the man-reptile three miles away, the human awake and back in charge. Teigler looked back toward the clinic, his escape trail marked with bloody footprints. The desert, not kind to boots, let alone feet, would soon cripple him. Already feeling thirsty, he tried to remember Pepper's desert lore. He must survive to get back to her.

Using the serrated lion tooth, he cut leaves off a yucca. Hunkering down, the man chewed at the base of the leaf with his teeth, causing string-like fibers to detach. Rubbing the fibers together with his palms produced a strong thin cord. Teigler wiggled over to a cluster of large prickly pear. Scraping off the spines, he strapped a pair of size-eleven cactus pads to his feet. The new sandals would leave little in the way of recognizable marks on the sand or stones. A smaller pad, reduced to a pulp, served as a poultice over his appendix incision. He chewed more pulp and swallowed the liquid, spitting out the fibrous solids.

Next came shelter. The desert sun's heat would soon push his naked body beyond endurance. His captors would certainly pursue. About a football field away, a cluster of faded black boulders sprouted above the uneven gray and tan desert floor. The dense rocks would retain some of the evening's coolness.

He remembered Pepper's lizard project. The little dudes buried themselves in the sand during the hottest part of the day. Teigler found a cantilevered boulder he could work his head and shoulders under. Digging out a slender three-foot deep trench for his hips and legs, he flopped in, pushed dark sand and then the lighter stuff over his body. With his head to one side, he could see out through a small slit between rock and desert floor.

In the afternoon, he heard a jeep in low gear. It circled his rocks, making a slow circuit. A man walked in front, looked for sign. Another checked for hiding places among the boulders.

"Don' stick yer hands or feet under any a' them rocks. They're full of snakes and scorpions. Might even be a Gila monster or two."

"Your ass!" Lou shouted back.

"Well, it's no never mind to me if you get bit. My brother-in law had a Gila lock onto his thumb. Even after we cut off the head, it still wouldn't let go until after sundown."

"Did it kill 'em?"

"No, jus' sterilized him. A great relief to my sister, as they already had five kids and one in the oven."

"Don' see anythin', what do we do?"

"The blood trail disappears back there. The man mus' know a bit 'bout this desert. But, there's no way he can walk out. No water, no food. Let 'em bake a day. Tomorrow we come back with half a dozen of the fellas and sweep the area walkin' in a line 'bout a hundred feet apart. The doc has also got himself an airplane, Cessna single engine. Him in the air, us on the ground, damned if we don' find him."

Lou climbed up on the escapee's rock. He shouted, "Teigler, better come out. When I go back, I'm goin' to take special care of that redheaded woman of yours. Hope she likes it rough."

The jeep noise died off. The desert was quiet, too quiet. Someone a few yards out spit. They'd left a watcher. The rifleman fried in the heat for an hour, then stomped off. Teigler passed the day planning retribution and watching bees flit by his peephole. The busy little buggers all seemed to be going to the same place. Pioneer stories told of people being led to water by the insects. They needed liquid to cool off their hives.

The sunset came, the moon brought out nocturnal creatures. Kangaroo rats danced and leaped. Teigler thought of them as Harry, Moe, and Curly, or based on their antics, it might be Harry, Moe, and Carol. A sidewinder rattlesnake's forked tongue tracked their scent as it slithered around a mesquite bush, confronting the trio. The rats squeaked and kicked sand into the snake's eyes. Rod swallowed a chuckle. The snake advanced—the three split up and ran for cover. Curly ran directly into Teigler's hole. The man hissed and clicked his teeth. The fluffy rat did an about-face and ran out, directly into the snake. A strike, a final quiver, and the two-foot sidewinder unhinged its lower jaw.

Teigler pushed out from under the boulder, shedding sand. With the rat in its mouth, the desert snake offered no defense—the man bit down, then tossed the severed head, complete with partially ingested rat, into the bush. After a few mouthfuls, both of the man's personalities agreed it tasted a lot like chicken. Teigler scrubbed blood and fluids off his hands with sand. He walked off in the direction the bees had taken earlier in the day. Smelling water, he tracked a ribbon of moist air to a fissure on top of the largest rock. An arm extended shoulder length into a crack, and came back wet to the forearm. Runoff from the recent rains had collected in this natural tank. He palmed water, drank until satisfied, then headed back to the clinic. On his way, he captured half a dozen sand-colored bark scorpions and tied them with short lengths of cord to the end of a three-foot-long mesquite stick. Pincers and barbed tails flailing, they swung back and forth, a nightmare cheerleader's pompom.

All the compound's lights blazed. Even the runway was lit up. That forced him to circle around to gain access to the outbuildings, which lay outside the wire. The good doctor had placed two guards among them. Fat and foolish city men, they would never see another Cubs game. Teigler would have the element of surprise. The staff focused on keeping guests from breaking out, not breaking in. Reptile and human thought raced back and forth, interlocked, and merged, creating a hybrid creature with greater capacity. It tapped all the knowledge, skills, and instincts of the two. Unslinging the tooth, the creature moved without noise.

After pulling the bodies into the shadows, it found the backhoe parked next to a freshly dug disposal ditch, black garbage bags piled nearby. The human had driven a similar machine during college-summer construction jobs. Tearing open the bags exposed a mix of normal kitchen trash and medical waste. From among the refuse, he extracted five empty whisky bottles.

The creature slunk over to the airplane, a Cessna 195. The man remembered his military service. The Army used such planes fitted with skis for Arctic missions. The seven-cylinder radial engine was a real oil hog. The canvas cover removed, the creature raised the engine cowling and opened the petcock on the oil tank, draining its five-gallon reserve. It moved toward the pole barn garage, after filling the bottles with 100-octane avgas from storage drums, and stuffing the necks with strips torn from the engine cover.

On the way, the hybrid discovered his Dodge camper truck. He secured a Bic butane lighter from the glove compartment and Grandpa Mahoney's foot-long knife from under the driver's seat. Slipping into the garage, the knife punctured car and jeep gas tanks. The creature picked up duct tape and shop rags from the repair bench and headed for the generator shed, a strongly constructed corrugated metal building with one locked door and no windows.

The man-reptile clambered to the roof and started stuffing shop rags down the four-inch diameter exhaust pipe, using the uninhabited end of the scorpion stick to pack the cotton rags tight. It burnt its knuckles. The back-pressure would strangle the generator engine, causing it to shut down.

Four of the five gas-filled bottles were duct-taped to the backhoe digging-bucket. The hybrid stood by with the Bic. The generator sound grew rough and gaspy—it ground down and stopped—the lights went out. The backhoe started. The lighter flared and lit the canvas fuses on all the bottles. The bucket rose to window height. The machine trundled forward. A flaming trail of sparks arced from the tractor cab to the garage. Bottle number five smashed, starting a fire that spread explosively through the earlier spilled vehicle fuel.

The reptile was enthralled. The beauty of it, a streak of fire across the sky and then rushing blue-yellow blossoms of flame engulfed the vehicles and shed. Its mouth dropped open, a nervous lick of almost sexual pleasure started in the neck, raced down the spine, quenching itself in an uncontrollable quiver of a phantom tail.

A memory of Nam surfaced, amber and blue tracers cycled overhead, parachute flares drifted, the flash, flash, flash from gun barrels. The drumbeat of helicopter blades and percussion of mortar explosions vibrated his body. The bitter fear-smell of enemy sweat as he crept closer, raising his machete—all so beautiful.

Dim lights clicked on at the corners of the fence and inside the building as the battery-powered emergency lighting system activated. The backhoe engine roared. Deep ribbed tires skidded, threw dirt and gravel as it breached the chain-link curtain wire, flattened it out, and pulled vertical support poles out.

One of the corner guard towers collapsed, the other bent over, both spilled their human occupants. Bumping along, over the inner yard, the tractor's extended bucket crashed into the window through which Teigler had escaped yesterday.

Bottles shattered, spilled flaming high-test gasoline onto broken-legged tables. Flames reflected off the half-dozen slender iron cylinders of hospital grade oxygen standing in a corner by the door. The fire flared up, flowed around the room, and leaped up the walls. The ancient structure had over one hundred years of layered crusted paint, and dried-out wooden floor beams and uprights. When the first floor supports burnt out, the upper floors would collapse into the flames.

The creature rolled out of the cab. The man diminished, the reptile welled up. It screeched, sounding like a combination freight-train whistle and fingernails scraping across a blackboard. A long-knife chopped through the heart of one of the fallen tower guards, the monster's shadow leaped and bounded toward the other.

The second tower guard shouted and limped toward the entrance shack. The Teigler-raptor trotted in the darkness along the front fence line, vertical eye slits fixed on the wounded guard. The prey moved into the umbrella of light near the front gate and collapsed. The remaining three outside guards converged on their comrade.

The guard captain kneeled, shouting, "You two get inside and put out the fire, I'll take care of Caparelli."

The injured guard's eyes jerked wide as he saw his boss's head flop down, spine severed, hanging by a thin hinge of neck flesh. The body twitched then fell. A naked man shook a flail of scorpions in Caparelli's face. Babbling incoherently, the prey raised an arm. The knife stuck him below the sternum and zippered all the way down to the crotch, jelly-slick innards spilled out between his legs. Screaming started.

Fire from the second-story windows danced amber-bright in reptile eyes. The flames had found their way through holes in the concrete floors, which allowed modern water, sewer, and electrical amenities. The Mafia-owned construction company had cut corners during the remodeling, not resealing the penetrations. Near the backhoe, clapboard siding, the porch roof, with its Victorian gingerbread decorations, ignited as fire clawed upward out of the window.

The creature spun, head down, racing to the entrance—it leaped the steps, and shouldered aside the partly opened front door. Smoke already began filling the upper hallway. The doctor and several men clutching fire extinguishers clustered around the door at the end.

"The key," Dr. Ralls shouted. "Who in the hell has the key?" He grabbed the doorknob, then leaped back wringing scorched hands.

One of the men shouted, "I'll get it." He ran back toward the main office. In the smoke and weak light, he mistook the bipedal silhouette for a member of the staff. The creature stiff-armed the man in the throat, pushed him into a side room. The knife pierced his heart and cut upward through ribs as though they were wet cardboard. The guard pig-squealed. The reptile dropped to hands and knees.

Alligator crawling on all fours to avoid breathing smoke, the hybrid entered a room, drawn by a familiar female scent. It scuttled under the hospital bed. The mattress springs squeaked, A man's naked feet slapped the floor.

"What in the name of Christ is goin' on?" Lou shouted as he hopped on one leg, pulling on a pair of white boxer shorts.

From under the bed, an arc of steel sliced through the Achilles tendons of both legs. The made man's shout cut off as his one hundred eighty pounds of flesh smacked flat onto the beige vinyl tile. The reptile straddled the Lou's twisting body, pinned him in place. Pulling the arms straight, one at a time, it cut the muscles and tendons at the elbow joints. The reptile stood, screeched to get the helpless prey's attention, and slapped the scorpion pompom against the floor. Under normal conditions, bark scorpions topped the crazy-anger scale of desert dwellers. Forced into each other's company, beaten, and smoked, these captured ones radiated rage beyond all limits. The reptile's hooked fingers raised the elastic waistband of Lou's boxer shorts and stuffed six of the most pissed-off venomous critters in the Chihuahuan into his crotch.

Teigler glided to the bed. A sedated Pepper lay quietly, still breathing. He swaddled her in the top sheet and oatmeal-colored waffle-weave hospital blanket. Slinging her across his shoulders, the man left the room, its walls and ceiling ringing with Lou's shrieks, curses, and futile begging. Unable to move, he would remain in exquisite pain as long as the consuming fire allowed.

In the hall, the doctor and nurse moved back a dozen feet. Dr. Ralls coughed, and then shouted, "Break it down!" Hand in hand, the pair turned and ran for the front exit abandoning the last of the guards.

Two men beat on the door with the butt ends of fire extinguishers. One of the oxygen bottles inside exceeded its safety limits. Valve cracked, the casing split. The gas violently decompressed, pure oxygen increased the fire's temperature by a magnitude of ten. Blast furnace heat and pressure blew the door and the men across the hall. Belt buckles, coins, and pistols began to melt and puddle together on the floor.

As the burdened hybrid creature stumbled toward the Dodge, he saw the Cessna increase speed and lift off the runway. Doctor and nurse airborne. Rod strapped Pepper into the truck's passenger seat. He locked the front hubs, jumped in, pulled the extra key from under the floor mat, and drove into the desert. The remaining oxygen bottles let go. The truck rocked from the explosion. The entire east end of the building had sheared off, offering new fuel and access to the fire.

~~~OOO~~~

Teigler sat in an aluminum-boned, strap-bottomed lawn chair near his camper's open door. From behind the truck came the rattle of an old-fashioned tower-mounted windmill. Its metal slat vanes powered a water pump that kept a 500-gallon galvanized steel stock tank full. Pepper lay in the camper bed, still asleep. She had bruises on shoulders, neck, and in some intimate places, but the woman was alive and not missing any parts. The sun finally dropped below the horizon. Zipping up a distressed-leather flight jacket, he turned up the valve on a Coleman propane lamp and tuned in a news station on the radio.

" ... refuses to comment on the mystery fire near the old town of Mendoza. Local ranchers who called in the blaze claimed the light could be seen for thirty miles in every direction. The area has been sealed off by order of the Brewster County sheriff's office.

"However, a confidential source has suggested murder and mayhem were involved. A number of dead bodies, some mutilated, were found at the site, as well as preliminary evidence of arson.

"In other news, a light plane crashed yesterday on the outskirts of El Paso. FAA investigators report the engine on the Cessna 195 overheated and seized up after developing an oil leak. The bodies of a man and a woman in the wreckage have yet to be identified.

"On a final note, friends of deceased Doctor George Phinias Jaeger, long-time Brewster County veterinarian, are reminded that graveside services will be conducted tomorrow at 6:00 p.m. in the cemetery of Our Lady of the Desert Catholic Church."

Teigler sighed, shut off the radio, and the lamp. The chair creaked as he shifted position, trying to ease his aches and pains. Overhead rotated familiar comforting constellations. He wondered if the ancients were right about the stars foretelling the future. Through the man's eyes, the reptile saw only chaos.

Monsoon Malarial Dreams 1967

> MEFLOQUINE (*Lariam*)—First used in the Vietnam War because
> of the emergence of malaria resistant to existing drugs, mefloquine's
> side effects include stomach upset, dizziness, vivid (good, bad,
> erotic, and otherwise) dreams, insomnia, and anxiety. More serious
> side effects, such as seizures and psychosis, are relatively rare.

Locked within hip-swaying pillars of rain
long-nailed Asian temple dancers
weave hands in sly-snake patterns.
Ankle bracelets shake, sun-break-silver,
above toe-ringed bare feet.

Drops lash our helmets, enamel
the smooth steel surfaces, their striking
sacrificial voices chorus-hum. Wind-lips
press against our black rifle muzzles, create
muted atonal metal flutes.

Jungle mud amoeba grasps our calves,
murmurs the seduction of Nirvana.
Without thought, our muscles resist. Minds,
thorn-pierced by killing, seek nothingness.

We are shredded, ripped leaves jinking
in the wind-borne water. Friends' faces
tatter, erode in the torrent. Stripped
to the seed, our souls' symmetry leached.

Group Therapy

Beth wheeled her VW Jetta into the veterans' hospital parking lot, pulling into the section reserved for employees. Its rusted fender clanked and shook for several minutes as two of the four cylinders kept firing even though the key was off. While she waited for the vehicle to finish its rumba, she read the sign positioned in the front center of her spot: Reserved for Dr. Elizabeth Mueller, MD. Only a month into her tenure at the VA, the paint remained bright and shiny compared to the weathered boards of her coworkers. After all those years of education and internships, her first job had blossomed into something better than expected.

Already the fruits of two paydays gave some weight to her new bank account. Most of the first check had gone for an apartment and the utility deposits, as well as some basic furniture. The second went for clothes befitting her new profession. The third would provide part of the down payment for a new car, well … new-used car. No more bang-bang Jetta.

She walked the half-block to her office, holding her skirt down from the attentions of a frisky wind. Pastel orange and brown leaves swirled, many accumulated in dead spots up against buildings and fences. Beth kicked a jumble of oak leaves away from the double doors of her building and entered. The old two-story Victorian had been the residence of a long line of hospital administrators, beginning in the late 1800s. The hospital behind it had been expanded several times—usually following major wars—when the demands of returning veterans forced the issue. Now, the detached house soldiered on as the Psycho-social Rehabilitation Recovery Center. Pushing the doors closed until they clicked, she turned and carefully wiped her feet on the large gray-ribbed rug at the entrance.

"That's a good girl," came a scratchy voice. "Remember the all-staff meeting at four today."

"Good morning, Alma," Beth replied. "It's on my list. I've got four veterans' wives arriving in an hour. Send them up as they check in."

The receptionist nodded her fuzzy hennaed head and turned back to her keyboard. "Oh," Beth added, "does your granddaughter have any Girl Scout cookies left? Let me have two boxes of the peanut butter and one of the thin mints."

"I'll bring them in tomorrow."

Beth chalked up a score in her mental account book. Getting and staying on Alma's good side could only help a new person. A senior employee with thirty years in the VA, the aging receptionist knew everyone and everything, good and evil, about the hospital. Her network had tentacles in every nook and cranny. If so inclined, she could cover your ass, or expose it buck-naked. Besides, as a product of a secretarial school of the fifties, she knew shorthand, a skill not taught anymore in this computer-rich age. The technique came in very handy on those occasions when the more keyboard challenged, like herself, needed a speedy document.

Beth loved her office. The honey-colored oak floors creaked faintly with human steps, a bit loose after a century of wear. Refinished a decade ago, they still looked good with the exception of a warped spot caused by a past window leak. The wooden desk dated back to WWII, but had come around with some polish and scar wax. A modern ergonomic executive chair paired with the desk, and a banker's lamp made an acceptable workstation. Lots of natural light flooded in through three floor-to-ceiling French windows to reflect off cream-painted walls. A braided blue-green wool rug surrounded by a well-broken-in couch and overstuffed chair completed the picture. The furniture's old dark leather exuded a classy scent.

Several ladder-backed chairs rested against the north wall's rail molding, providing extra seating. Beth owned the framed Monet reproductions on the walls, one of green-washed water lilies and the other of purple irises overflowing a garden. Her own bentwood rocker, a three-generation heirloom, allowed her to come out from behind the desk and join clients for a more relaxed atmosphere—an informality especially needed today.

She would be conducting an initial group therapy session with four Vietnam veterans' wives. Although of varying ages, all had children. Beth selected some items from a blue enameled toy box in the corner. She carefully placed a Raggedy Ann doll with frilly apron, several well-used Tonka trucks, and Legos of various colors centrally on the rug. Perhaps this new group would feel more relaxed, more talkative with these decorations, even though children would not be present. They also helped calm her shaking hands— this would be her first group for wives.

"Get them settled, ask your questions, and don't talk, just listen," her mentor and boss, Dr. Waszlowski, had said. "They aren't here to get caught up on the latest psychobabble bullshit."

"What if they ask me to comment, or make a judgment?"

"Many questions will be rhetorical. They don't expect an answer. Just acknowledge the communication and pencil a note in your book. If they specifically want a response, ask them what they think. Alternatively, if they persist, trust your instincts. If you don't feel comfortable answering, say so."

A fluttery knock at the door scuttled her replay of yesterday's advisory session. At her invitation, three women entered, all with either coffee or tea—Alma's acts of kindness. They took seats, one at each end of the couch and the third in the overstuffed chair. Nervous eyes roamed over the office and took in Beth's features. They raised cups to their lips simultaneously, noted the synchronized movement, and laughed together.

"We're expecting one more person," Beth announced, settling in. "How about this weather? Anyone blown off the road?"

A litany of complaints and wind-related stories followed, that expanded to fill the next five minutes. The conversation ended, the room quieted. Beth tried to think of something to say. Her sweat glands started stressing her deodorant before a tap on the door saved the day.

"Sorry, a semi-truck overturned on the highway ... down to one lane," a pixie-cut redhead said, swooping down on one of the ladder-back chairs. She dropped a green faux-leather shoulder bag on the floor and extracted a bottle of Evian water.

"I hope we will all freely share our thoughts and concerns as we get to know each other," Beth announced hopefully. "Let's get started by giving our first names and telling something about ourselves and our families. Who will start first?"

~~~OOO~~~

After the session ended, the mind-numbed psychiatrist eased back in her chair and slipped off her high heels. Alma entered, handed her a cut-crystal glass of cold orange juice, and departed. It felt like heaven going down a dry mouth and throat. Beth moved to the desktop keyboard and started typing notes. Let's see, she thought, first there's Elena, a thin California-born Latina with a migrant picker's second grade education, two middle school boys, and a husband who spent a tour in Nam as part of the Ninth Marines.

"Not an ex-Marine," Elena said. "Once a Marine always a Marine, and that, honey, is the trouble."

At his worst when drinking, Humberto would rage and threaten his wife and kids. The family remained entirely dependent upon Elena's earnings from hotel cleaning. Although jobless, he had refused to help with household work or child rearing. However, her situation was improving. The VA finally qualified him for a 100 percent disability pension—provided he attended PTSD therapy and stayed on his meds. He now spent his days helping with the children and working with other needy vets.

Then came Marge, the mousy brunette Ohioan with blonde highlights, a fifty-pound overweight high school grad with one Down syndrome child, which she blamed on her husband's exposure to Agent Orange. As an Army engineer, her man had received more chemical exposure than most. Phil suppressed his war-guilt and feelings of responsibility for his child's condition. He insisted on working night shifts. Sleeping during the day provided him an excuse to keep from interacting with family and friends. Emotionally numb, he spent his free time in the basement staring at a wall decorated with his medals and pictures of Vietnam. Fearing another Down syndrome child, Phil would not have sex or be intimate.

Number three, Janey, the blonde (probably), once a fashionable trophy-wife, now an out-of-style mess, some college, with a son and a daughter. An American classic, married the captain of the football team, sent him away to war, and got back someone with a rewired brain. Jack grew upset when Vietnam was mentioned and refused any meals containing rice. A perfectionist, he lost job after job arguing with his supervisors over procedures. Brimming over with survivor's guilt, he told her if he had only paid more attention to detail, he wouldn't have lost so many men in Nam. He now worked in the family business, whose members barely put up with his obsession. Very harsh and controlling at home, he recently broke down crying and sobbing when his son left for college—Jack felt unable to protect his son from his veteran's perception of a horrific world.

The last woman, Kathleen (nickname Pepper), told a much different story. She had stunning red hair, a master's degree in biology, a two-year-old girl baby, and a west Texas accent. She married a two or maybe three tour Vietnam Army veteran—former Lieutenant Teigler wasn't sure himself. Her husband's behavior was, in many ways, typical of PTSD afflicted veterans.

Emotionally stunted, he admitted to only having enough capacity to love one person. Pepper believed this, since when he played with their child, he remained cool to her; and when affectionate with her, he ignored the baby. She attended family and church functions alone. Not able to stand the pressure of social gatherings—his misery obvious to all attending—Teigler would either abruptly leave or start an argument. At random intervals, he would disappear to deal with his war-guilt and rage alone. Although not able to work with others, he wrote and sold stories and magazine articles, achieving a modest income and recognition.

But, something very scary intruded on this relationship. At times, Pepper felt threatened and fearful when his personality seemed to change. During these periods, he seemed more alert and high energy than normal. His musculature, posture, and responses reminiscent of, and she would shudder, "… of a wild creature." Being a trained biologist specializing in lizards, she labeled this behavior *reptilian*. Sometimes this transformation would occur during intercourse, frightening her deeply. Or, as she said, "Imagine having sex with a Komodo dragon." Her family pressured her to seek a divorce, fearing Teigler might harm her or the child during one of his episodes.

After the other women in the group went home, Pepper had stayed behind to relate a personal reoccurring nightmare. She lay in a hospital bed located in a smoke-hazed surreal room. A naked Teigler pinned a strange man to the floor, attacking him with her grandpa's old trail knife. The victim screamed as he was chopped apart, as one would quarter a chicken for the pot. Beth arranged for private sessions with Kathleen after future group therapy meetings.

~~~OOO~~~

April lived up to its reputation, bleak rain leaked out of a dark evening sky, gained velocity, and pelted against the tall windows. Beth clicked on the overhead lights. Six very busy months had passed since her arrival. She couldn't call herself a real VA fixture yet, but felt satisfied to be on the downside of the learning curve. The last appointment of the day was about to begin. At the completion of her March meeting with Pepper, the two decided the next step would be a solo interview with the husband. If that went well, they would advance into couple's therapy. A knock at the door startled her out of planning mode.

Alma held open the door for the twosome. Pepper held the baby with one hand, the fingers of the other hand entwined in Teigler's. It had been difficult to convince him this trip was necessary and she wasn't about to let him back out now. The man, over six feet tall and likely two hundred pounds, dressed informally. He wore a Black Watch tartan shirt and blue jeans—his black Wellington boots matched the distressed-leather bomber jacket he held in one hand. Around his waist, he wore a wide leather belt featuring a tooled representation of a snake, complete with imprinted scales. The heavy brass buckle displayed an inflated cobra head with fangs that fit into leather holes. The man's hair, black with sprinkled gray, had begun a gentle retreat on the sides. The former soldier's face was lean and olive skinned—and his best feature, his very deep, very dark brown eyes, were alert but apprehensive.

"Dr. Mueller, this is my husband Rod Teigler. Rod, this is Dr. Beth Mueller."

They shook hands, the man, face-neutral, nodded. Beth motioned him toward a chair in front of her desk. She would sit behind it for this interview, putting her in a superior, more professional position. The advantage might be needed given Pepper's disclosure of her husband's Mensa range intelligence.

"Rod … may I call you Rod?"

He managed a hesitant nod as he sat at attention in the chair, his jacket placed defensively across his lap. "We are here today to get to know each other better and to determine whether it is time to start couples therapy. Are you and your wife willing?"

After a pause, "Yes, I understand and we are willing."

"Let's get started. Tell me about your life, starting with your earliest recollection and advancing to the present."

~~~OOO~~~

Teigler, Pepper and child, and Alma sat out in the entry, waiting for Beth to finish her notes. It was well after dark. Given the high-risk neighborhood surrounding the hospital complex, it would be better for them to proceed in a group to the parking lot.

The interview had stretched longer than expected, but progressed better than expected, with even a few chuckles. When she pointed out how suspicious and negative many of his perceptions were, he responded, "Doc, throughout history all human groups have birthed their share of paranoids. And, sometimes they're right. The trick is to know when."

Teigler displayed many of the characteristics of PTSD. The major ones included anxiety attacks, flashbacks or intrusive memories, reoccurring dreams, emotional numbing, and difficulty displaying intimacy. His two-and-a-half years in Nam had exposed him to much heavy combat. He lost friends to bullets and a fiancé to a Dear John letter. He belonged to no clubs or associations and had no hobbies, writing being his sole outlet. Only one strange occurrence popped out, when questioned about feelings of suicide.

"Yes, I've considered it many times. Tried it once by attempting to drive my car into a truck at interstate speeds. And I've sucked on the barrel of my .45 Colt often enough."

"But you haven't been successful."

"Someone always stops me."

"Someone or something?"

"I can't really say."

"You mean you don't know?"

"I can't really say."

Beth sensed an opening to something major. She bombarded him with a battery of fast questions. His shoulders started to shake. The muscles in his face reconfigured themselves into a rigid mask. Lips parted and emitted a whisper-hiss. He twitched and twisted in the chair, an internal battle raged. Teigler gasped and relaxed back in the chair, sweat-faced, the session obviously over. She tapped in a final sentence, clicked on *Save,* and then the *Shut-down* icon on the computer. She grabbed her purse and coat on the way out the door.

The foursome walked along the shadow-streaked sidewalk in a column of twos, Pepper, baby, and Teigler in front, followed by Alma and Beth. Misty cold drizzle collected on the surrounding trees and bushes, occasionally dripping onto the group.

A black van caught them in its headlights, switching to brights and then back to low beams. It speeded up, then screeched to a halt. The doors slammed open, fragments of *Gangsta Rap* arrowed through the air *...capped him in his ass, no time motherfucker...* Five men in baggy pants and hoodies tumbled out—one carried a baseball bat.

The women froze. Teigler reacted, spreading his arms wide, he herded them back away from the street toward the buildings. Between Beth's office and the hospital proper, an alley opened. The women ran past a metal dumpster before stopping up against a chain-link fence. They were trapped in a cul-de-sac. Instinctively, Beth and Alma formed a human shield, pushed Pepper and the two-year-old behind them.

Beth watched Teigler back slowly into the alley, positioning himself between the gangsters and the women. She could hear him sob, and then it stopped—his body seemed to swell and then compress. The shoulders came down, he leaned over at the waist, knees bent and balanced, left arm extended palm out. He pulled off his belt, wrapped it around his right hand, leaving the snakehead buckle dangling from two feet of thick leather strap.

His body began twitching to the rap beat. The lead gang member pulled back his hood and motioned for the others to stand back. His hand came out of a sweatshirt pocket. Beth saw a silver flicker of reflected light off an eight-inch blade. The homeboy moved low and held the knifepoint upward, sidling forward in an experienced blade fighter's stance. Teigler forced his opponent to step with the beat of the music. The two men moved with the rap, back and forth, side to side, with the grace of dancers in an MTV video. The knifed-man leaped on the beat. Arm locked straight, blade pointed up, aiming to penetrate up under the ribs into the heart.

Teigler broke the rhythm, throwing the man off balance. His left hand fastened on the gang boss's forearm, pulling him forward and to the side while the veteran's right hand slapped the belt up around his opponent's head. The brass buckle's snakehead fangs caught in the flesh of his opponent's left cheek. Teigler's body twisted as he jerked back the belt. Beth heard a crackle and a short ripping sound. The man screamed. The knife clattered on the concrete. His hands covered his face. Blood gushed down, the soft tissues of the nose only attached to the bridge of his forehead by a thin string of flesh.

Teigler stooped and recovered the knife. The hood with the baseball bat lunged forward, swung the weapon left-handed. With a sinuous flexing movement, Teigler moved inside the swing, taking the blow from mid-bat rather than from the sweet spot. His quilted leather bomber jacket absorbed some of the force, but Beth thought she heard a rib crack. Teigler's right arm came down, pinning the bat. Instead of letting go, the man leaned back, tried to tug it away. A spark of light turned into a streak as the blade in Rod's hand flashed over an exposed throat. The bat dropped to the left, the dying body to the right.

The screams of the first man continued to mix with the rap lyrics … *blew him away, took his bad bitch* … a third gang member fumbled in his belt, freeing a short-barreled automatic pistol. Just as two hundred pounds of Vietnam veteran smacked into him. They rolled on the ground. The pistol skittered across the alley. Beth's jaw dropped, Teigler leaped up, and the man lay prone, unmoving, only the knife's hilt visible against his ribs.

Teigler bent forward and screeched at the remaining gang members. The sound was like metal-tipped claws on a blackboard. In the cold night air, a thick stream of white vapor, snot, and spit blew out of his mouth and nose. The screaming gang boss ran by the two remaining homies.

His gurgling, "Oh God, oh God, oh God," still chanting just the right harmonizing rhythm. The rest broke and ran, slammed the van doors, and left ribbons of dirty tire smoke down the street and around the corner.

Beth pulled a cell phone out of her purse and dialed 911. The beeps made Teigler spin in his tracks. He pulled the knife out of the body and rushed her. Left hand fastened on her neck, lifted her to tiptoes. The right hand holding the knife flashed forward, paused within an inch of one eye.

Gangsta blood dripped off the blade, ran down her cheek, and stained the collar of her rain-specked gray trench coat. If there was a hell, Beth was looking into the face of one of its denizens. She thought, Pepper is right. It is a reptile. A tinny voice floated up out of the dropped cell phone, "Hello, what is the nature of your emergency?"

Beth couldn't breathe. She pushed against Teigler's body. It was all springs and wires. Her hands clawed at his choking fingers, and she felt steel cables contracting.

Pepper shouted, "Rod, Rod, no. Goddamn it, no!" The redhead pulled at the knife hand. In Beth's side-vision, a rectangular black shape swung forward and slapped against the side of the soldier's head. Alma was using her purse. The snake cocked its head, looked surprised, then confused. The purse struck again and bounced off. The man's body relaxed. His arms lowered, the knife rattled on the alley's hard surface. Beth collapsed, gasped. The reptile was gone.

~~~OOO~~~

Beth sat in the back of Judge Joseph C. Walter's chambers with Pepper and Alma. Pepper stood, held the toddler to her shoulder, and shifted slowly back and forth, one foot to the other, rocking the fractious child to sleep. The judicial quarters were old-fashioned with walnut-framed squares forming the wainscoting, the uncomfortable chairs fashioned of heavy wood. She suspected that was on purpose, so conferences would be short. With dusty oak blinds on the double windows closed, only a few underpowered floor lamps offered weak indirect light. Judge Walters sat behind his desk facing a foursome.

A detective sergeant was just completing his report. An intent female assistant district attorney listened beside him. Teigler and his attorney formed a second pair. Unruly course white hair and matching curly eyebrows decorated the judge's craggy face. Food stains blossomed like mushrooms on his tie, and the cuffs of his white shirt were frayed. The room smelled of old man sweat and cigar smoke, hinting that its occupant never strayed far from its comfort.

Beth had followed the progress of Rod's case. It hardly seemed like two months had passed since he had been booked, fingerprinted, and processed by the police. Seventy-two hours later, he stood mute at the arraignment with his court-appointed attorney. Not responsive to the manslaughter and assault charges, the judge defaulted his plea to not guilty. Unable to meet the bail set, the former soldier spent his time in the county lockup awaiting events. The state news media went wild with the story. Most editorialized that Teigler's sole defense of women and a child against five gang members with felony records was heroic. To his benefit, the publicity resulted in the top criminal law firm in the state agreeing to represent him *pro bono*. They would bask in the media limelight with him, gaining future business from the free publicity.

His high-powered attorney speedily brokered a plea agreement with the district attorney, who by now despaired of finding a jury not prejudiced in the defendant's favor. Teigler's law firm pointed out how completely the state penal code on non-criminal homicide fit this situation. The lawyer quoted Chapter 9, Section 31:

> *The belief that force was immediately necessary as described by this subsection is presumed to be reasonable if the actor knew or had reason to believe that the person(s) against whom the force was used was committing or attempting to commit aggravated kidnapping, murder, sexual assault, aggravated sexual assault, robbery, or aggravated robbery.*

The gang members had been in the process of attempting to commit not only one or two but all of the above. Also pointed out, the defendant had fulfilled the code's proscription of a general duty to retreat before self-defense could be considered justifiable homicide. They had retreated as far as possible before being caught in a cul-de-sac with the criminals blocking the only exit.

Teigler would get off with a slap on the hand from a provision in the law called a deferred sentence. If the judge agreed, the court would accept the plea and not find the defendant guilty. If Teigler faithfully complied with all the provisions in the agreement by a set review date, all documentation of a plea would be expunged and he would not have a record as a convicted felon.

"Let me see if I have all the facts. Five gang members set upon this man, three women, and a child. Men the DA's office have long suspected of doing hit-and-run muggings and rapes, one such attack resulting in the death of their victim. It appears the tables turned in this instance. Mr. Teigler put up a defense, resulting in two gang deaths and one man mutilated, who you arrested later at city hospital getting his nose sewed back on."

The detective sergeant suppressed a chuckle. The ADA frowned and responded, "That's generally correct, Your Honor."

"And, today we need to finalize the plea agreement or determine whether any further action is to be taken against Mr. Teigler."

Beth saw Teigler's attorney lean forward. "Your Honor, my client is an honorably discharged war veteran, holding two purple hearts, a bronze medal for valor, and the rarely awarded Vietnamese Government Distinguished Service Medal. He served over thirty months in that country, where he experienced considerable combat. Our soldiers are trained to kill, not disable. In the incident in question, he used skills acquired in that conflict to defend his wife, child, and two other women from the worst kind of crime. After the action, the EMTs diagnosed him with a broken finger, a broken rib, and two other cracked ribs. If any charges are pressed, my client can count on an unassailable defense.

"He is also a commercially published author. His books of poetry and prose have won national awards. I note that a copy of his first book of poetry resides on the shelf behind you."

The judge swiveled in his creaky chair and pulled out the book of poetry, studied it a moment, then looked up. "What does the district attorney's office wish?"

The young ADA straightened her Armani gray mist three-button jacket, and opened clenched sweaty hands. "Given the verified facts of the incident, we don't believe any jury in this community would convict him, nor would any jury in any community. Therefore, we believe a *deferred sentence* is appropriate.

"However, in checking his history from Vietnam to present, there are disturbing instances which indicate that berserker-like reactions to high-pressure situations are not uncommon for this man. We are not sure if it is safe for him to be wandering our streets. The plea agreement contains what we believe to be a satisfactory plan."

The judge replied, "I have reviewed the agreement and the psychological profile submitted by Dr. Elizabeth Mueller. In light of the service he has done for his country and this community, and the fact no charges can solidly be pressed, a court order will be issued, requiring Mr. Teigler to adhere to the agreement. He will report tomorrow to Dr. Edward Waszlowski at the VA's Psychosocial Rehabilitation Recovery Center. The doctor will assign a therapist and determine a schedule of regular therapy sessions, and medication, if needed. A monthly report will be sent to my office summarizing Mr. Teigler's progress.

"As a further protection for everyone involved, for the next six months he will reside in a community halfway house. At the end of that time, given a positive prognosis from his therapist, he will be released, but will continue regular treatment.

"Do you understand, son?"

Beth looked at Teigler, his head down, slumping in the chair. The ex-soldier nodded. He would agree to anything. In saving them, he had lost everything—his wife's decision had been made in the moments following the incident in the alley—yesterday, he received divorce papers.

"Are there any loose ends here? Anybody? Hearing none, this meeting is over. Son, if you feel up to it, would you sign my copy of your book?"

Memorial Day in the Garden

Weathered veins of brown, black, and gray
run deep into the bench's bleached wood.
Thinning oak slats creak
under my gravity-laden flesh. Bare feet

root into the grassy, humid earth.
A fountain splashes, rainbow-washed songs
muffle a mother's call, children's laughter,

husky bass rumble of a truck.
In the spring warmth, I breathe
mingled scents of new mown hay, lilac,
and berry blossoms. I sip fermented air,

smooth as the velvet of Irish whiskey.
A cold breeze ruffles the hair
on my arms, wrinkles skin. Sounds slow,
mix into a mush of radio static,
and decades-old military call signs.
Once more the slap of bullets, night flares,
mists of copper blood and sulfur smoke,
snare drum of monsoon rain.

I look up.
Under the pines, prone in lush shadows,
Death watches.
Dressed in soldiers' jungle camos
and green beret, he does yoga,

curling and uncurling.
We nod—old comrades. Branches shake,
a robin falls, lands in his lap.
The Angel lifts

eyebrows, tilts its head.
In the starless obsidian of his eyes
float the faces of fallen friends,
those remembered, and those forgotten.

Cerberus

Bullets hornet-buzzed around the foxhole. Some thunked into the double row of gray sandbags around its lip or tore up the red dirt on the sides. Others spanged off the steel road wheels of the M-109 self-propelled howitzer dug in nearby. Fragments blew backwards striking the upper backs and necks of three GIs sheltered in the hole. Friction-hot lead and copper bits pierced cloth and skin to lodge in underlying muscle. The men swore and slapped at the tiny wounds.

Lieutenant Rod Teigler cursed both the enemy fire and the fate that found him and his men among the mobile artillery unit during an unusual daylight attack. A battalion of North Vietnamese Regulars, augmented by local Viet Cong forces, had massed to overrun this small fire support base. He had known a strike of some kind was coming. The members of his signal intelligence unit intercepted increased radio traffic in the area. Direction-finding equipment tracked several company-sized units converging on this position.

The fight started at dawn with sappers carrying satchel charges breaking into the inner defenses. Due to Teigler's advance warning, alerted artillerymen stopped all but one, who managed to toss his explosives into the number five-gun turret. The twenty-seven-ton monster rocked on its fully tracked tank chassis. Black smoke, interior equipment, and bits of men blew out of its back doors and top hatch. Immediately afterwards, mortar shells began to explode in and around the base. Over four hundred enemy rose running and screaming from their start positions. Swivel-mounted fifty-calibers on the turrets of the remaining four howitzers opened up, sending hundreds of thumb-sized bullets into the charging enemy. Other GIs returned fire with M-60 machine guns and M-16 rifles. Here and there, a claymore mine fired, sending hundreds of steel pellets into the face of the attack.

Armed with a stubby M-79 grenade launcher, Teigler's eyes swept the battlefield looking for threats, especially RPGs. The M-109's aluminum armor would stop shell fragments and most small arms fire, but high-explosive anti-tank rockets fired by RPG crews would cut though like butter.

He spotted one, raised the short-barreled grenade launcher, and thumped out a round. It landed three feet in front of the target, exploded, and blew a cloud of quarter-inch long steel shrapnel into the two-man crew. They flopped back bloody faced.

The well-executed Vietnamese plan would still have carried the day if not for the lack of surprise and a new weapon. The 155-millimeter cannons mounted on the M-109's normally fired 98-pound high-explosive rounds as far as eleven miles. At short ranges, the rounds would not detonate, but the unit had recently received new beehive rounds with thousands of nail-sized flechettes coiled in each warhead. When fired, they spread the flechettes in an expanding "V" pattern across the battlefield, taking out anyone standing or kneeling within the weapon's fan-shaped kill zone.

Teigler watched as armored turrets rotated and 20-foot-long cannon barrels lowered to target concentrations of attackers. He blinked as pillows of hot gases from the guns' back blast smacked his face and body. Huge pie-shaped chunks of advancing troops disappeared. The volume of enemy fire dropped.

A dozen NVA regulars escaped the howitzers' shot cones and moved through the barbwire toward his position. The radioman next to him took an AK-47 round in the helmet. His head snapped back, then forward as the man slipped down. Teigler loaded a buckshot round in the breech of his weapon, raised it to meet the first enemy only fifteen feet away. The M-79 kicked against his shoulder.

Three attackers fell. More Vietnamese soldiers crawled over the bodies, bayonets extended and locked. Teigler fumbled with his .45-caliber pistol. A sweat-soaked body smelling of Nuoc Mam smacked into his shoulder. He felt the beast inside flash to the surface. Teeth bit into the neck of his attacker.

A voice said, "Sir, Sir … the library will shut its doors in ten minutes." A hand continued to shake his shoulder.

Teigler opened his eyes, smelled his own adrenaline-laced sweat, felt the agony of knotted muscles. Lights were blinking, signaling closing time. He hunched over, head in his hands. He was safe, just a dream. The reptile in him coiled and went back to sleep.

~~~OOO~~~

A Norther spawned wind wrapped around his ankles, legs, and buttocks. Icy claws slipped into the loose places between his clothing and skin. The fast-moving cold front had halved the eighty-degree daytime temperature. Teigler picked up the pace, pulled the two library books in one hand closer to his side. The other hand held six slippery plastic-boxed cassette tapes containing classical music: two of Boccherini and one each of Mussorgsky, Handel, Bach, and Mendelssohn.

Streetlights along the block flickered, warmed themselves to full brightness. Silvered candy wrappers, Styrofoam cups, and dead dry leaves danced in swirling funnels. He noticed two gawky boys, almost men, waiting at the corner. The streets and sidewalks on both sides of them were deserted. Teigler stepped off the curb and crossed the street, a better part of valor move. His companions moved with him, now closing the distance. He wondered if the twenty in his billfold would buy him passage. Not much else, no credit cards at all. Living in a halfway house, making a few bucks giving blood and doing odd jobs didn't accumulate much wealth.

Disappointed muggers frequently took out their frustrations on their victims. The creature in his brain stirred, stimulated by a rising adrenalin level. The two drew closer. Both dressed identically in khaki pants and red hoodies arranged to hide their faces. He could probably outrun the fat one, but the other, whipcord lean and long-legged, would catch him in a half block. The pair stopped, moved together to block the sidewalk.

The reptile moved into his frontal lobes. Lips parted and gave a barely audible hiss of warning. If Teigler's body possessed a tail with a rattle, it would be shaking. The two hoods received failing grades in reading body language. Fatty pulled out a sawed-off baseball bat with a carved handgrip from the back of his pants. Skinny snapped open a pocketknife's six-inch blade.

"Give it—the wallet, watch, whatever ...," the big one said.

"You boys so poor you can't afford a gun?" The reptile started dancing back and forth in his consciousness.

Skinny stepped forward, brandishing the knife. "No, asshole. Cough it up, or we take it off your fuckin' dead fuckin' body."

Rod felt muscles go tight as his inner creature fountained up to fill his flesh like a hand filled a tight glove. His body jerked forward, mouth open. A screech, part roar, part train whistle hurt the muggers' ears. Their eyebrows jerked up. They leaped forward.

Thrown cassettes hit the sidewalk under Fatty's feet causing him to slip and fall face forward. The creature raised a thick novel in one hand and held back a thin hardcover book in the other. As Skinny's blade slashed a book cover, the thin edge of the second book smacked into the nerve complex under his nose. He froze—shocked—the pain felt like his whole head was coming off.

Fatty lunged up, slipped again. The predator moved in to clutch him in a tight embrace, making him unable to swing his club. A crooked finger thrust into his eye socket, dug out his left eye, and left it to dangle down his cheek.

The bat clunked to the concrete. Fatty fell backwards screaming with pain and disorientation from eyes that now saw two vastly different images. Skinny never saw the kick that burst his gonads.

"Sometimes the simple things are best," the human thought as he assessed the reptile's last move. Air flushed out of its nostrils as the raptor with the man inside watched for any further moves from the two sobbing would-be robbers. The temperature continued to drop. The creature detected some motion in the shadows around them. Its breath turned to vapor.

Hooded bodies moved out from the bushes, from behind the alley's dumpsters, and the bus stop shelter. Teigler rotated, counting—twenty, at least, moving in. The reptile released control—leaving the problem for the man. No amount of fighting would get them out of this. As the strangers moved into areas illuminated by the streetlights, he noticed a difference. The newcomers dressed differently, their shoes, jeans, and hoodies, all black.

One of the men stepped up, looked at Teigler, and then down at the failed muggers. "That action kind'a reminded me of a deadly version of the Three Stooges. Are you super Moe?"

Teigler could sense the smile behind the words. The voice sounded familiar. He kept quiet as a flashlight played over this face making him blink.

"You police? Martial arts instructor? Ex-military? A pause, the flashlight beam centered on his face froze. "Jesus ... son of a bitch! It's the El Tee."

Teigler stood puzzled. The man pulled back his hood and switched the light to his face. "It's Okie, man! Okie. We served in Nam together."

The two men hugged each other, pounded backs, one out of relief, one out of joy. The other gang members looked confused, then relaxed and stowed their weapons into belts and hidden places. The pair separated. On the ground, Fatty started throwing up. Teigler looked down at the two muggers and raised his eyebrows.

"Not to worry, El Tee. These two are from the Roosevelt Street gang, and way out of their territory. We were about to take them ourselves. You gather your books and cassettes and come with me."

~~~OOO~~~

Teigler sat in one of four old, but comfortable, leather upholstered wingback chairs. The portable electric heater buzzing in one corner chased the chill out of his clothes. He rested in a second-story office located in one of the old corrugated-steel warehouses clustered around the railroad tracks. One iron-barred outside window opened to a fire escape. A row of windows starting waist high lined the interior wall. They looked down onto the floor of the forty thousand square-foot building. The glass vibrated softly in time to hip-hop music from a far corner of the building. The office walls looked freshly painted in what looked to be Victorian colors, slate-gray and pastel-cream.

Centered at one end stood an amber-oak desk partnered with a matching high-backed swivel chair. Behind those, lined up along the wall, leaned an old iron safe and several filing cabinets. Okie approached with two coffee cups.

"Well, *Thượng Úy*, or should I say, Lieutenant, where you been?"

Rod rolled the thick-walled porcelain cup between his hands. Navy style, he noted, no handle. The vapor rising from the black liquid smelled of cognac, a high-end brand, Napoleon, perhaps. He stalled. "You appear to have done very well for yourself."

"Mostly due to you. Those night conversations we had, the books you lent me. Raised my aspirations. *Aspirations*, nice word, not one you'd hear me use in the old days."

Teigler felt rhythmic vibrations rise through his feet. A train rumbled by outside, a homey relaxing sound for those who had grown up in railroad towns. "But you're still a gang member and high up in the command structure."

"Step up to the windows."

Rod rose. The two stood shoulder-to-shoulder looking into the warehouse.

"Look to your left."

One-quarter of the warehouse floor space was screened off. In geometric patterns, fifteen or so cars filled the area. Men and boys leaned under open hoods or moved wheeled mechanics toolboxes into position. Pneumatic hoses hung like jungle vines, socketed air tools chattered. He admired a brand new 1986 Lincoln Continental poised on a hydraulic lift, next to it a new model Mustang SSP. In separate bays, a couple of yellow Hertz rent-a-trucks received foamy high-pressure sprays.

"Used to be a chop shop, now it's the best fleet maintenance shop in town. Engine overhaul, bodywork, and customization—all legit. Now, over there." He pointed to the right.

The remaining floor space consisted of three areas, all with their own outside entrances. Teigler noticed a gun store with long glass counters, the walls hung thick with rifles and shotguns. Rotating floor-mounted gun racks displayed more offerings. Separated by ten-foot tall petitions, an adjacent pawnshop seemed about half-full of customers. In the middle, sharing common walls with all the other enterprises stood what appeared to be a combination cafeteria, arcade, and general hangout. Gang members lounged on couches, watched TV, and played cards. A few male bodies performed pinball ballet before flashing and dinging machines. Others took turns shooting an arcade rifle at a robotic bear that ran back and forth on a rail. With every hit, the bear would roar and change direction.

"Everything legit. I took my gang's natural propensities and talents and turned them inside out. The chop shop mechanics became real mechanics, petty thieves and burglars became pawn masters, and those fascinated with guns run a state-licensed gun shop. Now they receive better pay, longer life spans, and the sense of belonging to something bigger remains."

Rod tilted his head, looked at Okie. "Your boys still control the streets and fight with other gangs."

"We keep the bad ones out. The local businesses pay us a small monthly fee to support our foot patrol. They get real protection. Robberies and muggings are about nonexistent. People feel safe—can walk the streets. We have an unwritten agreement with the police; we keep crime down and they leave us alone. Enough about that, let's sit. I have more to tell."

The pair refreshed their coffees and slid into the oversized leather chairs. Rod learned that Okie had collaborated with another of their war buddies— Robert Bruce MacDonald, known among his friends as Caber. Red-haired, reaching six-foot-five and 230 pounds, born into the most populous of the Scottish clans, he was a power in an organization which had business tentacles in ventures throughout the world, both visible and undercover.

Okie and Caber had also connected with other friends from the old country, Uncle Ho and his grandson, Nam. No one knew Ho's real name. The elderly native with his traditional scraggly white beard and moustache looked like the spitting image of the great leader of North Vietnam.

The pair had latched onto the three soldiers when the old man and his thirteen-year-old companion were discovered begging in the local outdoor market. The sole survivors of an enemy attack on their village near the border between the Vietnams, the locals shunned the pair. Village gossip spread rumors that Ho was some kind of shaman who could see and talk with the dead. He turned out to be a good cover-your-back man with a shotgun during several of their joint combat operations. Grandfather and grandson fled their country with other "boat people" after the fall of Saigon. Sponsoring their immigration, Caber set them up in a small business selling Asian foods and traditional medicines to a growing Oriental population.

Teigler remembered how the five worked together to barely survive a company-size VC attack against a poorly fortified position manned by green village boys. His mind slipped into a memory of the aftermath...

...The sun burned bright, the air already stove hot. Teigler could smell his own stink, that leftover adrenaline stink, when he moved. The hands on his army-issue watch read 0830.

In the background, clean-up squads moved bodies and stacked captured weapons. Some tied cloths around their faces, mostly to keep out the flies, although the heat would soon push the odor past what a normal nose could endure. Leaking body fluids left slick red mud around the dead, requiring each foot to be carefully placed.

An enemy's crisped body still smoked where fougass flames had caught him. Teigler hunkered down for a close-up look. When skin and body fat had been consumed, the flames stopped.

However, fire hadn't killed this one. A tight spray of number four buckshot had blown away the muscle and flesh on the man's back, chopped his spine, and shredded a kidney. White bone shards stood out in contrast to the red and gray of tissue and organs.

Ho's shot rendered an act of unintended mercy. Burns this extensive were a soldier's worst nightmare—even morphine hardly dented the pain. Given the primitive medicine available to the Viet Cong, this one would have pleaded for death within the first hour.

Behind him, Teigler heard retching and Caber's voice. "Jesus Christ, Lieutenant, did you know what that fucking stuff would do?"

Nodding, the lieutenant stood and staggered through the gate, stopped outside the perimeter wire. He kept his back to the tower, not wanting to see more, but the burnt-shit smell remained in his nostrils. Teigler's eyes watered from the stench—mostly from the stench. He kicked at a tuft of grass clinging to the red soil at the top of the roadside ditch...

"So, El Tee, what do you think?" Teigler stumbled out of his flashback realizing he had missed a relevant part of the conversation.

"Sorry, I was back in Nam. Say again."

Okie watched him for a moment, then nodded his head. "For the last six months, we've been thinking about setting up a new operation—a security company. There's money to be made burglar-proofing both the homes of the rich and commercial buildings. Our ex-burglars will be experts. And, we've also got the numbers and street smarts to provide security at rock concerts and major public events."

"Sounds like good thinking to me. You and Caber have the touch. Base metal is turned into refined products."

"Yah, well the only one thing slowing us. We've outgrown our leadership ability. Running into you is perfect. You're the man to head up the new agency."

He shouldn't have been surprised. "I don't believe I'm capable."

"Hell, man, you're smart and a good organizer. You were always two steps ahead of me and one step ahead of Caber." He laughed. "And three steps ahead of the enemy."

Teigler sat for a long minute, staring into the black coffee, his nose tingling from the cognac vapors. Sweat started to prickle his skin. "There's something about me you need to know."

~~~OOO~~~

He leaned back in the Swedish modern lounge chair, hands behind his head, feet and legs elevated on a cushioned lower panel. "So, it's been a year," he mused. Things had moved at redline speed after his confession to Okie and Caber. Their reactions to the existence of a reptile personality in his brain mixed, but benign. Okie, nodding with a slight smile, replayed in his mind the action between Teigler and the Roosevelt Street gang members. The sinuosity of the former lieutenant's movement, the speed, and absolute lack of emotion fit snake behavior. Caber's face reflected surprise, then the face collapsed into a frown of disbelief. Neither reaction slowed the momentum.

The three partners placed contributions into the common pot. Caber provided the start-up capital in the form of cash, Okie the work force, and Teigler the daily management. They called the new entity Cerberus, after the vicious three-headed dog of Greco-Roman myth that guarded the gates of hell. As more contracts came their way, they moved into a two-story brick building located in a changing neighborhood of the old downtown. Numerous other renovations rapidly changed the area from slum to upscale.

High-pressure hoses spewing ground-up corncobs removed the old outside paint and dirt from their storefront, exposing red brick and decorative blue-yellow Italianate ceramic tiles. Shrunken double-hung oak windows had been replaced with modern triple-paned replicas. Modest gold letters on the first-floor window announced the company's name. The basement contained the gym and a small-arms locker adjacent to a three-position pistol range. The street-level glass door opened into a reception area furnished with chrome-legged Barcelona chairs and a reception counter. Behind a sound and bulletproof wall beat the heart of the company as men and women answered phones, scheduled calls, and paid bills.

The second floor became his lair, divided into an office and a two-bedroom apartment. Skylights let in natural light to reflect off walls alternating in peach-colored plaster and the natural red brick of the building's bones. He kept the office Spartan, table, ergonomic chair, good lighting, and live plants positioned along a cabinet top under the row of back alley windows. Folding chairs could be extracted from an armoire in one corner for conferences.

He thought about the office employees, from receptionist to the bookkeeper, a half-dozen normal-looking middleclass people. The customers and even their families remained unaware of their extra qualities. All employees were proficient with small arms and the company's own brand of martial arts. As satisfied as a restless mind could get, Teigler reminisced about the defensive hand-to-hand art he had developed. The borrowings came from many sources: Army Ranger and Navy Seal training, the best of the Asian disciplines, French Savate, and Israeli Krav Maga. Consisting of purely defensive maneuvers: pins, come-alongs, disarming moves (knives and guns), throws, and nerve punches, all had been selected to incapacitate without killing. He thought of the whole process as the *Gentle Way*.

The *Way* turned out to be perfect for bodyguard services. Their excellent record of low injuries to out-of-control participants at rock concerts brought them more contracts. Outside of bruises and sprains, the company's staff received few injuries, in great part due to close-fitting Kevlar armored vests. He'd also special-ordered DuPont fingerless gloves that extended back from the second row of knuckles to just below the elbow. These protected forearms and the back of hands from knife thrusts and slashes. The armored palms could actually be used to grab knife blades without damage to the flesh beneath. All this planning and training worked for his employees—but not for the snake. One relapse had marked this first year.

~~~OOO~~~

Teigler heard the little silver bell ring as he opened the door to the Vietnamese dry-cleaning shop. Uncle Ho knew and talked regularly with several generations of this family, many of whom had been dead for several centuries. According to him, the current owners gave good value for money.

"*Chào Bà*," he said in greeting to the grandmother.

"*Chào Bac* (Hello, Aunty)," he addressed the blossoming teenage granddaughter with the waist-length raven-black hair.

The grandmother cackled at the implied relationship. The girl blushed and reached across the counter to smack him in the arm. His nostrils twitched as he caught a whiff of her jasmine perfume, a welcome change from the smell of the petroleum-based solvents polluting the shop air.

Lips parted in a smile, Teigler bowed deeply and gave the correct greeting. He turned to the youngest male grandchild saying, "*Chào Em*. And how is

Chinh (he thought the name meant correctness or righteousness) doing in school?"

"He get big prize in math," Grandma announced. "You here for pick up cleaning?"

Teigler fumbled for his ticket. He heard the rumble-throb of a car's glass packs vibrate through the front windows. The special mufflers reduced backpressure, increasing a car's power, but the fiberglass insulation let a lot of noise through. A chopped-top custom Chevy pulled up into the loading zone.

The men inside wore gang colors—the wrong colors for this neighborhood. In spite of his company's advice, the shop owners made a bad practice of accumulating cash all week, only making a bank deposit on Friday—today. Someone else knew about this. The passenger in the car looked up and down the street, fumbled for something metallic blue-black in his waistband. Teigler grabbed a handful of red-striped Bic pens from a drinking glass next to the register and jammed them under the door bottom. He leaped over the counter and began pushing the surprised Vietnamese to the back of the store.

"Get out! It's a robbery!"

The four pushed their way under the mechanized overhead conveyer line that held hundreds of plastic-wrapped shirts, suits, and dresses. The women disappeared into the jungle of hanging clothes. The boy followed him. Teigler heard the door bust open. He found the switch activating the racks. A rattling chain noise started as the mechanism rotated hanging clothes around U-shaped tracks that twisted back and forth, taking up two-thirds of the building space. From overhead, it looked like a writhing snake holding its tail in its mouth. The conveyer noise and the whispering of the plastic bags masked their flight.

He heard a shout of frustration from the robbers. The front desk and cash register didn't contain the weekly deposit bag. The men raced after the owners, moving in the aisles between marching dry cleaning. They became separated in the rotating maze. The lead man fired a shot into the ceiling, bringing down gray dust and plaster chips. The reptile stirred. Sick to his stomach, Teigler fell to his knees. The boy tugged at his arms, desperate for them to move. The half-man almost-snake looked under the clothes, spotted sneakered feet approaching. Chinh felt the man's arm muscles turn into ropy steel. He let go and backed away.

A speed-blurred hand sprang from under the dry cleaning and jerked the leader's left ankle. He smacked the floor, the shock of the fall causing his gun to spin-clatter across the concrete. The stunned body disappeared under the moving clothes. Chinh watched as the creature punched two fang-like fingers into the soft flesh just below the robber's sternum. The snake-like movements reminded him of grandmother's tales of *the worm*, his people's *protector dragon*. He could see shiny silver scales on the man's skin, or was it sweat?

With adrenaline-powered strength, the victim, as limp as a ventriloquist's dummy, held upright by the reptile-man, was lifted and pushed through the moving racks of clothes. In the fourth row the number two gang member had only a second to recognize his boss emerging from the dry cleaning before the limp body crashed into him, pinning him on the floor. Another heavy body piled on—he felt hot burning breath and heard a mind-numbing screech in his ear. A thin-stretched plastic sheet torn from a garment bag conformed to his face, shut off the air to his mouth and nostrils.

The third armed robber found grandmother, granddaughter, father, and grandfather huddled at the back of the store. He shouted, "Where's the money?" Grandfather offered a yellow, zippered canvas bag.

The chain-driven conveyer gave out an overwhelmed metal-on-metal squeal. The four shocked Vietnamese stared over the man's shoulder as two shadowy shapes trundled round the last row of the conveyer. The gunman turned and looked into the pale unconscious faces of his two comrades, their bodies secured to the conveyor hooks. He froze, watching them being pulled down the line, ankles dragging on the floor. He spun around, muttered, "Who?" Then panicked and crashed through the back door into the alley. A fast-moving body whipped past the open-mouthed family and slithered through the door in pursuit.

"Granny, Granny," shouted Chinh as he rushed to grab her legs. "Is it the dragon?"

Grandmother's hands cupped his head. Outside, lightning cracked across the sky; its flash through the windows caused winged snake-tailed shadows to dance across their faces. An unexpected rain began. A soft rattle against the glass became a drumming, drilling downpour like the monsoons of their birth country. "The dragon," she thought, "of course ... the dragon brings the rain." She whispered into Chinh's ear the ancient advice of generations of Asian grandmothers, "Become like the dragon."

~~~OOO~~~

Teigler rubbed the back of his neck. Every act has consequences, but he couldn't think of any coming from the cleaning shop experience. Okie and some of the boys cut down and revived the two unconscious gang members. Terrified by their encounter with the reptile, they were allowed to return to their own territory as a warning to others. The third one had barely escaped in the get-away car, one rear fender embossed with long talon-like scratches.

He was wrong about the consequences. In repayment, Grandmother insisted on feeding him lunch the last Saturday of each month. It became a mixed blessing. To keep the weight gain down from all the forced delicacies he had to fast the following Sunday. The one consequence he didn't like, the members of the Vietnamese community now addressed him as *Rồng* Teigler, their word for dragon. Even worse, it was starting to catch on with the company staff.

We

flame inside, *fuego en la sangre*, fire
in my liters of blood wine. You flash
miles through me: pulse, touch, moan.

Intimacy whips fever. Blue and green tipped
flares singe our flesh. Your presence injects
pure high oxygen, blast furnace violet.

Embers incense flesh. Burn-smoke
releases the caress of orange-vanilla,
peach-cinnamon, sweet pinion-sandalwood.

Rushing before your hips the salt-hot scent
of ocean exploding over black cliff rocks.
Swollen rose petal lips whisper

the liquid jazz of far-out Coltrane.
Updrafts spin our burnt souls' lace.
Gray-black particulates glow, spark.

Our mingled warm ash bound with desire
smolders, swirls in fitful breaths,
seeks each other again.

Like Father, Like Daughter

He heard the whisper of air sliding over the aerodynamic hull of the Astra 1A1 private jet. Vibration from the fuselage-mounted twin engines came up through the soles of his feet. The pilots must be pushing it. The plane had a max speed of 465 mph, and they were probably at the limit.

Angel must have impressed her employees with the need for speed. It fit with the desperate tenor of her phone call. Teigler wondered how she came by his private number. He stared out into the black night. From twenty thousand feet, the human eye could only delineate the ground by the glimmering lights of towns and highway truck stops. He remembered stories of the old days of aviation, back when open cockpits and no instrumentation made night trips highly dangerous. Disoriented pilots could get turned upside down in turbulent winds and mistake the stars for ground lights. They would go higher and higher, thinking they were approaching land until they finally passed out from lack of oxygen and gravity spun them down.

Teigler turned on the reading light, changing the window into a mirror reflecting his face. Memories of Angel flashed into his mind. They had met in the 1870s in a small mountain mining town snowed in for the winter.

"Yah," he chuckled to himself, "a time traveler, it had to be me, on top of everything else." Angel, the reptile, and I killed five bank robbers over a hundred years ago. Not that they didn't deserve it. He drifted into his memories, how it all unfolded…

…Teigler felt sick, mouth tasting of bitter bile. The waves of nausea slowed, the thick black coffee helped. It reminded him of the stuff his German grandmother used to make. In the early hours, before the men got out of bed, you could hear her turning the crank on the old grinder. Grounds and water were placed in a blue enameled pot, which sat on the stove all day.

He knew what had just happened. It was the ambush in Nam all over again, him not in control of his body. His awareness crushed down deep inside by the reptile berserker, helpless, only seeing things far off, like looking through the wrong end of binoculars. He hated it.

One of these times, he would not come back, his body an eternal prison, confining his screaming soul. Maybe the police had it right. He was a blight on the land. Teigler examined the two women drinking coffee across the table. They had been abused and contused, especially the younger one who sported blatant facial bruises and a broken nose. Hair in tangles, she rubbed at crusty stuff in the corners of her eyes. In terrible emotional shape, she slouched over the cup, hands clenching and unclenching, staring into the black liquid. Angel, the older one, appeared much more experienced and able to talk sense. Medium blonde hair framed blue eyes and a wide mouth that seemed about to break into a smile.

Her body language radiated toughness. He took a second look and uncovered a professional, calculating face, one used to making customers think they were welcome, while being fleeced. That night she became his lover.

The next day, they worked as a team to survive. She took out one of the two remaining outlaws with a shotgun while he and the gang leader shot it out in the street. She slung Teigler, wounded and unconscious, across the saddle of his mule and led the three of them back through a time portal into the twentieth century. After seeing him safe at the hospital, she left for Las Vegas to ply the only trade she knew, one unchanged since her birth over a hundred years ago…

Now, after eighteen years, she was calling in his marker. Relaxing back into the soft blond-leather seat, he felt sweat induced by the old memories drying and cooling his forehead. Angel told him nothing over the phone, only that she must see him, and fast. The jet's pilots knew only as much as a taxi driver—where to pick up and deliver the fare. Burke, the third man, probably knew more.

The five foot ten inch, 170-pounder, sat by the access door with a bulge in his sport coat near the right armpit, marking him as a lefty. Occasionally Teigler felt green eyes boring into the back of his neck. Their initial handshake quickly became a sizing-up rather than a greeting. He wondered if the gunman harbored a romantic attachment to Angel. Jealousy? Glancing at his watch, he noted about an hour remained on their journey.

It was a bad time to be away. The company had grown as fast as they could train good employees. Okie managed mergers with several of the other city gangs. The event security portion of the business and the home security company had both been spun off into separate subchapter S corporations. Cerberus now served as the parent corporation and an investigative agency. The company would go public next month. Like turkey buzzards circling a dying deer, Caber's relatives frothed at the mouth, hardly able to wait.

Even with long working hours, the last five years seemed more normal than usual for Teigler. Except for one occasion, the reptile remained dormant. After that incident, Uncle Ho provided Asian herbal medicines and amulets, which seemed to keep the beast asleep. Teigler never felt so free.

Closing his eyes, he drifted into a recollection of the creature's last appearance. The Crossroads Mall consisted of parking and outbuildings spread out over fifteen acres, its northern and eastern boundaries delineated by the intersection of two multi-lane highways, one an interstate. The glass-domed central facility encompassed some 300,000 square feet of space, much of its volume open air. The cruciform structure's four wings met at a huge circular tower. The design allowed four anchor stores, one at each end of the cross, rather than the usual two at linear malls.

Teigler stood at the top mezzanine of the rotunda, looking down three stories below at the flow of bobble-headed people. They flowed past and around each other, carefully avoiding touching, reminding him of bees over a honeycomb. He sped up their movement in his mind. Not insects, dancers ... a ballet.

Cerberus provided Crossroads with mall cops on contract. Teigler had just completed a surprise inspection. Pleased with the results, he relaxed for a few minutes strolling with the other shoppers and inspecting the latest exhibits. The Hang Gliding & Paragliding Association had the run of the building, showing off colorful winged examples of equipment designed and built by their members. They also pushed calendars and membership brochures.

Teigler stopped to examine a delta-winged rigid-frame glider at rest on a shoulder-high scaffold, the fabric-covered wings cleverly cut and sewn to resemble eagle feathers. For a dollar, people could have their picture taken while strapped into the stationary flyer. A screen behind it painted with sky and clouds furthered the illusion.

He walked past the exhibit and moved to the rail. Close to noon on a Saturday, the numbers of shoppers and mall rats increased by the minute. The hand radio on his belt squawked as the guards near Sears reported the detention of a shoplifter. Something strange caught his eye. Two men—older teenagers rather—pushed a four-wheel cart into the ground-floor rotunda, a canvas masked the cargo. One of the wheels caught a corner of the cover and pulled it half off. The cart was full of double-stacked propane tanks with small, red bundles wired to the tops.

The hair on the back of his neck rose. Teigler grabbed a hand radio. "Zulu, zulu, zulu. This is Dragon. Possible bomb in the rotunda. Evacuation plan Bravo." He repeated the message.

"Break. Two men with a cart moving west from the rotunda. Suspects wearing black trench coats, one blond and one black hair." Light reflected from a shotgun barrel as the blond's leg parted the coat. "Suspects are armed."

He watched two of his mall security people approach. They pretended to not pay much attention to the men, hoping to get closer—it wasn't working. Teigler shouted as the men drew a cut-down shotgun and a pistol from beneath their trench coats. His mall cops pulled Glocks but couldn't fire through the crowd.

The other two cut loose into the shoppers. A man holding a toddler, a white-haired couple, and two middle-school girls dropped bloodied and lifeless. Blood sprayed across the closest people. They screamed and pushed into others still confused over what was happening, creating a human dam.

The firing continued. The men took time to pick specific targets. The security guards motioned people into stores or pushed them down.

An empty lane opened between the guards and the gunmen. The mall cops still hesitated. If they missed, their bullets would travel the length of the east wing and go into the store at the end. That area remained full of shoppers. The gunmen fired. Teigler felt a sinking feeling as a red blossom opened in the chest of a female guard. Her companion pulled her into the shelter of a large fiberglass planter.

Teigler's feet and hands went numb as the reptile in his brain rose. Their shared body ran back to the hang glider. Shoulders lifted the aluminum frame off the scaffold. Feet leaped up to the handrail and pushed off into forty-foot high empty space. The glider yawed and pitched as the reptile swung its body one way then another testing out how weight and position affected its flight. It mastered the wing quickly. Teigler remembered that some reptiles flew, pterosaurs and early-feathered ancestors of birds.

The hang glider did a wing over and descended. The two men saw a huge winged shadow move over them. The reptile dropped out of the glider into the open air, arms spread open with hooked fingers.

The 200-pound body falling at speed smashed the pair to the floor. The sawed-off shotgun twisted up into the armpit of the blond and went off, leaving the man's arm hanging by a tendril of flesh and muscle. The reptile left him to bleed out. Black Hair flipped over and brought the pistol up to his attacker's face.

The reptile's right hand flashed forward. It crammed the fleshy wing between its thumb and forefinger into the space between the gun's cocked hammer and firing pin. The blocked hammer fell with no result. The creature's pinioned hand closed over the trigger guard of the automatic and twisted it out of Black Hair's grip.

Not done yet, the man pulled a hand-held electronic detonator from his belt. He flipped the safety switch arming the device. Black Hair's thumb fumbled near the red firing button.

A reptilian foot slammed down, breaking his wrist. The device dropped and skittered across the mosaic ceramic floor. A second foot smashed down on Black Hair's neck, driving the Adam's apple into the spine. The reptile stepped back, crouched, and hissed, watching its victim flop. It found no signs of a renewed attack.

It looked around. Surrounded by too many people and their ammonia monkey smells, the reptile became nervous and retreated. Teigler took over, secured the detonator, and began to administer first aid to the gunmen's victims. Outside the mall, ambulance and police sirens grew louder.

~~~OOO~~~

Even though the herbs and amulet usually kept the reptile repressed, there was no stopping the myth. He had not conceived of how frequently snakes and reptiles interwove into religion and culture. Teigler received numerous gifts. The first, a wooden Vietnamese dragon some three feet long. The four-footed, five-clawed writhing body glowed green from individually carved scales of jade. The second, a reproduction of the Tantric Buddha guardian *Vajropani* cast in bronze and gilded with mercury, a snake draped around its neck. A soapstone carving of *Jormungand*, an offspring of Norse god Loki squatted on a shelf. The Vikings had believed it stretched around the world holding things together by biting its tail.

A Naga crystal paperweight, the half-man, half-snake of Hindu stories, graced his desk. Nagas were rumored to be able to take human shape and to predispose babies in the womb to be born with snake characteristics. Teigler wondered whether he had been so influenced at the time of his mother's pregnancy. It made a strange, goose-bump raising kind of sense. The latest acquisition, he disliked the most. It now graced the wall behind the receptionist where he would see it the least. Commissioned in Mexico, it featured a portrait of him on black velvet, standing with one hand held out, palm up. Coiled around his waist and chest with its head coming out over his right shoulder the Aztec *Quetzalcoatl,* as a feathered, winged serpent. To the grateful Mexican-American gift givers, he must have seemed like the *Quetzal,* flying the feathered hang glider down the Crossroad Mall's rotunda.

Overruling his wishes, Caber and Okie encouraged the gifts, believing the growing myth a benefit to the business. There might be no end of it. A check at the library showed hundreds of references to dragons, and reptiles in cultures around the world.

"Please fasten your seat belts," the pilot's voice jarred him out of his snake thoughts, "we will be landing in five minutes: 9:10 a.m."

~~~OOO~~~

Burke, carrying a soft-sided green duffle, and Teigler with black leather briefcase walked toward a stretch limo parked in the morning shadow of one of the small airport's hangars. As they grew nearer, Burke slowed allowing the distance between the two men to grow. As Teigler reached the car, two men with the build and waddle of football linemen stepped out from the hangar sidewall, jerked his arms back, and slammed him over the trunk. A quick efficient pat down relieved him of his wallet, keys, three-bladed pocketknife, and chrome Cross pen. One of the men kept Teigler pinned, the other addressed Burke.

"Give me your piece. After we leave, you get rid of the luggage."

Burke dropped the duffle near the briefcase. He handed over the gun grip first. "Make it look good," he said.

"Raise your arms," the man commanded. He punched Burke in the ribs, left then right. Teigler's former escort responded with grunts and clenched teeth. "That'll leave some nice bruises."

The lineman stepped forward and snapped Burke's head back with a punch to his left eye. "The shiner and a roll in the dirt should complete the picture for Angel. You fought like hell but were overcome."

The two men pushed their prisoner into the limo backseat, sandwiching him between them. Teigler looked around. Blacked out car windows and privacy shield between the backseat and the driver isolated the three. He heard no outside noise, which testified to a lot of soundproofing. Sprung soft, he could feel when the oversized vehicle maneuvered. After thirty minutes at highway speeds, the limo slowed, sometimes stopping then moving again. They must be in an urban area with traffic lights. The two musclemen sat silent, heavy solid biceps holding him like bronze elephant bookends. He needed help to get out of this.

"You guys ever play for the Packers?"

"No questions. No talking."

"Just looking for autographs."

A heavy knuckled hand smacked Teigler in one temple. His eyes watered. "No questions. No talking."

The threesome sat quiet for fifteen minutes, Teigler counting the time between stops. With the timing down, he reached up to pull the reptile-restricting amulet from around his neck. The man on the right slapped his hand.

"I just want my Saint Christopher medal."

The slapper raised a fist. The second man, who must have been Catholic, spoke for the first time. "Let the man have his medal, you want the Pope to get mad?"

An image of the broken-nosed, thick-necked man dressed in an altar boy's red cassock and white lace-trimmed surplice rose in his mind—no way—he grinned. Teigler pulled the gold anti-snake amulet and chain over his head and grasped it in both hands. He felt the reptile stir in the back of his brain, the barrier between it and his fear now removed. The limo stopped. He dropped the medal on the floor between his legs. As he bent to retrieve it, the reptile filled his body.

The two linemen tensed up, then relaxed as Teigler fumbled with the medal. The muscles in his body aligned. Feet pushed, calves and thighs, stomach and back muscles rippled. He shot up and back in the seat, arms out parallel to his body. The knife-edge of his forearms smacked into the throats of the two guards.

They grabbed their necks. Teigler's arms reversed. Hooked hands jammed into their groins, squeezing two sets of testicles in a vice-grip. The men gasped and bent forward, muscles locked in pain.

Teigler climbed over the convulsing man on the right, opened the car door, and stepped out into the street. He barely had time to shut the door before the blacked-out limo accelerated with the green light and crossed the intersection.

He watched it drive off down the next block and out of sight. It'd be a few more minutes before the occupants recovered. The reptile crouched, turned, nervous. Too many cars crowded the streets. Too many people packed the sidewalks—no way to secure a perimeter. The smell of chilies and cooked meat assaulted its nostrils. It hissed and twisted between a blue-faded Buick Riviera and a low rider candy apple red Impala. The reptile pushed its way through multicolored human traffic and moved into an alley. It quickly retreated into its safe corner of their brain, leaving Teigler in control.

So ... where was he? Vegas, surely. They must have landed at a private satellite airfield. He retained no hint of Angel's location, although he remembered her telephone number. He needed to move before the linemen returned. The kidnappers had kept his wallet and other possessions, therefore no money, credit cards, or identification. Not entirely without resources, Teigler stripped off his cobra-headed belt, unzipped a thin compartment built into its backside, and removed five tightly folded twenty-dollar bills.

Exiting the alley, he entered a nearby bodega, to be greeted with a pleasant, "Buenos dias, señor. ¿Como esta?"

"Esta bien, compadre, ¿Donde esta el centro, por favor? Ah ... estan los casinos?"

Teigler received directions to the downtown and an offer to get him a taxi. Politely refusing, he bought a bottle of water, a sandwich, and two candy bars. The food lasted as long as a brisk four-block walk, which placed him at a clothing store named Garcia's La Tienda de Ropa. *Los vaqueros*, jeans, *la camiseta*, a black t-shirt with an Aztec sundial on back and front, and *sandalias*, brown leather sandals went into a shopping basket. He also purchased a camouflage-patterned backpack to hide his regular clothes and shoes. A *sombrero basbal*, baseball hat, and *los anteojos de sol*, sunglasses selected from the displays near the register completed the disguise. Emerging from a changing room, he wandered to the front door, slipped on the sunglasses, and stepped out onto the sidewalk. Joining a stream of walkers, he adjusted body posture and stride to mimic their rhythm.

The late afternoon sun felt hot on his neck as he entered Caesars Palace. Recently remodeled, the twenty-year-old grand dame casino retained its original class. Teigler wandered among the one-armed bandits. The dinner hour hadn't reduced the traffic much. A fog of cigarette smoke and stale human perspiration pinched his nostrils. One-arm bandits glittered, flashed, and belled. Plump overdressed, over-jeweled, over-painted women inserted coins and pulled levers to some kind of assembly line rhythm.

The pace broke occasionally when they stopped to take a drink or to squawk when rattling, clinking payouts occurred. He popped coins in a row of nickel slots working his way towards a bank of wall phones. With every pull of a crank, he watched for anyone that might have tailed him or was displaying too much interest. He hesitated for a few minutes while a maintenance man set up a ladder and replaced a light bulb. The show went on twenty-four hours a day with repair people establishing temporary little islands in the ebb and flow of dreaming, drugged humanity.

The second from the last machine paid back his investment. He scooped fifty dollars worth of coins into the backpack. Teigler left the stool and wandered slowly over to a phone. His heartbeat rose as he inserted money and punched in Angel's number.

"Hello," responded a female voice, rusty from crying and a lack of sleep.

"Angel, this is Rod." He paused, heard a gasp. "Are you alone?"

She caught on quickly. "No." Teigler listened as she ordered one, maybe two others out of the room.

"I was abducted ..." Angel tried to interrupt. "Hold on, let me finish. I managed to escape. Where is Burke?"

He reported in after the kidnapping and she sent him home to recover from the beating.

"That man and maybe others on your staff are working for the other side, whoever that is. Here's what I want you to do. Have you had your office and telephone checked for bugs, microphones?"

Angel indicated Burke had supervised a sweep a month ago.

"I want you to go to his office and call me back on his phone at this number (731-7130). It's unlikely he bugged his own phone."

~~~OOO~~~

Angel sat behind the wheel of a Chevy Malibu rental car, her blonde hair covered by a long black wig and a pastel-pink headscarf. Dark makeup, borrowed from her Mexican housekeeper, hid her pale skin. She and Maria had exchanged clothes and identities. They giggled together as the gringa disappeared and a larger-hipped (with the help of some padding) woman of obvious mestizo descent took her place. The new Maria escaped with little notice by the watchers. Only a brief thought crossed the mind of the leader of the stakeout, the housekeeper was leaving past her usual quitting time.

Forty-five minutes later, waiting at a red light at the corner near the bus terminal, she flashed her brights three times. A man stepped out of the crowd and entered the passenger side of the car. She caught a brief illuminated glimpse as the interior lights switched on then off as the door closed. Teigler appeared much as she remembered, even down to the five o'clock bristle on his cheeks. He looked a little thinner with numerous white highlights on his temples.

Teigler relaxed back into the car's bench seat. He hadn't recognized Angel through her disguise. He sniffed. She smelled the same. The spicy thyme and rosemary scent of Pear's soap tickled his nostrils. The reptile's eyelids opened, its head cocked to one side. A link to her past, Pear's soap had been manufactured for over two hundred years. It must have been one of few familiar comforts to a woman finding herself in a strange and distant future.

Stopped in the back parking lot of the Flamingo Hilton, the couple embraced. Through tears of relief, Angel told her story. She had done well since arriving in Vegas eighteen years ago. Plying *the trade* by herself the first three years allowed her to accumulate the capital to expand. She became the first to organize a high-class escort service. Angel attracted the best talent with a package of benefits and schooling in the courtesan arts previously unheard of in the market. Students displaying a high degree of proficiency worked in an on-call only agency. Others trolled for business at the casinos and clubs.

In the next two decades, Angel gained control of seventy-five percent of the escort business and fifty percent of the casino trade. The profits rose proportionately. However, as with any such nuggets, someone always wanted a cut. For a year, she resisted increasing pressure from a man who first tried to buy his way in and then resorted to rougher means. Angel received threats. Some of the girls took beatings. She investigated through her mob connections. They knew Tommy Bassiloni. A distant cousin to one of the Chicago Mafia leaders, he had been exiled from his home turf for being too greedy and ham-handed. The locals tolerated him as long as he didn't impinge on their regular business. However, if Angel found a way to put him down, they would not object. In their opinion, the man was a loose cannon. The situation, of course, continued to deteriorate.

"Rod, two days ago they kidnapped our daughter."

Teigler caught the pronoun. "*Our?*"

Angel began to cry again. "I didn't want to tell you. I never meant to tell you."

She waited. Teigler remained silent.

"Carrie's almost eighteen, tall, my coloration, except your eyes—very independent. I've had her home schooled and tutored. She's scheduled to start the fall semester at Berkeley."

Angel rattled on, afraid to stop for his reaction. "Carrie's got your athletic aptitude, a dancer and gymnast. Well liked, except she can go into strange rages when threatened. I had to pull her out of public school. Her psychiatrist prescribed tranquilizers. She's my only link to my past and you. You must help get our baby back."

The reptile in the man's brain stirred, curled into a ball, vertical pupiled eyes glowed as it remembered the mating. Teigler felt horror—whose daughter was this? Had his contribution to the child carried strange seeds? Would everything he touched be debased?

Teigler struggled to digest the flood of comment and failed. He mentally regained focus. "What does Tommy want?"

"The business, all of it."

"Are you willing to give it up to get her back?"

"I've worked for years to get this far. I came from nothing, owned nothing—I can't go back to nothing now. Besides, he isn't going to release her so I can go to the police with a witness."

"Do you know if she is still ... unhurt?"

"I talked to her earlier today on the phone. They'll keep her alive until they get the papers signed. Their attorney will have them ready in two days. Once I've signed over the business, I'll be as good as dead. Tommy doesn't leave loose ends."

~~~OOO~~~

Angel and Teigler sat in a cheap musty motel room located on the outskirts of south Vegas. They had initiated a plan earlier to see if anyone in her top circle, besides Burke, was on Bassiloni's payroll. Separate calls connected her to Bill, her in-house accountant; Jake, the second in command of security; and to her private secretary, Anne. Sworn to secrecy, all three had been notified that Angel would be meeting Teigler. Each were told a different location and time. The pair of plotters staked out the Kung Fu restaurant at Third and Fremont at eight p.m., the City Lites Dinner Theater at nine, and the Riviera's Café Noir at ten. Bassiloni's men only showed up at the last location. Anne and Burke would not be allowed into the office tomorrow. Jake changed all the locks and conducted a new sweep for bugs.

Teigler remembered Angel didn't sit around during an emergency. A mob friend and regular customer from her early days leaked the location of Tommy's headquarters, an old mining property, fifty miles out into the desert. She procured copies of the plans and an aerial shot from the county planning office.

Teigler sat at the motel desk and looked through pictures of his daughter: a baby in a pink bassinet, a laughing toddler in flowered Oshkosh bibs, a serious preteen in a leotard and jazz shoes wielding top hat and cane, and a contemporary picture of a young woman in a black cocktail dress with swept-back hair and well-shaped eyebrows. Her nails caught his eye, longer than usual and painted blood red, all filed to a point. The reptile inside blinked approvingly. All pretty pictures, he thought. A brief flare of fatherly feeling crept over him. Teigler hadn't believed himself capable of such feelings. Though given his history, it was better he hadn't been a factor in her life.

He gave up trying to bond with pictures. Gently placing the scrapbook on a side table, he turned to the problem at hand. They must achieve the element of surprise, a force multiplier. They needed a rolling series of surprises—one unexpected event generating another. There must be no way the enemy could anticipate or react in a timely fashion. He studied the aerial pictures and floor plan. A gated gravel road branched fifty yards off the main county highway and allowed vehicle access to the property. The most obvious approach would be heavily guarded. He would come overland on foot.

Improvements to the site consisted of a cavernous corrugated steel structure used to store mining equipment—it had a small, one-story office attached to its front. Between the office and the front gate stood a tall radio antenna supported by guide wires. The mine entrance was a hundred yards off to the rear. It looked to be barred and locked. A ten-foot high chain-link fence topped with barbwire surrounded the entire complex. Only two gates allowed entrance, one at the road with guard shack, and one at the rear, near the mine entrance. Strategically placed light poles lit the perimeter at night. Add some alert guards and it would be a tough nut to crack. There would need to be distractions. A plan was beginning to form. He started scribbling a list of needed things.

~~~OOO~~~

Teigler shut off the slow chugging engine and stepped out of the dune buggy. The light atop the mine radio tower blinked on and off about a mile away. He would go the remaining distance on foot. The cool desert night and his excitement raised goose bumps. He checked his equipment one more time. Apache-style deerskin moccasins strapped up to the knees allowed him to move noiselessly through the scrub. Repeatedly washed cotton pants and shirt dyed to match the desert dirt permitted maximum range of movement without making any rustling noises. Several layers of athletic tape covered his forearms. Soaked in water, the tape became a hard armor-like cast—useful weapons in close combat.

Completing the gear, a soft-brimmed bush hat covered his head, while all exposed skin became paint-camouflaged with the products of an army surplus kit. A black L.L. Bean combination hunter's watch and compass graced one wrist. Strapped upside down on Teigler's upper left chest rested a sheathed KA-BAR knife with a seven-inch blackened blade. He had spent an hour honing the razor-sharp edge to his satisfaction.

Wrapped several times around his waist, a gray muslin cummerbund held three tiny voice recorder chips and a pressed flat quarter brick of C-4 with a radio detonator. The layers of tightly bound cloth would double as bandages in the event of an injury. Grabbing a canvas shoulder bag from the vehicle, Teigler moved off in the direction of the tower's blinking aviation warning light.

He slow-trotted through the darkness. Fully developed night vision allowed him to move around clumps of cactus and waist high creosote bushes. No moon, but countless stars filled the great bowl overhead. As his muscles warmed, he moved faster. The reptile felt pleasure at the working of arm and leg muscles. It leaned the body forward to get more speed. It felt awkward, remembered there was no tail to counterbalance, and eased back into the less efficient primate gait. Even so, the pair's exhilaration grew as dark shadows of rock and vegetation flashed by on both sides.

The creature rushed forward, the target swelling larger. Ten yards before entering the bubble of light from the perimeter lamps, a shadow dropped prone and began a slow crawl-stop, crawl-stop to the rear gate. Taking advantage of brush and irregularities in the ground to shield his approach, Teigler froze every few yards to check for any movement both inside and outside the compound.

Periodically, a quarter-sized flare illuminated the face of a guard in the shack at the front gate—a man musing about the wonders of the universe instead of paying attention to the perimeter. Teigler allowed himself a moment of envy. He gave up smoking over twenty years ago, but still felt the desire. Only habit forming, they said, not narcotic—my ass it isn't.

His eyes spotted and followed the power lines in from the highway. As in the aerial shot, the last pole hosted a transformer. The power source for the complex was its Achilles heel, the line of poles being outside the chain-link fence. He wiggled over and removed the C-4 from his waist. The smell of tar on the sun-baked wooden pole almost made him sneeze. Teigler planted the charge low on its inside face. When it blew, all power to the complex would go and the pole would fall across the fence, taking it down. This would leave another escape route, if needed.

Checking again for patrolling guards and sensing none, he wiggled to the back gate. Secured by a thick logging chain and padlock, he recognized the double-keyed lock as almost unpickable. A wrap-around steel shield protected the shackle from hacksaws and bolt cutters. Such high tech, just what his company would have recommended. It would take too long and too much noise to defeat it. Teigler reached into the shoulder bag and brought out his answer to the problem, a compact stainless steel vacuum bottle with a sprayer tip. Angel's folks had bought it from a surgical supply house at his request.

The flat black Dewar thermos contained a liter of liquid nitrogen. Normally used by doctors to remove warts and carcinomas, the fluid made normal materials, especially metal, brittle and fragile. He first saw its properties demonstrated in high school chemistry class, when the teacher froze a hot dog. A hammer blow and the normally soft sausage shattered into rock-hard fragments.

Teigler lay in the dust and gravel near the gate trying to resist scratching his nose. He checked his watch. The first of the distractions should be forthcoming. Right on time, an old Ford Fairmont pulled off the two-lane highway onto the gravel shoulder, right rear tire flapping.

A man exited, cursed, and slammed the driver's door. As he raised the trunk, a woman yelled something out of the passenger side window. They argued back and forth. She turned up the car radio. A Kingman station blared country music. He recognized Dolly Parton's voice belting out "Rocky Top."

The guard at the gate flicked his cigarette, a little meteor spun in a short arc and popped out a burst of sparks as it hit the ground. He phoned for reinforcements. Two men with rolled-up shirt sleeves stepped out onto the stoop, and glared at the couple.

While they watched the man fumble with the jack and yell back at the woman, Teigler raised the sprayer. It hissed. Frigid liquid not found in nature coated the chain. He shut off the bottle and jerked the chain, a link cracked into fragments. He pulled the gate open and slipped through, closing it behind him. Covered by the continuing argument from the couple at the highway, the invader slunk across the open space and worked his way between the parked cars and the office wall. Body pressed against the metal siding, Teigler looked through a window's skewed curtains.

The entire inside space consisted of a large open room, sparsely furnished. The remnants of an interrupted poker game decorated a round table. Blue-backed bicycle cards fanned face down, high-necked brown beer bottles, and small stacks of white, red, and blue plastic chips marked the spots of four players. Two men remained seated, impatiently drinking beer. A man with wide shoulders and dark, slicked back hair sat in an overstuffed chair, whiskey glass on the table beside him. Probably Bassiloni. A TV with the sound set low flashed reports from the news channels.

The refrigerator in the corner by Teigler's window turned on, vibrating the sheet metal wall and window glass. He stiffened as he spotted his daughter lying dormant on a twin bed with her wrists and ankles bound to the bedposts. He wondered if she had been drugged. One hand moved. Sharp nails made a sawing motion across the cloth binding.

He smiled—still some spirit in her. Teigler slipped back along the corrugated wall until he found a metal door leading into the connected garage. Liquid nitrogen on the deadlock snapped the bolt and allowed him to gain entrance. He waited a few minutes to maximize his night vision.

Around him, squatting on the concrete slab floor, abandoned mining equipment rested like giant insects. Massive trucks with dump beds that once hauled ore to mill sites, conveyer buckets, an enclosed cab tractor with a scoop bucket, and some unrecognizable specialized machinery slept in neat lines under the two-story roof. One of the machines resembled a thirty-foot-long low-slung scorpion. A large fixed scoop formed the first ten feet of the vehicle. Two gathering arms operated by hydraulic pistons were mounted, one on each end of the scoop. The operator drove the machine into piles of loose ore blasted out of a vein's face, and used the arms to pull the fragmented rock into the scoop for transportation to the surface.

Teigler found the inside door into the front office unlocked—time for distraction number two. He detonated the C-4, a loud bang shook the building and rattled the windows—the lights went out. Entering the now blackened room, he turned sharp left and counted off the distance to the bed. He almost got smacked in the face. Carrie had one hand free.

"Your mother sent me. I'm here to get you out," he whispered.

She relaxed. He pulled the KA-BAR. The knife blade sliced through her remaining bonds as though they were tissue paper. Around them, men shouted and knocked over furniture. A glass shattered on the floor. Father and daughter went through the door into the storage building just as the cursing became inspired. Cigarette lighters and a flashlight flared. The men spotted them.

Well, Teigler thought, Clausewitz had it right. *No battle plan survives first contact with the enemy.*

Outside, immediately after the explosion put out the perimeter lights, the couple in the car pulled silenced weapons. The man put a 30-06-rifle slug through the chest of the gangster in the guard shack, whose flashlight provided an excellent aiming point. Almost simultaneously, the woman fired a burst of nine millimeter rounds from an MP-5 submachine gun aimed at the front door of the office where the two men watched. One went down with a bullet in the hip and the other caught one in the neck. Those guns had a tendency to lift their barrels when on automatic fire. Two of the slugs pierced the front door and caused the people inside to duck.

The rifleman braced his weapon across the hood of the Fairmont. He peered through the light-gathering night scope mounted on his customized Remington 700 and fired just-to-be-sure rounds into the two huddled bodies on the front stoop.

Inside, Bassiloni shouted, "Get the girl, they'll have to stop."

His remaining two men followed the fugitives into the cavernous storage building. Teigler hoisted Carrie into the cab of one of the trucks. He pulled the tiny voice recorders from the cummerbund folds, switched them on, and pitched them in different directions.

He waited. Bassiloni's men worked their flashlights around as they moved to cover the exits from the building.

A tinny voice near one of the pursuers shouted out, "Freeze ... FBI! Drop your weapons."

The closest man turned and fired a shotgun.

A second voice shouted, "Drop 'em! Drop 'em! You're under arrest!"

The second crook blasted away in a new direction with a pistol.

A third voice cried, "Take 'em down!" and what sounded like hundreds of gunshots, both single and automatic, came from all directions. Echoes off the corrugated sheet metal walls and roof raised the intensity of the sounds to ear-shattering levels. The two mob gunmen crouched, emptied their weapons, firing at shouting voices and imagined silhouettes.

Teigler moved from machine to machine, starting their motors to increase the confusion. Sitting in the driver's seat of the scorpion-armed ore loader, he watched the two Mafioso come to a stop, fumbling to reload weapons. He recognized the two musclemen who had kidnapped him earlier. With a grim smile, he pressed the accelerator and pulled levers until the gathering arms activated.

The vehicle lunged forward. The pair turned, one tried to raise a shotgun, the other slipped and fell. Spines cracked, heads flew back as metal arms hit them from behind and swept them into the open cargo bay. The lower edge of the scoop caught one at the ankles and the other at the knees. Sharpened by the action of thousands of past loads of rock abrading metal, the machine cut through flesh and bone without pause, leaving amputated legs and feet twitching on the floor. The men screamed at first, but not even a soft whimper remained when Teigler shut off the machine.

He hopped out of the cockpit and moved back to where he had left Carrie. A heavy body materialized out of the dark and smashed into him. Teigler felt a pistol barrel bruise his side. A muffled bang, a metal-jacketed round pierced his left pectoral muscle, grazed a rib, and exited through his scapula.

The man-reptile honked, took advantage of the enemy's forward motion. It bent low at the knees and moved its good arm between the attacker's legs. The creature straightened, the arm lifted, the attacker sailed up and over, landing on the concrete floor, stunned. The gun flew out of his hand and clattered off to stop beneath a miniature caterpillar tractor. Weakness grew in Teigler's left arm. Dizzy from the wound, he felt like vomiting.

The morning sun's glow began to come through the skylights providing enough illumination for Teigler to recognize the man on the floor as Tommy Bassiloni. The man leaped up, pulled brass knuckles out of his pocket, and bear hugged his opponent. His fist battered Teigler's ribs, one of which cracked. One punch to the head with those nucks would break his skull like a smashed egg, and the fight would be over. Teigler hung on.

He grasped Bassiloni tighter, smelled whiskey-soured breath. In this position, he couldn't get to his knife. He couldn't maintain his grip long. The reptile provided some energy.

One-handed, Teigler pulled the sprayer out of its bag. He smacked the metal cylinder against his enemy's temple. Bassiloni's head flew back. The sprayer hissed liquid nitrogen, as cold as the frictionless vacuum between planets, into his opponent's eyes.

Bassiloni shouted in a quavering falsetto, "It burns! It burns!"

He released Teigler and stumbled back, hands to his face. The empty stainless steel thermos bonked on the floor and rolled away. A wrung-out Teigler dropped to his knees.

A slim lithe body leaped off the hood of an ore truck and clung to Bassiloni's back. Hands clawed the man's face. Fists smacked his frozen eyes. Ice-solid dry-crumbles of eyeball ran like sand from their sockets. The man's screaming grew to high pitched squeals.

Carrie shrieked in harmony, exposed her teeth, and dropped her head to Bassiloni's neck. She bit down, shook her head; bright arterial liquid and a chunk of flesh spun out of her mouth. Her tormentor collapsed, blood pumping out onto the floor. The she-creature stood over his body—head tossed back, flexing clawed hands—open mouth giving a nonhuman victory squeal.

"Carrie," Teigler mouthed softly as she spun to assess the threat.

"Carrie," he said again, addressing the repressed human in her.

She sensed his weakness, crouched, and stalked forward hissing. He marshaled all his strength, filled his lungs, and shouted in the command voice he honed in combat, "Carrie! Stand down!"

The reptilian rictus faded from her face. She started shaking, then recovered and walked to his side. He leaned against her, arm around her waist, as they moved to the ore truck cab. Teigler felt the warm support of well-toned dancer's muscles.

The cummerbund now wrapped around his wounded shoulder, Teigler watched from the passenger seat as Carrie slammed the massive R series Mack dump truck into gear, floored the accelerator, and blew out through the side of the storage building. Behind them, the roof collapsed.

The truck's four-foot tires rooster-tailed gravel the length of the driveway before crashing through the chain-link double gate, leaving their frames bent into abstract shapes. Acquiring Angel's folks in the Fairmount, they drove toward Vegas.

In the truck cab, two pairs of personalities, human and reptile, admired each other.

Reflections

Reflections in the shaving mirror,
my body crouched in jungle fatigues,
blood splatter on my cheeks.
The rifle breech spins golden brass.

Reflections in river ice.
Under the bridge, my comrades
in fusty ragged uniforms huddle
by a smoky barrel fire.

Reflections on the curved glass
of my intravenous bottle.
Drip, drip, drip,
Agent Orange seeks its level.

Reflections in my car hood's
flaking blue-pearl paint
of a speeding 18-wheeler bumper,
a gift of suicide by trucker.

Reflections in the sunglasses
of a fur-voiced priest.
The sound of gravel
ratting on my hollow coffin top.

Toe Poppers

arrie crouched, one knee down, behind the three-foot thick trunk of an old-growth ponderosa pine. She scanned the trail behind them in slow sweeps, eyes seeking any nearby threats before checking the middle distance, and then as far out as she could see. If someone hid in the forest or along the trail, they would have to be masters of camouflage to elude her scrutiny. She peered around the rough-barked tree trunk to see her father, Rod Teigler, still hunkered over the carcass of a deer.

The man remained in the same frozen position. One hand rested on the creature's bloody neck fur, the other gripped the hilt of a sheathed eight-inch bowie knife, duct-taped upside down on the left shoulder strap of his backpack. A stray breeze carried the mixed ammonia-shit smell of shredded innards. Body torn apart, something had broken the mule deer's neck, snapped off antlers, and ripped out the liver and heart.

The early morning shadows of northern Montana pines, hemlocks, larches, and fir trees suppressed sunlight and sounds, leaving the space at their bases dark and silent. Carrie lifted the anti-shine leather flap off the face of her watch—there was something wrong. Rod—she still had trouble thinking of him as father—hadn't displayed more than a muscle twitch or flare of nostrils in the last ten minutes. She leaned back.

Six months had passed since her long lost old man, reacting to her mother's emergency call, rescued her from probable death by a bastard offshoot of the Las Vegas Mafia. During that episode, it became apparent she was indeed her father's daughter, as the inner berserker reptile she had inherited rose to kill the gang leader. Afterwards, mother hired father and his security company, Cerberus, to train her in self-defense and physical security. They uncovered natural talent. She could drop a bullet right into the bull's-eye with any gun placed in her hands, and her dancer's muscles and moves translated easily into the company's brand of mixed martial arts. This wilderness trip was both a graduation exercise and an opportunity for them both to know each other better. However, the first two days Carrie had gained little insight into her father.

The route of their outback hike had been determined by Orienteering Gaia, an international not-for-profit organization promoting backcountry treks. They selected her father, as the CEO of a large donor company, and a companion of his choice, to test a new route before confirming it as the site of their next annual event. Carrie discovered orienteering was a competitive international sport, combining cross-country racing with precise navigation. Participants use only a compass and map to plot paths through unfamiliar terrain, stopping at control points along the way—to verify a completed control point, an orienteer uses a punch hanging from the control flag to mark his or her registration card, the specific route between "controls" is left entirely up to the competitors.

Using the tickets provided by OG, they flew Delta Airlines to Missoula, Montana, and then went by private plane to Libby, a small town of 2,600 in the middle of the Kootenai National Forest. A waiting car and driver took the pair and their gear to a trailhead about six miles west. The trail initially followed Cedar Creek, a tributary of the Kootenai River, past the two lakes it fed to its mountain headwaters.

The first day, they made the five miles to Lower Cedar Lake and reasonable rainbow trout fishing—8 to 10 pounders. The fillets, shaken in a bag of flour and spices, sprinkled with slivered almonds, and pan fried over a wood fire formed the centerpiece of their first wilderness meal. The old man surprised her with a couple of miniature airline-size bottles of Chardonnay wine cooled in the lake. For a vegetable, he had collected two cups of the tender fiddleheads of forest ferns, sautéing them in a small amount of oil. Whether it was the food or the mountain air at 6,000 feet, she responded to his questions with a lot of personal stories and secrets. Mostly a monologue, Carrie hesitated to push him to open up.

They spent a second day and night on the shore of Upper Cedar Lake, before pushing into the unmarked Cabinet Wilderness Area, stopping frequently to consult the contour-lined OG geological survey map. Although they used military-grade lensatic compasses, her father also showed her how to determine direction during the day with a shadow-tip and during the night by locating the North Star. Day three contained lessons on how to make cordage out of bark, and how to use the cords to make animal snares and fishing line. Under supervision, she started fires with flint and steel, and foraged for the edible roots and tubers of spring beauty, columbine, and bitterroot to supplement freeze-dried rations from their packs.

Carrie learned many things, but the most important questions remained unanswered. Who was this strange father? How did they resemble each other? Would he let her in? Not right away though, she thought, clenching her fists. Today, they practiced silence on the trail, using Teigler's made-up sign language, a blend of the military hand signals of Army Long Range Reconnaissance Patrols and Native American sign language. His last flurry of signals had posted her to watch their back trail while he examined the dead deer to their front.

Fifteen minutes passed. Carrie peeked around the tree. He remained frozen in position. She made a last slow scan of the countryside. Advancing a step at a time, she stopped about five feet from man and carcass. Sweat slipped down from Teigler's hairline to form heavy drops, which dripped off his eyebrows and nose. Patches of dark wetness made Rorschach blot patterns on the chest and underarms of his green-dyed t-shirt.

After another long look to make sure they were alone, Carrie stooped and picked up a thumb-thick dead branch. She bent forward and poked her companion's backpack. The man's body came alive. The heavy Bowie flashed out of its sheath. He lunged, and sliced the branch neatly and cleanly into two pieces just a few inches from her hand. She stumbled back and fell, avoiding a second slash. Propped on her elbows, she stared into eyes black and cold as obsidian. She gasped. The eyes faded into a warm brown.

"Carrie, what the hell are you doing?"

Teigler lifted her with one hand twisted in the loose cloth of her shirt. They ran back, left the trail, and settled behind a fallen log. He stabbed the Bowie into the ground, raised a hand, and bit the side of his index finger.

"Rod ... Dad, we have to talk. What happened there?"

He held up a hand. "Give me a sec."

"Jesus, don't hide from me anymore."

"I was back in Nam. The death smell, that death smell—the rotting animal flesh took me back to Vietnam."

"Tell me!"

Teigler pulled an army green bandana from a backpack pocket, wiped his eyes and forehead.

"They sent me to Kontum on temporary assignment. They needed someone expendable. I took along heavy firepower. An armory sergeant, a relative of your uncle Caber, provided me with an experimental fully automatic version of the M-14. The design included a muzzle stabilizer, a straight-in-line stock with rubber butt pad, fold-down bipod legs, and fore and rear handgrips. The twelve-pound beauty could make four-inch groupings at twenty-five meters, and seven-inch ones at a hundred. The eighteen 7.62 MM rounds in each magazine consisted of a mix of ball, tracer, and armor piercing rounds.

"A colonel from Military Intelligence met me at the helicopter pad. We sat in an empty perimeter bunker away from prying ears."

"Lieutenant Teigler, I believe someone in the command structure holds an intense and genuine fucking dislike of you. Only Sun Tzu's perfect warrior is apt to survive this mission."

"I'm sure you're right, at least about the first part."

"So, here's the deal. We need to stop the stream of pure heroin which is finding its way through Kontum Province into the hands of GIs all over South Vietnam. Guys hooked on one hundred percent junk go crazy when rotated back to the States where the local dealers dilute the product. In the war zone, they are ineffective warriors who frequently fail their units in combat.

"Originating in Burma, our spy planes have tracked drug shipments being transported on boats down the Mekong River past Thailand, then overland across the toe of Laos. They emerge north of here in the vicinity of Dak To, a part of the friendly Republic of South Vietnam."

"How do they get past the North Vietnamese and the VC?"

"Palms get greased, frequently in the form of war supplies that come down with the shipments. Also, our enemy is well aware of the addiction's ability to decrease their opponents' combat effectiveness."

"I imagine our allies here also share in the largess."

"Not only the locals, but some of our own soldiers must be cooperating. At any rate, you will do a helicopter insertion into the jungle tomorrow with one of our long range recon patrols — five men plus you."

"Well, at least they'll know the territory and watch my back."

"You'd best watch your own back. The three most experienced members of tomorrow's LRRP returned from two previous missions hauling the dead bodies of your predecessors."

"Well, third time's the charm, isn't it?"

~~~OOO~~~

In the darkness almost a week later, Teigler remembered the colonel's warning. He lay prone in a cutout in the grass and brush lining the top of a saddleback ridge. His M14E2 rested on its bipod, muzzle aimed at a well-used trail seventy meters below. Extra magazines rested to his right, butt down within easy reach. On the other side, he positioned the aluminum tubes of three parachute flares. To his left lay a dead member of the patrol. To his right, the last two live ones lay trussed with the Army's version of duct tape. One squirmed and let out a muffled complaint. Teigler drew his KA-BAR and cut a four-inch slice across the man's cheek. The warm blood ran down in dribbles. The man quivered and sank into silence.

Getting here had been a nightmare. On the second day after insertion, one of the patrol members stepped into a *pungi* pit, sharpened shit-covered stakes went through an ankle and calf. An unhurt man was detached to take him back, leaving Teigler alone with the grinning threesome and a suspicion that they had made this happen. On day four, he escaped attempts to lure him into a spiked pit and a deadfall. The trio were unaware that being red-green colorblind meant Teigler saw booby trap camouflage as off-color blotches dropped on neutral groundcover.

The three let their agitation show on day five as they neared the Laos section of the drug route. After a C-ration supper of beans with meatballs, Teigler retrieved a roll of toilet paper from his pack, left his rifle, and wandered into the rainforest. Twenty paces in, he hung the roll in plain sight on a bush and faded into the undergrowth. The soft scrape of jungle fatigues against elephant ear leaves approached and passed him. Teigler slid through the low grass coming up behind a puzzled man holding the toilet paper in one hand and a machete in the other.

A knee bent the traitor's body back. A hand went over his mouth and nostrils. As an eight-inch blade spiked the man's right kidney and twisted, Teigler whispered, "Here I am."

Circling the campsite, he stopped and kneeled. Sweat dripped, soaking the ripstop nylon fatigues covering his thighs. The reptilian thing within him stirred and sent his pulse racing. Something was trying to get out. A mindless rage swelled up from his spine and lower brain. The knuckles on his hand turned white as Teigler squeezed the handle of the machete liberated from the dead traitor. The struggle resolved itself—back in control, he silently crept close enough to hear the remaining two talk.

"Shouldn't we wait to be sure?"

"No, the fucking lieutenant is dead. It's getting dark. Put up the all-clear sign. Let's get our money."

The man pulled a small folded banner from a pocket and shook it out—a gold star on a red background—the North Vietnamese flag. He left to hang it from a tree near the trail. Returning to find his friend stretched out as if napping, he stepped close and bent down. The flat blade of a machete smacked against the cloth boonie hat covering his head.

~~~OOO~~~

No moon, no stars, the jungle squatted in blackness. Lack of light did not affect the thousands of rainforest-spawned insects. Teigler let them crawl, bite, and tickle. Slapping sounds would carry too far. Fortunately, most of the six and eight-legged visitors were just exploring. Many legs moving in unison pinched the skin on his right forearm. Slowly moving his left hand cross-body, he curled his fingers and flicked off a four-inch long poisonous centipede. The reddish-brown bug's bite was not the kind of distraction he needed now.

Teigler felt a tremor come up through the ground to tingle his belly skin. He listened. There was a whisper of sound coming from up the trail. The vibration grew. Something heavy was coming. The noise level increased, became a plodding, marching rhythm.

He raised one of the flares and popped it. The rocket shot up. A burning phosphorus star dangled from a parachute. The scene below on the trail made no sense. Three huge mirrors floated ten feet above the ground reflecting the drifting flare.

Teigler heard shouts. Upturned faces reflected the light. His finger on the trigger tightened. Starting in the middle, he fired repetitive bursts of six to eight rounds. Mechanically, he reloaded as each magazine emptied. The rifle's muzzle moved right and then left. The screams of men and … animals came back. Animals?

He fired another flare. Lying on its side, one of the huge shadowy shapes became illuminated. It was an elephant. He resumed firing. The damn fools were using elephants to pack opium and supplies—the phantom mirrors were corrugated metal building sheets strapped to their backs.

Teigler heard trumpeting sobs from the rear elephant. He moved the gun over and fired a burst into its massive body. The noise stopped. He tried not to think about the way armor-piercing rounds would devastate so much flesh.

Teigler let up on the trigger, in the quiet aftermath, he heard rustling in the brush—a few of the Viet Cong remained alive. The M-14E2 tracers had guided the survivors to him. Leaving the gun smoking on its bipod, he crawled backwards into the underbrush, leaving the last three members of the patrol, two squirming and one quiet. He drew his family's .45-caliber pistol. Three VC rushed up from the left flank and emptied Ak-47s into their three collaborators.

Teigler felt very light-headed, his vision grew dark. Something snakelike wiggled up from deep inside him, filled him like water fills a vessel. The pistol fell to the ground. The VC jumped and screamed as a hissing wraith leaped out of the bush.

A machete blurred down on one fumbling to reload. A head popped off, spraying blood into the eyes and faces of his comrades. The blinded men had time to take a breath, their final one. The chopping of steel on bone continued long after the last shriek.

~~~OOO~~~

Teigler stared at his shaking fingers, rubbed his chin, and said, "That … that was the second time the berserker reptile personality completely took over."

Carrie's stomach churned, remembering her own bloody experience. She placed a canteen in her father's hand.

"Where does it come from? Did you inherit it from your parents?"

"No, there's no hint of anything like this in the family tree. I think it all began with army enhancement experiments." He paused, took a drink.

"Four of us volunteered for a program designed to increase our physical capabilities."

"I've read the military did a lot of crazy human experiments during the Vietnam War, even using LSD and other drugs."

"It wasn't like that. It seemed pretty tame. We recited nonsense syllables and strings of incomprehensible numbers while watching complicated asymmetric patterns flowing across a screen. Periodically, we took written tests. They exercised us until we became exhausted, and then we repeated the numbers and patterns again and again."

"So, what did they accomplish?"

"It seemed at the time the experiment had failed. The scientists intended to create new more efficient brain circuits. They hoped for a fifteen to twenty percent increase in muscular reaction times, better hearing, improved day and night vision, and enhanced detection of scents, all combined with a higher pain threshold."

"None of the training took?"

"The general-in-charge closed out the experiment. After administering a 'no-tell' oath, they transferred us to regular units. Except for a slight detectable increase in learning ability, nothing materialized."

Carrie picked up the doubt in his voice. "But you think otherwise."

"I believe the circuitry is there, just not assessable by the conscious human mind. When the reptilian portion of the brain takes over, it has access to those enhancements. And, I think as an unintended consequence, the program's conditioning opened the way for the ancient snake in us to rise."

"I wasn't part of the experiment. Why am I affected?"

"I'm only speculating, but the Army was always giving us vaccinations and inoculations. They may have injected us with something which locked the changes into our DNA, allowing me to pass the curse on to you. Maybe they wanted to raise new generations of improved soldiers—at no cost to the government."

Around the fire that night, the pair ate reconstituted Chili Mac with sides of dried apricots and dates. They sipped from a hipflask of Jack Daniels while

Teigler told Carrie his life story mixed with tales of their common ancestors, both the noble ones and the black sheep. Laughter and tears alternated.

~~~OOO~~~

At the start of the next day's trek, the hikers paused briefly at the deer corpse. Flies rose to greet them. Teigler huffed the gut-liquefying smell out of his nose and grimaced as the reptile in him spasmed. Although he knew better, he wondered if he himself might have killed the creature in a forgotten berserker moment. The way the body had been butchered and then mutilated—very wrong for a cougar, wolf, or bear kill. The hair pricked on his neck. He did a 360-degree slow scan. Someone watched them. His knuckles faded to white as he raised his hiker's staff and smacked it against the ground.

Carrie spoke, "You feel it too."

"Let's move on. Stay alert."

Father and daughter moved cross-country, stopping at intervals to consult the map. They found a control point and recorded the location and time in a logbook. Deep in the mountains, they discovered an open meadow forty yards across where the next flag should have been. Low tree stumps in the open area showed chain-saw marks, all brush and saplings over three feet tall were cut down. Ground level grasses and plants lay bent over in a swirled clockwise pattern, a faint perfume of kerosene tainted the air.

All the observations came together, Teigler turned to Carrie. "It's a rough country helicopter LZ—landing zone. I've carved similar ones out of the jungle while in Vietnam."

"Who in the hell would construct something like this? Forest service? Military?"

"Not likely. And at this altitude the land won't grow much, not good for pothead plantations."

Staying within the tree line, the two circled the artificial clearing and stumbled across the beginning of a well-used path on the south side.

"Another thing that shouldn't be here—there's no trail marked on the map. I'll take point, you follow twenty-feet back."

Carrie followed her father's example, moving slowly, placing feet carefully to make no scuffing sounds. Quieter than usual, the lack of normal bird sounds and movement made her feel like they pushed through heavy gelled air. A morning cloud-mist gloved the upper branches of the forest. Here and there, fog tendrils floated, obscuring open places between tree trunks. Her nerve ends became more sensitive, the creature inside her stirred and raised its head. A frisson licked up her spine, someone or something kept pace and watched. At her father's signal, Carrie moved a few feet off the trail and knelt.

Teigler sniffed, lowered himself to hands and knees, and sniffed again. A faint outhouse odor came from the sides of the trail. Moving closer, his color-defective vision detected man-size oval shapes among the grass and plant litter covering the trailside. One hand carefully slid under the camouflage, discovered a pit, and loosed the nose-pinching aroma of human excrement. Pungee pits in the mountains of Montana? His lips curved into an ironic smile.

Advancing a few yards down the trail, his color blindness detected twenty rough-edged six-inch circles interlocked in triangular patterns arranged on the path and to its sides. He laid prone, face close to the first circle. Picking up a short twig, Teigler cautiously brushed away pine needles and bark chips exposing a fist-sized olive-drab cylinder. He recognized a military issue M-14 toe popper mine. He nodded to himself, blew the dirt and dust off the top of the can-sized mechanism exposing the yellow arrow on its top locked into the armed position. He glanced up. On the far side of the mines, farther up the path, came a reflection of light off a dew-covered spider's web hanging from a transparent, almost invisible tripwire running eight inches above the trail. A detailed eyeball of the sides of the trail disclosed the mottled green-plastic body of a claymore mine hidden behind leaves and refuse.

Teigler signaled Carrie forward. She crawled up to his position. In a low voice, he pointed out the pits alongside the trail, then the small mines and the claymore tripwire.

"Imagine a line of men walk down this trail, the point man may step on one of these toe poppers. They contain one ounce of tetryl explosive, enough to blow your foot into rags. If he misses these, he would brush against the tripwire setting off the claymore—a shotgun blast of seven hundred steel balls would wipe out the first three or four men. The others would instinctively take cover on the sides falling into the pungee pits. This is definitely Vietnam era tech and tactics."

"Can we circle around these off the trail?"

"Unlikely. They will have placed more claymores on the flanks."

"Who's done this?"

"Someone has something to protect. We should leave, but there are three people blocking our back trail. They've followed us since the helicopter LZ."

"How do you know that?"

"They have shitty smoke and water discipline. The breeze carries the scent of their cigarettes and their half-filled canteens gurgle when they walk."

"So what now?"

"You follow me, step exactly where I step. There are probably more men ahead. We'll split their forces by putting the minefield between us and the ones behind us."

Teigler paused at the claymore tripwire, watched Carrie negotiate the last of the toe poppers. He pointed to the wire, stepped over its eight-inch height, and took a few paces to clear the area.

Carrie followed, lifted her feet over the tripwire. She froze. Her father's body quivered, his eyes focused on a flicker of movement coming toward them. He motioned her behind a tree, gave the hand sign for *watch our back trail*.

Two men approached, almost marching in step, shoulder to shoulder, one short and thin and one tall and thick bodied. Twenty feet distant, they stopped. Teigler noticed the left man was actually of average height and weight. He only looked smaller next to his grizzly bear-sized companion. That one stood at least six-four and must weigh two-sixty.

The shorter stopped and motioned the taller one to advance. Teigler felt the snake in him come to attention. A pulse in his forehead throbbed. His two personalities detected something both familiar and threatening.

Pausing at a ten-foot distance, the bear-man spoke, "You took your time gettin' here, Rod. The female baggage delay you?"

The addition of the voice solidified the identification. He nodded. "Mack the truck. Where *have* you been since our army days?" Teigler's right hand made the signal for *danger*, then *wait*.

Carrie kneeled, removed her pack, and pulled a skeletal-framed skinning knife with a three-inch blade from an inner boot sheath. Increasing pressure from her reptile personality made her hand quiver as she used the gut hook projection on the blade tip to cut her bootlaces. She could move faster barefoot.

"This meeting isn't an accident, is it?" her father said.

"The Orienteering Gaia invitation, fake—the airline tickets, maps, not from them. All from us. Led ya by the nose. We have a deal to offer."

Teigler looked around. The reptile persona began to swell in his mind. It tensed his muscles, knees bent, shoulders lifted. Across from him, the other man's eyes turned yellow as he hunched. The two berserkers hissed and displayed teeth. Behind them, the other man raised a chrome-plated coach's whistle to his lips and blew three short blasts.

Men cradling weapons emerged from between trees to form a perimeter around the meeting place, one pair stopped behind Carrie. The three men who had followed them from the LZ came up the trail and stood on the far side of the minefield. Teigler's alternate personality relinquished control, deciding that an attack at this time would be useless. The big man shook.

His short companion shouted, "Mack, Mack, drop it!"

The internal struggle continued. Mack's face contorted, and then relaxed. "That was a bad 'un, Rod. I almos' didn't come back."

"Mack, you need help."

"Ya know, the others from the experiment didn't make it. The bastards used us up in Nam. Used us up! Sent Stevens out on one fuckin' mess after another till he let the VC kill him. William Coffee, same ol', same ol'. He disappeared in the Delta, probably still there, killin' natives and screwin' crocodiles. I went AWOL."

Teigler spread out his arms. "What is all this?"

"You could say I've fallen inta bad company. These mothers are neo-Nazis."

They're gatherin' strength here in the backcountry, trainin' people, then sendin' them home until the time comes for the insurrection. Three or four hundred so far. They admire what I can do when I get crazy. I told 'em 'bout the experiment, 'bout you. The *Gauleiter*." His head jerked toward the man behind him. "Says you're ta join up or you and the pretty one will never leave."

Gauleiter? Teigler fished out an obscure reference from his memory—the title referred to province governors appointed by Hitler. Most had been overbearing butchers, killing Jews, Poles, and Russians in conquered territories without mercy.

He took a count, a motley assortment of ten men armed with an even more motley assortment of shotguns, M-16 variants, and Mini-14s stood around waiting for orders. Not too alert, not too disciplined. Feeling confident in their numbers, some drank from canteens, others opened cans of Skoal to replenish tobacco wads held between lips and teeth. A few even leaned their weapons against nearby tree trunks.

The two near Carrie made kissing sounds and whispered comments about what they would do, both singly and together, to her body. Her upper lip curled, a dodgy odor of stale unwashed clothes and crusted skin reached her.

"What's with the helicopter LZ and the mines?"

Our leader has contacts and resources. There's lots 'a powerful folks who don't like the way the country's goin'. The mines keep out the curious and any Fed's prowlin' around. They was also a test—to see if you still had it."

"I recognized your work—on the mule deer back there."

The big man leaned forward and whispered, "Rod, I need ta know how you've done it. I'm at the end of my rope. A couple more berserker plunges and I won't be able ta come back, the thing in me keeps getting stronger." A tic started in his cheek, shoulders slumped and shook."

"Mack, I had help." Teigler remembered the Apache witch woman and the sacred *Kiva* where he and his internal lizard had fought to a standstill. "Let's get out of here. I'll do everything I can to get you stabilized."

A shout from the *Gauleiter,* "What the hell's goin' on? Mack, is he with us, or no?"

"Time's up, my brother berserker. There's only one way out of this. They won't let either of us leave any other way. Ya joinin'?"

Teigler's right hand signaled *get ready.* Carrie shucked off her boots and socks. Bare toes dug into the spongy forest carpet of decomposing pine needles. She unbuttoned her shirt, allowing the free movement of her body.

"You and I took an oath, Mack, *I will support and defend the Constitution of the United States against all enemies, foreign and domestic ...*"

Teigler's right hand signaled Carrie, *attack! attack!* The reptile personalities in the men burst forth. Two male bodies slammed together. The flesh-bone smack echoed off the trees.

"Don't shoot," screamed the leader. "Mack will take care of him."

Teigler felt himself being shoved back, his boots pushing up dirt and leaves as he resisted the bigger, more powerful man. He had his hands full just avoiding the Mack-creature's teeth.

Carrie spun around, leaped, and kicked. The heel of her extended right leg pulped the first man's testicles against his pelvis. He bent over with a silent gasp-whine.

The second man froze for a second too long. Her little knife plunged into his right eye and wiggled in the brain. The body dropped. She returned to the first man, holding his head while she stuck the knife into his neck. The gut hook at the point of the blade caught the artery and sliced it open on the backstroke.

She stopped, tore off her shirt. The reptile personality didn't like the elastic confining thing around her chest. Sports bra peeled off, naked from the waist up, Carrie disappeared into a remaining tongue of morning mist.

The Mack-reptile lifted Teigler off his feet and squeezed until he felt his opponent's lungs stop filling. The skinheads around the periphery cheered and watched intently. Arms free, Teigler slammed the palms of his hands together, one on each side of Mack's head. Stunned for a second, he allowed the former friend to slip free and back-pedal.

Mack rushed forward. Using his enemy's momentum, Teigler pulled on Mack's arms, rolled backwards, stuck his feet into the big man's crotch, and flipped him head over heels.

Carrie raced around a tree trunk, leaped up on a skinhead's back, her left arm closed from the rear in a chokehold. Supported by her grip on his neck, her hips pivoted up allowing her feet to connect with a second man's chin. She felt and heard the jaw fracture.

Planting her feet, she bent over to hip-lift the first man off the ground, her forearm acting as a garrote. She used the knife on the collapsed male bodies to ensure no live enemy remained behind.

The Mack-creature staggered to his feet, faced his opponent, his back now to the minefield. Teigler rushed forward, the impact pushed the bear of a man backwards. His boots broke the tripwire. The claymore exploded.

Standing in the path of the funnel-shaped cone of steel ball bearings, the three men on the back trail disappeared in a cloud of blood, weapon fragments, and chunks of flesh.

Carrie used the blast as cover to take out two more of the men, both of whom seemed mesmerized by her bare breasts. Making the most of their hesitation, she used her teeth on their throats. The female reptile raised a bloody mouth, mewed, and crawled over the cadavers seeking the last enemy.

The Teigler hybrid straight-fingered Mack in the solar plexus, buying another pause in the big man's response. This would be the last chance. He hadn't damaged Mack much yet, just kept him off balance. There was time for one more move before Mack's superior strength and weight ended the contest in his favor.

The Teigler-reptile leaped forward, hugged his opponent around the upper chest, right foot swept Mack's feet out from under him. Locked together, the two fell into the minefield, Teigler on top. Separated by split seconds, he heard *blammblammblamm*.

The man beneath him shouted as their joined bodies lifted, then settled. Mack convulsed, gripped him tighter, then relaxed. The toe popper mines had blown holes the size of fists through his back, into heart, stomach, and a kidney. Muscular hairy arms became dead weight and fell to the ground.

Teigler pushed up, stared into his friend's face. He could see no sign of the reptile in it. Mack smiled, tried to say something. Bloody froth leaked from his nostrils. The eyes closed. Teigler felt a last puff of breath caress his cheek.

Teigler rose and turned to face the gauleiter, now only five feet away. The camo-dressed man drew a pistol. The reptile hissed as its human personality recognized a Walther P-38, a nine-millimeter automatic pistol of WWII German design, the exterior hammer cocked. The gauleiter looked puzzled. It was too quiet. What had happened to his men?

A sliver of fear worked its way up his spine. He concentrated on the creature before him, to look away would be madness. The Nazi's finger tightened on the pistol trigger.

From his right, he heard a three-round burst of automatic rifle fire; irrepressible instinct pulled his head toward the distraction. A rush of wind, the pistol slapped out of his hand, he felt himself being lifted—teeth found his neck—and then he was tossed aside. The gauleiter lived for only a half dozen seconds, hands pressed against the blood spurting hole where his larynx used to be.

Teigler collapsed. Arms and legs drooped as the reptile drained back into the medulla, their mutual body now paying the price for the high intensity, high adrenalin activity of the last ten minutes. He was now the last survivor of the experiment, but not the last of his kind. Teigler looked for his daughter.

Carrie held the last skinhead, legs dangling off the ground, up against a tree trunk with his rifle pressed sideways across his neck. The man's legs kicked, his own weight strangling him. The movement slowed to a twitch and the body fell like a sack of potatoes dumped off the back of a delivery truck. Reversing the weapon, she smashed the butt several times against the man's skull.

It took almost a full minute before Teigler realized that she was not wearing a crimson t-shirt.

Changeling

We pace in the sauna-hot Saigon sun.
Khakis, washed by village women,
smell of thick brown jungle rivers.
Sweat forces out the stink
of rotting plants,

animal piss and mold.
One hundred men, aroused lovers,
worship the taxiing bird coming to
take them back to "the world."
We almost float without weapons,

ammo and paddy mud on our boots.
A crowd of wrinkled, silence-chained
replacements move off the plane.
The two groups repel each other —
the north poles of magnets,

not able to touch.
Shouts, prayers, and cheers
from the loading veterans lapse
into catcalls and "you'll be sorry's"
tracered at the green troops.

A few muffled "fuck you's" come back.
On the return flight men twitch
in REM-sleep, sharing bloody
guttering dreams—clearly,
we are not finished

sacrificing for our country.
At a stateside airport,
we roll on the ground,
dogs in misplaced ecstasy, and
kiss dusty tarmac that smells

of oil, vomit, and chewing gum.
The drive home takes us
through the Iowa countryside.
The car is not in a convoy.
Unblinking eyes scan the tree lines

for the barrels of AK-47s.
In wooden masks, my parents say
I move too quietly … not the same.
Their child is lost,
replaced by something

hollow—it is helpless.
In dry-acid heaves, it feels
repressed fear snake-squirm loose.
The bedsheets weep into shrouds
for the dead it can never leave behind.

Les Fantômes

The military police at the convoy collection point waved Lieutenant Teigler's truck into position behind a gasoline tanker.

Teigler's head and right shoulder jutted out of the passenger window. "Can't you put us someplace else?" Teigler yelled, visions of his little vehicle being engulfed in a huge fireball during an enemy ambush.

The MP sergeant turned, smiled, and moved his head from side to side. "Luck of the draw, El Tee."

Rod suspected he did so with hidden relish. Second lieutenants got little respect. His driver, Corporal Morgan, pulled their three-quarter-ton M37, the Army's slab-sided version of the full-size pickup truck, up behind the 88th Transport Company's tanker. It would take another thirty minutes for the fifty-vehicle convoy to form for the trip through Ambush Alley, a nasty fifty-mile section of unsecured road subject to daily firefights.

Stepping out of the Dodge-built four-wheel drive vehicle, he walked past the olive-drab tanker trailer. Rainy-season mud squished over the toes of his boots; the disturbed ooze smelled of rotted vegetation and animal excrement. A soldier stood with one foot up on the running board of the connected semi-truck.

The man turned and came to a rough semblance of attention. He said, "Sur," and started to salute.

Rod broke in, "No saluting, friend, relax. I just as soon the enemy didn't know my rank. What have we got here?"

The man's muscles loosened. In a voice containing all the honey and velvet of the Deep South, he replied, "The bes' of the bes', sur. A Peta-bilt 281 diesel fresh off the ship."

"I'm more interested in what's connected to it. How many gallons are you carrying?"

"A little over five thousand gallons of reg-lar U.S. A'my gas-lean, complete with pow-ful engine cleanin' additives."

"How big a boom will that make?"

"Wal, the chem-es-try of the sit-u-a-shun is this. Only the fumes of gas-lean explode. We are runnin' full, so any metal, such as bullets, piercin' the sides will allow the contents to leak out—but prob-lee not go bang. Now, if we get hit with a RPG, all bets are off. Do not worry 'bout that, 'caus' in that event we will not have time to bend over and kiss our asses goodbye befor' in-cin-er-a-shun."

"And where did you learn all that?"

"I'm a hell of an engineer, or I should say 'bout half a' one."

The phrase sounded familiar. Teigler added that to the southern accent. "You're 'a rambling wreck from Georgia Tech.'"

The soldier started to sing, "I'm a rambling wreck from Georgia Tech and a helluva engineer ..."

The lieutenant joined in, "A helluva, helluva, helluva, helluva, hell of an engineer, like all good jolly fellows, I drink my whiskey clear."

The pair stopped and laughed. "I only completed two years before runnin' outta' funds, but I'll go back on the GI Bill afta' my honorable term of service. How do you know the song?"

"It was one of the favorite drinking songs at the beer blasts we suffered through in college."

MP whistles and shouting interrupted. Men mounted up, the convoy started to move.

~~~OOO~~~

The truck *rock 'n rolled* over the rough dirt road. Teigler's back and kidneys started to ache after the first twenty miles. He supposed he should be grateful for small favors—the M37 had a split seat, allowing his short driver to be closer to the wheel, while his own six-foot frame could keep the passenger seat fully back. Overall, the truck was a commendable workhorse. Its tried and true T245 straight, six-cylinder engine matched an equally reliable four-speed manual transmission. The mechanical marvel also possessed some cross-country capacity. Fender wells high up on the sides allowed the wheels considerable play over uneven terrain.

Rain pattered down on the canvas roof, leaked through insect- gnawed holes, and wet his left side. Being on the butt-end of the monsoon, ragged spits of rain came down throughout the day. He shifted his lucky 40-millimeter grenade launcher to a drier spot between his legs.

The truck carried about seven hundred pounds of supplies, including a precious case of real eggs. The crated goodies had come thousands of miles by truck, train, and refrigerator ship—then by truck again to reach them. Some of the contents would be bad, shells cracked or too old to eat. The lieutenant guessed about twenty percent or so, but the rest would be quickly devoured along with C-ration ham doused with Louisiana hot sauce. The taste would be pure heaven for men who had been eating out of cans for months.

He felt the bullets strike before he heard the gunshots. The hail of clinks and clangs announced the penetration of the thin, steel sides of the M37's bed. He and his driver bailed out of out of the truck and rolled onto the ground.

The vehicle continued to move forward, coming to a stop after bouncing off the bumper of the tanker to its front. The engine coughed, sputtered, and lugged to a halt.

Enemy fire was coming from the tree line on the driver's side. Teigler crawled up to take shelter behind the engine block, it being the closest thing to armor the pickup possessed.

A standard ambush, the VC concentrated fire on the first and last units in the convoy. The disabled vehicles kept others from driving out of the kill zone. The enemy would be sorry if they didn't.

Leading the convoy was a refurbished WWII M-42, a fully tracked tank chassis with twin forty-millimeter Bofors guns mounted in an open turret. If they opened up, the enemy would be smothered with high explosive, fired at 240 rounds per minute, effectively ending the ambush.

He peered over the hood. The VC switched from primary targets to secondary—the tanker was at the top of the list. A machine gun fired from the trees. Sheet metal blistered open in a long line across the tanker's curved shell. Gasoline sprayed out in rivulets on both sides.

Teigler let out his breath. The Georgian was correct, no flame yet. Leaning over the truck hood, he raised his personal weapon, the M-79 grenade launcher, and tracked the machine gun's green tracers back to the tree line. The short-barreled gun went *pfumpt*, the round arched out, exploding shrapnel into the trees above the VC line. Fire from the machine gun hesitated and then restarted.

He broke open the shotgun-like barrel, pulled out the smoking cartridge case, and inserted a fresh round. He aimed a bit lower. This time the round landed directly in front of the machine gun, spraying shrapnel into the gunner's teeth. The automatic weapon went quiet.

Someone got the twin guns at the front of the convoy into action. Chunks of trees, body parts, and metal tumbled in the air along the tree line. The ambush ended.

Teigler found Morgan on his back at the rear of the truck, soaked from the waist down in a mess of clear egg-jelly striated with strings of yellow yoke. Frothy blood bubbled up from a wound in his chest—a sucking chest wound. Teigler unwrapped the man's individual bandage, pressed the plastic cover over the bullet hole, and held the thick wadding on top. Tilting the man into a sitting position, he wrapped the long tails of the dressing around his back and pulled them tight. The wound must be sealed to prevent the soldier's lung from collapsing.

The corporal pawed at the sticky mess on his groin, grunted, and muttered, "Fucking eggs."

The smell of the spouting gasoline burned Teigler's nostrils, and the fumes they were inhaling made him cough. He grabbed Morgan by the armpits and dragged him out of the vapor cloud. With his corporal stabilized, Teigler walked to the front of the tanker looking for the driver. A body lay sprawled in a wide puddle by the truck's open door. A great sadness came riding up out of the fumes to pale his face. The boy from Georgia, gas-soaked clothes sticking like another skin to his body, had only half a face. A large caliber round had fragmented his skull. There would be no effort to find all the pieces. The country had lost one *helluva engineer.*

~~~OOO~~~

Teigler heard a door open and slam shut. His mind and body swam up out of the past, out of the gasoline-drenched dream. Shaking hands held open a copy of *La Tribune*, the French capital's business rag. A drop of sweat fell off his nose to splat in a sun-pattern on the newsprint. He guessed he had been staring at the same page for the duration of the flashback. He barely had time to wipe his forehead before Chuck Cardoza, one of his Cerberus staffers, approached. The man's heels made a snappy tap-dance sound as he walked across the polished oak floor.

"Good Morning, Chief. May I join you?"

Teigler folded the newspaper, rested it on his lap, and pointed to a Louis Quatorze chair, a heavy ebony piece with upholstered seat and ruby velvet back. "You look chipper this morning in blue polo, khakis, and Nikes." His voice only quivered a little.

He tasted his coffee, found it cold, and poured more for himself and some for Cardoza from a silver pot resting on the *centre table* between them. It was *café au lait,* strong espresso coffee, which needed to be mixed with hot milk. The tray offered other temptations. A baked-this-morning crusty baguette rested next to butter and jam. In consideration of the American guests, yogurt, grapes, and strawberries had been added—no sausage, bacon, or eggs. The French staff refused to bend that much.

Cardoza ranted on, "Caber had a great idea about renting this … chateau … as a temporary headquarters for our entrance into Europe. It's a perfect location, only forty miles from both the German and Swiss borders. It even has its own private airfield and helipad."

"Not a chateau, my friend," Teigler replied. "Architecturally, it is a castle. In addition, as usual, Robert Caber MacDonald kept the deal within the family. Even though he doesn't bear the name outright, the manager, or castellan as they are called in these parts, is part of the MacDonald family tree. The connection being through an ancestor who fled from Scotland to France in 1746 with Bonnie Prince Charles. Yet, it is a marvelous place."

The pair sat in a cluster of furniture at one end of a very large ballroom. Meticulously restored to the style of Louis the XIV, the room featured tall French doors lining the south wall. Their ancient wavy glass let in ample light but distorted the view of the adjacent outside patio and stairs leading down to the formal gardens. Shoulder-to-shoulder mirrors ran the length of the three inside walls. Above them, framed paintings and tapestries covered all the remaining available wall space. Ten-foot diameter wrought-iron chandeliers swung in counterpoint to a ceiling painted in colorful prancing characters from ancient Greek and Roman myths. Teigler tried to imagine silk clad men and women twirling on the hardwood floor, couples spinning off periodically to dally in the gardens.

A door silently opened and shut. He looked up to see a quaint figure walk across the hall. A man dressed in the light blue, tight-fitting servant's livery of the Sun King's court, even down to a short-bobbed powdered wig. Goose bumps formed on Teigler's neck and arms. Something was wrong. He scowled, looked more closely, and caught it. The man left no image in the mirrors. The apparition passed through the door at the end of the ballroom. The touch of fear caused the reptile inside his brain to stir in its sleep.

Misinterpreting a break in the conversation, Cardoza injected a comment, "What's the history of this pile?"

Teigler licked his dry lips and swallowed. "Castle Beaubien is built on the ruins of an eleventh century fort, hence the slanted stone wall foundations. The two towers at the front were added during the Hundred Years' War. The remainder of the structure consists of add-ons built during more peaceful times."

"Wow! I've noticed antique swords, maces, and spears hanging on the walls of the entrance hall. If we're attacked we could defend ourselves."

"Not very well, I'm afraid. Too many indefensible entrances." He motioned toward the French doors. "Although, I suppose you could seal yourself up in one of the towers for a while. They've preserved a few of the cross-shaped cutouts designed for archers and crossbowmen."

Cardoza glanced at the copy of *La Tribune* crumpled in Teigler's lap. "There's an excellent story about Cerberus in the newspaper. I'm feeling good about us being able to pick up a tasty chunk of the physical security business in Europe. Sécurité EU has had a virtual monopoly for too long."

Teigler heard his watch begin to chime. He rose. "I've got a meeting with the castle's management. Any complaints, compliments, or adjustments I should mention?"

"Everything good to go, so far. We'll have the proposal for Euro Disney ready tomorrow."

"Now, that'll piss off Sécurité."

~~~OOO~~~

Teigler stepped outside on the front lawn, smelled newly-mown grass, and took another look at the ancient structure, now a hotel and conference center. The later buildings, topped by numerous tall chimneys and pointed roofs, appeared to be squeezed in-between the two older asymmetric towers, giving it a strangely distorted gothic ambiance. A phantom breeze brought up a shiver from his tailbone to his neck. He turned and walked briskly to the outbuilding containing the office of the facility manager.

He knocked, and welcomed by a cheery shout, entered Guy Chevalier's office. The manager motioned him to a chair and offered a cut-glass bowl of Jelly Bellies. "An American affectation, I know." He spoke perfect English. "A trifle brought back from my university days in your country. I received my degree in hotel management from the University of Michigan."

Teigler picked out a few of the orange ones. "A good choice, Monsieur Chavalier."

"Call me Guy, my friend." He pronounced it the French fashion, which rhymes with tea. "Are the accommodations working out?"

"Quite well, everyone has a private room with bath. The offices are light and airy. The food disappears as quickly as it is served—great butter and cheese. I'm going to schedule exercise times for my people or they will weigh a great deal more when they leave."

"The place is entirely yours, so have them take advantage of the tennis courts, riding stables, and the fitness center. Unfortunately, the swimming pool is under repair. We'll be pouring a new concrete floor two or three days from now. Anything else?"

"Yes, two items. We'll need to use the central gallery, and on occasion, the ballroom for business presentations and receptions."

"No problem, we can set them up in any configuration you wish. Our man Pierre can assist with any audiovisual requirements. Oh, will you need services scheduled on Sundays in the chapel or will a list of local churches suffice?"

"The list, please. This is a pretty diverse crew."

Guy nodded and made a note on his desk pad. "There is a second item?"

Teigler hesitated, lips pressed tight. "I wouldn't bring this up if it was just me, but with a dozen of my folks here ..." The manager's eyebrows rose in anticipation. "In the ballroom earlier, I saw a man wearing a wig and period clothes walk in one door and out the other. The strange thing ... he left no image in the mirrors."

Guy rubbed his cheeks, stared down at the blue desk blotter. "Hmmm, I can't think who he could have been. I'll check with the staff. Perhaps the mirrors on three sides and all the light and reflections coming in from the outside simply masked the reflection."

~~~OOO~~~

Teigler sat on a Roche Bobois gray leather *grand canapé*, sipped a young, but good wine from the castle's vineyard, and listened to Pappy Wallace finish a joke:

"I reached down, picked up that frog, and slipped her into my shirt pocket. She stuck her wart-speckled green head out and said, 'I don't understand. I said if you'd kiss me, I'd turn into a beautiful princess and be your sex-slave forever. Why won't you do it?' I looked down at the little darling and replied, 'At my age, I'd rather have a talking frog.'"

Laughter rose and bounced off the high ceilings, echoes returned to fill the space, as though the jolly gods and satyrs on the ceiling were joining in the mirth. Someone standing outside would have thought the room held three times its dozen occupants. Pappy was always telling jokes about his age. A three-war veteran, the almost seventy-year-old remained as active as a much younger man, except for the cane he used when his old war wound acted up. He served as the team's weapons expert and trainer. The next oldest person, besides Teigler, was a thirty-year-old computer expert, so Pappy took his fatherly role seriously. Only a stupid person would threaten any of his charges—a short-lived stupid person.

Teigler stood, raised his wine glass, and made a toast to the group before leaving. "Your very excellent work has landed us the Euro Disney contract, exposing the incompetence of our competitor Sécurité and opening the Euro Zone to Cerberus. To everyone here, *a votre sante* and a night of pleasant dreams."

He jogged up the stairs to the fourth floor of the oldest tower, entering his suite of rooms through the bedroom. Beyond, behind a sliding pocket door, lay a sitting room with couches, chairs, and plants facing a floor-to-ceiling arched window, which caught cream-colored morning light. A modern bathroom and a small office completed the floor plan. The whole thing was called the Gaubert suite, after the medieval noblemen who built the towers. Over the fireplace in the bedroom hung a very old oil painting of Aalis, the last countess of that family to walk the halls and gardens. Recently restored and cleaned, the blonde lady of the castle appeared serene and beautiful, until you noticed the eyes. Those slightly slanted and sensuous lidded orbs gave away the passion hiding within. She must have been some package.

The centerpiece of the room was a four-poster, oak-paneled bed, complete with dark-brown velvet curtains that could be drawn to keep out drafts. The antique had come with the castle, passed down from one succeeding owner to another. The mattress, however, had been modernized. Could this be the bed Aalis and the count had shared? Teigler pondered the thought as he shed his clothes, slipped between the sheets, and started to catch up on his business reading.

Three hours later, he woke with the papers scattered across his chest. He tossed them on the floor, shut off the light, and rolled over. He jerked awake again in the early hours, confused, breath stuck in his lungs.

Gasping and choking, he tried to rise. An invisible presence held him down, its heavy weight filling the curves of his body, pressing him deep into the mattress. A few more moments and he would pass out. Teigler started to panic from the lack of air—he couldn't even twitch. Dark circles formed and scrolled inward from the rim to the center of his vision.

From a deep spirit-well within him, fire blew forth. The reptile personality flushed into his mind and body, filling every organ and muscle. The weight disappeared. The body leaped out of the bed to land on all fours, butt wagging as though lashing a phantom tail. Lungs filled. Golden vertical irises scanned the room, breath hissed out in challenge. The reptile saw nothing, detected nothing. Apparently, only humans could see ghosts.

Deep inside, Teigler peered forth. He watched the bedclothes writhe and hump. Sweet voices murmured. A man clothed in a long gold-brocaded dressing gown opened the door and stumbled toward the bed. His pale featureless ovoid face caught the moonlight through the window.

A clenched hand held a long poniard or dagger. The shadow plunged the two handed weapon down into the bed, thrusting again and again. He heard a tinny muffled scream followed by silence broken only by the killer's heavy breathing, then nothing.

The reptile stared, confused by the terror felt by the man-portion of its awareness. It had not and could not detect any threat. It returned to its mental lair, leaving the naked man shivering against the cold stone floor of the empty room.

~~~OOO~~~

"The anniversary," Guy muttered after hearing Teigler's ghost story. "The anniversary. *Mon Dieu!* As you may be aware from popular writings, many old castles have their ghost myths. Beaubien is normally free of such hauntings, but every one hundred years, at least for a few days, we get spectral visits. That is the story handed down. As a modern, educated man, I did not believe it myself, but perhaps there is some truth in the old tale."

"Any danger to my people?"

"No, no, none whatsoever. No injuries have ever been reported. *Les fantômes,* the otherworldly visitors, appear, do their thing, and ignore any humans not in their way. You should not worry."

"Who the hell are they?"

"It's Jaques. Count Jaques de Gaubert inherited the castle and grounds from his father. In spite of his power and immense wealth, he failed to retain the love of his new wife, Aalis. She took a lover, who would visit her chamber."

"The room and the bed I am currently inhabiting?"

"Yes, yes, of course. Jaques became mad with jealously after listening to the sounds of their lovemaking. The couple was murdered, supposedly by the count's own hands. Shortly thereafter, the man deserted the castle because he could not bear the noises made by the ghostly lovers. But it may have been Jaques' own guilty conscience."

"No. It was the sounds. He is still trying to silence them."

"Do you want to move to another suite?"

"I think I'll stay in this one. I'm intrigued by the story."

~~~OOO~~~

Teigler raised his head from the pillow on the couch in the sitting room. The lovers were at it again in the chamber next-door, and he felt a little bored. The players hadn't deviated from the ten-minute script—lovemaking and then the dagger—for the last three nights. Since he had moved out of their playground, they ignored him completely. He heard the usual tenor and alto moans and groans and an occasional, "Ooh, la la." He fluffed the pillow, laid his head back, and closed his eyes. It would end soon.

Above, around, and beneath him, the tendons of the ancient dwelling cooled and relaxed. Its cooks, maintenance men, and managers had disbursed for the day to villages and cottages outside its spacious grounds. From an opening in the west tower eaves, small hairy bodies fluttered out on silent wings headed for insect-heavy vineyards and woods. Castle Beaubien and its human guests on the second and fourth floors slept, all except for an old man, his rubber-tipped cane making no noise as he walked the pain out of his legs. Fractious clouds threw ragged curtains over the full moon, shadows dripped over the building's façade like inky tears.

A tawny owl sat next to her nest watching pin-feathered chicks fight over the juicy parts of a field mouse. Her head swiveled. A blacked-out van drifted up the castle's gravel drive and rolled to a stop. Men exited from the rear doors. The owl's head tilted, muscles tensed, as she assessed the risk to her brood, then relaxed as the invaders moved toward the structure, which had been a part of the lives of thousands of her ancestors.

The scuff of Vibram-soled boots on the castle's stone steps made a low-key susurration. Shadow-men dressed in black battle dress, black watch caps, and camouflage face paint moved from dark spot to dark spot.

Short-barreled weapons equipped with silencers held at hip level probed empty spaces. The men divided into three pairs. One set guarded the first floor entrance, another staked out the second floor living quarters. The last two moved in short measured rushes up the tower stairs, stopping and listening, then advancing.

At the fourth floor they slinked down the hall and cracked open a door. They listened. Their teeth glistened, exposed in Cheshire cat smiles, as they caught the sounds of male and female bodies in motion. Their target would be much too involved to resist.

The first man entered and approached the bed, motioning his comrade to watch the door. He raised the weapon, aimed at the writhing blankets, and fired a burst of slugs. A fat tube on the automatic's barrel suppressed the flash and sound. Thick stonewalls kept the popping noises from alerting the next closest humans two floors away. The sighs and humping didn't stop. The assassin stepped back amazed, and then emptied his weapon into the bed.

The accomplice at the door squeaked, *"Capitaine!"* in a strangled voice. The killer spun. A man with a maniacal face walked toward him holding a long knife. The captain pushed the ejection button allowing the empty banana clip to clatter on the floor, inserted a new magazine, jacked back the bolt, and fired. The bullets passed through the attacker, killing the accomplice at the door.

Back-pedaling, the team leader fell on the bed. He watched the dagger rise. Stomach muscles clenched anticipating the knife's entry. The blade came down, then again and again. The assassin gasped. The ghost vanished—the room quieted.

The man pulled off his gloves and felt for blood and wounds. There were none. He relaxed. Scaly hands slapped around his head, pulling it back to expose the neck. Teeth tore out a chunk of the aorta. The Teigler-reptile held the body until the feet stopped twitching.

The captain's head fell limp to one side. The man-creature rose and strode barefoot past the second body lying half-in and half- out of the door, pausing only to pull an eight-inch knife from the dead one's boot sheath. It slipped down the two flights of stairs to the second floor.

Glancing over the railing with lizard eyes, it spotted a shadow-man holding a shotgun on one of Teigler's employees. Pappy Wallace stood slightly hunched over in wrinkled pajamas with right hand up. The left grasped the head of his cane. A second assassin stood on the landing directly under the reptile.

The Teigler-creature chirped and leaped over the banister. Pappy's guard looked up. Moving faster than any old man had a right to, the prisoner's empty hand came down on the cane head, drew out a two-and-a-half foot hidden blade, which moved in an invisible arch to slash across the guard's throat.

Pappy caught the man and lowered the body softly to the ground. He looked toward the stairwell as Teigler finished jamming the combat knife through his target's spine at the back of his neck. The assassin staggered two loose-limbed steps. The reptile caught him by the collar and the belt and lowered the dead body to the floor. Both actions had taken only seconds with no noise.

"So the dragon's loose, is it?" Pappy whispered. The creature paused. A tongue licked out to taste the old veteran's scent. The man inside argued against killing him.

Pappy picked up his former guard's shotgun. "Son of a bitch, an AA-12 fully automatic 12 gauge. I am a happy pappy. Three hundred rounds a minute of heavy titanium shot in twenty round drum mags."

The creature disappeared down the stairs.

"That's right, Dragon, you find 'em, I'll watch your back."

Listening and tasting the air, reptile senses picked up two more invaders in the entryway, their backs turned to each other as they watched for threats. It slithered along the wall, stood, and lifted a seven-foot-long poleax off its wall hooks. It appreciated the brutal efficiency of the fourteenth century weapon, a hammer and axe affixed to a pole with a nine-inch iron spear on top.

The reptile drew on Teigler's memories of army bayonet drills. The weapon felt a little off balance, the ash-wood haft was probably longer originally. Holding the poleaxe horizontal at hip height, it stepped out into the ten-foot space between the two enemies, the ends of the weapon within a few feet of each.

It stamped a foot to attract their attention. They turned. The poleaxe haft bounced off one man's belly, arms increased the return velocity of the weapon's head, planting the spearhead into the opposite enemy's sternum. The reptile levered the heavy metal head back and forth, slicing up the man's heart.

The weapon extracted, the body fell. The poleaxe reversed in a vertical circle. Moonlight glistened off its bloody metal. The first man recovered his breath and started to raise his Uzi. The axe blade swept down, smoothly detaching his arm from his shoulder. Shock slowed his shout, allowing the silent decapitation of his head as the sharp-edged weapon quickly looped back. The body fell forward spurting black blood over the ivory-swirls of the centuries-old Italian marble floor.

In the quiet aftermath, Teigler heard the rumble of a vehicle outside. His bare feet made no noise. He reached the door and flashed a glance out. Forty feet away, a heavy-duty van spewed powdery diesel exhaust onto the gravel driveway. On its top, a cut-down machine gun mounted on a roof swivel covered the castle's entrance. It looked like the driver and gunner were all that remained of the hit team.

If he could only get near them. The reptile mind warred with his, wanting to rush out. They'd never cover the distance before the gun opened up.

He'd pretend to be one of them. Teigler pulled a long dirk off the wall and stuck it through his belt in back. Maybe they'd let him get close enough. He strode out the door, trying to look nonchalant, as though he carried a message from the inside team. Clouds, which had been blocking the light of a full moon, cleared. The gunner shouted and muscled the gun around, moving it to point right between Teigler's eyes. He thought it was the largest borehole he had ever seen.

A roar filled his ears as a weapon went fully automatic, teeth clenched, eyes closed, he waited for jacketed slugs to fillet him. No bullets hit. The firing noise came from behind and above him, not in front.

Eyebrows up, he watched the men and the Mercedes van erupt in chaos. Chunks of flesh, metal, and Kevlar armor blew back in funnel-shaped patterns, the van and its occupants literally being chewed to bits. The roar stopped. He heard a click as Pappy, in the second-floor window, inserted a fresh magazine of armor-piercing ammo into the AA-12.

The driver moaned and fumbled with a shoulder holster. The firing began again.

---OOO---

Teigler stood on the steps outside the front door of Castle Beaubien. Guy and the staff lined up along the driveway to wish them goodbye on their journey to Cerberus's new permanent headquarters in Brussels. Company staff piled into limos for the drive to the airport. No smiling faces there. His dozen had worked like mad people to clean up the devastation inside and outside the castle before Guy's people reported for work in the morning. They seemed to have succeeded. The bodies, guns, and much of the debris lay buried in the dirt beneath the swimming pool floor waiting for the concrete trucks to arrive today. They had used the vineyard's tractor to tow off the chewed-up van. Fill dirt and fresh-cut sod covered the remains of the Mercedes, now resting in a ditch well back into the woods.

As best they could tell, Sécurité had hatched the assassination attempt. The entire foundation of their business threatened by the better-trained and more innovative Americans, they thought they would embarrass the newcomers. The attack would prove Cerberus couldn't even protect themselves, let alone any customers. Teigler was sure his competitors would scour the news media for days waiting for the attack to be reported. A case of nerves wouldn't hurt them. He wished he could be there when they finally accepted that their hired assassins had disappeared. His competitors would never know how lucky they were that none of Cerberus's people had been hurt or killed. The gang mentality resting just a scratch below the surface of his organization would have extracted a terrible vengeance.

Teigler took one last look at Beaubien through the tinted window of his limo. He would miss the ghosts. After all, Aalis, her lover, and the count had saved his life. He raised a micro-recorder to his ear and pressed a button. Out of the little speaker came moans, groans, and an "Ooh, la la."

Kill-Zone Requiem

We wade through jungle shadows. Sweat drips
off our tiger-striped fatigues to wet red jungle soil.
Boots scuff, release fermented biting odors.
Butterflies blink wing eyes, shimmy dragon tails.

Insects in droning click-bodied clouds flutter,
nip, creep. Saw-toothed leaves and vine thorns
scarify our necks and arms. The clack of toucans,

the chortle of long-tail macaques set the tempo.
The bass drum beat of mortars firing slaps
our cheeks. Wind shakes triple canopy trees

their creaking limbs a pizzicato of violin and cello.
Bodies crazy-dance to the brass cymbal screech
of slicing shrapnel. We hear the tremolo drumstick

smack of jacketed bullets pierce canvas, cloth,
flesh. The splintered oboe thunk-grunt of metal
embedding in wood creates jittering chords.

Smoke-curdled air quivers with the clarinet warble
of blunt-nosed ricochets. We dying give up
a final fugue of voices. Jumbled echoes fade,
weep off elephant grass, strangling fig, twisted lianas.

Ransomed

A tall man with fiery-red hair pushed aside the heavy curtains of the second-story window and examined the street below. Long lines of cars, buses, and motorcycles fought for space in the crowded thoroughfares. The colorful patchwork of their hoods and roofs were only occasionally broken by the black and white of a police vehicle. The buildings he could see were no more than five stories tall, most weren't even that. Painted signs in Spanish advertised auto repair, pharmacy items, money exchange, and Coca Cola. One newer addition stood out like a red and yellow pimple on a nose, featuring a glass-enclosed playground budded off a Burger King. He had smelled its hamburger and fries aroma intertwined with gray car exhaust and the *aji* and *rocoto* peppers of the flanking native restaurants when the group arrived five hours ago.

Somewhat less than graciously, the embassy had provided this safe house for his team's urban headquarters. Pulling family economic and political strings got them this far. Robert "Caber" MacDonald wondered if it would be enough. Three months had passed since the kidnapping of Rod Teigler, the CEO of Cerberus, the MacDonald conglomerate's physical security company. His capture occurred during the fulfillment of a consulting contract. The job required their company to develop security plans for several new regional soccer stadiums under construction in the country's hinterland. La Manera Del Sol, a Mao-inspired rebel group, ambushed their three-car convoy, leaving six government guards scattered dead among the wreckage. Teigler disappeared, stolen away for ransom.

Caber thought about his friend and partner's situation. He respected the man. They had saved each other's lives many times during their tour in Vietnam. He wasn't sure, however, that they liked each other. The man had returned from combat with what the VA doctors described as severe multiple personality disorder. At least two distinct personalities shared the same mind and body, the one acquired in Nam, nasty, very nasty. Great fear or rage—life and death situations turned it loose.

The private clinic drugs and Asian medicines that kept the beast quiet would have run out by now. Caber wondered if the kidnappers had discovered the hidden death yet. Capturing Teigler was like bringing a deadly snake into your home and then locking the doors. No, not a snake, more like a two hundred pound sickle-clawed raptor.

The Macdonald's took care of their people. They received the *liberation money* demand along with the first two knuckles of a little finger. The fingerprint proved to be Teigler's. Working through intermediaries, the company paid the $750,000 ransom, but the captive was not released. Management immediately raised the stakes. Volunteers for a rescue party, pared down from the many who applied to a six-man squad, lounged around the room, drank the local thick black coffee, and waited for the next briefer. A biology professor from the university had finished his bit earlier. Caber remembered his words with trepidation.

"Your area of interest is one of the least explored parts of the Amazon rainforest, a place where the ill-defined boundaries of three countries come together. In your North America, a diverse forest contains twelve to fifteen species of trees to the acre. The same space in the jungle contains 300 species of trees and another 300 to 400 of lesser plants. One would not think it so, but the Amazon is a crowded place with some 2,000 species of birds and mammals, 800 varieties of reptiles and amphibians, over 2000 types of fish, and insects beyond counting."

The shuffling of feet and scraping of chairs, as his team resumed their seats for the next presentation, intruded on his recollection. A panel of three men continued their education. Major Juan De Castro, a representative of the country's air force presented a short history of the La Manera Del Sol guerilla group. Once powerful and insinuated throughout two-thirds of the country, they had fallen on hard times, mostly through their own fanaticism. Their many assassinations and the destruction of peasant markets, which they felt smacked of hated capitalism, turned the native population against them. A vigorous government effort, backed by money and equipment from the U.S.A., decimated their ranks and forced them back into the thinly populated jungle. Occasionally, the remnants found new energetic leadership and the kidnappings would start again.

After the major, a short, dark-skinned man in a police uniform with sergeant's stripes introduced himself as Vincenté de los Mashco-Piro, a native of the target area. "My people do not desire contact with the outside. Illegal oil workers, missionaries, and loggers have already brought problems into our homeland." He rubbed a pockmarked cheek. "We do not have immunities to so-called civilized diseases. Your rebels have been avoided for this reason; that and the fact that they are too heavily armed." He ran his fingers through his raven-black hair. "My first suggestion, you drop your plans and go home. The rainforest is no place for amateurs."

Caber stood up and broke in, "Do you have a second suggestion?"

"I am in harmony with what you want. The desire for justice is strong among us also. If you insist on going, I will be your guide."

With a nod, Caber sat. "We gratefully accept."

The last briefer, an intelligence officer from the embassy named John Smith, probably not his real name, gave them what he knew. "We cannot say whether your man, Teigler, is still alive. Our sources of information are limited to intercepted signals and an occasional night flyover by aircraft equipped with infrared and heat sensors. Six weeks ago, we could have given you the location of their base within a quarter mile.

"However, in the last four months they have moved three times. Each time they move deeper into the rainforest. They appear to be reacting to pressure from some unknown opposing force. We determined this after intercepting several panicked radio messages."

A half-laugh came from the back of the room. Pappy Wallace, the Cerberus weapons master, stood, pumped a fist, and shouted, "The dragon is loose!"

~~~OOO~~~

The reptile-man lay half-in, half-out of the bole of a massive tree, feet pressed against the smooth bark of the trunk, body stretched out on a thick projecting limb. As still and motionless as an ancient stone god, only half-lidded eyes moved, its head shifted slowly so not to disturb the myriad of birds, insects, and monkeys.

The body had finally adapted. Woefully soft and awkward at the beginning, insects found its blood easily taken. The sharp-edged leaves of jungle plants left oozing infected cuts everywhere on its flesh. Prey escaped its clumsy thrashing. But, it had learned. Skin darkened and grew tougher. Feet, hands, and knees developed thick-layered calluses, and senses sharpened. Thirty pounds lighter, whipcord muscle moved it easily through the three dimensions of the rainforest. Its diet suited it well, bird eggs and squabs robbed from high nests, *paiche* and *piranha* fish caught in pools and tributaries, tree and vine fruit, and the meat of snakes, lizards, and occasional capybaras. Its toe and fingernails grown long, the reptile-man sharpened them against rocks and trees. They broke too easily, but they were what he had.

A trio of romantically inclined butterflies twisted and jinked. Prism-shaped scales on the interior of the wings generated a neon-blue flash with every flap. Their erratic mating flight made it difficult for birds to snatch them from the air. One settled on a branch, closed its wings, and disappeared— the insects' outer surfaces camouflaged to match jungle dappled greens and browns.

An eight-inch long walking stick rested on a leaf nearby. A dragonfly dodged a large butterfly, landed on the man-reptile's flank. A muscle twitched. It flew off. The butterfly came to rest in the long hair on the hybrid's head. It winked wings as big as a man's hands, displaying two large oval spots, mimicking owl eyes.

The reptile froze, all its senses collected information. Something approached. The signs were slight, a displacement of humid air, the almost noiseless placing of a paw on the spongy jungle floor, and a change in the motion and interaction of birds and animals. At the edge of its vision, ground-level leaves moved where there was no breeze. Pushing through the undergrowth, a jaguar paced past. A black-spotted domestic piglet dangled from its jaws. The reptile-man's brain flashed pictures of the rebel camp five miles to the south. The cat had stolen from the men.

It remembered. Pale silky scars running across the reptile-creature's butt cheeks, back, and belly ached with memories, lashing whips, slashing knives .... The evil ones had inflicted torture on their captive until its escape. The creature's little finger on its left hand itched as it grew back. It was good to be a reptile.

Over the last eight weeks, it stalked and killed camp men every two or three days—one at a time—their bodies dragged off and hidden in deep dark places, buried under rotting wood and vines. A hundred yards away, a troop of howler monkeys cut loose a barrage of warning hoots and screams as the spotted cat entered their territory. Leaves drifted down in bunches as the troop raced to higher, safer elevations.

~~~OOO~~~

Five squad members hunkered behind their individual displays of equipment as Caber conducted one last inspection. Weapons, clothing, boots, and various pieces of equipment lay neatly arranged on folded jungle-camo ponchos. Everything, including the radios, worked. That's not to say that they would last long once assaulted by the fungus and bugs of the jungle. Most of the squad was ex-military. They had been drilled without mercy for the last week to get their skill levels back. The training schedule also included rappelling from the Merlin helicopter that Major De Castro provided. Their insertion into the rainforest would be down a hundred feet of rope into a tiny drop zone macheted out by Vincenté's people. A seven-mile hike from there should put them where native scouts had located the current rebel camp. Every night for the last week, helicopters flew over the area getting the rebels used to the sound of the machines passing overhead. Tonight, when the chopper flew in, it would stop for five minutes over the drop site, and then quickly move out. Hopefully, the rebels would categorize it as just another flyover.

Caber looked up and down the squad line, mentally shook his head. He studied the crazy quilt configuration of faces, ages, and body types. Pappy Wallace, an aging three-war vet with experience in the jungles of the Pacific Islands and Southeast Asia, displayed an AA-12 automatic shotgun and a KA-BAR knife. Uncle Ho, native of Vietnam, stood behind his WWI Remington pump action shotgun, complete with long-bladed bayonet. These two would be the base element. They would operate the long-range radio and serve as a reserve. If, on the way back, rebels pursued, the two men would set up an ambush, allow the friendlies through, and cut down the enemy.

Nam, Uncle Ho's grandson, took leave from the Army to become a member of the team. After the two fled their country in the seventies, Nam gained his U.S. citizenship learning to be a Green Beret. Skills he gained as the honor graduate of the military's toughest jungle training school would come in handy. He carried a customized M-16 assault rifle with attached forty-millimeter grenade launcher.

As the third partner in Cerberus, Okie possessed an unchallenged position in the group. Both he and Caber had served with Teigler in Southeast Asia. A fair radioman and close-in fighter, he served as the second grenadier in the squad, armed the same as Nam.

Their number five was as odd as they came. Teigler's oldest daughter, Carrie, possessed expert shooting skills. He didn't know how she did it. Give her a weapon that threw a projectile and she could put its slug anywhere within its range, dead on, first time, every time. She became one with the bullet, riding it to the target. Appointed the team sniper, a fiberglass-stocked, short-action Remington 700 in caliber .308 suited her perfectly. That was scary enough, but her choice of personal hand-to-hand weapons turned out to be one of the strangest ever. They looked like a pair of mutant brass knuckles. Inserted within each camo-painted knuckle were three-inch razor-sharp claws, like talons, that could be raised and locked into a cutting position. Carrie demonstrated what they could do on a pig carcass—nothing but spare ribs and pork chops when she finished.

Of the remaining two members of the team, Vincenté came armed with an AK-47 and Caber had equipped himself with an MP-5 submachine gun and a nine-millimeter Browning Hi-Power, both heavily suppressed.

Besides tiger-striped jungle fatigues, soft wide-brimmed hats, and leather and nylon mesh boots, everyone's kit included a CamelBak water bladder, machete, first-aid package, extra socks, and a roll of jungle-green duct tape. The four older ones also packed two hand grenades apiece and a claymore mine with clacker detonator and tripwire mechanism.

Their two radios came with self-destruct thermite grenades attached. The canisters contained a compressed cake of powdered aluminum and iron oxide. When ignited, they produced temperatures in excess of 4,500 degrees. Burning about half as hot as the surface of the sun, the mixture produced its own oxygen, allowing it to work even in a vacuum or under water. A pull-ring would activate the little suns, destroying the equipment rather than allowing it to fall into enemy hands.

Other preparations included eating native meals consistently the week before to ensure their sweat smelled right, butch haircuts to foil parasites, and no deodorant, toothpaste, or soap three days before kickoff. The group suffered through all the long hours with only one request, which he granted for morale purposes. The entire team, including Vincenté, had received a tattoo of a dragon wrapped around their right bicep.

~~~OOO~~~

The reptile-man tried to make a decision. Should it take one or two? The creature crouched in the undergrowth on the bank of a river tributary upstream from the six men it stalked. Camped behind a massive kapok tree at the water's edge, their fire of mostly green wood smoked fitfully. The sound of coughing drifted on the water as the jungle breeze died, letting the smoke and fumes hover in place. Part of a regular resupply effort, the men humped backpacks and A-frames of food and equipment to the rebel base camp. At their current rate of progress, the reptile estimated it could prey on them for two more days before they reached the uncertain safety of their base.

Unguarded approaches to the camp were limited. Thick stands of cecropia trees ringed most of the tributary's banks. Stinging ants lived in their hollow stems, ready to attack any creature disturbing the clusters. The insects and plants formed a millennia-old partnership. Downstream, the reptile heard a tapir splash into the water, probably fleeing one of the larger jungle cats. From the sound, a heavy one—the long-nosed creatures could grow to five hundred pounds or more. That size usually protected them from predators until they weakened from disease or old age. The reptile froze. The tapir swam past, breathing heavily, using its prehensile snout as a snorkel. An opportunity. The snake-man slithered silently into the water and began driving the gray-black tapir toward the men.

The odd couple slipped through thick floating mats of blue-flowered water hyacinth and six-foot wide lily pads. Reaching the shallows, the reptile clawed the shorthaired creature on its fat rump. With a squeal, the pig-shaped beastie exploded out of the water, rushed around the tree and straight through the men's fire, scattering smoking logs and embers. It bowled over two humans on the far side and raced off through the jungle.

The muzzles of weapons flared as the men emptied their weapons in its general direction. Using the cover of the distraction, the reptile leaped from the other side of the tree. One hand drew back the head of the rearmost man. Clawed fingers ripped out the rebel's windpipe and larynx.

The remaining men turned in time to see a shadow disappear into the brush, carrying the body of their comrade over its shoulders. Once out of sight, the reptile-man veered right, putting the trunks of large trees between itself and the enemy. It stopped and tucked itself and prey into the shelter of the lichen-covered buttress roots of an immense strangling fig tree.

In a few seconds, weapons reloaded, sprays of bullets zipped through the undergrowth. The creature heard the *whack* and *thunk* of projectiles burying themselves into the wood of saplings and trees. When the firing stopped, the reptile jogged deeper into the rainforest. The body he carried grew cooler. The dead meat felt much heavier and bulkier than when it was alive.

~~~OOO~~~

Five miles away, the rescue team settled in for their first night in the jungle. The group kept a cold camp, no fire, or lights. Fishnet hammocks strung between trees held humans and their gear off the forest floor. Caber noticed Vincenté standing in a listening posture near a clump of saplings at the campsite's edge. Pappy Wallace's command voice cut through the camp noises.

"Well now, you've never been to any Scottish Games, have you? If you had, you'd know how he got the name Caber."

Several voices murmured back.

"All right, imagine this. Cut yourself a nineteen-foot-long, 175-pound piece of timber. Grasp one end with both hands, holding it upright. Then run forward and flip the damn thing end-over-end. And that's what they call the caber-toss, friend."

Questioning sounds drifted out of the group.

"Hell, I don't know why they do it. Probably something some highlander invented to scare the shit out of the British. Any rate, the man can hoist and throw one of them toothpicks twenty-five feet or more."

Caber felt a light touch on his shoulder and turned to face Vincenté. "I have an up-to-date report." A leaf near where the native police officer had stood trembled in the still air. Members of the man's tribe must be all around them. He hoped the rebels weren't as skilled at moving that quietly.

"I think your man is still alive, but ..."

"But what?"

"The shamans don't feel he is human. Given the actions of the rebels and his response, they believe he is a sending from the *Amaru,* the snake spirit who controls the underworld. My people leave him offerings of food, *chicha* beer, and *warmi,* young women. So far he has ignored them and focused on his mission."

"Mission? What mission?"

"To kill the rebels and protect the *Huaca,* the sacred place."

~~~OOO~~~

Caber examined half a grapefruit-sized pod being passed around the group. Inside the shell, brown-orange segment-shaped sections lay arranged in a circle. He gave a grunt of recognition. He now knew the origin of Brazil nuts. The team was finishing food provided by the natives. Tribal women had stacked wooden bowls and leaf-wrapped meats at the far edge of the campsite, avoiding coming close to the foreigners. They even stayed upwind, so they wouldn't breathe the same air. With refugee-like appetites, team members disposed of *sopa de choclo, cuy, juanes,* and various exotic jungle fruits. Those in the know wisely refrained from disclosing to the ignorant that much of the cooked meat came from domesticated guinea pigs.

In addition to the food, Caber digested Vincenté's full report. If they were to continue, the team's goal must be monstrously upgraded. His stomach twitched and acid rose in his throat. He swallowed. Chasing after Teigler would give him ulcers.

The team leader coughed. "Gather around, friends, we have a decision to make." The seven made a tight circle.

"I really don't know how to present this to you." He rubbed three-day-old prickly whiskers on his chin. "Anyway I say it, you'll think I'm crazy. So, I'll just lay it out. The locals believe an event of truly world shattering consequence is about to happen. To their minds, the Teigler kidnapping and our presence is not a coincidence.

"Their legend begins five hundred years ago. Pizzaro's Spaniards with their diseases, steel, and native allies kept defeating the Incas in battle. Great Incas and their followers kept retreating farther and farther into the jungle until they reached this area. In desperation, their *Huillac Uma*, high priest or pope equivalent, located a spot where the normal world and the underworld touched, separated only by a few feet of soil and decaying vegetation. They built a fortified city around it to make their last stand.

"Over the hole in the *Kai Pacha*, or this middle earth, a stone tower in the cross-section of the Inca cross, the *chakana*, rose to imprison a creature the Inca priest called forth from hell. A being whose touch could shuck the life force out of any living thing. Basically, a last ditch doomsday effort. If the Spaniards destroyed the empire, The Great Inca would loose the *Killer of Worlds.*

"Priests kept the beast confined in the tower, binding it with daily rites while waiting for the release-command from the last Inca royal. The word never came—the last emperor and the high priest were assassinated in a surprise attack by the alien conquerors. The remaining lesser priests and guards of the lost city intermarried with the local natives, their descendents maintained the restraining rituals and kept watch. No one among them knew how to send the demon back to hell.

"The current problem, the La Manera Del Sol rebels have possession of the fortress-city. The restraining rites are not being performed. The creature is gaining strength. The fool guerrillas are attempting to break into the *Huaca* tower, because they're thinking it contains treasure. When they open it, the creature will be unleashed upon the world."

The first to close a gaping mouth, Pappy, broke into the stunned silence. "Say we believe this tale, how do we destroy the world-killer?"

"When the creature materializes on this plane, it can be hurt. It becomes vulnerable to our laws of physics. However, Vincenté believes neither we nor the rebels are carrying anything that would cause it more irritation than a mosquito bite."

"This is insane. Our primary reason for being here is to rescue my father," a female voice injected. "I can't go along with any change of priorities."

"Your old man is being drawn to the *Huaca*. The natives believe he is an angel-demon sent to save them and the world. We'll find him there."

Okie spoke. "So what can we do?"

Vincenté spoke, "The world-killer is blacker and colder than anything humans have ever experienced," Vincenté replied. "It is an enemy of *Initi*, the sun god, and can be thrown back into hell only with light and heat."

Caber decided to ramp up the ante. He pulled the radio codebook out of his pack. They would request an air strike from Major De Castro. He figured about six sticks of phosphorous impregnated napalm would do the trick— goodbye rebels and supposed monster. The team would penetrate the fortress, snatch Teigler, and retire covered by the air attack. The old stone walls of the city would hold the 2,000-degree fire like the sides of a frying pan. The good major would only be told about the rebels. There was no time to convince a rational air force officer about the supernatural aspect.

~~~OOO~~~

The team moved down an almost invisible trail led by Vincenté. Tribal warriors scouted ahead and ranged on their flanks—they would be the best warning if there were any sign of the rebels. Rain had come rattling down before sunrise. Water still dripped and ran off the triple-canopy of leaves and limbs wetting everything and everyone. The dappled green light sifting through thick plant material made it hard to tell if the sun was shining.

They had a plan. The attack would begin at high noon. Caber presented it with confident speech, although internally he felt shaky about their prospects—too many wild cards, not enough intelligence. In Vietnam, Teigler had taught him the truth of Clausewitz's basic rule of combat, "No plan survives first contact with the enemy." A hand signal from the point man caused the group to crouch, weapons pointed in alternate directions.

He advanced to confer with Vincenté. "We are within 500 yards of the rebels. My people have found a freshly killed body—not your man, one of the Sun Path rebels."

Caber signaled for Uncle Ho.

~~~OOO~~~

The team and their allies maneuvered closer to the objective. Caber felt better now. When they first adopted Ho and his grandson in Vietnam, the two were destitute. The locals believed the grandfather could talk to the dead so they avoided any contact with the pair. Vincenté's people appreciated this talent. Several of their shamans also claimed to conduct conversations with the dearly departed, although usually they needed help from *wachuma* cactus buds. Ho examined the body. He reported his conversation with the dead soul.

Part of a six-person rebel resupply mission, the man and his comrades had been picked off one at a time by some kind of jungle wraith. Ho felt sure this referred to Teigler. Further questioning determined only forty frightened men remained to garrison the lost city. Their weapons consisted of a variety of rifles, two machine guns—only one of which worked—and a few hand grenades. Under constant but random assault from Teigler, twenty of their comrades had disappeared, and with each loss the morale and unit cohesion of the rebels weakened. The guerrilla leader had recently shot three of his command for desertion. In Ho's opinion, only two things held them together, the fear of meeting their shadowy stalker and the possibility of Inca gold, the sweat of the sun, from the *Huaca*.

Caber scratched his nose as he moved the last few yards toward their objective. He felt immersed in a nightmarish dream that grew worse the longer it persisted. What normal person would believe in the existence of a reptile-man serial killer, an interrogation of the dead, and a 500-year-old lost city inhabited by a demon from hell? He must suspend disbelief or he would run off into the jungle gibbering and tearing out his hair.

Behind him, Pappy and Ho carried a handmade weapon they hoped would distract the demon. A miniature caber, it consisted of a ten-foot-long, fifty-pound sapling stripped of branches and leaves with the team's two thermite grenades duct-taped to one end. Cords ran down from the pull-pins of the grenades, their ends tied to a stick. The hope being that Caber could run forward holding the pole as he did in the Scottish games, the stick in his mouth. Once tossed, the cords would pull, activating five-second fuses. Hopefully, the weapon would pinwheel and land on the creature. The intense heat should kill it, or at least slow it down.

For over five hundred years, the jungle had grown up to lap over the old city's walls. Tree roots a foot thick wrapped around tight-fitting Inca stonework. The rebels had not cut back any of this natural camouflage. The rescue team spread out in a line abreast, weapons at the ready, and advanced the last few yards to the city's main gate. Their native allies moved to surround the place cutting off any escape routes. Dead, limp, and still warm at the foot of the wall, they found the bodies of two sentries. One lay bent over a fallen tree, his blood soaking into the jungle humus, throat showing a ragged slash. The other sat propped against a bush, eyes open, looking as though he might rise at any moment, except that his head was twisted at an impossible angle. They had missed Teigler by minutes. He was already inside.

Nam and Okie made wall-top nests for themselves on each side of the gate. They would cover the others with rifles and the grenade launchers slung beneath the barrels of their weapons. Carrie entered the city and climbed to a sniper's position on top of the remains of a stonewalled building. Caber and Vincenté advanced, Pappy and Ho served as escorts on each side, shotguns ready.

Grown careless in their greed, a dozen of the rebels gathered near the apex of the tower. The remainder formed a half-circle at the bottom, staring up. The work party at the top pried and tugged at one of the smaller dark stones of the structure. About two feet of its width stuck out from its smooth-faced tight-fitting brothers. The leader shouted. Sweating men took a break. The stone would be out in minutes.

The stone plug moved by itself. It stopped, then moved a few more inches with a grating stone-on-stone sound. The men's body language showed shock and disbelief. The ground shook.

The stone plug suddenly blew out like a champagne cork. Rebels pinwheeled off the structure. A black viscous substance vomited out. Cold winds whirled around the tower. Clouds formed and rose in massive dark pillows, eclipsing the light of the sun.

A huge amoeba-like lump grew, rising upward, first to twenty feet, then to forty feet high. Black frost formed on the plants at its foot. A wave of cold advanced, shriveled plants, and dropped insects, coating them with obsidian-colored ice.

Vincenté whispered, "*Yana Supay,* black devil."

Following directly behind the freezing curtain, the creature's odor smashed into the humans. It felt like breathing razor blades—it was the smell of death. New death with its urine, blood, and shit meshed with middle death's putrid syrup of liquefying flesh and open intestines.

Swirling amidst these, old death's miasma of acrid, musty bone dust and the rotting shrouds of ancient tombs and graves. Caber choked and lowered his head. Uncle Ho scowled and held a packet of scented herbs to his nose. They heard a gagging noise. Pappy chucked out his breakfast.

Gasping, the oldster said, "Don't tell the others."

Rebels yelled, fired rifles. Bullets disappeared into the monster's great mass. One threw a hand grenade. The creature's trunk flowed over it. The explosion made a great bubble in the monster's stalk that burst, splattering out some of its substance.

The creature formed a mouth and bellowed. The vibration shook human muscles and bones. The hole created by the explosion filled in. Tentacles flew out grabbing the rebels. The mouth sealed.

Caber and his team watched. Black tar-thick material flowed over the guerrillas, cocooning them from ankles to necks. They screamed. Inside the covering, millions of thin microscopic wire threads penetrated the pores of their skins.

The tips of these filaments burst the walls of muscle and blood cells as they worked their way inward toward the organs. The men ran out of breath. Their bodies began to bend and unbend in an obscene parody of set-ups. The creature forced them to take air into their lungs so the screaming could continue. It pumped the bodies, bringing forth atonal choral music from its insane choir while it sucked out their life cell by cell. It would take a long time.

Caber stood close enough to throw the thermite weapon, but there was no opening. The world-killer must be distracted and pinned in place until they could find Teigler. Pappy slapped his shoulder with the handset of the radio. Major De Castro's three aircraft circled overhead.

"This is Pachacuti flight to Pachamama. Come in Pachamma. We have homed in on your radio beacon. Over."

"This is Pachamama. Can you deliver the strike? Over."

"This is Pachacuti One, I have three fast movers capable of dropping two sticks each. We can loiter fifteen minutes before bingo fuel. Currently low clouds over the target give us zero visibility. Over."

"Pachacuti One, this is Pachamama, standby. I'll see what we can do. Out."

Caber wiped away cold crystallizing sweat. Something must be accomplished soon. Rhime ice formed on the barrels of their weapons. The intense jungle humidity warred with hellish cold. Their uniform cloth lost flexibility as their sweat froze and stiffened the fabric. He shouted, "Open fire."

He heard the *thumps* as the grenadiers opened up. The grenades penetrated the tarry mass of the demon, exploded bubbles inside with little effect. No mouth opened.

Carrie started killing the encapsulated rebels to reduce the screaming—not for mercy. Perhaps the loss of its singers would aggravate the monster.

Caber and Pappy threw hand grenades. The resulting explosions went unanswered, still no mouth. They positioned and set off two of the claymores. The concentrated shrapnel opened tears in the demon's sides that sealed quickly. Bullets and tracers continued to penetrate the creature causing dimples and ripples on its surface.

Nothing was working. Caber thought about saving a last bullet for himself, rather than become a singer. Out of a clump of blackened bushes on the side of the tower, a tan body launched into space. The figure looked dwarf-sized up against the monster. It smacked against demon skin—clawed feet and hands cut a slit as it slid down.

Caber shouted and ran forward, raising the thermite-topped pole. Pappy and Ho opened up with their shotguns on either side, the concentrated shower of double-aught buck kept the slit open.

A tentacle grabbed the reptile-man by the ankle. Caber tossed the pole. The pins pulled out of the thermite grenades. The sapling trunk rotated like a slow-motion propeller, reached its peak, and dropped back, entering the open sore in the monster's hide just before it closed.

A flash of tiger-stripe battle dress caught his eye. Carrie raced past. She leaped upwards and grasped the tentacle holding a writhing upside down Teigler. The three-inch razor-clawed nucks in her hands spun around the diameter of the pseudopod, cutting it loose from the creature's body. She and Teigler fell together. The isolated fragment of the monster dropped away.

Pappy skipped sideways, placing himself between the monster and a stunned Teigler. His AA-11 on full automatic sounded like a pneumatic jackhammer. Titanium shot opened lace-like patterns in the fiend's black skin.

The demon danced and roared. Its body quivered and bounced as the thermite ate its substance. Tentacles opened and writhed, the bodies of its victims fell and landed like sacks of mush. Caber motioned his team out. If they could only order the strike now, but thick clouds still hung too low.

Ho stopped to reload his shotgun. He pulled shells out of loops on bandoliers, thrusting them into the weapon's loading port. A tentacle smacked into Pappy, reflexively wrapped around his waist, and lifted. The man shrieked as the creature squeezed and snapped his spine. Kicking legs went limp. Pappy's shook his head, still the combat veteran, Caber could see him taking stock of the tactical situation.

Ho shouted a chain of words in Vietnamese, fired his last three shots, and rushed forward, his shotgun with sixteen-inch bayonet extended. The rest of the squad charged forward. They had all gone crazy, Caber thought. Trying to rescue a comrade at close quarters, they would all be killed

Pappy watched the rush of friends from his high perch. He looked down at his body—paralyzed from the waist down, kidneys, liver, and most organs damaged beyond repair. The only thing keeping him from going crazy with pain was the nerve damage. He would not survive, not even if the demon released him. One more casualty and his squad-mates wouldn't have enough strong backs to haul everyone out.

Caber watched Pappy's face grow calm. He waved goodbye and spun the AA-11 around. The barrel went under his chin.

Caber screamed, "No! No! Goddamn it!"

The blam of the gun froze the humans. A headless corpse jiggled in the tentacle's grasp. Caber moved among his men, shouting and punching, forcing them toward the exit. They wanted to recover the body. They wanted revenge. He bent down and hoisted Teigler up onto his back. Behind them the demon continued to buck and roar.

Through the ancient city gate came a strange trio. A man wearing a headdress and tunic adorned with gold ornaments held a staff topped by a sun symbol. On his right walked a woman clothed in a purple cotton tunic worked with gold thread. Hand-sized sun symbols dangled from each ear. The third person wore a pure white loincloth and a rayed gold mask. Obviously a warrior, he carried a club with a solid gold spiked head and a square shield with intricate designs picked out in thousands of tiny red, yellow, and blue bird feathers.

"Leave them," Vincenté commanded. "They have a job to do."

Caber stopped outside the gate and looked back. The priest and his party halted twenty feet from the twisting demon and began chanting. The priest raised his staff. The clouds thinned, the noon sun showed through. The monster shuddered as the sun's rays and heat played over its glassy blackness.

Behind him, he heard Vincenté on the radio, "Pacachuti One, this is Pachamama. Proceed with napalm drop. Over."

"This is Pachcuti One, visibility increasing. Drop in progress. Out."

Caber's eyes teared. Pappy gone. The priest, the virgin, and the warrior would be next. All sacrifices. Caber turned, motioned to Carrie, and ran. He raced behind her with Teigler splayed over his shoulders.

He tripped and fell to one knee. Behind them, the first two sticks of napalm tumbled over the lost city walls. The 750-pound bombs broke open and spread roiling mountains of flame over an area as wide and long as a football field.

Carrie grabbed Caber's arm and helped lift him and his burden upright. They rushed on. Fire blossomed out of the lost city gate, forming a long, thick tongue of oily flame that narrowly missed the last two team members and their burden.

The shadow-silhouettes of a second and third aircraft flitted across the ground, homing in on the flame mushroom still growing within the walls.

~~~OOO~~~

Freshly showered and clothed, the team gathered, drank the local brew as guests of Major De Castro's Officers' Club, and rehashed their adventure. The mission had been successful, but no one was celebrating. They had all attended a memorial service for Pappy that morning. Caber felt the loss. His lips twitched as he imagined Pappy in the room. He would have been belly-up to the bar, slapping backs and leading the singing of dirty lyrics he had created to the tune of "Louie, Louie."

The rescued Teigler had required treatment. The ankle grabbed by the demon had swollen to twice its normal size, but it would heal. The tough part was getting his mind back into balance.

In sole control for months, the reptile personality did not want to let go. Uncle Ho and the village shaman filled Teigler full of various herbs and drugs. The two spent hours praying and "laying on hands."

Caber shook the memories out of his head. Picking up three long-necked cold Cuzqueña's from the bar, he walked over to the table of a sober twosome. Carrie held her father's hand. A clear-headed Teigler, clad in blue shirt and khakis, one bandaged foot up on a cushioned hassock, waved—his little finger completely grown back.

Wonderland

Alice, did you slip down
the rabbit hole and discover yourself?
each adventure a reflection of humanity.

Pursuing the White Rabbit:
a mirage, the Holy Grail
that you were not pure enough to catch.

Eat me, the label read.
Drink me, uppers or downers,
you were not able to "just say no."

You are so like us, Alice running fast
as you can to keep in the same place
"Faster!" screamed the Red Material Queen.

From cup to cup, from cult to cult, you move
with the Mad Hatter, the charismatic holy man,
whose failure to know God ends in Waco or 9/11.

We pray, that like you, a protective angel
will appear for us. Our hope, that its Cheshire
smile will be one of compassion—and not madness.

Supermarket Takeout

Prologue

Blinding high-low flashes of headlights flooded the car's interior. The long blare of a truck horn shocked him out of the nightmare, and by reflex, his arms twisted the steering wheel. The car screeched back into its proper lane, rocking back and forth. The air-conditioning fan blew across sweat-soaked clothes, raising a bumper crop of goose bumps. Teigler shook the dream's remnants out of his head and concentrated on keeping the vehicle within the highway's white lines.

The nightmare occurred day or night at random times. It opened with him alone staring at his reflection in the mirror-black surface of the cabin's sliding glass doors. A shadow moved close in the outside darkness. Teigler's stomach churned. A ten-foot-long reptile thing leapt up, slammed its clawed pads and scaled muzzle against the glass. The metal frame groaned and deformed with the weight. Its thin Y-shaped tongue licked the corners of the panes, summoning him. Knees shaking, he collapsed through the glass, merging into the creature—two drops of liquid mercury becoming one. Their muscles elongated as they turned to stalk the adjacent farmland. The yellow-eyed head moved back and forth, a carnivore's flicking tongue tasted the scent of nocturnal humanity.

He forced his attention back to the traffic. The subcompact buzzed along, another ant in an unending chain of similar-looking vehicles. The rental agency had come off a busy day, and this was all they had available. Left with no choice, the deal lubricated with a healthy discount, Teigler agreed to take the diminutive hatchback.

After the first fifty miles, he discovered its good and bad points. The five-speed manual transmission made for peppy acceleration, reaching highway speed more quickly than most of its breed. Built with a tight suspension and rack and pinion steering, it handled just a cut or two under the sports car he once owned. The car also lacked the syrupy nicotine smell of most rental vehicles. On the bad side, the shocks transmitted every bump, large and small, to passengers.

He watched dark fields and small town lights spin past as the radio played Joplin's hundred-proof, fried voice. She belted out a late 60's blues tune—a tribute to his lost generation—many of whose soldiers still hid in woods and wild places. It seemed that Teigler was always a single breakdown away from joining them. Like the others, Vietnam had rewired his brain.

At the VA, the psych doctors said multiple personality disorder, but were confused because this should only happen if you were abused as a child. Teigler told them where it lived—coiled inside the back of his brain. They didn't know about the dream that returned again and again.

One of them had it right. This doc theorized a separate berserker creature, blind to everything but its immediate focus, cut off from all human emotion, a throwback to our ancient reptile ancestors. The medication they prescribed made him feel like he was made of wood. He quit taking it. So, it's in there, quiet for now. Looking through his eyes … waiting.

---OOO---

The way he moved, back straight, measured steps, arms swinging with a relaxed rhythm through the supermarket parking lot, caught her attention. She guessed him at over six feet and near two hundred pounds. The muscles through the faded t-shirt and stonewashed jeans rewarded the length of her gaze.

It was difficult to tell more in the shadow-spotted lot, the two of them moving in and out of foggy blue circles cast by mercury-vapor pole lights. A chill ran over her skin, contrary to the heat and moisture still radiating out of the concrete and asphalt, stored up by a hotter than normal day. Taking her cold flesh as a warning, Alice stopped, scanning the lot. They were the only occupants. Besides their two vehicles, a scattering of cars at the far end marked the employee parking area.

The quiet made her nervous She listened, the man visible but moving silently—probably rubber-soled shoes. She reached into her purse, fingered the keys to her white VW Rabbit, paused, and then decided to continue her original errand. This was the only store open this late and it closed in half an hour, the downside of living in a small town recently evolved into a bedroom community. The moment of fear could be a premonition or just something her mind dredged up from voraciously reading hundreds of murder mysteries.

Her footsteps started again, clicking noises marked the progress of her composite heeled loafers. Once inside, in full light and under the eyes of the staff, she would feel silly about this moment. The outside doors swished open, exposing a line of interlocked grocery carts. She tugged at one. It stuck. A second tug failed. Two long-fingered hands grabbed the cart, startling her. A sharp jerk separated out the end cart. She looked up at the man from the parking lot. His forearms were hairier than most, the soft, faded brown cotton shirt molded to his chest.

She experienced a light-headed moment, imagining him in a wet t-shirt contest. His eyes were very brown and very deep. She froze for a moment, a bird paralyzed in the hypnotic glare of a snake. The cold metal frame of the cart brought her back. Older than her first guess, his age made apparent by lines and wrinkles around his eyes and lips, and black hair highlighted with random touches of white.

Exposing no teeth, he gave her a quick tight-lipped smile and turned to select a plastic red shopping basket nested in a stack near the inner door. Her sniff disclosed no distinctive scent, no cologne, or deodorant—perhaps he was allergic. Wouldn't block the pheromones anyway. As he marched into the produce section, she noticed the high gloss of his leather-topped Nikes. Ex-military or law enforcement, she thought. The casual interest budding in her leafed out as her final calculation placed him in his middle fifties.

The conclusion, a bit alien to her small-town experience … but interesting. Lonely for a long time, she felt a visceral attraction. A well-maintained body spoke of discipline, or at least good genes. Might be a bit of the bad boy in there also. What to do next? She wanted to express interest but not seem too brazen. If the man felt her cat claw thoughts in his mind, he gave no indication, continuing to twist a green wire tie around a plastic bag of red and yellow striated apples. Cartwheels squeaked as she waltzed past the checkout counters, manned at night by a clerk and a bag boy.

"Hey, Alice," the boy shouted, "how do you like the music?"

For the first time she noticed the usual elevator music had been replaced by the classics, and not rock'n roll classics either. "Oh, for Pete's sake, Wagner's 'Gotterdammerrung.' Erv must be the night manager," she shouted back. "Matty, Bobby, you'll just have to bear it."

A less than happy Matty rested her broad backside against the checkout partition. She pointed upward, directing Alice to look to the partial second floor. Alice could just see the top of Erv's head through the business office window. She imagined he was probably bent over the opera's score, trying to harmonize with the singers. Erv was her second cousin. As a relative, she felt obliged to listen to him try to convert all and sundry to be fans of such music. His dream of becoming an opera star, taking triumphant tours of foreign lands, would never materialize in this hick town. Not that he didn't have a good enough voice for the church choir—a role that would probably be the height of his accomplishments.

"When you come back through, I've got some good dirt to pass on." Matty wiggled her eyebrows. "Oh!" she added, "Jack Barker's escaped from federal prison!"

Moving on, Alice caught something more about Mr. Benson and the neighbor lady through the now-booming music. Bobby picked up a folded-over copy of the local newspaper and penciled in a number on the Sudoku of the week. The kid, a third cousin and a numbers genius, worked at the store during summer vacations from MIT. His often-expressed goal in life was to work out the math for a hyper-drive engine, which would allow faster-than-light travel to the stars.

Alice turned into the cereal aisle with the thought that everyone in this damn town must be related, except Mr. Benson and the neighbor lady. So, if they were entangled, at least it wasn't incest. Then it registered. Jack Barker busted out of the pen after fifteen years. He'd been a nasty one, worked his way up from school bully to car thief, to burglar, graduating to bank robbery and assault. His last victim still walked with a cane.

She caught a flicker of motion as the tall man crossed the aisle near the meat department. As predicted, she felt foolish about being so spooked in the parking lot. The overhead fluorescents flooded the store with soft white light, bringing out the reds, blues, and greens on the cans and boxes with their buy-me messages. She moved with a relaxed step, trying to ignore the music and the rhythmic squeak of one of the cart's wheels. A mélange of scents tickled her nostrils and made her mouth water as she entered the spice section. The smell grew more intense and she put a finger under her nose to keep from sneezing. Someone must have spilled pepper.

The town was lucky to have a store this large, only made possible by the interstate highway connecting them with the state capital some thirty miles south. Over the years, suburban residential construction had crept north. A recent housing development finally prompted the construction of a real supermarket. A glance at her watch indicated fifteen minutes left until closing time.

The store was part of a small regional chain still owned by the original family, who not beholden to stockholders, closed on Sundays. She needed a few more items to tide her over until Monday's 8:00 a.m. certification test. For more than a year, she had been classified as a Basic Emergency Medical Technician. Her boss finally convinced her to try for the next level, EMT-185. This weekend was set aside to study.

Passing through the dairy department, the cart grew heavier with the addition of a gallon of skim milk, a few containers of yogurt, and a bottle of orange juice. Jelly and peanut butter completed her list. Alice moved up the bread aisle toward the checkout. She'd hang out talking with Matty until the t-shirt guy came through. Maybe she could think of a flirty opening line to try on him. Just before turning the corner, she heard shouting over the music.

The threatening sound of male voices made her pause. She moved in front of the cart to peer around a pyramid of stacked boxes at the aisle's end. Three men moved among the employees. An older man riffled the cash drawer. A second man, overweight with dark hair and a broken nose, watched Matty, standing very close. The third man, a young blond, stood back a few feet with a hand on Billy's shoulder. Alice glanced up at the office, noticing Erv being jerked to his feet by two guys, one bald and the other in a red shirt. Baldy grabbed a handful of the manager's hair then smacked a pistol down on the bridge of his nose. Red Shirt fumbled with something on the desk, the opera music cut off.

"Johnny," the old man by the register chuckled, "member, a broke nose'll sure make a man co-op-er-ate." The blond boy's cheeks turned pale. "Now, let's see what we got here," he said, pinning Matty's arms behind her back and securing them with duct tape. Her mouth opened. The man in front moved closer, jammed a hand between her legs. The cold steel barrel of a gun pressed into the curve under her left ear. Her intended scream lapsed into a half-gasp, half-sob.

Bobby couldn't stand by. He leaped forward, slipping out of the inexperienced young guard's grasp, an instinctive, non-thinking reaction to protect a female of his tribe. The boy's fists beat against the back of the dark-haired man. His target spun around, grabbed a handful of Bobby's clothes, and thrust the gun, as though it was a knife, into the boy's body just below the sternum. A muffled *BAM*, the bullet went through a lower lobe of the boy's heart and blew bits of flesh out the exit wound.

Most of the splatter left a patterned spray over the front windows—some coated the blond's left arm. In the stunned quiet, they could hear the metallic *ting* of the ejected cartridge as it bounced off the floor tile. The body slid off the counter.

NASA would have to wait for hyperdrive.

Alice opened her mouth. No sound came out. Her subconscious decided at light speed to shut down her vocal chords—survival demanded silence. As her body shrank back, a hand knocked a box of crackers out of the stack, causing the pyramid to collapse. For a few seconds, she and the three men at the register stared at each other. She turned and ran back down the aisle, abandoning her cart and purse. The click of her heels on the hard tile sounded like panicky dance steps.

"Johnny!" the old guy shouted. "Get'er! Son'a bitch, don' jus stan there."

The blond boy reacted to the command. The goods on the shelves blurred together as Alice picked up speed. She turned the aisle end corner at too high a speed, lost her footing and fell, sliding across the floor.

Her body thumped against the cold stainless panels of the meat counter, and she lay there, stunned. Too soon for her to recover, the blond rounded the corner and stopped. He straightened and might have tried to say something, but any words were cut off.

Alice's eyes widened as her parking lot companion stepped up beside her captor, his right hand held a heavy Pyrex pie dish. His arm, backed with all his body weight, swung the tempered glass plate. It caught the boy in the middle of his throat, crushed his larynx, and dropped his dying weight like a sack of potatoes. If the plate had been sharp edged, Alice thought, the head would surely have sailed off the body. She could only imagine the speed at which the dish's thin rim had connected. The blond boy lay choking, face turning dark, unable to breathe or talk. The man, plate still in hand, motioned her to follow.

Repulsed and overwhelmed by the killings, she felt faint and paralyzed. He stepped forward, sat the plate on the meat counter, grabbed her under the armpits, and lifted. On her feet again, her legs reluctantly decided to work. She leaned on him as they scuttled toward the back of the store. It'd only be a few moments before the other convicts found the dead boy.

He guided them through double swinging doors into the unloading docks. Spotting the back exit doors, they picked up speed. The pair hit the crash bars and bounced back unexpectedly. They could see a chain laced through the outside door handles. The man let her stand, alone and shaking, while he checked the overhead truck doors, which allowed entrance to the loading docks. Both were jammed.

Alice started to ask what they were to do. He raised a finger to his lips and hissed. She shivered. She wanted some words of assurance, wanted to know his name, wanted a plan. The bad guys had a plan. They weren't going to let anyone out. The store was now officially closed and no one would expect it to open until Monday. The four remaining criminals had the perfect well-stocked hideout for the next thirty hours, plenty of time to finish off the remaining store employees and the two customers.

She looked for the man. A light came on in a closet off the open area. Alice moved in that direction, thinking how she was ridiculously dependent upon this person she knew nothing about. Since he refused to talk, she would call him "Soldier." Noticing a wall phone, she grabbed the handset and raised a finger to punch 911—no dial tone. She let it drop.

In the utility closet, the man read labels on the store's gray metal electrical boxes. He pulled the levers down on the switches controlling the parking lot lights and outside store signs. The one marked *refrigeration* he left connected—the compressor noises would help conceal the sound of their movements. A large box packed with circuit breakers transferred power to the inside fixtures and air conditioning. He switched off the panel's master breaker. All the lights went out. Covered with goose bumps, Alice shivered in the eerie darkness.

They felt their way out of the closet. Battery-powered emergency lights flickered on. In the dimness, Soldier closed and locked the door. Picking up a box cutter from a nearby shelf, he jammed the tip of its blade into the keyhole and broke it off. Alice understood they would be safer in the dark. The pair moved back into the store.

The emergency lights cast shadows everywhere. Shadows they could move in—hide in. Her heels clicked and echoed. He stopped and pointed at her shoes. She nodded and noticed for the first time that he was barefoot. The shoestrings of his sneakers tied together and looped around his neck. Shoes off, she slipped and almost fell, the nylon feet of her pantyhose slick against the recently waxed floor. Handing him her shoes, she tugged the hose down to the knees, almost falling in the process. They became tangled. She finally had to lie down while he peeled them off. With a low grunt of disgust, he stuffed the wadded-up hose into his pocket.

Up by the registers, a barrage of loud talk and cursing let them know the gang was still fumbling around, trying to become organized. As they made their way to the farthest corner of the store, Soldier would stop and leave her to collect items from various shelves as they passed. They holed up in a corner of the soft drink section, the surrounding shelves stacked high with aluminum cans and plastic bottles of Pepsi, Coke, and generic brands of soda.

The man laid out his treasures, her panty hose, a box of black drawstring trash bags, two 10-ounce cans of ground red cayenne pepper, and a grapefruit knife. To Alice's eyes, the knife didn't look like much of a weapon. Almost eight inches long, half its length consisted of a round steel handle. The narrow scoop-shaped blade's curved edges were notched with small teeth and terminated in a short sharp point. Circles of light played across ceiling—the criminals had finally found the stock of flashlights.

A voice shouted, "Where the fuck is my brother Johnny?" It continued, "Gramps, you and Frenchy check out where he went. Jack and I will watch our guests. See if you can spot the woman."

Lights fluttered down the aisle, marking the two men's progress. "Shit! We found him, boss." A few minutes passed as the two examined the boy's body. "Goddamn, son' a bitch! Karl, your brother's dead." Grabbing the corpse's hands and feet, they dragged the body to the front of the store and lifted it to the counter.

Karl worked his flashlight over the corpse. "There's no marks on him. Did anybody hear anything? How did he die? How could a woman do this?"

The men turned and flashed their lights outward in jerky nervous patterns. Karl raised his automatic. "You two, get back out there and find her!" The two reluctantly moved forward in a slow crouch, heads scanning.

Soldier pulled a black trash bag from its box, fluffed it open and carefully poured in the cans of pepper. Partially pulling out the drawstrings, he tied them into a slipknot. Making two parallel cuts three inches apart in the right pocket of his jeans, the man threaded the grapefruit blade in one cut and out the other—a makeshift sheath. He placed the pantyhose in his other pocket. Bag in hand, the man rose. Alice started to get up. A hand squeezed her shoulder and pushed her back. She was to stay.

The two men turned into the first aisle. Frenchy bumped into Alice's cart and stopped to investigate, opening her purse to examine the contents. Gramps continued down the aisle unaware he now walked alone. Almost to the end, he heard his companion yell, "I found 'er purse. 'Er ID an' cell phone in eet."

"Bring it here," Karl shouted back.

Gramps spun around in time to see him disappear. Something black and slick slipped over his head, tightened, and shut out the light. His fingers jerked. The gun in his hand fired, blowing open three cans of peaches, their contents splattering shelves and the floor.

His adrenalin-pumped muscles demanded oxygen. The old man's lungs expanded and sucked in fiery pepper. Gramps' wide-open eyes filled with the stuff, vision blurred. An explosive sneeze, he immediately inhaled another measure of the spice.

The gun clattered to the floor. Soft tissues burned, replaced only by deeper burning. He tried to scream while he ran blindly down the aisle, that is until he bounced off Alice's abandoned cart. Body and cart spun out into the open area at the front of the store.

Unable to breathe, Gramps tore at the bag. Its quilted strength stretched and resisted tearing. He blindly staggered a few steps toward the checkout counters, fell, and groped the darkness. With his final breath, the bag molded to his face.

Alice jumped and almost panicked at the gunshot. Thoughts of Soldier wounded or dead blew through her mind. Should she stay or find him? As an EMT, she might help. She didn't want to be alone. The conflicting arguments kept her motionless. A familiar shadow materialized. She grasped his hands in relief. They felt strange, the skin dry, flexible, and almost scaly. He kneeled and shook as he handed over the flashlight taken from the thug.

Soldier choked and whispered in a little boy's voice, "It's … it's loose."

She moved her lips close to his ear. "What's loose?"

The body next to her hissed. Alice massaged his neck and back. Amazingly, there was no sweat. The muscles felt like wire ropes and squirmed away from her fingers. She heard shouting again. Soldier stiffened.

Karl's voice went up an octave. "What the fuck! Jesus! Is that Gramps? Who in the hell is this woman?" He shook the contents of the handbag on the counter. "Jack, hold your light here." After studying the driver's license, he said, "Who is Alice Krantzmeyer?"

"We went to high school together," Jack responded. "Last I heard she worked at the clinic. I can't believe she could do this shit."

The gang boss raised his head and howled, "Alice, Alice … you're dead. You bitch! Fucking bitch!" He tore at the card. Slammed it on the floor. The men stepped back. Karl paused, wiped spittle off his chin, and regained some control. "You two, Jack, Frenchy, go kill her. Don't come back till you do or I'll shoot you myself."

As soon as they were out of sight, Frenchy grabbed Jack's arm. "Jac', ma grand-mere, she tell us kids bout the *whitigo*. Es person who change shape… kill, drink blood. I have ver bad feelin'."

"Relax, man. This isn't some fucked-up bayou swamp backwater. There ain't no gators, snakes, or boogiemen. I grew up here."

"You go first. I watch yer back."

Jack moved, one slow step at a time, trying to be silent. He shut off the flashlight and signaled his companion to do the same. She wouldn't be able to track their movement by the glare. He noticed the emergency lights starting to dim. Their batteries normally only lasted long enough to let people evacuate the store. The one at the end flashed on and off. He motioned to Frenchy to keep up, the distance between them kept growing. Frenchy must be scared shitless. He whispered, "Goddamn you. Stay close." Jack turned the corner and moved along the meat display cases. Pushed out at right angles to the main aisles, several shorter rows of shelves led to the far wall of the building. The first walkway featuring pet food was empty. Dim light from spots reflected off the polished floor.

He kneeled at the entrance to the second row and leaned forward just enough for a quick look and pulled back. A shadow huddled in the corner! Someone touched his shoulder. He jumped, and then relaxed as he caught a whiff of Frenchy's bad breath.

"Damn, don't you ever brush your teeth? All right, I'll go down this aisle, you go down the other, we'll catch her between us."

About halfway down, and she hadn't moved. Jack waited a few more seconds to make sure Frenchy was in place. He raised the flashlight. On the other side of the shelves, he heard shoes rasp the floor, then jerky scraping noises and a heavy flopping sound.

What the fuck was Frenchy doing? Jack clicked on the flashlight. The woman leaped out of his field of vision, flushed like the pheasants he and his father used to hunt. Startled, he fired twice, missed her, and exploded several half-gallon plastic bottles of Diet Pepsi.

"Frenchy," he shouted, "she's on your side. Shoot!"

Jack raced around the corner, slipped on the pool of soda, fell and broke the light. Jumping up, he limped down the dark aisle, tripped, and fell on top of a warm, still body. He felt around in panic. The face had a broken nose.

He found the second flashlight and pushed the "on" button. Frenchy's neck tilted at an unnatural angle. Jack pulled at the strange brown loop around the corpse's neck. As it came free, he recognized it as pantyhose tightly twisted into a rope. The hair on the back of his neck lifted. He could feel eyes watching him. His companion had been right. There was a monster loose in the store.

He must escape. But, Karl guarded the way out. A decision came quickly. He'd rather kill the boss or be killed by him than stay in the dark with whatever killed Frenchy. Looping around the back of the store would put him in line for a back shot. Karl would never see it coming. Jack would take the register money and get out.

Alice squeezed in-between two of the meat cases near the fruit and vegetable displays, directly under a blinking, dying emergency light. Face and right arm sticky with sprayed Pepsi, she attempted to control her breathing and slow the escalated thump of her heart. Events had moved too fast for her—the shots, the dead body, and the race to escape. Where had Soldier gone?

Maybe it was better for him not to be near. A man who could kill like that, she couldn't have imagined it a few hours ago.

A shadow moved directly toward her. "Jesus, help me," she whimpered. The overhead spotlights blinked. "Oh, hell." She recognized Jack Barker's stained teeth smiling gruesomely.

Jack had spotted a pair of feet sticking out, their polished toenails evident, even in the dim light. Jack liked them. He had always been attracted to female feet. Fifteen years without a woman—too bad he was in a hurry. Jack glanced up, "Hello, Alice."

The emergency light flashed ON—for a moment, there was Soldier's face behind Jack, a pale oval growing larger—Flash OFF—the criminal straddled her body, savoring the moment. Flash ON—white light reflected off her rescuer's cheeks, eye sockets black shadows—Flash OFF—Alice heard two sets of heavy breathing—Flash ON—Jack raised his pistol, leveled it at her head—Flash OFF—an unseen hand came up and around Jack's face. The three bottom fingers clamped over his mouth, the thumb and forefinger pinched his nostrils shut. The two bodies came together like lovers. Soldier's knife spiraled up. All four inches of the blade entered Jack's right side just above the belt—Flash ON—she could see both faces. Jack's looked like a contorted wooden mask. Flash OFF—over Jack's right shoulder, the eyes of his killer glowed neon yellow, like a night predator caught in headlights.

The dying body brushed her feet as the creature lowered it quietly to the ground. Alice got up to run. Two sinewy hands closed on her neck, cut off her air, lifted her up on her tiptoes. Her eyes bulged, face turning red.

This wasn't a man any longer. The transformation complete, this creature would kill anyone without hesitation. The reptile paused. What it held wasn't male. It lowered its head and sniffed ... sniffed again. The hands relaxed slightly, allowing her to breathe.

Puzzled, it stopped to consider. The scent revealed the captive was a female in season. Lowering its head, it licked her cheek. The sweat contained chemical encouragement. It began to feel aroused. The female's body responded. Her temperature rose, breathing doubled. She could smell and feel its reaction.

One hand left her neck and clutched her waist. The other locked in her hair. Its lips came down on her neck. Teeth nibbled. Alice let out a long gasping,

"Ahhhh." The night's shock, fear, and exhaustion were too much. Barriers fell. Rushing up out of her medulla, primitive instincts took control.

A series of gunshots came from the front of the store. Bullets crashed randomly through shelves and glass cases. Reptile heads snapped around to face the threat.

"Jack, Frenchy, where are you boys? Dead?" Karl answered his own question. "They're dead!" The emergency lights faded to candlelight level. A car drove by, its high beams made a shadow race across the length of the store. Karl fired again and again. "Come get me, you bitch. I've got something for you."

Dropped from the reptile's embrace, a receptive Alice lay on the floor. She watched her companion crawl toward Karl's location. The creature's body moved, suspended off the floor on arms crooked and held out to the sides, palms down flat. Hands and knees alternately pushing it forward with a slinking side-to-side motion. She thought it resembled the way she had seen alligators or Komodo dragons move on TV.

Reason returned to her with a simple understanding—something must be done. This madness must stop. Looking up at the ceiling, an inspiration came. The sprinkler system! If activated, it would set off an automatic alarm at the firehouse. Damn, it was too high. She could never reach it. Alice's thought process focused. The meat department, with its lower ceiling, might be the answer. Pulling herself up, she concentrated on advancing one shaking leg after the other.

Just enough light remained to see the sprinkler heads. They were closer, but still too far away. She grabbed a push broom, leaned against the butcher block, and tried a swing. Not quite enough. A bullet ricocheted past. The last bad guy continued to fire at shadows.

Alice levered herself up to stand on the meat-cutting block. She stood firmly and swung, almost connecting. She started giggling. It was ... *piñata* time. She tried again and nailed it. The holding link broke off, pinging on the floor. Water sprayed out, drenched her, and made everything slippery.

Her giggle grew, leaping into shrieking laughter. It grew louder and louder. She couldn't stop. The water-distorted demented sounds blew out of the meat department, echoed off shelves, ceiling, and vibrated the front windows.

Surrounded by hideous noise, Karl began shaking uncontrollably. His bowels let loose as a shadow detached from the floor and leapt upon him. The master criminal quivered, too frightened to speak, move, or lift his hands. His screams didn't start until teeth started working his flesh. The man felt himself being lifted. Body tossed like a rag doll against a front window. Karl crashed through to rest on a pile of glass shards carpeting the parking lot asphalt.

He heard a siren, saw a pair of Nikes crunch past him through the broken glass. A car door slammed, an engine started, and a car drove off. Moments later, a fire truck and the sheriff's patrol car pulled up to the front doors.

Epilogue

Sheriff Charles Krantzmeyer stroked his bristly mustache and took a sip of highly sweetened coffee. Two FBI agents stared at their untouched cups and the gray file folder that lay on his desk. It contained a mystery of major proportions, now three months old.

The agents looked almost as alike as Tweedledum and Tweedledee. Both wore dark navy suits, white shirts, and red power ties. Even similar haircuts. The only difference being the older one clipped his side arm on the right side and the younger on the left. The ancient window air conditioner rattled on, giving the illusion of cooling without any of the satisfaction. Over the coffee smell, he picked up the odor of Old Spice. Damn, he thought, they even use the same deodorant.

The sheriff spoke up. "I believe it's time to close the file. Too many questions—not enough answers."

The head agent inhaled the stale cigar smoke in the office, grimaced, and said, "Let's do one more run-through."

Chuck ran a hand through short-cropped gray hair. "We have one dead local boy, whose murderer has been identified. Four criminals also put to rest, and the surviving witnesses completely confused about who killed them. You fellows have the gang leader, any progress there?"

With a sour look, the junior partner responded, "Karl Berghoff is under heavy sedation. He's in isolation at the federal psychiatric hospital. You know his thumb, index, and middle fingers of both hands were bitten off? Fingers we have never found, by the way. He still isn't coherent and will only say, 'Don't kill me, don't kill me!' finishing with peals of hysterical high-pitched laughter."

Krantzmeyer started checking items off a list he had scribbled out earlier, "Matty, the checkout clerk is doing better, but still doesn't remember anything past Billy's murder. Erv, the night manager, from his position, bound and gagged behind the counter, claims to have seen nothing, except some animal-like thing leaping on Karl at the end. Alice swears a strange man killed the criminals, but outside of a very generic description, she doesn't know who, what, or where about him. Not even much about the kind of horse he rode in on."

The senior agent broke in with a grunt. "I'm afraid, no forensic evidence of any kind has been discovered in the store or parking lot to support the existence of this mystery man, no fingerprints, clothing, blood, tire prints, etc. Only Alice's recollection that he drove a dark-colored hatchback, like millions of others."

The sheriff nodded. "Well, we do have a few smeared bare footprints, but lacking a database to search, they can't be identified. The grapefruit knife used to take a core sample of Jack Barker's kidney had a few threads stuck to it from a pair of generic Wal-Mart blue jeans. So, where does that leave us?"

Both agents lifted eyebrows and stared at the sheriff, their lips compressed. He pushed up straight in his chair, the casters making squeals of protest. "You can't possibly imagine my niece, Alice, took out the criminals. She's lived in this little town all her life, possesses no military or martial arts training, and has sworn an oath to save lives. Oh no, there was someone else. Someone who, without leaving nary a trace, wiped out four full-grown killers, one at a time with the most primitive weapons, in ways that drove a hardened criminal insane with fear. I'm closing the local file. This is your problem now. And if this man or creature is out there … you had better damn well be afraid!"

All The Thousands 1964 - 1975

I hear your voices in the . . .

    shush of my Bass Boat wake rocking
        thick mats of pale river lilies,

    splash of Koi tails in an Imperial Palace
        tile-lined garden pond,
    lap of a rough pebble-skinned water buffalo's tongue
        in a ruddy paddy field,
    drum-rattle slap of the monsoon — a million tons
        a year into the Mekong,
    drip, drip, drip of your water off vines
        and elephant ears making red mud.

I see your faces in the . . .

    relentless dream flames consuming logs
        in my fireplace,

    yellow flicker under steaming family rice kettles
        in a thousand brown villages,
    roaring cheek-blistering sear
        of zippoed thatch-roofed hootches,
    napalmed triple-canopy jungle acres
        of roiling liquid hell,
    white, white, white sun of the welding torch
        sealing your stainless coffins.

*From the Book *Remembering Willie*, Published 2003

Last Day Trilogy

The wind, a frigid-Norther birthed in Canada, rushed south without pausing at the artificial lines drawn on maps. Racing over a hilltop, it dashed down a wooded ravine and hummed through the bare branches and brush at the bottom. Its passage thinned the feathered-breath of wet-nosed, whitetail deer sheltering in a tangle of woods. Lacy veils of snow spun up across the backyard of a gray farmhouse and swirled around a red-blotched barn The wind stripped cakes of snow from the pine trees, and from the side of the barn facing the road, exposing the faded remnants of fancy curlicue letters spelling out Coca-Cola.

The tail of the gust threw a last flick of snow in a static rattle against the windows of the farmhouse den. Inside, a lean white-haired man sat at a Mission oak table. The headset of an old tan push-button phone slipped from his hands, making a loud plastic clack as it dropped on the receiver. His granddaughter, Carrie's girl, wanted a favor. A fine athlete, she excelled in track and field in high school. Upon graduation, she received a full college athletic scholarship. He remembered the bobbing blonde ponytail, red track shorts, and flashing Nikes as she broke the ribbon during the last iron woman marathon. Rachael had some legs, all right.

In many ways, she was the treasured child. The only one from his genes he had been allowed to help raise. This daughter of his heart and flesh worked alongside him on the farm, remembered his birthday, and generated the spontaneous laughter that kept the bad memories locked away. He frowned at the phone. In an excited voice, she had let him know her activated National Guard unit would soon serve in Afghanistan. She wanted to carry the family .45-caliber pistol during her tour.

He wondered if her ancestors' war guilt and curse were contagious, whether the plague passed from father to son or daughter still existed, waiting to blossom on the battlefield. Perhaps it took generations before the infection died out.

Teigler picked up a pistol barrel and bore brush from the table, then laid them down and looked up, huffing the smell of gun oil out of his nostrils. He raised his arms over his head, stretching the wrinkles out of his faded flannel shirt. He scanned the room, nerves burning from Rachael's request. Cream-colored plaster backlit the floor to ceiling walnut bookshelves fixed to three walls. On shelves, clusters of books crowded framed photographs, tarnished plaques, and trophies. Across from the windows, the fourth wall displayed large color maps of the United States. They ranged from ancient cartography blobs to an early twentieth century map any contemporary American would recognize.

Rod Teigler glanced down at the blue, brown, and chrome weapons nestled on stained frayed towels draped over the table. The envy of the local survivalists, the gun collection consisted of thirteen automatic pistols, examples of the world's most historic military handguns. Normally stored in a gray steel lockbox at the bank, he unleashed their destructive power a few times a year at the firing range. Surprisingly, ammo could still be found for the rarest pieces, a testimony to the popularity of man's deadliest sport.

On the table nested Walthers, Lugers, Tokarevs, Colts, and Brownings, all except one, finely machined and finished. Rod picked up the king of them all, a scarred and worn army-issue .45-caliber Colt 1911A1. In a flash of fantasy, the gun's stocky body and large bore morphed into a great white shark, scattering the lesser fish on the table.

A faithful family retainer, the forty-five had accompanied three generations of Teiglers into combat. In between conflicts, it slept and dreamed. In the gray light from the windows, it seemed to glow. A frisson worked its way up Teigler's neck. He wondered whether the gun absorbed some spiritual remnant of those it killed. If so, the pistol's old iron must be close to brimful. Mother hated it and had made her feelings clear to his father.

"Absolutely not! Bill, that damn thing will not touch my son's flesh," a pause between each word accented her anger.

"Elaine, for Christ's sake, it's a tool. Rod needs to know how to protect ..."

"Just like it protected you and Granpa Chuck? Hell, since you returned from Korea, we can't even sleep together. I get soaked with your sweat. And the night I fought to break the grip of your hands choking me. I don't know who is behind your eyes. The only time you'll bring that thing near our son is if I'm dead."

Mother passed when he was six. The house's ten-foot ceilings grew cobwebs in the corners, dust gathered on the hardwood floors. It seemed larger, as if it had increased in volume with her absence. Only touches of perfume, jasmine and Chanel, remained. The smells released when Rod opened long-sealed drawers and trunks.

Her scents retrieved gentle memories, the legs he grasped the first day of kindergarten, the soprano chuckle of her amusement over his drawings. Most of all, he remembered her hands, fingers tucking a stray lock of hair back in place, lifting him to her embrace, and walking down the steps after church in a tide of knees, her hand an anchor keeping him from being swept away. The memories meshed to knot in his chest. Rod absently rubbed his sternum in a futile effort to relieve pain. His father, Bill Teigler, honored her wish for a year and then started educating his son about the pistol.

"Rod, my son, you're not ready to shoot this bad boy, but not too young to take apart, study, and reassemble it. This gun could save your life someday." His father's voice deepened, raspy with memory, " … like it did mine."

~~~OOO~~~

Bill Teigler felt someone tug at his arm—stopped again, his body and mind winding down from lack of sleep and the intense cold. It made him stupid and slow to react. The tug came a second time.

"Lieutenant, gotta keep movin'," the sergeant said. "The Chinese'll catch us. We've los' contac' with the rear guard comp'ny."

He shivered—the two of them—alone and unsupported. "Let's hustle, Sergeant Davis. They won't hold a ship just for us."

The Marines were maneuvering toward the Korean coastal city of Hungnam where Navy transports waited. It seemed like months rather than nine days since the withdrawal from the Chosin Reservoir. Bill remembered his shock that first morning, when he learned a Chinese force, rumored to be a million men strong, surrounded them. Members of the Corps didn't give up. They picked up their wounded and dead, and fought through the People's Volunteer Army, lashed by a bitter mountain winter that tried to destroy both friend and enemy with equal ferocity. Yesterday, his men stumbled across a failed enemy ambush, a hundred frozen Chinese dug in along a ridgeline—blue-veined marble hands still gripping rifles and machine guns.

Bill took a clumsy step. Sergeant Davis noticed. "Better let me take a look at them feet, Sir, may lose 'em to fros'bite."

"No time, no time," the lieutenant mumbled through the ice-crusted wool scarf bound around his mouth and nose.

The sergeant glanced back then dropped to his knees. "Jesus, Sir, we got a chink squad on our ass!"

Davis unslung his carbine and pushed Teigler into the ditch at the roadside. The officer pulled at the flap on his holster, it resisted, stiff in the thirty below zero weather. The first two Chinese trotted over the rise.

"Fuck! Fuck! Fuck!" Davis cursed as his cold-locked carbine refused to fire.

Teigler pulled out the forty-five, his movements slowed by layers of clothing and the cold. The enemy fired. The pistol was sheathed in ice. He blew on the spur hammer. His thumb forced it back to full cock.

The Colt boomed. Pieces of ice flew off to sting his forehead like little razors. Burnt powder singed his nostrils. The first Chinese soldier dropped. Bill felt a heavy blow against his chest. Rocking back, the gun leveled and fired at each of the enemy in turn. It was magic. He pointed his wand and the puppets' strings were cut.

Bill groaned. A bullet had ricocheted off the frozen ground and lodged in his left pectoral muscle. At least it didn't require a bandage. His own frozen blood sealed the wound. Where was Davis? He rolled over. The sergeant sat on his heels, hands twitching, staring blankly ahead, his face a shattered wooden mask.

Teigler's lips quivered as he realized the man's lower jaw had been completely shot off. The sergeant should be dead, but the cold ... the goddamned cold had stopped the bleeding.

The .45 became weightless. It lifted his hand and arm stopping in line with Davis's heart. Bill struggled to keep from crying—tears would freeze his eyelashes shut and he would be blind.

--~OOO~--

Over the next two years, Rod grew to know each of the gun's fifty components and how they fit and worked together. He never failed to be intrigued by his growing understanding, the way the parts meshed at rest and how they moved under the explosive pressure and heat of firing. One hand pulled the heavy cast-metal slide back, then released it to feed a live round from the magazine into the breech. The barrel's machined flanges locked into grooves in the slide when fired, and then unlocked to eject spent brass. The thick recoil spring that rode under the barrel returned everything to its original position after each firing sequence.

The gun featured three safeties, a half-cock on the spur hammer, a small thumb-worked locking lever, and a grip safety—the Army's attempt at idiot-proofing. In theory, the hammer must be pulled completely back, the safety clicked down, and the pistol's grip squeezed firmly before it would fire. Rod smiled tightly, remembering times when the systems failed.

In Nam, standing orders required all weapons to be emptied before entering buildings. Once, a Green Beret sergeant shot himself in the ass when the safeties failed as he slapped the supposedly empty gun back into his shoulder holster. A bad location to take a round, since army myth inferred such wounds could only be received when running from the enemy.

A second incident had hit closer to home. The night shift communications officer paused outside the officers' barracks, removed his forty-five's magazine, and worked the slide several times. Thinking he'd removed the bullet in the chamber, he pulled the trigger to release the hammer. The gun fired and the slug penetrated the outer wall, passing through four internal partitions before lodging in a wooden framing stud. Fortunately, Rod and the others were in their cots—the round passed over their sleeping bodies.

When they felt he was ready, his grandfather, Granpa Charles, took over his training. The boy could never tell in advance what mood possessed Granpa. He remembered good times, sitting on a red-cushioned coffee shop bench pressed next to a hand-waving Chuck, talking with his cronies about corn yields, presidential candidates, and the price of hogs. The old man's frosted eyebrows and hair pale in contrast to his farmer's tan. The smell of cinnamon rolls, strong coffee, and manured boots spiced the spaces between words. The moments of connection grew fewer as Granpa aged, his conversations frequently interrupted by daydreams marked by muscle twitching, whispers of unknown names, and a retreat into memoried places where others could not follow. On his ninth birthday, Granpa Charles took him out to the barn.

"Rod, I want you to hit the anvil with this five-pound hammer using slow steady blows. Try it first with the right hand and then switch to the left. It will simulate the Colt's recoil. We don't want you frightened of its mule-kick. In combat, it will be one of your best friends," the old man's eyes moistened. " ... maybe your only friend."

~~~OOO~~~

"Charles A. Teigler, Private, U.S. Army, Serial Number RA 149623507 ... Charles A. Teigler, Private, U.S. Army, Serial Number RA 149623507," he repeated the words over and over. It helped keep the panic manageable as the nightmare ride in the Higgins boat grew more intense. It was D-Day. Along with thousands of others, they raced toward Omaha Beach. Most of his companions were sick. The diesel fumes, the up and down slap of the hull, and the splash of cold sea water soaking uniforms pushed soldiers' stomachs past any normal endurance.

On his left, one of the company's nine boats disintegrated in an eruption of water and a globe of orange fire—bits and fragments of boat, men, and weapons rattled down. Chuck slipped to his knees and vomited.

A sergeant's callused hand grabbed him, pulled him upright. "Unbuckle your pack straps, idiot. If we end up in deep water all the extra gear you're packing will drag you down."

"It's almost upon us, lads," Captain O'Flannery shouted from up front.

The landing craft bottom hit something solid and jerked to a halt pitching men forward. The front ramp dropped. The captain waved his arm and took three steps. Bullets chewed into his body, he danced for a moment before his dead meat dropped.

The men behind him melted away, a stick of butter in a hot frying pan, as German machine gunners fired 800 rounds a minute straight into the open hull.

"Over the side," the sergeant yelled over his shoulder. His feet disappeared.

The private followed. Cold water shocked his flesh. He sank rapidly. Chuck dropped his M-1 rifle and slipped the sixty pounds of gear off his shoulders. His mouth gaped as it regained the surface. Seawater rolled over his tongue tasting of salt, iron rust, and the metallic copper burn of blood.

The quiet he'd experienced underwater contrasted with the battle noise above. Bullets spanged off the boat and steel beach obstacles, men shouted and screamed, enemy mortar teams walked rounds up and down the beach, each explosion throwing up sand, rocks, and chunks of human flesh.

High velocity anti-tank guns fired repeatedly into the incoming boats.

Farther up the beach, a Sherman amphibious tank burned, stored shells exploded in its interior as flames reached the ammunition racks.

Chuck low-crawled out of the surf and scrunched down behind a pile of bodies. Bursts of slugs swept the beach, thunked into the dead, making the bodies jerk and quiver. He whimpered.

A familiar hand slapped the back of his head. "Where's your weapon? Get a weapon, damn you." The sergeant from the boat squatted next to him. "We need to get up under the bluffs. They can't hit us there."

The private reached for a holstered .45-automatic pistol strapped to one of the bodies. He pulled on the corpse's legs to free up the gun belt. The body rolled up against his chest. The dead man's Vaseline slick, red-gray intestines slithered out of his belly, flopping over Chuck's hands and forearms. He screamed.

The sergeant squeezed his neck. The pain brought him back under control. He pulled the blood-sticky pistol out of the holster. Arms pumping, the two of them ran through explosions, the smoke, and dust.

Gasping, the private dove into the sheltered area beneath the bluffs. He gagged, the sewer smell of the gutted officer clung to his hands and clothes. "Sarge, we made it, we made it! Sarge?"

He glanced to both sides. Back down the beach, the sergeant crawled toward him, leaving a bloody smear in the sand. A mortar shell landed so close to the non-com to make the question of whether or not it was a direct hit moot. When the sand settled, only a pair of brown army-issue shoes remained, still filled with feet and ankles.

Chuck ground his teeth. A fire ignited inside his skull. The Colt .45-pistol grew roots into his hand. Ahead, a shallow rocky gully ran toward the German positions. "No mercy," he thought. "They gave none, they will get none." Alone, he began to crawl.

~~~OOO~~~

At twelve, Rod began shooting the three-pound weapon. The adults insisted he shoot equally well with either hand. In the following years, he mastered the quick reload, allowing gravity to pull empty magazines out of the gun held in one hand, while the other slapped in a full one.

At seventeen, Grandpa taught him how to work the piece with one arm, pushing the automatic into the trouser cloth over his thighs to jack back the slide, and then letting it slam forward to strip a cartridge from the magazine into the firing chamber. An enemy couldn't stop you by wounding or breaking one arm.

At twenty-one, the calluses on Rod's palms and fingers matched the pistol's imprint. He thought he knew how to keep the gun operable in every conceivable situation.

~~~OOO~~~

White, nostril-burning, eye-watering smoke blew across their position, the little circle of OD-clad soldiers coughed and gasped. Grass and brush burned in the large clearing to the east, where air strikes had loosed napalm. Lieutenant Rod Teigler loved it and hated it. The smoke made it difficult for the enemy to find them, but their own troops couldn't locate them either.

He heard isolated groups of Viet Cong and North Vietnamese Army troops stumble through the surrounding jungle. At this late stage of the battle, confusion gripped both enemy and friendlies—communication, always chancy in the thick growth, had completely broken. Bombs, artillery, and helicopter gunships shredded any large group of enemy soldiers, but didn't stop them. They continued to pour out of caves and holes, attacking the Air Cav landing zone.

Teigler had made a mistake, a great bloody bastard of a mistake. The battalion's most aggressive platoon leader, he had pushed his men forward, losing contact with the rest of the unit. Overrun and chopped to pieces, he and eight others appeared to be all who remained of the twenty-six airlifted into the clearing.

They huddled together in an irregular depression in the ground, roughly twenty feet by twelve. He heard a final grunting exhalation from Corporal Rodriguez on his left.

"Doc," Rod said emotionally, pitched in a voice low enough not to carry.

The medic thumped down next to him. "El Tee, he's gone. No blood, no plasma ... nothing we could do. How's the arm? Sure you don't want morphine?"

An enemy slug had broken Teigler's left arm. Using a couple of dead troopers' belts, the medic had strapped it to his side. "Doc, I really fucked up. I really fucked up getting us into this mess." His unbound hand covered his eyes. He began to shake.

Blood splatter peppered on his bare arms and face, Doc leaned forward and half-whispered in his ear, "Lieutenant, I don't give a rat's ass about what you think happened. You are the only leader we have left. You son-of-a-bitch, don't abandon us now."

Teigler's mind stopped whirling. He swallowed a tablespoon of stomach acid. "Is Private First Class Moros the senior man left?"

Moros crawled back after doing an inventory. "We don't have much, El-Tee. Only five of us can still pull a trigger. The water's long gone. I've redistributed our remaining twenty rounds of 5.56mm. Other than that we have three non-issue hunting knives."

Two magazines remained for Teigler's forty-five, one with two rounds and one with a full load of seven. He placed the full one close between two crumbly red rocks. Surely, this would be over soon. Rod waited. The smoke thickened. The jungle waited.

A whistle blew and the sound of men rushing through the undergrowth came from their front. Another attack going in against the battalion, but it would sweep over their position in passing.

Moros shouted, "Fire!"

The stutter of M-16s ended almost before it began. There were shouts and curses in Vietnamese. The first enemy stumbled over the lip of the depression and fell face down. Rod fired the pistol, putting a round into the back of the soldier's head. A second leaped out of the smoke. The forty-five boomed, knocked the man on his back, the slide locked open on the empty magazine.

Rod pressed the release button. The empty fell out, tinged on a rock. He gripped the barrel of the gun between his knees, burning the skin on both sides. From the landing zone behind them came the crash of American and Vietnamese weapons.

The lieutenant palmed the reload into the pistol butt and depressed the slide latch charging the gun. During the next flurry of seconds, he dropped two more enemy soldiers, one by one as they came out of the smoke, their last wide-eyed expressions registering surprise.

The lieutenant's men had nothing left. One more sweep by the enemy would finish them. He thought the pistol contained four, maybe five rounds. The smoke started to disperse.

In a few minutes, they would be naked. He heard approaching troops, this time from the flank. Moros stood up, left cheek and neck scratched and bleeding, his fists half-raised. Teigler lifted a shaking forty-five. Black rifle barrels pushed aside blood-dewed elephant grass. Teigler coughed out the last of the smoke.

"Wal, hell, tha' sounds lik' a Yankee coff," a Deep South voice drawled.

~~~OOO~~~

Teigler eased back, rubbed his forehead with a gun-oil scented piece of old cotton t-shirt. Even after fifty-five years, his personal horror kept returning, still full of pain, sweat, and stink, and with it the soul-twisting rot of his long-ago failure. With the death of Sergeant Major Moros six months ago, the last of his Air Cav platoon was gone.

Teigler focused on the framed pictures displayed on the bookshelves, one showed Moros at his promotion party. Tailored army dress blues and white gloves set off his weightlifter's body, his right shoulder pushed forward to show off the new golden stripes, three chevrons on top and three rockers on the bottom, a five-pointed star in the middle.

The new sergeant major smiled as his left hand pointed to the symbol of rank, a smile that could welcome friends or strike terror in the minds of raw recruits. Agent Orange had finally claimed him. At the end, his emaciated body lay tangled in the sheets of a VA hospital bed. He still wore an undiminished smile.

Doc had died in a car accident the year before. In the picture next to Moros, a tux-clad Doc and his new wife waved as they drove off in a rented green convertible, cans tied to the bumper with brown baling twine clanked and rattled. Reflected in the frame's dusty glass, a best man's dried-out carnation lay sealed in a plastic bag.

The waiting green-clad spirits of the two men and twenty-four others called him, his platoon reporting for duty once again. There were others, those who had lost their lives defending him: Private Willis in Vietnam and Pappy in Peru—and all the enemies he and his alter ego had snuffed. His entire life spent sending men to their death. The desire to join them—to ask forgiveness, to find peace—grew overwhelming.

Wind pushed against the northwest corner of the house. In the silence, he could hear the two story's wood-on-wood frame creak and moan. In his late seventies, Rod felt physically worn, but given the strength of the family genes, he might live alone with the guilt for a couple more decades. All his friends gone, Rod would be alone, even the war-spawned reptilian creature who shared his mind had grown old, decrepit, and ready for the quiet of eternity.

Now Rachael, the only child he had permitted himself to love, was going into harm's way. If her ancestors' experience of war followed true—if she survived—she would come back a very different person. He must warn her.

Rod gathered the forty-five's parts and clicked them together. With a loaded magazine inserted, the gun made a familiar metallic thump as he placed it on the table. The lightly oiled metal reflected the amber rays of the late winter sun through the frosted windows at his back. His fingers caressed the scarred checkered walnut grips. The pistol felt comfortable and reassuring in his hand. "Of all my friends, you are the best and the last."

A muffled boom and shattered glass shook the quiet.

Something moving fast whiffled through the frigid outside air. In the gully, startled deer broke out of the tangle wood, the buck pushed three does in front of him. They raced across the pasture. One slipped on an icy patch. Sharp cloven hooves scrabbled. As they ran, thick foggy breath spewed from their nostrils.

A spatter of red blood and a curved piece of bone rested on the powder-dry snow beneath the farmhouse's broken window. The snowmelt caused by its warmth refroze, jeweling the fragment with crystal.

www.ingramcontent.com/pod-product-compliance
Lightning Source LLC
Chambersburg PA
CBHW070926260626
47162CB00007B/2802